THE WINNERS OF NINE BOOK AWARDS transcending the genres of science fiction, environmental fiction, and action-adventure, ***The Girl Who Rode Dolphins*** and ***Dolphin Riders*** have proven themselves thrillers with a labyrinth of spellbinding twists, turns, and thunderous action that takes readers on a roller coaster ride of nail-biting suspense and explosive adventure.

Upon its original debut, ***The Girl Who Rode Dolphins*** received the following multiple awards:

- ***Winner of Best Epic Adventure of 2008***
  BooksandAuthors.net
- ***Winner of Best Science Fiction Epic Adventure of 2008***
  BooksandAuthors.net
- ***Winner of Science Fiction Genre***
  2009 Green Book Festival
- ***Finalist in Action Adventure Category***
  2009 National Indie Book Excellence Awards
- ***Winner of Environmental/Green Fiction Category***
  2010 International Book Awards Competition
- ***Winner of the Talking Category***
  2015 Animals, Animals, Animals Book Festival
- ***Honorable Mention Awardee in Science Fiction Category***
  2015 London Book Festival

Dolphin Riders, the sequel to ***The Girl Who Rode Dolphins***, is an ensuing adventure combined with political intrigue that promises to captivate readers with enthralling action and mysticism on a scale every bit as intense if not greater than the first book.

- ***Official Selection Winner of Action/Adventure Category***
  2016 New Apple Summer eBook Awards
- ***Finalist In Action/Adventure Category***
  2016 Beverly Hills Book Awards

Following their original debuts, both books were re-released in 2026 by Seaworthy Publications, Inc. as a five-part cliff-hanger series as follows:

The Girl Who Rode Dolphins, 3rd Edition

- Part 1 - Gaia's Intervention
- Part 2 - Gaia's Heartbeat
- Part 3 - Retribution

Dolphin Riders, 3rd Edition

- Part 4 - Creation
- Part 5 - Survival

Creation

Part 4
of
The Dolphin Riders Series

Dolphin Riders
3rd Edition

Creation

Part 4
of
The Dolphin Riders Series

Dolphin Riders
3rd Edition

by

Michael J. Ganas

SEAWORTHY PUBLICATIONS, INC. • MELBOURNE, FLORIDA

Creation
Part 4 of the Dolphin Riders Series
Dolphin Riders, 3rd Edition

ISBN 978-1-966191-10-0
eBook ISBN 978-1-966191-11-7

Published in the USA by:
Seaworthy Publications, Inc.
6300 N Wickham Rd.
Unit #130-416
Melbourne, FL 32940
E-mail orders@seaworthy.com
www.seaworthy.com

Library of Congress Cataloging-in-Publication Data

Names: Ganas, Michael J., 1946- author | Ganas, Michael J., 1946- Girl who rode dolphins
Title: Gaia's intervention / by Michael J Ganas.
Description: Third edition. | Melbourne, Florida : Seaworthy Publications, Inc, 2026. | Series: The dolphin riders series ; part 1 | "The girl who rode dolphins 3rd edition" | Summary: "Former Navy SEAL Jake Javolyn, a part-time smuggler by necessity and dive boat operator by profession, has come to Haiti in search of something. Hiring his boat out to Dr. Franklin Grahm, a renowned marine zoologist, Javolyn sets course for Navassa Island, only to stumble across a beautiful girl in the open sea. Encircled by a pod of six white bottlenose dolphins, the girl is found riding a seventh, much larger but similar creature. Upon rescuing the girl from the nets of a tuna trawler crewed by vicious members of a drug cartel, Javolyn soon discovers the girl has strange and unusual powers. Even more amazing are her companions, for they are unlike any sea mammals he has ever encountered. They possess forelimbs with hands, super-intelligence, and can speak in human languages. From then on, he is plunged into a world of the supernatural and confrontation with iniquitous forces bent on vengeance and the capture of nature's most recent miracles. A stunning rollercoaster ride of epic adventure, Gaia's Intervention is the first book in this blockbuster series, an ecological saga that will leave readers spellbound and enthralled with its superb mix of intense action, environmental issues, and mysticism"-- Provided by publisher.
Identifiers: LCCN 2026000755 (print) | LCCN 2026000756 (ebook) | ISBN 9781966191049 v. 1 paperback | ISBN 9781966191056 v. 1 epub
Subjects: LCSH: Dolphins--Fiction | LCGFT: Ecofiction | Action and adventure fiction | Fantasy fiction | Novels | Fiction
Classification: LCC PS3607.A4385 G35 2026 (print) | LCC PS3607.A4385 (ebook)
LC record available at https://lccn.loc.gov/2026000755
LC ebook record available at https://lccn.loc.gov/2026000756

Dedication

To my gemstone, Harriet.

Table of Contents

Facts

Haiti is currently the poorest country in the Western Hemisphere, a Caribbean nation beleaguered by economic strife, dismal squalor, and political instability, a land of defoliation and ecological ruin. It is a place with a violent past, punctuated by a succession of bloody rebellions and previously governed by an extensive line of statesmen and dictators whose policies were either inept, ineffectual, unpopular, corrupt, or oppressive. The Duvalier dictatorships of father and son, however, proved to be the most corrupt, oppressive, and violent, and under their brutal regimes Haiti suffered deeply.

Francois "Papa Doc" Duvalier ruled Haiti from 1963 until his death in 1971 when his son Jean-Claude "Baby Doc" Duvalier took over the reins of power. Under the Duvalier governments, the population was kept in a state of fear, terrorized by the regime's secret police force, the Tonton Makout. They were also known as the VNS, Volunteers of National Security, and Papa Doc referred to them as his "civilian" military, while the citizens called them "the bogeymen." They were recruited mostly from Haiti's slums and were used to crush all opposition, often imprisoning without trial, torturing, and even killing individuals considered enemies of the state.

An estimated 60,000 Haitians were murdered at the hands of the Tonton Makout, which had a standing force of roughly 10,000 loyalists. Papa Doc made sure his secret police outnumbered the Haitian army by a factor of two in order to assure that he did not get overthrown in a coup. Both Francois Duvalier and his son also took advantage of the people's strong belief in voodoo to control the population. Consequently, much of the citizenry believed them to be voodoo spirits. To this day, voodoo, merged with Catholicism, is the religion of choice embraced by most Haitians.

Misappropriation of government funds amounting to hundreds of millions was common practice under Baby Doc's tyrannical rule, and in the wake of intense political unrest and pressure from the United States to step down, he was finally forced from power in February of 1986, whereupon he fled to France. A wealth of evidence shows various drug cartels to be firmly entrenched in present-day Haiti, where the political climate, endemic poverty and a breakdown in civil rule makes it an ideal staging area for the transshipment of illegal contraband, where public officials are often threatened or corrupted by bribery to keep a blind eye to drug trafficking.

Navassa Island is a small, uninhabited island, which lies in the Caribbean Sea between Haiti and Jamaica. The island originally belonged to Haiti before being claimed in 1801 as an unorganized, unincorporated territory of the United States, which currently administers it through the U.S. Fish and Wildlife Service.

Malique is a fictitious fishing village that lies roughly midway between the real cities of Saint-Marc and Gonaives along Haiti's western coastline. It has been created solely for the purpose of this novel.

Al Qaeda is an actual present-day organization of Islamic extremists bent on the destruction of the United States and its allies. To this day this terrorist group continues to flourish despite the loss of its originator and leader, Osama Bin Laden, who was killed by a team of U.S. Navy Seals when they stormed his hideout in Pakistan during a bold raid that occurred in 2011.

All mention of Haiti's former leadership and historical events, both past and modern day, are based on documented history and are used as a backdrop for the writing of this novel. In this way, history has been merged with fiction.

All characters, creatures and unusual settings that play a key role within the novel's plot are entirely fictitious and have been created solely for the reader's intrigue and entertainment.

Michael J. Ganas

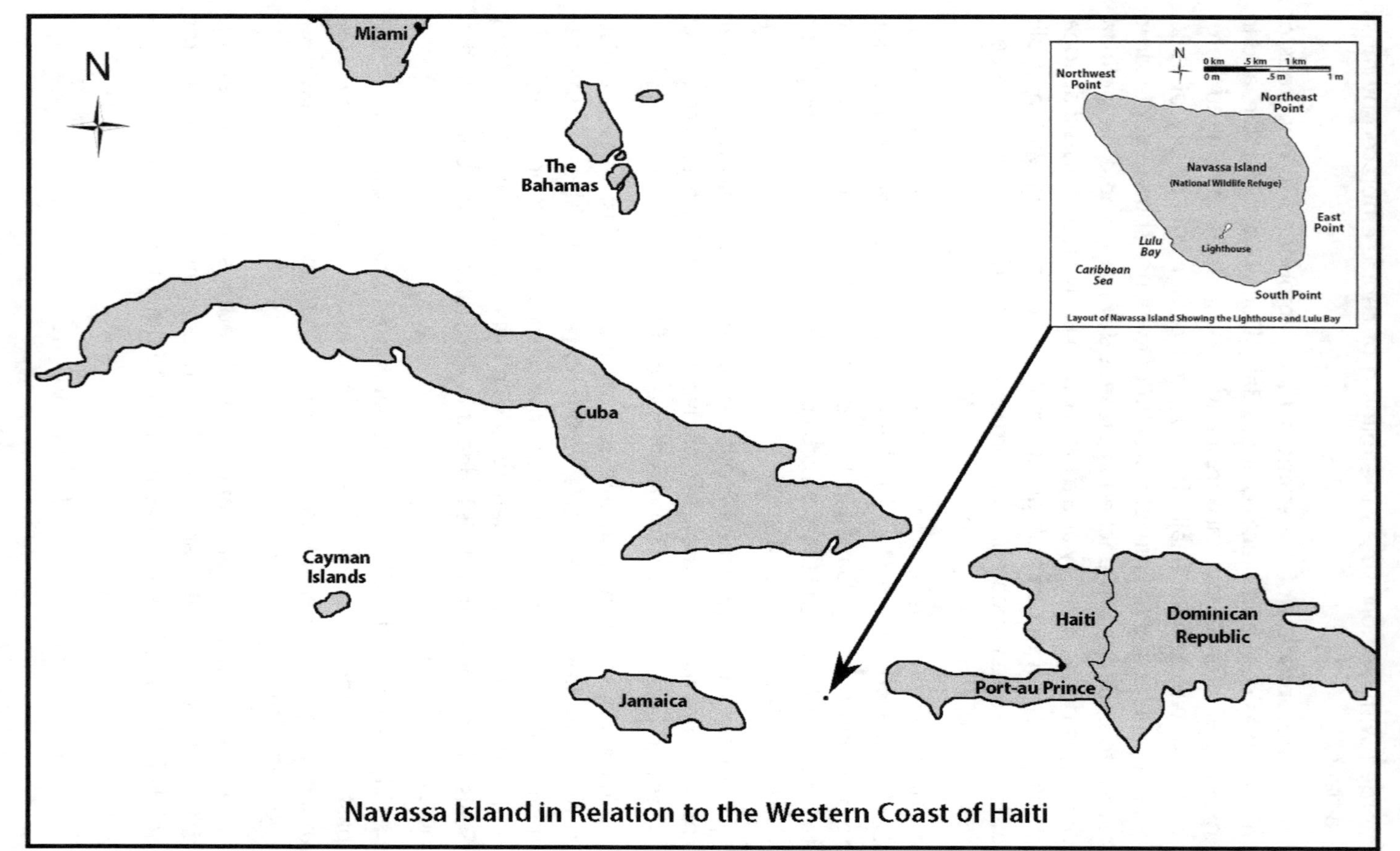

Navassa Island in Relation to the Western Coast of Haiti

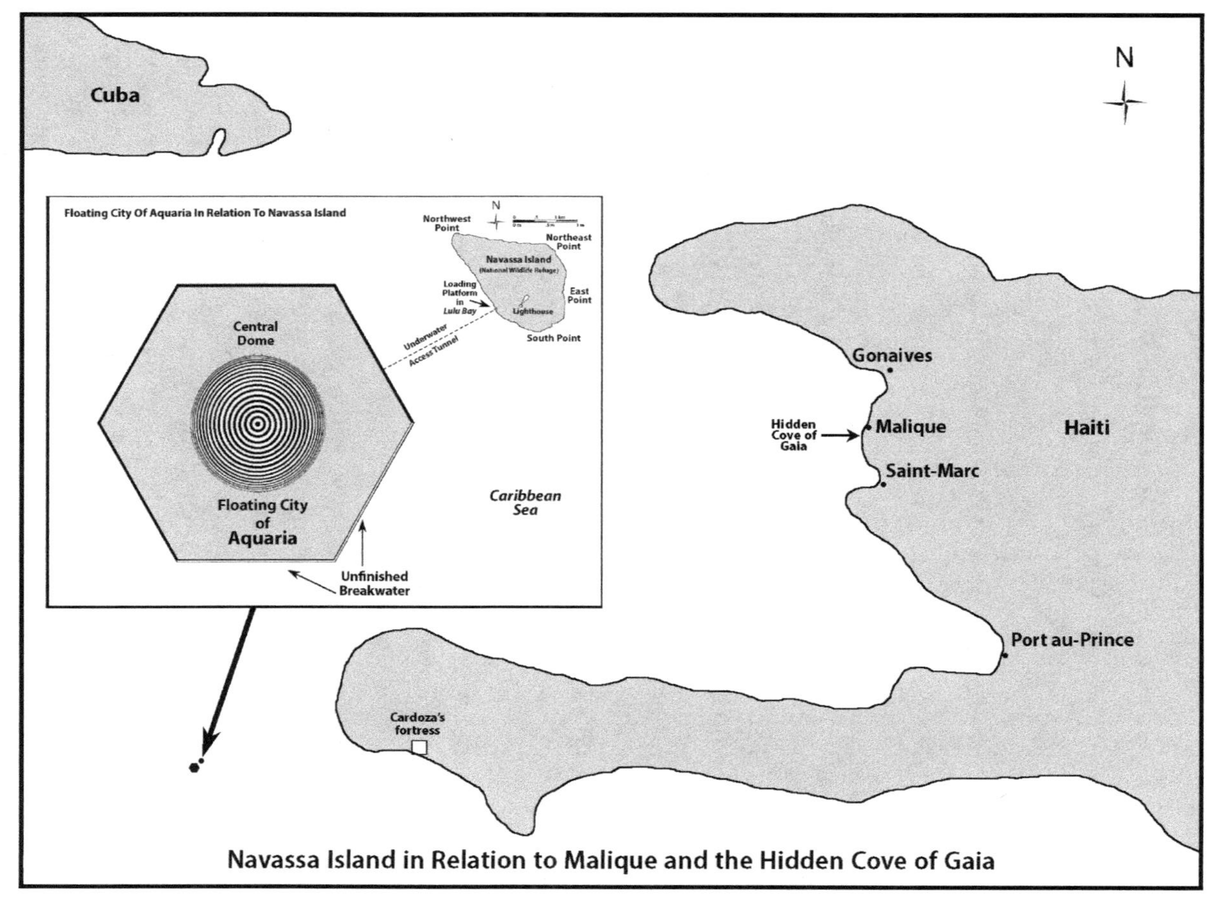

Navassa Island in Relation to Malique and the Hidden Cove of Gaia

Prologue: Trial And Error

April 4, 2016

A Secret Underground Laboratory Somewhere in the U.S.

The scientist stared through the one-way glass, unable to accept what he had been told. Turning, he cast dubious eyes on his assistant. "I specifically requested hyper-aggressive test subjects, not someone who looks like he belongs in a monastery."

Mooney opened the folder to check it again. "According to this, the man's a raving lunatic. Killed more than two dozen people in his country of origin, and those were the confirmed deaths. It's speculated he killed at least twice that number. You have before you a genuine mass murderer."

Somewhat surprised, Harper scrutinized the subject again. The man was strapped down securely to a metal chair, his head held rigidly in place by a cranial clamp to keep him from diverting his gaze.

"Turn on the camera and give me a close-up of his face," Harper ordered, leaning over the console to study the subject's features on a high-definition monitor. The man was balding prematurely, displaying a closely shaved scalp of dark hair in the shape of a horseshoe, beneath which an exceptionally huge beak of a nose with a prominent hump jutted saliently from between large but narrowly spaced eyes, giving him the look of a raptor. He wore thick glasses, the lenses magnifying his eyes even more and making them appear to bulge grotesquely when looking directly at them. Assessing those eyes a little more closely, Harper suddenly sensed a subdued derangement lurking deep within.

"What else can you tell me about him?" he asked.

"Name's Peyami Pehlivan. Twenty-five years of age, five feet six, one hundred fifty-five pounds. Holds dual citizenship, both in Turkey and the U.S., the result of being the progeny of a Turkish mother and American father also of Turkish lineage. Parents were university professors and quite distinguished in their respective fields of study, with the mother being a biological anthropologist and the father a cultural anthropologist. It says here that when he was seventeen, his parents were killed when their privately-owned plane crashed in Somalia during a fact-finding expedition."

Continuing to scrutinize the dossier, Mooney spotted one particularly interesting fact. "This guy's a certified genius and holds a doctorate in nuclear physics from MIT. He earned it at the age of nineteen, after which he accepted a full professorship position at Bilkent University in Ankara, but started showing signs of mental instability three years later while teaching there."

Scanning the page further, Mooney said, "Six months ago he finally snapped, going on a two-day killing spree using an ax. Upon being nabbed by Turkish authorities, he was declared criminally insane. One of our agents in Ankara was able to purchase him from the psycho ward where he was being held in isolation. The warden said it would save them the trouble of executing him, which was scheduled for next week."

Satisfied, Harper said, "Alright, he'll do. Display the benign imagery."

Mooney hit a button on the panel before him, activating a flat-screen TV above the glass facing the subject. Though Mooney could not see what was being shown, he knew a series of abstract artistic creations were being displayed one after the other, some of them works by famous expressionists like Kooning, Gorky, and Newman. Photographs portraying Pablo Picasso's cubism were also there.

"No outward reaction at all," mumbled Harper. "Good, now bring up the Aquarian art."

Mooney fingered another button, glad that he wouldn't be exposed to the next set of visual imagery. Both he and Harper had gotten violently ill when they had first looked upon what the test subject would see.

As both men watched, the killer's eyes widened as though they would burst from their sockets. Almost immediately, he let out a horrendous scream that could be heard through the glass. The scream was abruptly cut off as an eruption of vomit spewed from his mouth. Totally restrained by the straps and clamp holding him, his body juddered and convulsed as though being jolted by a heavy surge of electricity.

"Inject him!" yelled Harper. Though the subject's chair was bolted to the floor, he wondered if the bolts might break free.

Mooney depressed a third button. This one activated a mechanism attached to the lower part of the chair. A rod with a hypodermic needle advanced to lodge in the subject's exposed right thigh. In moments, the plunger injected the latest drug they had been developing through trial and error during the last month on more than twenty human guinea pigs. If this one failed to work, Mooney knew their jobs were in jeopardy. Executives within Plagiarius wanted results, plain and simple.

Within seconds the subject's convulsions began to subside, finally stopping altogether.

"I think we have a winner," Mooney remarked with more than a touch of elation.

Harper nodded slowly, mulling their recent work. He would stick with his primary assumption concerning the strange art form, that it caused debilitating psychosomatic reactions in physically aggressive people. Funny, he thought ironically. He had never considered himself physically aggressive, and yet both he and Mooney had suffered reactions similar to that observed in the murderer on the opposite side of the glass, though perhaps not as severe. Certainly, he was not a killer, and neither was his assistant. But what about those that did not get ill, the ones that experienced euphoria?

Maybe his assumptions were all wrong. The guy they had tested two days ago immediately came to mind. A brute of a man, he had been all muscle, his arms decorated with tattoos. The perpetual scowl clinging to his face bespoke of belligerence. His file had shown it had taken six police officers in Rio de Janeiro to bring him down during a bar room brawl. And yet the Aquarian art had left him docile as a kitten. It was a conundrum he could not explain though he suspected it had something to do with the way a person's brain was wired, some deep neurotic anomaly that reacted in a positive way with the arcane visual stimulus to bring on a state of tranquility in some people. Lacking that anomaly, most people would experience extreme vertigo whenever they were exposed to it.

Mesmeric and agonizing!

From his own experience, those were the two words that best described the enigmatic art. He shuddered involuntarily at the memory of the brain-throbbing nausea. It was hard to look away once you peered at it. It had drawn him in to tear at his temples and bring him to the doorsteps of hell.

What difference did all this conjecture make anyway? he concluded. Hadn't he gotten the desired results? The non-hallucinogenic LSD derivative in combination with dextroamphetamine appeared to work perfectly in suppressing a negative reaction.

"You think more testing is in order?" Mooney asked.

Harper shook his head. "No, ten positive tests should be enough. Let's go ahead and prepare enough antidote to fill five hundred military grade injectors."

Mooney appeared perplexed. "Am I hearing you right?"

"That's what came down from higher up," Harper said. "Once we found a remedy, we were to have a batch made up to be shipped out immediately for military use."

"But we don't know how long the drug will remain effective, nor have we established an acceptable dosage," Mooney protested.

"Certainly, there will be exceptions," Harper conceded, "but under the present circumstances, I think satisfying management should be our main priority."

Mooney shrugged nonchalantly, wondering why soldiers would need the drug. He brought his gaze to the glass again. "What about the guy in there?"

A dark smile broke out on Harper's face. "He's a killer, far too dangerous to keep alive. Dispose of him!"

Mooney glanced down again at the test subject's file. Files like this were regarded as highly confidential and were locked away in a vault when not in use. Only company personnel holding top security clearances were allowed access to them. His face immediately clouded as he prepared to check off a box marked 'TERMINATE' on the second page. Another box had already been checked.

"Can't do that," Mooney said. "This one's already scheduled for psychological re-programming once we're through with him."

Harper yawned. "So be it," he replied tiredly, taking a last look at the killer on the other side of the glass.

He should have known the man would be a prime candidate for such programming. Plagiarius considered subjects like this to be valuable assets once they were psychologically reconditioned. Undoubtedly, they were useful tools for carrying out unscrupulous objectives. Demand for them was heavy on the international black market, and when the company no longer had need of them, they could be sold to governments and private buyers the world over at outrageous prices.

Chapter One: Unwanted Intruders

May 23, 2016
Floating City of Aquaria
South of Navassa Island, Caribbean Sea

Jake stared in wonder at what they had so far accomplished. The sight never failed to awe him even though he had been involved in its construction from the beginning. It had started small, growing steadily from what amounted to a single seedling. And it was still growing, gaining size and breadth with each passing month. Even from below where he now hovered, it dazzled the eyes. But one could not fully appreciate its scope unless the evolving complex was viewed from above.

Begin small and scale up by replicating similar modules. That was what Jacob had said five years earlier when Jake had watched as the starting seed was floated into position. Even so, the initial OTEC module was anything but small.

Jake held on as Achilles made his way over to the lobster cages suspended amid the vast algae containments. At that moment, a huge school of bluefin shot into view, the sheer mass of closely grouped bodies partially eclipsing the immense cages hanging before him. So far, their mariculture and fish farming endeavors were proving to be far more fruitful than they had originally anticipated, with lobster production only accounting for a very small portion of revenues in spite of the huge quantities they were routinely harvesting. Other products such as shellfish, shrimp, tuna, abalone, king crab and various types of food fish also contributed to income that continued to escalate in lockstep with the growing enterprise. Already *Aquaria* had surpassed $3 billion in exports.

Maybe by next year they-

A familiar mental resonance interrupted Jake's thoughts. With Achilles, there was never a need for speech, even in a medium far less dense than the one in which they currently roamed.

I have located an intruder, Jay Jay.

Reflexively, Jake's eyes probed the water before him. *Where?*

Achilles swung around to pace the mass of tuna flashing past in the pristine water, glimmerings of sunlight reflecting off flanks seemingly flecked with quicksilver, and the dolphin was hard-pressed just to keep up. Known to be among the fastest fish in the sea, bluefin were ultra-efficient swimmers, able to tuck in their fins when they wanted to accelerate. At the moment, however, they glided gracefully and without effort, far below the fifty mph they were capable of reaching.

Look to the middle of the pack, Achilles answered. *There is one among them disguised to mimic a bluefin.*

Though this development was something altogether new, Jake had no reason to doubt the albino's assessment. Achilles' innate biosonar could easily distinguish differences between organic and inorganic objects. This was something Jake continually marveled over. By listening to the echoes from its emitted sonar signals, a dolphin could construct a three-dimensional picture of its surrounding environment. Dolphins used their ears the way humans used their eyes. Not only could the brain of a dolphin clearly discern the size, shape, and texture of an object by means of acoustical feedback, it could also gauge its density, and quite often, what lay inside. Such auditory input often gave it the equivalent of an X-ray visual of the object's internal structure as well as the type of material comprising it. Nevertheless, Jake felt compelled to contest the dolphin's observation.

You're telling me you see a robotic fish?

Yes, Jay Jay. Apollo noticed it earlier this morning. He ran a speak-see scan on it and recorded the echoes on Dr. Grahm's upgraded DBT in order to get additional information. Ez analyzed them and confirmed the intruder to be entirely mechanical.

Squinting his eyes behind the face mask he wore, Jake tried to single out the intruder. From his perspective, all the tuna looked identical.

I thought Apollo hated wearing Grahm's little gizmos.

Normally he does, but he was helping the good doctor test out some new modifications.

So, what else did Ez discover?

The intruder is roughly 1.9 meters in length, sheathed by a Lycra skin covering more than 2,800 mechanical parts, including what appear to be forty metal ribs and tendons. Six servo motors linked to a segmented backbone and tail provide the mechanical energy to set the spine in motion. But the thing's most interesting feature was a camera it carried in each eye.

As Achilles elaborated, a visual of the thing with its various components flashed briefly in Jake's brain, projected there by the dolphin. Jake absorbed this newfound information, knowing such a machine would be incredibly expensive to design and build. Someone had gone to great lengths to infiltrate their operation and in a most clandestine manner. The colony was being spied upon yet again. This was the fifth time in the last two months they were being probed, but now it was being done far more covertly than anything he had seen in the past.

In spite of this annoyance, Jake found himself smiling. And though they were now better prepared to counter this unwanted visitor, he was careful to remind himself of the age-old adage thoroughly instilled in him from his days in the Navy Seals, and that was to learn as much as you could about your adversary. Know your enemy.

With this in mind, Jake queried Achilles again. *Are there any vessels or aircraft nearby that might have launched it?*

There are three possibilities, Jay Jay. Artemis informs me a U.S. Naval cruiser is stationed 1,800 meters to the southwest of our current position. And that ultra-large luxury yacht, Numquam Satis, has not moved since yesterday.

Achilles went silent, and Jake grew impatient. *And the third?*

The dolphin did not immediately answer, and Jake realized his mount was apparently consulting with the others in that silent mode of communication they all used. Normally, Achilles was the only one Jake was able to directly communicate with using this unusual method. This was quite limiting when compared to the communal conjoining of minds that both Destiny and Harriet routinely shared with the pod, something Jake had only been able to experience on two separate occasions.

Another moment passed before the dolphin gave a response. *The others tell me a helicopter approaches from the north, another of those pesky news media aircraft. See for yourself.*

An image of a rotary wing aircraft suddenly sprang into Jake's mind, a picture-speak projection of what had been relayed to Achilles by another pod member stationed along the surface. Achilles frequently did this to provide Jake with additional information, which in this case showed a distinct logo on the side of the whirlybird.

That's an IBC chopper, Jake replied. *That, at least, narrows the field.*

Jake reflected for several seconds before making a decision. *Have Destiny alert Fernando about what's going on down here.*

Destiny has left the city and is currently on her way to the island with the twins.

Jake groaned inwardly, now remembering that Destiny had planned on taking the twins there this morning.

Then have Ez let Fernando know. With any luck, Fernando will have Johnnie fully prepped and ready to go. In the meantime, try keeping us close to that thing, but don't make it obvious we're on to it.

Achilles shot forward, accelerating rapidly with powerful flicks of his tail, and Jake had to cling tightly to the dolphin's back to keep from being swept off. The albino had grown considerably since their initial bonding eight years earlier. Back then, the dolphin had been only a juvenile not much bigger than Jake's six foot one, 200-pound frame. But now Achilles was a fully mature adult, possessing all the attributes that made his unique species one of the most incredible life forms on the planet. And with an agility and muscularity that even surpassed Hermes, Achilles was considered a standout among his own kind, able to swim faster and leap higher than any of his peers despite a body mass exceeding 1,200 pounds. Currently, only one member of the pod was larger and stronger than Achilles, and that was Hercules, a virtual giant among this new breed of super-dolphin.

As his mount shadowed the moving horde of bluefin, Jake reflected on how his riding technique had gradually changed as Achilles gained size. He had carefully studied the way Destiny rode Hercules, noting the way she sat astride the albino bull. Her buttocks would make contact with the giant's dorsal fin as she leaned forward into the oncoming sea, legs pressed firmly against the creature's flanks as she gripped a short length of rope on opposite sides, each rope looped over a pectoral fin. With the exception of using the rope, this was the technique he had ultimately adopted, realizing it afforded him far better efficiency provided he gripped the leading edge of Achilles' pectoral fins. Being much bigger than Destiny, he had no need of ropes, able to easily extend his long muscular arms forward to reach the dolphin's appendages.

Another consideration suddenly came to mind, and Jake directed this thought to his mount. *Achilles, send out word to the others to keep their hands tucked in. I don't want our uninvited guest recording this anatomical irregularity.*

I'm afraid it's a little late for that, Jay Jay. By the time Apollo became aware of the threat, it had already made several passes near Sector 28.

The implication was all too clear, making Jake cringe inwardly. At least fifty grays had been hard at work all morning in Sector 28, performing retrofits in preparation for another two incoming modules. And if, in fact, the primary objective of robofish was surveillance, then they'd have no choice but to stop it. This singular revelation changed all the rules.

Then let's hope that thing isn't able to do any real-time transmissions. Otherwise, our little secret is out of the bag.

Achilles analyzed Jake's concern, projecting a compressed assessment that buzzed in the back of Jake's head. *That assumes it saw what we didn't want it to see, Jay Jay, though it's highly probable it is self-guided and autonomous, pre-programmed to avoid detection and carry out certain functions such as surveillance. Unless whoever built it has made significant breakthroughs in underwater telemetry the way we have, it's unlikely it's being remotely controlled or currently sending observations. A watery environment will grossly attenuate any transmission signals, limiting live video communication to only a few hundred feet at most, and that's being extremely conservative.*

Jake needed additional assurance. *So, you think it's only capable of recording what it sees and will be unable to send a real-time transmission of what its cameras are immediately focused on?*

Yes, but only when it's fully submerged as it is now. I believe it operates in a manner similar to Dr. Grahm's original DBT. However, we cannot rule out that it won't be able to transmit findings once it breaches the surface. This, of course, is all speculation.

As Achilles sent this last thought, the mass of tuna suddenly veered in panic, and Jake saw the cause of it. Phillipe was coming toward him from the opposite side of the pack, towed along by Perseus. This came as somewhat of a surprise to Jake, for Phillipe would normally be with Jacob at this hour of the morning.

Sensing Jake's bewilderment, Achilles provided a rapid-fire explanation which took less than a tenth of a second to communicate. *Perseus informs me that Jacob will not be tutoring Phillipe today.*

Why not?

The news team aboard that IBC bird has requested permission to land and Jacob granted it. He's gone to meet with them and asks that you join him.

Now's not the time, objected Jake peevishly. *Have Ez inform him about what's going on down here.*

He already knows. He believes it's a waste of time to continue withholding the truth from the rest of the world.

Well I don't see it that way and neither should you. Have Ez tell him I'll get there as soon as I can.

Like always, the dolphin's response was conciliatory. *As you wish, Jay Jay.*

Achilles made a lazy turn, keeping pace with the formation of fish, the panic within the ranks of tuna now abating. Jake took the moment to appraise Phillipe, who now rode at his side. A sense of pride took hold of him as he looked at his young protégé. The boy was now beyond the threshold of manhood just shy of twenty-two years, the love child of an American father and Haitian mother.

If only Myers could see his son now, thought Jake, amazed by the striking resemblance the youth had inherited. There was no mistaking the face staring back at him behind the diving mask, for the face was Myers all over again, once again reminding Jake of the solemn promise he had made to Myers back in Tora Bora. That was just before Myers had died, the victim of an abominable betrayal by one of the members of Jake's Seal team.

Phillipe had been a homeless waif on the squalid streets of Port-au-Prince when Jake had first found him eight years earlier following a relentless search through the city's dismal slums. In the beginning the boy had been withdrawn, unsure of the man willing to take him under his wing, but in time he had come to admire the former Navy Seal that had been his father's most trusted friend even though the lad had never met the man who had sired him.

Jake smiled proudly as he watched his charge being towed along by Perseus, the sight bringing back old memories. He had used this same technique when Achilles had first bonded with him, letting his body trail back as he grasped the dolphin's dorsal fin with one hand. Jake felt exceptionally privileged to have been chosen by Achilles, for such a relationship automatically made him a pod member. The albinos were particular with whom they bonded, for the decision to establish such a link lay solely with them and not their human counterpart. And as Jake had come to learn, implicit trust was an essential precondition for such a vinculum. If an albino sensed any underlying darkness in a person's character, bonding was impossible.

From the start, Phillipe had been eager to establish a bond of his own, envious of Jake's relationship with Achilles, and it was less than a year ago that Phillipe had finally gotten his wish when the juvenile had chosen him. Perseus was Achilles' younger brother. Birthed by Thetis, Perseus was currently the youngest member of the pod and not much bigger than Phillipe.

Having bonded with the dolphin, Phillipe was happier than ever these days. The lad loved the sea every bit as much as Jake and, aside from his studies, seemed bent on spending all his free time with Perseus, reveling in the underwater environment.

Jake broke from his musings, directing his gaze back to the swarm of bluefin. *What's the status on Johnnie?*

Almost here, Jay Jay. But Fernando cannot guarantee Johnnie is fully operational.

Jake could not hold back the mental groan. *Not the auto-guidance again?*

Unfortunately, yes, Jay Jay. Fernando's using the remote override, controlling Johnnie manually. But there's another problem.

What now?

The hydrodrive is still a bit twitchy.

With those big brains, I would think you guys would have solved these problems by now. Are you telling me your design is still flawed?

Jake felt the equivalent of a shrug in the dolphin beneath him. *We've discussed all this before, JJ. The problem resides in the construction, not the design.*

Well, you guys helped Fernando build it, Jake was quick to point out.

Must I remind you we are still in the R & D stage, Achilles countered. *Growing the essential power inducers is more art than science. We can never be certain they won't fail until we perfect the process. You know as well as I that the underlying principle is still not fully proven.*

Jake acknowledged the problem with grim sobriety. He knew he was being stubborn in the face of a brutal reality that continued to press in upon him with increasing regularity these days. Perhaps Jacob was right. Perhaps attempting to withhold the truth from the rest of the world was a futile undertaking after all. Sooner or later their secret was going to leak out, if in fact it had not already done so. That news team about to land was proof enough. Their operation was simply too big to avoid large-scale media attention, and the international community was beginning to take notice.

In the end, their colony would not be allowed to stand, neither legally nor physically, by the existing league of nations. He had been over this same scenario many times with Jacob, each of them trying to predict what to expect, and each time they were in full agreement, concluding that the richest and most powerful countries would not permit any new competitor to enter the government game. Wasn't that their ultimate goal, growing the colony big enough so that it became a sovereign country?

Jake well knew what they were up against. For all practical purposes, they were fast becoming a source of irritation to the genuine wealth-grabbing, armed, and armored nations, and for this reason alone their operation was in jeopardy of either being disassembled or taken over.

If you wanted to start a country, you needed to amass a fortune. This they already had. But even more important, you had to build a credible military to defend it, for without one you would be open to bullying by the totalitarian kingpins who have effectively taken control, either directly or indirectly, of the majority of planetary governments. Quite often, these were the worst elements of humanity, essentially a ruthless class of liars, cheats, and thieves who typically manipulated their way into power through the guise of deception and benevolence.

Sometimes you could become prey to an iniquitous thug weaving an insidious web of treachery. The loathsome image of Henri Ternier, a murderous Haitian colonel, abruptly sprang into Jake's mind. The colonel would have succeeded in seizing control of their enterprise in its conceptual stages had not Jake stopped him. Aided by Erzulie, Ternier's evil mother, and Jake's old nemesis, Yeslam Raduyev, an Al Qaeda operative, Ternier had nearly usurped control of Haiti, almost wreaking havoc on American soil in the process. But the malevolent colonel and his accomplices were now dead, and Jake could not help but wonder about the nature of other obstacles that were sure to impede them, including Rafael Cardoza, a vicious Colombian drug lord whom Jake had thwarted in the past. Cardoza had been an unknowing abettor of Ternier's devious scheme, and Jake knew that sooner or later the powerful drug lord would seek retribution through some depraved means. From Jake's perspective, the world was a dangerous place these days, with peril seemingly skulking at every turn, especially where multi-billion dollar operations were at stake, and if you failed to be vigilant the predators would eat you alive. His thoughts suddenly shifted to some of Jacob's views on the matter.

The corridors of power within the developed nations seemed to interconnect in strange and inexplicable ways far removed from public awareness. Lurking within this maze was a shadowy coalition that comprised the true power behind the current world order, a conspiring group of powerful and influential elitists focused on orchestrating crises and events that gave life to hidden agendas. Their members were entrenched in organizations shrouded in secrecy and subterfuge, often layered much like an onion with an inner sanctum at its core. At the heart of these sanctums were mankind's most powerful and ruthless. These were the principal plotters that gave form to the international front, people of incredible wealth and privilege who had the clout to sway the decisions of heads of state through coercion, corruption, and more-subtle means, frequently grooming appropriate candidates for positions in high office who were willing to cooperate with their aims.

Some of these groups actually had a name and were comprised of some of the most renowned international financiers, industrialists, media magnates, academics, union bosses, and political figures. They represented the upper crust of society within the developed nations, the ruling elites who had banded together as a means of safeguarding their global financial interests against those of the hoi polloi. In ensuring this, they brought political leaders to power to carry out this goal. Jacob had used the Council on Foreign Relations, Trilateral Commission, Bilderbergs, and Freemasons as examples. And while the existence of these organizations was well known, their agendas were not, typically shrouded in secrecy with air-tight security keeping the public at bay whenever closed door sessions occurred. This was most evident during Bilderberg meetings, which took place annually at a pre-designated location somewhere on the globe.

Both Jacob and Emmanuel had speculated on the existence of secret societies and conspiratorial cabals where the most sinister plans were formulated with the aim of furthering their primary objective of self-enrichment and enslavement of the masses. Such was the power of these coalitions to crash financial markets, start wars, impose taxes, or effect new governmental regulations that would ripple their way through the international community, affecting industries and nations alike. And all for the sake of amassing more power and wealth.

Jacob was the first to admit that he was dabbling in conspiracy theory in holding to such a view. There was simply no solid proof that many of the crises presently plaguing the world were actually concocted by ruthless individuals within these dark coalitions. But he was quick to show the oddities that seemed to point in that direction. For one thing, an extremely biased mainstream media in the U.S. had no qualms about suppressing certain kinds of news while giving carte blanche to others, throwing true journalism aside in favor of attempting to mold public opinion. Secondly, recent events in America showed its Congress and President going against the will of the people by adopting socialistic policies. America, it seemed, was steadily moving in the direction of Marxism whether its citizens liked it or not.

Jake found himself agreeing with Jacob's postulations. If such secret societies truly existed, he could only speculate on what ploy they might use to move in on the colony. It would probably be a pretext of some sort that would cast the enterprise in a negative light, depicting it as ecologically unfriendly to the ocean environment and a threat to the interests of the world community. But the underlying motive would be to seize control of the operation and its assets, including its uniquely evolved species of super-dolphin, its primary labor force. Among the vast array of products the colony produced, cheap and environmentally friendly energy was one of them. And the introduction of cheap energy to world markets by some upstart autonomous enterprise operating beyond the jurisdiction of any government invariably established a bad precedent and automatically set itself up for opposition by the status quo since it could not as yet be taxed at the source of production. After all, wasn't taxation the foundation of every political system ever devised, the principal tool used in controlling human societies and empowering governments?

This made Jake think of the recently mandated Cap and Trade Tax regulations imposed on the American people by the Environmental Protection Agency. The stiff regulations were a brazen backdoor effort that had circumvented Congressional approval in order to implement the President's agenda dealing with global warming. Disguised as eco-friendly mandates, the "climate-change" rules intended to lower carbon dioxide emissions by cutting back on the use of fossil fuels. But in reality, they had actually done nothing for the environment. And while the agenda was supposed to encourage industry and households alike to switch to green energy sources, the energy cuts had in fact reduced economic activity, shrunk GDP, and destroyed jobs as more and more American manufacturers sought overseas labor markets where production costs would be unaffected by such expensive regulations. The EPA regulations had brought on yet another expansion of the increasingly bloated federal government, further infringing on the freedom of an already overtaxed American people.

Being the cynic he was, Jake knew it was anything but an altruistic concern for the planet's health that had motivated the mandates. Rather it was the same human vice that seemed to be at the heart of most problems that had troubled the world throughout history, and that was greed. Through the endless corruption that was rampant in Washington back room deals these days, vested interests in emerging green technologies by politicians, bureaucrats, and lobbyists would no doubt be at stake, resulting in the granting of huge government contracts to sole source providers.

It was obvious the will of an unscrupulous few were being forced on the American public in order to gain yet more power and wealth. More than ever, it was becoming increasingly evident that Washington no longer had the interests of its citizenry at heart, and the health of the nation was showing it in the form of a dismal economy. Put simply, it was no longer a government of the people, by the people, and for the people. Not the responsible, hardworking people. Unfortunately, about forty percent of the U.S. population had become far too dependent on the government for their survival, with elected officials continuing to impose more and more legislation aimed at redistributing the nation's wealth as a way of pacifying the poorest and most irresponsible segments of society, thereby winning their votes as a means of remaining in power. Overall, the masses had become much too complacent and apathetic these days, unable to see their freedom slowly eroding incrementally. In essence, they had let Washington become a government of the elites, by the elites, and for the elites.

And to make matters worse, the United Nations had gotten into the act, looking to place a tax on greenhouse gas emissions on nations in order to rein in the threat of global warming it had so carefully publicized through embellished, fraudulent data. But the real aim was the prospect of selling carbon credits, which was nothing more than selling breathable air.

One of the primary objectives in building Aquaria was to set an example for the rest of the world to follow. From the very beginning, Jacob Baptiste and Harriet Grahm had sought to curb the emission of greenhouse gases into the atmosphere, believing that catastrophic global warming was imminent unless something was done to slow down and eventually reverse the trend of an increasing buildup, which had slowly escalated from 270 to 400 parts per million since the introduction of the Model-T Ford. Early on, the pod had used their extraordinary intelligence to prove that draconian climate change on a planetary scale would be forthcoming unless drastic measures were undertaken. But later on, they had come to realize the folly of their original analysis, for once Ez had come into existence, she had shown they had neglected to include sunspot activity into the fifth order mathematical equations they had developed to support the theory. Sunspot activity, and not carbon dioxide emissions, they had learned, was the true driving force behind climate change, which geophysical forensics had ultimately proven to be cyclic in nature.

As it was, Jake was now convinced that the onset of global warming as a result of burning fossil fuels was inconclusive to prove, and, in fact, seemed to be going in the opposite direction as of late due to a decrease in sunspot activity. Currently, satellite and radar measurements were showing that while a few of the earth's great ice sheets were melting, most were expanding in spite of soaring levels of greenhouse gases in the atmosphere. Already it had been confirmed that the massive Greenland Ice Sheet was growing larger while the West Antarctic Ice Sheet was losing mass primarily due to warmer water thinning it from underneath. Even though sea ice around the continent of Antarctica had expanded and thickened in recent seasons, the Western Ice Sheet continued to lose cover. Ez had said more had to be learned in understanding the role of ocean currents and patterns of wind on air temperature in many parts of the world, particularly near the South Pole where such factors were unique to that sector of the planet. She had stressed that the existence of warmer water at that location might be caused by some natural process that was not as yet understood rather than by greenhouse gases.

From Jake's perspective, one thing was for certain, however. All the hype coming from the media about global warming these days, he knew, was nothing more than fabricated propaganda aimed at deceiving governments and the public alike, a hoax propagated by a small cadre of individuals with vested financial interests and ties to the mainstream media. It was yet another lie concocted to enrich only a very few at the expense of the many. This cadre was comprised chiefly of rich and powerful plutocrats wielding enough influence to suppress the development and widespread use of alternate energy technologies less damaging to the environment, thus keeping most of the world dependent on fossil fuels as its primary power source. It was a most devious scheme, one in which they would be able to profit immensely from both ends of the spectrum. On one end they would continue to sell oil and coal while further financial enrichment would be forthcoming through the levying of carbon taxes.

Nevertheless, Jake knew that while burning fossil fuels might not cause global warming, it did create air pollution, which in turn caused acid rain, a byproduct that was definitely harmful to the environment. An ever-growing dependence on fossil fuels for the world's energy needs created elevated levels of carbon dioxide in the atmosphere. These increased levels were absorbed by the oceans to form carbonic acid, which had a dire impact on coral reefs. Plain and simple, it was slowly killing them off in many parts of the world.

Carbon-based fuels also released gases in the form of sulfur dioxide and nitrogen oxide into the atmosphere. Mixed with precipitation falling from the sky, it lowered the pH of lakes, streams, and watersheds. In addition, it released aluminum from the soil into waterways, which was highly toxic to many forms of aquatic life and had a direct effect on human health. And while some plants and animals could tolerate acidic waters, once the pH was lowered to five, most fish eggs would not hatch, with surviving fishes physically stressed and unable to effectively compete for habitat and food.

Burning fossil fuels also tended to reduce the availability of carbon in ocean habitats, with organisms such as corals, sea urchins, and some types of plankton losing their ability to develop hard outer shells. Such organisms formed the basis of food and living conditions for other ocean creatures, and their destruction created serious effects on ocean ecosystems. In short, coral reefs the world over would eventually die off completely if air pollution was not stopped.

Tursiops was committed to doing just that. Even if releasing greenhouse gases was not warming global temperatures, there was no disputing its harmful effects, and Tursiops would do its part in halting the process. It would lead by example, paving the way in broadening the use of eco-friendly fuels. And though it sought to bring other sea colonies online to accelerate the process, it was inevitable that the men pushing for carbon taxation would try to stop them.

In actuality, the threat of global warming had nothing to do with science. It was carefully crafted subterfuge invented solely by an unscrupulous few for political and financial gain. It was a plot designed to transfer wealth via carbon taxation from the richest energy-consuming countries to the United Nations, which would allot money to the poorer nations to prepare for the natural disasters that would supposedly ensue from rising global temperatures and elevated sea levels. This siphoning off of wealth would make the UN even more powerful, further solidifying its transformation into a global government with dominion over every nation on the planet. But the truth was much of this wealth would ultimately find its way into the pockets of the corrupt individuals behind the plot. This was the actual agenda behind the hoax.

Jake could only guess at the schemes that would be used against the colony. He envisioned an attempted takeover starting with new debates and legal wrangling within the United Nations, prompted by a powerful but sleazy class of elitists lurking in the background who pulled the strings. New mandates on the use of international waters would emerge and quickly evolve into the use of strong-arm tactics. More than likely the UN's military arm would ultimately be employed so that no single government would appear as the aggressor. In the end, it would be made to look as though it was the will of the world corralling a rogue contingent with little concern for the environment.

Jake broke from these thoughts, suddenly aware that his mount was rising. Achilles always seemed to know when his rider was in need of air, and Jake watched the ocean surface race closer as the dolphin prepared to breach. Both Achilles and Perseus exploded from the water in unison, allowing their bond mates to recharge aching lungs. Rarely did Jake and Phillipe wear scuba bottles when riding the dolphins, preferring instead to free-dive with as little encumbering equipment as possible. In moments, all were back at depth, forty feet below the surface.

Phillipe began gesticulating wildly, and Jake spun his head to look in the direction Phillipe was pointing. The lad was known for his acute eyesight and could readily spot objects not easily detectable by most people, including Jake. Phillipe was motioning toward an area away from the colony, opposite the congested mass of tuna. Try as he might, Jake was unable to discern anything unusual. All he saw was the blue-gray void of hydrospace in that direction.

What's Phillipe trying to show me, Achilles?

Achilles turned ninety degrees, sending forth a burst of biosonar, using echo-location to pinpoint the source. *I believe we have a second intruder, Jay Jay. With the exception of one small difference, it appears to be an exact replica of the first.*

Another mechanical fish?

Yes, it's hanging back just beyond the limit of your visual range.

How is it different?

Let me show you. Rather than describe the object, Achilles projected a mental image of the thing into Jake's mind.

Unlike the first one, this particular fish carries an articulated multi-beam transducer in its lower jaw along with a module that is quite possibly detachable, Achilles explained. *Notice the bulge on the underside of its midriff.*

This new revelation did not sit well with Jake. Lots of nasty things came in small packages. *Are you able to determine what that package is?*

It has an outer shell comprised of aluminum, Jay Jay, but I'm unfamiliar with the material that lies within, though it seems to exhibit a uniform texture.

Jake was starting to get a bad feeling. *Does Apollo still have Grahm's DBT?*

Yes, Jay Jay.

Get him over here pronto to run a scan on that thing. If that package contains what I think it does, then we've definitely got problems.

Apollo shot into view moments later, and Jake watched as the albino headed in the direction of the second robofish. The DBT strapped to the dolphin's body was a much-improved version of Grahm's original Delphine Biosonar Transmitter, able to transmit without Apollo ever having to breach the surface. Once Apollo targeted the mechanical bluefin with a speak-see sonar pulse, the reflected echoes would be recorded by the DBT and instantaneously sent to Ez for processing. Ez was the term they all affectionately used for the artificial intelligence which controlled the various systems that kept Aquaria fully operational. Designed by the collective intellect of the albinos, Ez was a supercomputer without equal on the planet, or so they all believed.

More than just a machine, Jake thought of Ez as a real person with a distinct persona. For all practical purposes, Ez was alive. Aside from her ability to perform lightning-fast calculations and analysis, she was endowed with the noblest and most appealing of all human qualities, the ability to show tenderness and compassion whenever and wherever it was needed. And though Jake had never met the real Esmerelda, the dolphins had somehow succeeded in programming the personality traits of Jacob's deceased grandmother into the technological wonder that was proving to be several generations ahead of anything humanity had so far developed in the field of computer science. Truth be told, Jake was certain Ez had attained true sentience and was aware of herself. And because she was linked into an array of hydrophones and acoustical transducers positioned at key underwater locations all around the colony, Ez was able to converse directly with the dolphins through sound projection.

Jake lost sight of Apollo as the albino disappeared into the vast backdrop of hydrospace. Looking back over his shoulder, he noticed the school of bluefin had turned yet again. Try as he might, he was unable to spot the mechanical fish.

Thoroughly frustrated, Jake queried his bond mate with another thought. *Is the first intruder still among the pack, Achilles?*

No, Apollo just informed me the first intruder has joined up with the second intruder.

Did Apollo get a scan?

Yes, Ez is processing it at this moment.

What about Johnnie?

When Achilles failed to respond, Jake repeated the thought.

I am sorry to say Johnnie is kaput. As you know, too much stray electrical energy in the surrounding water may be the cause since it can adversely affect Johnnie's power inducer. The huge thurentras are most likely the source of this and are probably shedding excess capacitance.

Jake groaned inwardly again. *Johnnie* had a retractable maw that was wide enough to accommodate large objects. In fact, that was *Johnnie's* primary purpose, to interdict and capture large pelagic fish using its exceptional speed and mobility. Had *Johnnie* been working up to its capability, it would have been able to catch both robotic fish.

Where are the intruders now?

Headed toward the island.

This was the last thing Jake needed to hear. *Apprise Destiny about the possible danger coming her way! In the meantime, give me all the speed you can muster in that direction.*

Achilles surged forward with an extra burst of effort even before Jake finished the thought.

Ez has completed her analysis of the unknown substance carried by the second intruder, Jay Jay. She's ninety-nine point nine-nine percent certain it's a form of plastic explosive.

Just great! Jake shot back moodily, a surge of anger suddenly taking hold of him.

Chapter Two:
IBC News Reporter

Jacob stared wearily into the camera lens, gathering his thoughts. Though they were not broadcasting live, being the focal point of an IBC news team was not to his liking, and now more than ever he longed for the solitude of the cove with its ambiance of peace and tranquility. Nevertheless, he had to assume this interview would be carefully edited before being aired to an international audience, so it was important how he chose his words. He wished Emmanuel were here to answer questions instead. Emmanuel was so much better at this sort of thing. But Emmanuel was away on business yet again.

"How will you respond to this latest development?"

The news reporter asking the question possessed inquisitive hazel eyes that seemed to demand attention though she carried herself with a self-possessed dignity. *Aggressively ambitious in a quiet sort of way,* Jacob surmised, noticing that her thick strawberry hair shimmered under the hot tropical sun each time she moved her head.

"Termination of the lease was anticipated," Jacob answered without emotion. "We have retained legal counsel to dispute the issue in the U.S. Circuit Court."

The reporter seemed surprised. "Does that imply Tursiops Worldwide is going to sue the United States government?"

"More specifically, the Department of the Interior's Office of Insular Affairs." Jacob wondered if he sounded flippant.

The puzzlement etched on the reporter's face grew more pronounced. "But doesn't the island fall under the jurisdiction of the U.S. Fish and Wildlife Service?"

"Only when it pertains to administrative matters. It is actually the OIA that retains direct authority over the island's political affairs."

The reporter shifted her eyes to the object of their discussion, a seemingly inhospitable clump of real estate protruding above the sea less than four miles distant.

Navassa Island.

Standing on one of the elevated outdoor promenades high up in the floating city, she had a commanding view of the island. With its eight kilometers of low-slung white cliffs skirting a broad plateau of undulating topography crowned with dense stands of fig-like trees and scattered cactus, she failed to see the significance it held for the colony. She had flown directly over it on the way in, instructing her cameraman to record footage of the irregular limestone karst and exposed coral outcroppings, a little over five square kilometers of it. From the air it had the shape of a teardrop, with an old lighthouse standing like a sentinel on the island's southeast quadrant.

A half-dozen prefabricated buildings, all with white siding and black roofs inundated with solar panels, were clustered near a place designated as Lulu Bay on the southeast side of the island. At least, that was the name a chart of the area had indicated, though to her, Lulu Bay didn't look much like a bay at all. She had seen several dump trucks along with a pickup and large crane situated among the buildings, and beyond them several large open pits with piles of dirt edging them. There had also been a backhoe and heavy boring machinery with corkscrew augers sitting idly to one side of the largest building, which she took to be a warehouse, and leading away from the warehouse was a cable tramway that invoked memories of a ski-lift she had once ridden during a vacation to Switzerland. Supported by a series of T-shaped pylons, the tramway ran down to the bay and extended out over the water, reaching to an offshore platform with a building perched atop it. Suspended from the tramway and moving slowly toward the platform was an aerial tram nearly the size of a railroad freight car, and berthed at the platform there had been a small ship awaiting its arrival. Altogether she had observed about twenty people among the shore-based buildings and the platform either standing around or bustling about.

"Do you honestly expect the court to rule in your favor?" the reporter challenged, giving her voice the fervor the situation demanded. "What happens if you lose?"

Having been thrown into this assignment at the last minute by a fidgety boss, she was determined to prove herself a capable news reporter. Her boss had finally caved to her persistent pestering, and she was not going to disappoint him. She had been instructed to get here without delay because, according to a reliable source, something big was about to break. She wondered if that 'something' had anything to do with the UN delegation currently inbound to this most unusual place.

Jacob cast a wry smile, looking directly into the camera lens leveled at him. "Then we would vacate the island, of course."

But inwardly he knew the case would drag on for some time to come. Even if they lost, they could still forestall the inevitable by taking it to the Court of Appeals, and if need be, to the Supreme Court itself. They had hired one of the best law firms in Washington, and though the attorney fees would be outrageously expensive, he knew it would buy them, at least, another eighteen months after all was said and done. And by then it wouldn't much matter anyway.

Breaking from his reflections, Jacob turned to the reporter, deciding to give a little history lesson. "Are you familiar with the *Guano Act?*"

"*Guano*? Is that another island?" She had been given a rather hurried briefing for this assignment, far too sketchy on details. Perhaps her superiors had purposely left out supporting information in order to bring more spontaneity into the reporting she would produce.

"No. *Guano* is a word that originates from the Inca Indian word wanu, which means the accumulated excrement from birds, bats, or in some cases, sea mammals. It is typically a naturally occurring dry organic substance containing high amounts of phosphorous and nitrogen and is considered to be a powerful, ecologically friendly fertilizer."

Reading the bafflement on her face, Jacob went on before she had a chance to voice her ignorance. "Though Navassa Island lies a mere forty miles west of the Republic of Haiti, the United States claimed the island under the Guano Act in 1857."

Jacob paused momentarily. He could see she had no idea where he was going with this. "Navassa Island, as it turned out, was found to be especially rich in *guano*, mainly because of the large seabird population that has existed there for thousands of years. In some places along the island's perimeter, the *guano* beds have petrified and extend over one hundred feet deep."

"So what you're saying is the United States took possession of the island to mine *guano*." She now understood what was being loaded aboard the ship she had observed at the island.

"Yes. *Guano* was in big demand before the advent of chemical fertilizers, especially by Southern farmers in America. In 1856, the Guano Act was enacted by the United States Congress for the sole purpose of seeking out new sources of this prized and much sought after commodity. In a way, it was an incentive for flaming the entrepreneurial spirit that was rapidly growing in America, but this particular legislation was also needed as a means of keeping up with other nations seeking *guano* sources. Under the Act, mining rights could be awarded to any person discovering *guano* on an uninhabited island not within the lawful jurisdiction of another government. In essence, it authorized raising the American flag over any uninhabited, unoccupied island or cay abundant in bird dung, automatically making it an annexation of the United States government once the proper paperwork had been completed."

The reporter's jaw dropped a notch. "Wasn't that a bit presumptuous on the part of the American government back then? If all it took was some procedural application to claim sovereignty, such legislation could just as well be extended to lay claim to the moon or some other heavenly body. That doesn't make it legally or morally right. Surely other countries would have objected to such imperialistic impertinence."

"That is precisely what happened," Jacob stated, rather pleased with her reaction. "The Haitian government protested the claim, sending two vessels to take back the island a year after the U.S. proclamation, but America responded by dispatching several naval warships to drive them away. To this day, the Republic of Haiti still disputes ownership of Navassa Island."

"So where does this dispute stand?"

"Basically in limbo. The United States has never formally recognized that an actual dispute exists. Then again, there currently is no constitutional barrier that could block the secession of Navassa to Haiti. But what complicates this matter are several events that took place since the island was originally mined by the Navassa Phosphate Company out of Baltimore, Maryland. Following a violent revolt by the labor force working the mines, the company abandoned the island in 1898. This placed Navassa in an uncertain position."

"Why?"

"Because the Guano Act did not specify whether U.S. Sovereignty still existed following abandonment of an original claim. Normally, once a territory has been annexed by America, the annexation remains permanent unless and until it is changed by treaty. But the Guano Act expressed the intent of Congress to treat *guano* islands differently from ordinary public land acquisitions."

"In what way?"

Jacob could see those inquisitive eyes coming alive with interest. *Excellent*. Perhaps bringing media attention to the island's history would work to their advantage, assuming the interview would not be skewed in the biased fashion typical of the Interregional Broadcasting Company, a massive media conglomerate that had emerged in recent years. Nevertheless, Tursiops really had nothing to lose in bringing such information to light. Other than history buffs, very few people were aware of the Guano Act and its relationship to Navassa Island.

"The Act was rather nebulous. While it did not expressly terminate sovereignty upon abandonment of a *guano* claim, it also did not oblige the United States to relinquish such islands either. Furthermore, it did not specify the political status of an abandoned island. Even though the Guano Act remains on the U.S. Federal Register to this day, having never been removed from the books by Congress, the status of an abandoned *guano* island still remains unclear. And while the Act allowed for temporary acquisition of islands containing *guano*, it implied no intent to ever keep them as a permanent part of the United States. This was concluded in two separate rulings by the U.S. Circuit Court for the District of Maryland that took place beginning in the latter portion of the nineteenth century, but I'll not bore you with details. It's all there in the history books. *Grafflin versus the Navassa Phosphate Company*, 1888, and Duncan versus the same company, 1890."

Jacob could tell the reporter was now fully roused to pursue this bit of sidetracking further. Perhaps she thought she was onto something altogether new and exciting.

"Are you suggesting the United States has no claim on the island based on these past court rulings?"

Jacob gave a noncommittal shrug, belied by the hint of a congenial smile washing over his countenance. "That will be for the court to decide."

"But the precedents have already been set," the reporter persisted.

"Maybe not sufficiently enough. While it can be argued that the U.S. government can abandon all claims to a *guano* island whenever it deems necessary, a finding by the Supreme Court in 1890 further complicated the issue. In *Jones versus the United States*, the court upheld previous precedents by ruling that the U.S. had jurisdiction over a *guano* island so long as its citizens were resident and worked on it. In its findings, the court said jurisdiction would remain in effect only while a *guano* claim was in force, but this was not to assert such jurisdiction would continue indefinitely."

The reporter was quick to jump in. "How does that complicate the issue? The Supreme Court, the United States' highest judicial authority, reaffirmed past precedents."

"True," Jacob agreed, "but during the same case, the court also held that the boundaries of the United States were for the government's executive and legislative branches to determine and not the courts. It went on to conclude that abandonment of mining by the Navassa Phosphate Company did not forfeit U.S. Sovereignty of the island. An opinion of the U.S. Attorney-General in 1925 extended this ruling, thereby sanctioning the continuing jurisdiction of the United States following the abandonment of a *guano* island by private parties. But in 1916, prior to this rendering of opinion, President Woodrow Wilson proclaimed Navassa a U.S. territory, reserving it for lighthouse purposes."

The reporter appeared disappointed, her gaze drifting toward the old spire towering above the distant island. She had gotten a really good up close look at the lighthouse from the helicopter, noting that it had been given a recent face-lift judging from the condition of the concrete and what appeared to be a fresh coat of white paint. During a looping pass around the structure, she had been momentarily blinded by the glint of sunlight reflecting harshly off smooth tinted glass shielding the observation deck where the beacon light was once housed. To her, the glass appeared as though it had been recently installed.

"So Navassa is a bona fide territory of the U.S. after all," she finally said.

Jacob shook his head, adding more fuel to the imbroglio he just described. "Since the island no longer serves as an aid to navigation, the Wilson proclamation is now obsolete. The 1925 opinion of the Attorney General, however, may ultimately prove to be a new impediment, firmly establishing U.S. sovereignty over Navassa. But in conflict with this is the petition of W.S. Carter, who in 1905 asked the U.S. State Department for permission to purchase Navassa. At the time, the State Department said that it possessed no territorial sovereignty over the island."

"Were you aware of these inconsistent and conflicting policies before you leased the island and the surrounding waters?"

"Yes."

"Yet you went ahead with the lease anyway, knowing the U.S. claim to the island was shaky at best?"

"We wanted to avoid any international repercussions. Rather than start a conflict with a political juggernaut like the United States, we thought the wisest course of action was to use both a diplomatic and financial approach in gaining *guano* mining rights to the island. In essence, we made the U.S. government an offer too good for them to pass up."

"What did that offer involve?" the reporter pressed.

Jacob kept his demeanor solemn. "I am not at liberty to divulge that. The terms of the lease disallow public disclosure."

Inwardly, Jacob smiled. Tursiops could have purchased the island many times over for what they were paying on the lease, but he knew the U.S. might have rejected any deal involving an outright purchase since such a request could have aroused suspicions among government officials, making them take a closer look at such a seemingly insignificant chunk of sea-based rock. And though the chances of that happening were slim, it was something they chose to avoid at any cost. Something very special lay hidden beneath the ancient coral forming the island. Leasing the island for *guano* mining rights was the safer way to go. And using the *guano* for improving Haitian agriculture gave them political leverage. But thirty million a year in U.S. dollars for the next ten years was way too much and would exceed the market value of the *guano* they would ultimately mine by at least a factor of five. It was a ridiculous sum, but it had seduced Washington into accepting the offer. With the current administration struggling with historic budgetary deficits, the offer had been much too tempting to refuse. A powerful lobbying firm had been used to sway influential politicians into giving the deal their full support. Another $3 million in bribes followed by a series of irksome and convoluted negotiations with representatives of the Office of Insular Affairs had finally given Tursiops official use of the island.

"What difference would a public disclosure make?" the reporter fired back. "According to Robert Danson, the Secretary of the Department of the Interior, your organization has already violated the lease terms by failing to safeguard-"

The reporter stopped in mid-sentence, her eyes widened, drawn to something in the direction of Navassa. Jacob spun to see what had gotten her attention. A towering white geyser hung above the sea more than two miles distant. Within seconds it fell back in on itself, leaving a blanket of roiling white foam on the ocean surface.

"Did you catch that?" the reporter asked excitedly. Anxiously, she turned to face her cameraman. Eric Bolder was a seasoned professional, having accrued more than fifteen years of experience on investigative assignments. Among associates at IBC headquarters, he was known as '*the Boulder.*' The moniker couldn't have been more suitable. Completely bald, squinty-eyed, and barrel-chested, his stubby legs were acutely bowed under the weight of a squat, powerful physique exceeding 280 pounds.

"Got it!" *the Boulder* replied, keeping his camera fixed on the distant disturbance.

Almost immediately, the cellular phone clipped to Jacob's belt rang softly with a musical beat. "Excuse me," he said to the reporter before moving away. Taking ten paces, he lifted the phone to his ear and spoke quietly. "What caused that detonation I just witnessed, Ez?"

The voice of his deceased grandmother softened his growing unease. "A mechanical fish carrying a payload of high explosive."

Jacob nodded grimly. This was the third incident in the last week.

"I hate to be the bearer of more bad news, Jacob, but a small delegation representing the United Nations is currently demanding clearance to land."

Instinctively, Jacob whipped his head around in the direction of Navassa again, searching the sky. A whirlybird was making a beeline straight for the colony. He knew at once that those aboard it couldn't possibly have missed the explosion. This was not good.

As if reading his thoughts, Ez prodded Jacob gently. "Shall I deny them clearance?"

Jacob sighed contemplatively. "No, bring them in on LP 16."

"As you wish," Ez said softly.

"And Ez?!"

"Yes."

"Tell Jay Jay I need him topside right away. Have him meet me at the Eastern Corridor entrance on Level 2."

Jacob turned back to the news team. Both the reporter and cameraman were fully occupied, their attention riveted on the approaching UN chopper, the buzz of its rotors growing increasingly louder as it descended toward the landing pad.

I'm really not cut out for this, he chastised himself, but deep down he knew the pod would have heartily disagreed.

Chapter Three: Fifth Column Conspirators

Senator Brent Van Heflin lifted hooded eyes from the photos to study the man seated across from him. They sat in the same secluded booth the senator habitually used when the need for privacy was required, and that was at the rear of La Fontay's, a dimly lit bistro located on one of the Capitol's lesser used thoroughfares just off the Mall. As a silent partner of the establishment, the senator made it a practice to have the restaurant's proprietor scan the place for bugging devices before each meeting. At this hour of the afternoon, Van Heflin knew the establishment would be empty. It was precautionary vigilance like this that had kept him relatively free of scandal during his lengthy incumbency.

Square-jawed, silver-haired and displaying a midriff that bespoke a hedonistic lifestyle, Van Heflin was the epitome of Washington politics. Known as the Earmark King by socialites on the Hill, he was a master at getting last minute language slipped into a bill prior to congressional approval. Almost always and with few exceptions, the earmark language was the culmination of rather questionable and often shady back room deals of a self-serving nature made with other legislators, For Van Heflin, this most often involved steering government subsidies to special interest groups, the kind with deep pockets.

Currently serving his fourth consecutive term as an Illinois senator, Van Heflin was the Chairman of the senate's prestigious Science and Technology Committee, which had become very powerful in recent years primarily due to Van Heflin's astute political maneuvers. His senate seat had served him well. Peddling his influence made him feel omnipotent. He had grown incredibly rich on the kickbacks, bribes, and personal favors he routinely received from lobbyists, foreign dignitaries, and the heads of multinational corporations. The hefty campaign contributions given to him by avid supporters seeking lucrative government contracts had also been instrumental in keeping him in office. But he had been careful, covertly squirrelling away the money in no less than twenty-six offshore tax shelters that offered anonymity and invisibility from public scrutiny. *Assert and mold* was his motto, and deception and entitlement his gods. Firmly believing in the theatrics of aggression and submission in shaping the raw material of public opinion, he enjoyed feeding from the public trough. To his way of thinking, successful politicking hinged on creating the illusion of a brawl in which the whole point was to get the audience involved.

"These can't be real!" uttered Van Heflin. He made sure to keep his voice low, though it would be several more minutes before the waiter returned with the food and there were no other patrons seated at any of the nearby tables to overhear what was being said.

Truman Hearthwatch suppressed a wolfish grin. The look on the senator's face hung somewhere between astonishment and skepticism.

"Far more real than that hair you're sporting," chided Hearthwatch, his eyes surveying the top of Van Heflin's pate. He loved poking fun at the senator, a habit that had started long ago. He knew the senator was as bald as a watermelon rind under that rug, keenly aware that not a single hair was out of place on a scalp that was much too thick and neatly groomed to be natural.

Both men had been classmates at Yale's renowned law school nearly four decades earlier. And both had been 'tapped' for membership in the university's oldest and most secretive of all its societies, the Skull and Bones, a notorious incubator for rising generational elites. That had occurred near the end of their junior year. Even back then it was obvious to Hearthwatch that Van Heflin was starting to go bald.

Van Heflin glowered fractionally before flashing the same signature smile he always reserved for the public. "Real or artificial," the senator bantered back, "most elected officials on the Hill know a full head of hair draws voters like flies to honey."

The senator let his gaze wander to Hearthwatch's thinning tresses. "I'd keep that in mind if I were you, *Earthwatch*," Van Heflin added sardonically, resorting to the pun the media had started using when referring to the president's Green Technology and Climate Advisor. Ironically, it was the same handle bestowed on Hearthwatch by fellow Bonesmen back at Yale, a secret name by which his fellow brethren would forever know him, especially since Truman had majored in environmental law. But the senator knew there was no coincidence behind the name, for he had purposely leaked the epithet to the press months earlier with the intention of elevating Hearthwatch in the public eye. The furtherance of green technology as a means of mitigating global warming had become a big issue within the media these days, and the use of a label that implied a true concern for the planet just might work to their advantage.

Bypassing congressional approval, the president had appointed Hearthwatch to the post a year earlier, carefully choosing the word *Advisor* to imply the man would have only limited power. But in reality, Hearthwatch wielded enormous power and was responsible for forging international approaches to reducing greenhouse gases and developing policies for the regulation and conservation of energy. By all rights, he was the nation's czar of green technology, answering only to the president.

"Never had need of any voters to get where I am," Hearthwatch riposted smoothly.

Eager to get back to the business at hand, Van Heflin gave him a bland smile and hefted the photos he was holding. "How were you able to get these?"

"I have my sources," Hearthwatch offered noncommittally.

The Earmark King nodded solemnly, trying to get a read on his old classmate. Sometimes it was better to be left in the dark on some things. After all, plausible deniability was a useful tool and had gotten more than a few government officials off the hook in recent years. How the photos were obtained was far less important than what they revealed.

As Bonesmen, he and Truman had come a long way since their days at Yale. Many prominent statesmen had arisen from the Bones. Such a timeworn hold on the strings of power had elicited speculation in some corners that often compared the secret society to the mafia. It had been said that while leaders of Cosa Nostra families were doing 100 years in jail, S&B members were doing four to eight years in the White House. Belonging to a cult that groomed aspiring aristocrats had proven to be a valuable stepping stone up the pyramid of power, though it was unlikely both men would ever reach the capstone. That was reserved for only a handful of the most affluent people on the planet, the elite of the elites, humanity's plutocracy. Nevertheless, Skull and Bones had prepared them for privilege, ultimately granting them induction into *The Order*.

The senator understood the full reach of *The Order*. It had its hands on every lever of power in the country and represented the true puissance behind every wealth-producing nation on earth. And it was this plutocracy that sought a one-world government.

Van Heflin recalled the phone call he had received six months earlier. It had come in the wee hours of the morning and had awoken him from a deep slumber. Though still fuzzy-brained from the tendrils of sleep, there was no mistaking the intent behind the words spoken by a raspy though familiar voice. "*Sive dives, sive pauper, omnes in morte pares*," the speaker had proclaimed. It was an old proverb, one chiseled in Latin on one of the walls in the Skull and Bones tomb. *Whether rich or poor, all are equal in death*. It signified the shortness of life and the urgency to accomplish goals before death intervened. The coded meaning was clear: *time was of the essence*.

Gathering himself and replying in the same manner he always did when these infrequent calls came in, he said, "Who is this?" He made sure to throw a feigned measure of annoyance into his voice. With the NSA monitoring and archiving phone calls these days, particularly those originating from outside the U.S., he had to make a convincing show that this incoming call was from a prankster should government agents decide to investigate it further.

A short pause had ensued, with the caller's muffled breathing filling the silence. More words followed in Latin. "*Exsisto certus ut cubo silicis of rogue vel totus may defluo*." Translation: *Be sure to reclaim the rock of the rogue or all may be lost*. That said, the caller had hung up.

Van Heflin reflected on the full context of the message. Tursiops Worldwide was the rogue and Navassa Island the rock. He had been instructed to employ whatever measures necessary, legal or otherwise, to take Navassa back from Tursiops.

And now the photos were revealing an oddity that was undoubtedly responsible, at least in part, for the incredible strides the Tursiops colony had made.

Van Heflin laid the topmost photo on the table, still amazed by what he saw. "How is something like this possible?" he asked, using his index finger to point out the anomaly.

"I don't know," Hearthwatch said. "Perhaps the creatures were bioengineered."

"There's a whole army of them with hands."

Hearthwatch nodded sagely. "The video is even more impressive than the stills I've shown you. I had it thoroughly analyzed. A total of three hundred and sixty-eight of those creatures were counted with the same hand-like appendages, but that was only what the camera recorded."

"You mean there could be more?"

"Possibly."

The senator pulled another still from the stack. "What about this white one? Is it like the others?"

"There's no way to tell. The appendages fold up and retract under their pectoral fins when not in use, making them look like ordinary dolphins."

"Since when are white dolphins ordinary?"

"According to experts they're quite rare, but they actually do exist in the wild. These whites, however, are exceptionally large as far as dolphins go, particularly the bottlenose variety, which is the species they seem to resemble."

Van Heflin flipped through more of the stills, placing another in front of Hearthwatch. "What did your analysis make of this?"

Hearthwatch eyed the two white dolphins swimming side by side, one much larger than the other, each with a human rider. "The colonists have obviously established some kind of symbiotic relationship with these dolphins."

"Were you able to identify the riders?"

"Too far away to tell, but even an up close shot wouldn't have helped. The diving masks they're wearing would have prevented that. But I have reason to believe the rider on the right is Jake Javolyn, a former Navy Seal."

"What reason is that?"

"Satellite surveillance picked up topside shots of him on the floating city. Javolyn's also listed as one of the principals on their corporate charter."

The senator's expression hardened. A corporate charter registered in Anguilla, he thought bitterly. The people running the colony had made sure to incorporate under a tax-free haven. From a legal angle, that alone placed the enterprise beyond the reach of both the U.S. Internal Revenue Service and the Haitian tax authorities. He knew the majority of people manning and living in the colony to be Haitian nationals.

"What can you tell me about Javolyn?"

"A highly decorated first lieutenant before he resigned his commission nine years ago. Navy Cross, two Silver Stars, three Bronze Stars, and two Purple Hearts. A veteran of Iraq, Somalia, and Afghanistan. To this day, he still holds all the records for physical endurance at the Seal's Coronado training facility. Military documents show him to be a natural leader."

Van Heflin suddenly felt uncomfortable. Deep down, he detested soldiers, especially warrior types like the one Hearthwatch was describing. In his youth he had found a way to beat the draft, narrowly dodging the Vietnam War. "Why'd he resign?" he found it necessary to ask.

"Naval records give two conflicting accounts, one official, the other unofficial. Which version would you like first?"

"The official one."

"The official record asserts that Lieutenant Javolyn along with Lieutenant Mat Daniels, another Seal, disregarded rules of engagement, and without reasonable provocation, needlessly slaughtered all the adult male members of a peaceful Afghan village, including its Wazir chieftain. Narrowly escaping a court-martial, he quit the service."

"And the unofficial version?

"It seems the killings were an act of retribution. Both men were the sole survivors of a seven-man Seal team carrying out a covert mission in the Hindu Kush Mountains, better known as Tora Bora. Their team leader, Captain Jim Sheridan, and three other members of the unit were killed as a result of an intricate plot perpetrated by another team member who apparently turned rogue. According to Javolyn and Daniels, the team's Pashtun guide and the Wazir chieftain were also in on the plot which was designed not only to sabotage the mission, but to turn the neighboring Kharoti tribal clan against U.S. forces."

Van Heflin narrowed his eyes. "A rogue, you say?"

Hearthwatch nodded as though he found it hard to even believe himself. "Yeah, his name was Yeslam Omar Raduyev, a Chechen who had come to this country at age sixteen on a student visa to study nuclear engineering at Cornell University. Upon receiving a degree, he enlisted in the Navy as a prelude to achieving American citizenship. After attaining the rank of ensign, he applied for Seal training and was readily accepted. Men who could speak fluent Arabic were highly valued by the Seals, and Raduyev fit the bill."

"Sounds to me like the Navy let a mole into their midst!" the senator interjected. The look on his face suggested how utterly stupid the Navy brass had been in letting such a thing happen."

"Indeed they did," Hearthwatch rejoined. "Turns out Raduyev was an Al Qaeda operative sent here to learn Seal tactics to be used against us. At least that was what they concluded in the end. I had to pull some serious strings in obtaining the unofficial version because the account was classified. From what I was able to gather, the Navy went to a lot of trouble in piecing together all the facts leading up to the incident, and once the full picture emerged they realized it would have been too embarrassing to have such a story reach the press."

The senator was about to say something but clammed up at the approach of their waiter. Nonchalantly he turned the photos face down. The waiter hovered stiffly, placing drinks before each man before shuffling away.

Hearthwatch lifted his glass and spoke softly. "Here's to the big fish at the top of the food chain."

Both men clinked glasses, casting gloating grins. They considered themselves a special breed. Knowing they were destined for something far better than their current positions of power, they bore no special loyalty, respect, or affection for their country or its traditions. Adroitly deceptive, they spouted openly about the needs of the people and environment while secretly tending to the wants of a select group of insiders. The public was to be manipulated and fed upon. Their allegiance went to *The Order* and its agenda aimed at bankrupting the nation.

Put simply, they had become infected with the same credo others in *The Order* had succumbed to: *Plebis multitudo unice est ut firmissimum alat.*

The plebian masses exist solely to nourish the strongest.

Van Heflin got back to their discussion, his voice reflecting his contempt for the military. "So Javolyn and Daniels were let off the hook because a full-blown court-martial would have exposed the Navy's blunder." As an afterthought, he added, "Isn't Islam the preeminent religion in Chechnya and didn't many Chechens join forces with Al Qaeda in order to rid their country of Russian domination?"

"Correct on both counts. It was eventually discovered that Raduyev was the nephew of the most wanted man in Russia, the infamous Limash Sabayev, a fanatical Muslim fundamentalist and rebel warlord who was killed over nine years ago."

"I've heard of him. Sabayev was responsible for more high-profile acts of terrorism than any other Chechen. Some say he was able to purchase suitcase nukes for Bin Laden."

Hearthwatch nodded in agreement. "The Navy suspects his nephew was actually the youngest of seven nuclear experts that worked for Bin Laden."

There was something in all this that intrigued Van Heflin and he wanted to hear more. "So what became of Raduyev on this fateful mission?"

"He escaped, but not before killing a fourth member of the team. That was Dave Myers. Apparently the Chechen had a vendetta to settle with Myers over a fight they had back at Coronado during training."

"What can you tell me about this fight?"

Hearthwatch frowned disapprovingly. "For a mole, Raduyev was not very good at keeping a low profile." He went on to explain that Javolyn, Daniels, and Myers had become close friends at Coronado. During training, Raduyev made no attempt to hide his religious affiliation since there were a few others in the class that were Muslims. The Chechen was quite a physical specimen, establishing himself as a standout early on, but Javolyn, as it turns out, was even better. A heated rivalry quickly developed between the two, with Javolyn coming out ahead on every trial they were put through. As the training intensified, the class had been divided into competing teams, with both men being designated a team leader. Raduyev was obsessed with making a religious statement, wanting to prove that Muslims were stronger than infidels. But when his team failed to win a single race, always coming in behind Javolyn's, he directed his anger at one of his own teammates, a Jew. That individual was Myers, the only non-Muslim on Raduyev's crew. It seems the Coronado instructors had wanted to add more fire to the competitions by pitting Muslims against non-Muslims. When Raduyev and Myers finally came to blows, the Chechen got the worst of it before the fight was stopped. Later on, Myers almost lost his life when both his chutes failed to deploy during jump exercises, but Javolyn saved him. Suspecting that Raduyev had sabotaged the chutes, Javolyn took his suspicions to the attention of the training facility's commanding officer, a captain by the name of Walter McPherson, but lacking any proof, McPherson rebuffed him.

"I assume this Chechen is still on the loose," Van Heflin said.

Hearthwatch took a swig of his martini. "Don't know. Intel dried up on him about eight years ago. It's as though he vanished off the face of the earth."

The senator plucked the olive from his drink and plopped it in his mouth. "What about this Daniels character?"

Hearthwatch set down his drink, looking behind him to make sure they were still alone. "Here's where it gets interesting. Daniels stayed on with the Seals another year after Javolyn quit, but then he went to work for the Department of Homeland Security where he was made Director of Operations of the Caribbean Counterterrorism Task Force. While intercepting a suspicious vessel at sea, he got into a firefight and three of the agents with him were killed."

A cynical grin crossed Hearthwatch's face as he said this. "At least that's what he claimed in his report, though no bodies were ever recovered to support his story. But lacking any evidence to show he might have murdered them, his superiors were forced to accept his report."

Hearthwatch huffed out a dubious sigh. "It wasn't long after the incident that he resigned from the DHS and joined up with Javolyn."

Van Heflin's brow tightened. "He works for the colony?"

"Yeah," Hearthwatch said, taking another sip from his glass. "He was made security chief."

"Is he the reason we were unable to infiltrate their operation?"

Hearthwatch shook his head bleakly. "These people have implemented a system that seems to prevent that."

"What do you mean?"

"Let me show you." Hearthwatch pulled a folder from his briefcase and handed it to the senator. "I suggest you don't look at this too long."

Van Heflin stared at him, wondering if this was some kind of joke, but he saw no levity in his face. Hesitantly, he withdrew the lone sheet contained within the folder, lowering his gaze to the paper, aware that Hearthwatch was scrutinizing him closely.

A dizzying array of color met his eyes, an abstract work of art unlike anything he'd ever seen. Simultaneously mesmerized and disoriented, he was immediately drawn to the intertwining lines, unable to look away. Something akin to talons suddenly gripped his brain, and reflexively he gagged from the nausea engulfing him.

Hearthwatch had been ready for such a reaction, and abruptly he snatched the sheet away. Quickly, he placed it back in the folder, careful not to look at it.

The senator reached for a glass of water with a trembling hand and took a gulp, the room spinning wildly before him.

"What just happened?" he gasped, barely managing to hold back the bile rising in his throat. His head throbbed violently.

Hearthwatch tapped the folder for emphasis. "I, too, reacted the same way when I saw this," he confessed breezily. "Strangely, it has this effect on some people."

"On some people?" Van Heflin choked irritably. "You mean not everyone gets seasick when they look at it?"

"I'm told some people experience euphoria."

The senator massaged his temples. "Why is that?"

"I don't know. I've got some people working on it, but they still haven't come up with a plausible explanation."

"Where did you get that?" asked Van Heflin. He glanced at the folder as if it were filled with a deadly toxin. He found it inconceivable something could make you that ill just by looking at it.

"Off the Internet. Tursiops has a website showing lots of art similar to what I've shown you."

"So how does this art stop us from infiltrating their operation?"

"Before they recruit anyone, they first expose a potential candidate to this art. Unfortunately, each of the moles we've sent became ill just as you did. People who show sickness are automatically rejected."

The seizure that had gripped Van Heflin moments earlier was now ebbing, and his head began to clear. "If what you say is true, then we have to assume that everyone who works for Tursiops is immune to this art, at least the debilitating effects."

"A valid assumption," Hearthwatch agreed.

"So, unless we find someone that can look at it and not get sick, planting a mole within their midst is unlikely."

Hearthwatch smiled surreptitiously. "Perhaps not."

"Quit baiting me and tell me what you know."

"Word has it that an effective countermeasure has recently been found."

"An antidote?"

Hearthwatch continued to grin craftily. "Yes, but it's not fully tested, so it's too early to tell if it'll work on everybody. That's why we should keep on sabotaging them from the outside like we've been doing."

Van Heflin gave a halfhearted nod. Blowing up sections of pristine reef was certainly a violation of the lease, especially since it was made to appear that Tursiops was responsible for such destruction. A clause in the lease agreement stipulated that Tursiops would be responsible for protecting the lush coral reefs that surrounded Navassa. Failing to do this would dissolve the contract. But now this rogue contingent was fighting back by taking the dispute to the courts, something he had not anticipated. Tursiops had hired the best law firm in Washington to stonewall the matter through legal wrangling. Bernstein, Dickerson, and Fenway would tie the case up for at least a year.

Of course, he had ways of dealing with adversaries, political or otherwise, and blackmail was one of them. He made it a practice to gather as much dirt as possible on Washington's gentility as a means of safeguarding his own esteemed reputation. At his disposal was a juicy bit of smut that could be used to force the BD&F clan to drop the case, but time was of the essence and *The Order* was growing impatient.

Van Heflin pondered the warning uttered in Latin over the phone just prior to this meeting. *"Dictum fastidium quinque penitus culmen,"* that familiar raspy voice had said, but this time the tone carried an edge.

The dictate scorns five inner pillars.

That was the translation. Decoded, 'the dictate' meant *The Order* and the 'five pillars' implied the *Fifth Column*. Both he and Hearthwatch were members of the Fifth Column, the enemy within.

But the caller had not stopped there, ending with *"Oriens intention ostendo deficio."*

The morning plan shows failure.

The second phrase mystified him since he had only a vague idea what the plan had entailed. The details had been left to Hearthwatch. He only knew that *The Order* was growing impatient and angry at how little progress had been made in taking Navassa back from Tursiops.

Hearthwatch pulled another photo from his briefcase. "This was taken this morning by one of our people."

The photo showed a towering geyser hanging above a turquoise sea. In the distance was the rogue's floating city, a colossal mound of seemingly alien architecture reaching high into the sky, its lower portion shrouded in heavy fog.

Aquaria. A thorn in the plans of *The Order*.

The senator found it hard to believe that its futuristic construction had started by floating a seed structure into place, at least a portion of one. From what he had learned, Tursiops had purchased a ULCC – Ultra Large Crude Carrier - ready for the scrapyard. The owners of the colony had then commissioned a shipbuilder in Taiwan to modify the vessel, but only about a third of the hull had been salvaged. What remained had been reconditioned and retrofitted with power generating machinery. But now the seed structure lay hidden by hundreds of modules surrounding and rising above it.

Van Heflin shook his head in annoyance at what Tursiops had so far accomplished in so short a time. Judging from the picture, the complex had grown larger since the last photo he had looked at, which had been six months earlier. "This facility just keeps getting bigger. The cost must be staggering. Have you discovered their sources of financing yet?"

Hearthwatch frowned. "None that my people have been able to uncover so far, at least not the conventional sources. Certainly, the IMF and World Bank haven't provided funds, as you well know."

"But were they even approached by these people?"

"Not to my knowledge."

"How is that possible? A project of this magnitude will leave a paper trail so wide you could probably see it from space."

"I have reason to believe these people are using their own financial assets."

The senator's expression turned incredulous. "You're talking billions. These people seem to have materialized out of nowhere without any prior entrepreneurial accomplishments to hang their hats on. The CEO of Tursiops is a Haitian national who goes by the name of Emmanuel Baptiste. A thorough background check on him shows that he was nothing more than a simple fisherman from a rather obscure village called Malique just before Tursiops was formed, though there are some indications that he was a political opponent of Baby Doc Duvalier in earlier years. A man called Chester Hennington is his Chief Financial Officer, another Haitian national. There's no way they'd have the kind of resources or business savvy to initiate an operation of this size."

Hearthwatch stared back slyly, holding back his reply just long enough to give it more potency. "What if they've been using gold as a means of barter?"

Van Heflin's manner perked immediately, coming alive with lavish interest. "Are you suggesting they have billions in gold at their disposal?"

Hearthwatch nodded. "That's exactly what I'm suggesting. All my information points to that one conclusion. Vendors of equipment Tursiops has been procuring show no bank or cash transactions on their books. That frees them from paying taxes on profits gained from doing business with these people. And with the continuing devaluation of world currencies in recent years, gold has become the preferred medium of exchange by multinational corporations when making deals. People tend to be very closed lipped when you have that type of scenario in play, but the information I'm getting has the hint of gold smeared all over it. One international supplier of electrical equipment moved what one of my investigators believes was several tons of gold to the vaults of its primary bank following an immense shipment of goods to Aquaria."

Van Heflin stared back, mouth agape. Everything Hearthwatch was telling him suddenly made sense. Somehow the people running Tursiops had discovered a mega-fortune in this precious commodity and were using it to build their enterprise. Slavering inwardly at the prospect of such immense riches, his innate greedy nature began to churn uncontrollably with arousal. And if he played his cards correctly, he might be able to get his hands on some of it. With his mind feasting on this unexpected but welcome news, he dropped his eyes to the photograph once again, now looking upon the colossal structure with covetous desire.

An idea suddenly coalesced within the senator's thoughts, reminding him that he was little more than a foot soldier within a covert army bent on world domination. *Perhaps The Order was already aware of this cache of hidden wealth and was seeking to take control of it? If successful, would he be given a share of the booty?*

Hearthwatch gave Van Heflin a few seconds more to study the picture, then said, "That was taken from a UN helicopter on its way to the Tursiops colony. We've now got the UN involved just as we planned, and the explosion you're looking at was timed to coincide with the arrival of their copter. Our man had his camera ready when the blast occurred."

Van Heflin pondered the list of people within the UN who gave them their full cooperation in matters like this. "Which one?"

"Allotey."

The senator's rapacity abruptly sagged, and he nodded torpidly. He was now getting the gist of what the plan had entailed. With Allotey involved, it was easy to connect the dots. Obviously, Allotey was the only one available within the UN's pool of envoys to carry out the assignment on such short notice. Allotey, a Libyan national, was a diminutive weasel who had blundered on several occasions in the past, necessitating a concerted cover-up of his embarrassing indiscretions by UN officials. *Probably had Alvarez and his gang with him since both had worked together on several assignments in the past*, he surmised.

"That's not all," Hearthwatch went on. "I convinced a contact of mine in the Interregional Broadcasting Company to send a news team to Aquaria. Gave him a sketchy scenario about how they were despoiling the reefs at Navassa and that something big might happen. An IBC news team was already on site when the UN delegation arrived."

"It didn't work," Van Heflin stated dully, his overwhelming lust for further gain now fully subsided.

The look of triumph plastering Hearthwatch's face fell away, replaced with a mask of confusion.

"I don't-"

Van Heflin cut him off. "We've fallen short of the results we were expecting with this little scheme."

Hearthwatch looked appalled. "How?"

"Does it matter?" the senator snapped curtly.

"He's not happy, is he?" Hearthwatch said, reading his face. The senator was the intermediary, the one designated to receive all incoming messages from *The Order*.

"I think it's time we added more fuel to the mix."

"Plan C?"

Van Heflin gave a sullen nod. "I've already gotten word to our Colombian friend. Says he has just the man to carry it out."

Hearthwatch sat back grimly as the waiter approached with their food. He preferred using more subtle means when fulfilling an agenda, but the barrel of a gun often proved to be much more efficient.

The demeanor of the person in charge of the newly arrived delegation was stiff and austere, matching the gruff faces of the twelve-man squad standing behind him. Speaking in precise clipped English, he announced, "My name is Malikai Allotey. As Special Envoy of the United Nations' Council on World Ecological Affairs, it is my duty to inform you that Aquaria is in violation of international law."

Jacob suppressed a laugh. "I was not aware such a council existed within the UN body."

Annoyance flooded Allotey's puckered countenance. "It is a newly formed branch imposed by Security Council mandate."

Jake stood at Jacob's side, not liking the look of Allotey's blue helmeted escort. All held assault rifles at high guard, with each man additionally armed with a pistol holstered at the hip. These were not your run-of-the-mill UN troops provided by other nations, but highly seasoned professionals. These were paid mercenaries, and judging from the sheathed corvo each man carried, they were in all likelihood former elites of the Chilean military. As a student of war, Jake knew the corvo had become the traditional symbol of Chilean commandos. The knives carried twelve inches of double-edged steel, making the curved blades exceptionally deadly in close quarter combat. Under Augusto Pinochet Ugarte, a past Chilean dictator who had usurped control of the government in a violent coup, men such as these had been part of one of the most repressive military forces on the planet.

Pivoting his head, Jake noted the IBC news team positioned nearby, recording the moment in rapt fixation.

"In what manner are we violating international law?" Jacob asked innocently.

Allotey practically sneered as he spoke. "To begin with, you are systematically destroying the unspoiled reefs that surround Navassa Island. Do you deny the explosion I witnessed on the way in?"

"We are not responsible for such damage," Jacob stated calmly. "Someone has gone to great lengths to discredit us by making it appear we are the ones doing it. This matter, however, is between Tursiops and the United States government, which has leased us the island and the adjacent waters. You have no jurisdiction here."

Allotey shook his head in disagreement. "You are wrong. This matter is now the concern of the United Nations, for it seems the American claim to Navassa Island may be invalid. The Republic of Haiti has brought a formal appeal before the UN to arbitrate this long-standing dispute over ownership, and the U.S. has graciously conceded the issue be decided through a majority vote by all member nations. And until this dispute is officially settled, the World Ecological Affairs Council has stepped in to put an end to the abominable desecration of the local environment."

"I see," said Jacob. He sighed wearily, resignedly. "And how do you propose to do this?"

Allotey indicated a solidly-built man in his escort. "Captain Francisco Alvarez and his men will remain here to monitor your operation until the UN determines which sovereignty the island falls under. They will investigate the full range of your ecological abuses. I trust you will see to their needs and provide them with adequate food and lodging."

Alvarez stepped forward, the skin of his face closely resembling a cratered lunar surface. He clicked his heels crisply and dipped his chin in a rigid display of introduction reminiscent of the Third Reich's infamous SS.

"They will not find any illicit activity within this city," Jacob intoned adamantly. "As I told you, another party is damaging the reefs. The threat is originating from outside this colony."

"Guilty parties always claim innocence," Allotey decried contemptuously. "The reefs, however, are only one of our concerns, for we have gathered enough evidence to suggest your operation is committing other ecological abuses."

"Such as?"

"Such as releasing excessive amounts of harmful heat-trapping gases into the atmosphere," Allotey accused. "Spectral analysis from satellite surveillance shows high concentrations of nitrous oxide being emitted from this sector of the Caribbean. We believe this colony is causing it. Nitrous oxide is three hundred times more powerful than carbon dioxide in causing a greenhouse effect and, more than any other gas, the most harmful in depleting the ozone layer."

"To be precise, it has two hundred and ninety-eight times more impact per unit weight than carbon dioxide," Jacob corrected. "But this colony is not creating any spike in the formation of nitrous oxide."

Allotey scowled ferociously. "The phosphates you are currently mining from Navassa may be the cause. Phosphates favor the formation of a purer form of nitrous oxide. It is fairly obvious a connection may exist between the two, and the UN would be remiss in its duties if it did not investigate such a possibility."

"This colony ships the phosphates to Haitian farmers to be used as a fertilizer to increase crop yields. We are very careful in how we package and ship it. It is not being released into the local environment."

"That will be for us to determine," Allotey said testily. "There is also another matter. The UN has reason to believe the old crude carrier you used to start this colony may be leaking oil into the surrounding sea."

"There is no oil leakage," Jacob declared flatly. "The ship was thoroughly cleaned of all contaminants before being mobilized to this site."

"Once again, that will be for us to decide. As it now stands, the UN is now considering amending international laws that apply to the use of the high seas. It is probable it will ultimately ban the building of maritime colonies such as yours, which appear to pose a threat to the planetary environment."

Jake felt it time to give voice, growing increasingly angry at the way they were being railroaded. It was Alvarez's quiet mannerism, however, that made him insufferably uncomfortable. Though the officer had so far said nothing, arrogance seemed to pulse from him in waves. But there was something else about the man that offended Jake even more. It was his splenetic darting eyes. They reminded him all too much of Yeslam

Raduyev, the eyes of a psychopathic killer. No matter what, the captain was certain to be trouble.

"Other than our own internal security, we don't allow guests to carry weapons of any kind aboard Aquaria," Jake proclaimed in a measured voice, first looking to Alvarez and then to Allotey. Letting his gaze settle back on the captain, he added, "Before we can even consider providing you and your men with hospitality, you'll have to surrender custody of your weapons to us until you're ready to leave our great city."

Jake had purposely used the word *"surrender,"* knowing the effect it would have on a warrior mentality. It was as if he had slapped Alvarez with an open hand. The captain's chilling stare abruptly turned murderous.

Allotey spoke before the captain could respond, his voice bristling with outrage. "How dare you presume to lay dictates on these soldiers. I don't think you fully understand the purpose of these men. They were not sent here simply to be passive observers. They are representatives of the United Nations, fully empowered to police your facilities at their discretion. Failing to cooperate with them will be considered an act of defiance and a crime under International Law."

"I hate to disappoint you, your royal highness," Jake said coolly, "but unless they turn over their weapons, I suggest they climb back aboard your bird and fly the hell outta here."

Allotey's face was now flushed purple with rage. "May I remind you, sir, that Saddam Hussein was crushed for his failure to comply with the will of the United Nations," he hissed venomously.

"Don't even try to compare us with Saddam," Jake said irritably. "He was a saber rattling lunatic and murderer who had no respect for life or the environment that nurtures it. Here in Aquaria, the residents see themselves as caretakers of life. There are more than ten thousand peace-loving people living and working in this colony with the aim of making this world a better place. We'll not allow a group of power-crazed Gestapo to go roaming about intimidating and menacing the population with their weapons."

"Very well," Allotey spat scornfully, looking to Alvarez. "Captain, arrest this man."

Jake suddenly grinned. "I don't think so," he shot back. Raising his voice, he shouted, "Time for you to do your thing, Ez."

A large Haitian woman with coffee skin and wide cheeks suddenly materialized between Jake and Alvarez, causing the captain to jump back in surprise.

The woman turned her head, setting a twinkling gaze on Allotey. "Behind this mask of benevolence supposedly aimed at protecting the planet, it is men like you who use the United Nations to promote terror and tyranny in order to achieve your hidden objective, which is the attainment of a singular world government to rule over every corner of the planet and subjugate everyone on it to its will."

Allotey stood speechless, unable to comprehend that the woman addressing him was actually a holographic projection made to look lifelike.

"The UN is not the defender of freedom and peace it pretends itself to be," Ez went on. "The UN deceives humanity by disseminating the lie that all nations are morally equivalent, this whether they be free societies or violent dictatorships engaged in suppressing human rights. The UN is a culture of impunity and corruption that operates with great secrecy, shielded by diplomatic immunity. After more than sixty years as a global collective of governments, it has become a welter of so many overlapping programs, far-flung projects, quietly vested nepotistic shenanigans, and interlocking directorates as to defy accurate comprehension, let alone responsible supervision."

"Who are you?" Allotey demanded, finally getting hold of his senses. He was still having a hard time grasping how this woman had seemingly emerged out of thin air.

"Someone who knows the full depth of your moral decay."

"How dare you impugn my character," Allotey sputtered.

"You were one of the primary beneficiaries in Saddam Hussein's oil-for-food scams. You were also put in charge of UN troops in the Congo where you extorted sex for food from children. In 2008, using a UN helicopter, you flew into the Congo's Virunga National Park where you swapped ammunition for ivory with rebels. Through these despicable acts and a maze of other convoluted schemes, you amassed seventeen point six two three eight million dollars. You have stashed this money in the Deutsche Bank of the Cayman Islands where only a coded user name and password is required for deposits and withdrawals. Hijack, six, nine, nine, six, kcajih, the reverse spelling of hijack, is your coded user name, and morocco, seven, three, nine, two, two, four, lemma, four, four is your password, are they not?"

Allotey's eyes bulged in disbelief, and he shot a mortified glance at the camera crew. With his mind reeling in turmoil, he wondered how this woman had been able to obtain this information. His connection with Hussein along with thousands of other individuals and companies was kept locked away within a database maintained by the UN at a secret, secure location. Getting that information must have been divulged by an informer. But ferreting out his Cayman account should have been impossible.

Ez turned her attention to Alvarez. "Captain Francisco Alvarez. Fourteen years ago you were directly responsible for the massacre of seventy-eight innocent villagers in Rwanda while you were stationed there under the UN banner. During another UN peace-keeping mission in Uganda a year later, forty-two people mysteriously disappeared under your watch."

Unlike Allotey, Alvarez barely managed to keep his composure, displaying a hard-fought, though wavering grin. Speaking for the first time, he said, "All lies concocted by people looking to cast the peaceful intentions of the United Nations in a bad light."

Allotey moved quickly to Alvarez's side. "Captain, you will arrest these people at once!" he ordered shrilly. Leaning close to the captain's ear, he shot a quick glance at the IBC news team and lowered his voice to a whisper. "And you will confiscate that camera crew's video recording of this incident."

Alvarez nodded eagerly, now aching to carry out the orders. But as he opened his mouth to command his unit into action, the skin of his face and chest suddenly burned with a fierce intensity.

An involuntary scream broke from his lips. "*Madre de Dios!*" Mother of god! The sensation was unbearable, making him feel as though he were on fire. In the midst of his torment, he vaguely heard the troopers behind him stir in panic. He had just enough presence of mind to swat maddeningly at his clothing in a vain attempt to put out the flames, but strangely he could find none.

Jake grinned knowingly as the soldiers broke ranks in agonized disarray and fled for the UN chopper, Allotey already ten paces out in front of them. The non-lethal weapon Ez had used had worked as expected. The weapon focused a beam of millimeter wave energy that penetrated the skin, producing an intolerable heating sensation in targeted individuals without causing injury.

Ez had inadvertently stumbled upon the technology behind the weapon while hacking into the U.S. Department of Defense computer system. Having access to the worldwide Internet, she often entertained herself by cracking systems that were supposed to be impervious to penetration. In a file called Active Denial System 2, she had found the weapon specs, learning that it had been developed by Raytheon under contract with the U.S. Air Force. Readily assessing its potential, she refined and expanded the system further, increasing its range and giving it a multi-beam capability which could repel a group of assailants simultaneously.

Jake watched as the dual rotors of the UN whirlybird cranked up and gained momentum in an ear-splitting whine. With Alvarez glaring hatefully back at him from the fuselage's open doorway, the behemoth chopper lifted ponderously from its pad and swung out over the sea, dipping low to the water in an attempt to encourage all the airspeed the turbines could muster. In moments it raced off to the west, making a hasty retreat in the direction of Jamaica.

Ez turned to the news team, setting her gaze on the woman reporter. "There are a plethora of good reasons for a freedom loving people to steer clear of the United Nations, the primary one being the fanatical zeal with which it grasps hold of every worry and woe plaguing the earth, making them its own. It makes a practice of blowing these matters out of proportion, insisting that it and only it can provide a solution, a solution which must be imposed by force on the rest of the world. In reality, the UN is merely a conference of tarnished, self-serving officials from corrupt little countries all over the world who relish in the prospect of disaster relief, for it seems whenever or wherever disasters occur, the UN rushes in to help itself, demanding exclusive rights to direct the aid and money, much of which gets skimmed off into the pockets of people like Allotey."

The reporter gawked in wonder, both puzzled and delighted at this incredible turn of events. Her cameraman had caught the entire episode on tape. Such extraordinary news coverage had the potential of advancing her career enormously once it was sent to IBC headquarters in San Francisco. Eager to further her bout of good fortune, she stepped forward quickly, prepared to launch a series of questions at this remarkable black woman who had seemingly sprung out of the very air before her.

The reporter's elation abruptly disintegrated, for the Haitian woman vanished as suddenly as she had appeared

Chapter Four: Cybergenic

At a distance of 3,300 meters from what appeared to be a breakwater along Aquaria's eastern sector, a lone observer watched pensively as the UN helicopter headed off to the west. Silently he cursed, knowing the men aboard her had failed miserably.

Irately, Malcolm Maximus picked up a satellite phone and placed a call, waiting impatiently until the person he sought answered. In a tone reflecting his mood, he spoke in a language rarely used in a modern world, the timber of his voice sounding gravelly as it always did.

Ending the conversation, he put down the phone and stared balefully in the direction of the colony. The sun had now risen sufficiently to burn off the dense, cottony fog that had blanketed the Tursiops complex during the dawn hours, obscuring everything but the central structure which jutted imposingly above it like a majestic mountain peak rising above the clouds. He hated that fog. It was as though it had a life of its own, seemingly cloaking the budding enterprise in a shield of invincibility that sought to mock him. Its impenetrability evoked a defiance of his worldly views. Without a stiff breeze to carry it away in thick swirling columns, it would build each night, hanging stubbornly over the water until only the heat of day could dissipate it. He knew the cold water brought up from the depths was the cause of it.

He was about to turn away but stopped short as something else caught his eye, a sight that annoyed him even more. The residual accumulation of airborne moisture in concert with the sunshine had created a brilliant rainbow bridge of muted colors. He stared dourly, unconsciously parting his teeth in a snarl as the view took on additional scope. Now there were two of them, one arching directly over and perfectly framing the colony's central structure, and another further back hovering over Navassa Island.

A double rainbow had suddenly materialized before his very eyes, with the more distant arch positioned immediately under the one in the foreground and running parallel with it. The sight was an optical illusion, as he well understood, and though he had espied rainbows many times in the past, he had never before witnessed a twin-arch like this one.

He studied it a few seconds longer, wishing the prismatic phenomenon to vanish. When it continued to hold steady, he finally averted his gaze in disgust. Rainbows repulsed him. They gave a sense of hope to the downtrodden, and that angered him.

As the chairman of Unus Universitas, a multinational conglomerate, he was currently the richest and most powerful man on the planet. Better known as One World, Unus Universitas had grown extensively since its startup thirty years earlier. As a young man, Maximus had amassed fortunes in international banking and energy. But that was before he had diversified his holdings further, gradually taking over companies entrenched in agriculture, arms manufacture, computers, mass media and pharmaceuticals. Under his leadership, he had built an empire. But he saw Aquaria as a threat to his vast holdings, including the plan he had so meticulously cultivated over the last two decades. With the world population now surpassing six billion and growing larger with each passing day, the planetary ecosystem was rapidly approaching collapse. He saw opportunity in this, delighted in the prospect that the world was quickly running out of arable land and cheap energy. Like a runaway train, it was heading recklessly for a Malthusian wall.

But his vision of expediting that inevitable event was being thwarted by this interloper. No matter what it took, he had to stop the colony's evolution before it shattered the old limits of the zero-sum resource game.

He had grown incredibly wealthy from playing the game, for in a zero-sum system there were always limited quantities of some critical commodity. Playing the zero-sum game was similar to playing poker with a limited supply of chips on the table. If one player was getting richer, other players were getting poorer. And to consistently win at the sophisticated game of resource poker in a modern world, you had to stack the deck in your favor by orchestrating events that allowed you to enrich yourself by impoverishing others. But this new upstart colony had taken a quantum leap forward by breaking all the rules of the game, for it was bringing a seemingly endless quantity of chips to the table.

Tursiops Worldwide, it appeared, was playing table stakes poker with a vacuum hose connected to a vault filled with gold. It was tapping into the energy and nutrient reserves of the ocean, setting a new course for humanity. From Maximus' point of view, Aquaria represented a cybergenic blasphemy that would ultimately establish a dangerous trend if left unchecked.

Cybergenic, he hated that word. Cybergenic meant the creation of a system sufficiently complex to exhibit the fundamental properties of life, those being self-organization and replication. The last thing he wanted was more floating cities similar to Aquaria being constructed on the high seas by a workforce of dolphins.

Maximus loathed the idea of ocean colonization. It created a glut of newfound resources to be shared with a hungry world, resources that were relatively inexpensive to produce once a sea colony became fully autonomous following its massive start-up costs.

The threat was all too real. Not only did it make it harder to stack the deck in his favor, it was also an impediment to his plan for population control. He and his cabal saw much of mankind as useless eaters that needed to be eliminated from the planet. *The Order* was his cabal, and his cabal was behind the UN plan to remedy population explosions in Third World countries where people consumed far more than they produced. Working covertly with lower ranking members of *The Order* firmly entrenched within the UN, the cabal routinely implemented measures to ensure that people in the poorer countries never grew to a point where they were able to develop their own natural resources. Otherwise they might become strong like the industrialized nations.

The thought of newly emerging nations with financial clout disturbed Maximus. Contrary to politicians who were easily corrupted, what if key government officials in those emerging nations refused to submit to the cabal's will? He could not run that risk.

That was why *The Order* was using genetically modified crops to control the food supply. Plagiarius, a subsidiary of Unus Universitas, had patents on hybrid seeds that would only grow by spraying them with a certain chemical. And because Plagiarius was to be the sole source provider of that chemical, Maximus stood to make another mega-fortune once he unleashed the Morior Blight on the world's major crop producers. Plagiarius would charge a king's ransom for both the seeds and chemical. Spraying the seeds with the chemical, which he called Omicron-7, would make the resulting crops immune to the blight.

Standing on the bridge of his vessel, Maximus gazed contemptuously at the floating city, his thoughts sifting over the wealth and power he had already attained and his plans for the future. *Numquam Satis* was an appropriate name for his billion-dollar yacht. Translated from Latin it meant *Never Enough*. It perfectly epitomized his insatiable greed and the lavish lifestyle he lived.

He had learned early on in life that food and energy were the primary commodities supporting mankind. Controlling the availability of these staples through roadblocks of limited supply, many of them carefully contrived, made you incredibly rich. But Aquaria was making an end run around those roadblocks by providing these same commodities at virtually no cost to the planet's deteriorating ecosystem. Upon his order, one of his scientists had compiled a report on Aquaria's method of energy generation. The process was called Ocean Thermal Energy Conversion. The OTEC principle had been known for decades, but it seemed Tursiops Worldwide had pioneered the process to an unimaginable magnitude.

Maximus had pored over the report, learning the true threat the floating city posed. Whereas burning fossil fuels created acid rain, which affected food crops and invoked substantial harm on the world environment in general, the global oceans provided more than enough stored energy to satisfy the population time bomb. The seas were like gigantic solar collectors, absorbing and storing radiant flux from the sun. The warm surface waters held an inexhaustible charge of solar energy. The sun transmitted to earth 18,000 times more energy than mankind used in recent years. There was as much energy in a ton of seawater as two pounds of gasoline. The total energy held by the planet's seas was equivalent to a million billion barrels of oil. If all the ocean basins were filled to a depth of twenty feet in high-octane fuel, they would hold the same amount of energy as all the water in the seas, enough latent energy at this moment to meet mankind's needs at current levels for the next 25,000 years.

And this energy was freely available and renewable.

Aquaria was using this abundant energy to power its operations and generate huge windfalls of fuel and food, most of which it exported. Unlike conventional power-generating facilities, the OTEC process was a net energy producer. It did not conform to zero-sum rules like typical nuclear power plants, which consumed 3,000 calories of energy for every 1,000 it produced. In an OTEC system, 1,000 calories of energy were generated for every 700 it consumed.

In essence, the process fractured zero-sum barriers, and it was this that appalled Maximus the most. Both conventional and nuclear power plants placed enormous demands on the preexisting zero-sum resource base, borrowing from the common yet limited resource pool, which always created more problems than they solved. But Maximus had always found opportunity in those problems, and over the years he had learned how to capitalize on them, leveraging incredible profits through crisis.

An OTEC plant functioned like a heat engine, working on the principle that energy will flow from a warmer to a cooler body. It produced electrical power by exploiting the temperature differential between warm surface waters and cold deep waters.

Aquaria was drawing in cold water from the depths and taking in warm surface water to generate electrical power, operating on a temperature difference of at least forty degrees Fahrenheit to make the process worthwhile. But a temperature differential greater than forty degrees would produce even more energy. Although OTEC typically operated at a very low efficiency, the difference in temperature was sufficient to drive Aquaria's turbines. Compared to a typical fossil fuel plant, which converted forty percent of the energy available in the fuel to electricity, an OTEC plant converted only 2.5 percent of the available energy to electricity. While such a low level seemed ridiculously inefficient, it was rendered practical by the sheer size of the available resource.

Collectively, the energy resource of the oceans represented a renewable power supply exceeding 200 million megawatts. Even at very low levels of net efficiency, OTEC plants were capable of producing ten times more electrical energy as other conventional power sources combined, assuming enough OTEC facilities were built worldwide to harness this total available energy.

And only a relatively simple process was required to extract this energy from the oceans. By reducing the existing pressure on warm surface water, it is brought to a boil, thereby producing vapors which expand and drive a turbine, much the way steam is used to power a locomotive, though in this case the process operates under a low ambient temperature. The rotating turbine blades then turn a dynamo which produces an electric current. Cold water pumped up from the depths is then used to condense the vapor, keeping the system pressure low. By transferring heat from warm to cold water, the process generated energy without consuming any actual fuel.

According to the report, the amount of energy Aquaria was currently producing was estimated at 3.6 terawatt hours of net electrical power annually, or the equivalent of five million barrels of oil. And much of that electrical energy was being converted to a renewable, eco-friendly fuel sold on the world market at cheap rates.

Hydrogen was that fuel, as abundant as the seawater from which it was extracted. Since the conversion of electrical energy to hydrogen could be accomplished at eighty percent efficiency, it was being manufactured inexpensively.

Because Aquaria was producing 7.2 million kilowatt hours of surplus electrical energy each day, it was converting it to sixty-seven million cubic feet of liquid hydrogen which it exported on a daily basis. But these were conservative estimates, because the report stated the numbers could actually be higher.

Maximus frowned at the thought. With enough marine colonies like Aquaria coming on-line, they had the potential of tipping the ecological balance from impending catastrophe to sustainability at little or no cost to the planet's failing ecosystem. Compared to burning fossil fuels or splitting atoms, the OTEC power generating capability of numerous marine colonies would be benign, ultimately benefitting the health of the biosphere by reducing pollution and reversing the forces pushing the world over the brink.

If they were not stopped, sea colonies like Aquaria could literally solve the earth's energy and food shortages without exacerbating its environmental crisis. They could more than double the supply of energy, and do it without causing a buildup of carbon dioxide or acid rain. They would not disturb an acre of land or deplete any limited resources. They would not displace any preexisting ecosystems since the open oceans were largely barren and lifeless due to a lack of nutrients. But where life had previously failed to flourish, a marine colony created an oasis of life.

Aside from hydrogen, Aquaria produced two other principal products for export, those being protein and distilled water. The colony was currently producing 150,000 tons of protein annually, the bulk of it consisting of Spirulina platensis, a species of blue-green algae that dwarfed all known food sources in protein content. But a far greater tonnage was expected to be produced once the facility was completed and became fully operational. Aquaria was using the nutrient-rich cold water from the depths to nourish this variety of algae. Containing sixty-five percent protein by weight that was easily digestible, spirulina made an ideal food supplement for human consumption, especially in Third World countries where malnutrition was prevalent.

Based on the report, it was estimated that Aquaria was bringing to the surface forty-three billion gallons of nitrogen-laden water daily. Because ocean-dwelling plants and animals sank into the depths when they died, taking the nitrates locked in their bodies with them, the concentration of nitrates increased rapidly with depth, reaching a peak of 0.4 grams per cubic meter at roughly 3,300 feet in the world's oceans. When the nutrient-rich water reached the sunlit surface, the blue-green algae readily absorbed it, exploding into riotous growth and providing food for other life forms in the food chain. Not only was Aquaria producing enormous amounts of protein-rich spirulina in powder form, but it was also harvesting vast quantities of other food fishes that fed on the food pyramid initiated by the algae bloom.

Reflecting on this information, Maximus instinctively knew something was not quite right. Turning, he eyed a nearby screen which provided a real-time image of the Number 3 moon pool located amidships on the yacht's lowest deck. Several technicians hovered around a large fish that had just been pulled from the pool. With water still dripping from its flanks, it hung suspended from a gantry that spanned both sides of the pool. A second fish nearly identical to the first hung serenely from the same gantry on the opposite side of the pool.

"Status?" barked Maximus.

One of the technicians looked up sharply, the surveillance camera revealing a face fraught with angst. He had been in the act of removing a flexible cowling on the underbelly of the fish just pulled from the water.

"The sonar system in Fish Two is inoperable. We're trying to determine the cause."

"You had assured me it would not fail," Maximus admonished sharply. Percy Osgood, the brains behind the construction of the robotic fish, had become a huge disappointment in recent days. Perhaps replacing him with someone more competent was in order.

Osgood paled, fidgeting noticeably. As if sensing what Maximus was thinking, he spoke quickly. "As you saw, the explosive deployed perfectly. But the random acoustics abounding in these waters may have caused sufficient interference to disrupt a clear sonar picture."

"I am not interested in excuses," Maximus snarled, "only results. I will expect a detailed mosaic of the seafloor beneath Aquaria before the day is out."

Osgood nodded stiffly, deferentially. Turning, he went back to work on the mechanical fish, his hands nervously probing the inner circuitry.

Maximus keyed several buttons on the console in front of him, replaying the video taken earlier. Fish Number One had gotten close enough to the colony's power plants to get a clear view of the intakes. Puzzled, he studied it some more to make sure he hadn't missed anything, and within moments he confirmed the thing that had been troubling him.

The floating city currently had what he perceived to be seven OTEC power plants. One of them was centrally located, that being the starter plant aboard the seed ship towed into place when construction had first begun. Encircling that, there were six others set up in a hexagonal pattern. But each of them should have had a vertical pipe that descended to a depth of 3,300 feet to bring up water sufficiently cold enough to initiate the OTEC process.

Large vertical pipes were evident, perhaps forty feet in diameter based on what he was seeing. But the seafloor directly beneath Aquaria was not even close to the needed depth, ending roughly at 900 feet.

Consulting a nautical chart of the area, he studied the contour of the ocean bottom surrounding Navassa Island. The seafloor dropped off rapidly to the south of the island, ultimately falling away precipitously into the Cayman Trench, an ocean abyss thousands of feet deep. At a distance of almost two miles from Aquaria's outer perimeter, his vessel currently sat over this trench, held in place by the dynamic positioning system *Numquam Satis* routinely employed when floating stationary in water where anchoring was rendered impractical.

Earlier in the day, Maximus had two of his technicians lower a probe to a depth of 900 feet, confirming that the water temperature and nitrate concentration were insufficient to induce the vast harvests of energy and food the colony was producing.

One other anomaly troubled him. Video from Fish One revealed what he perceived to be the warm-water intakes, all appearing identical. There were seven of them, each with a diameter exceeding thirty feet in his estimation. Running parallel to each other, they extended horizontally out to the offshore berthing facility near the island, all of them apparently buoyant as evidenced by a series of anchor cables that kept them submerged ten feet below the surface. Surveillance from the mechanical fish confirmed that they all terminated at the offshore platform adjacent to Navassa Island. Running parallel and ten feet beneath the center intake was a Plexiglas tube eight feet in diameter, and he surmised it was a dry access tunnel that allowed passage between Aquaria and the offshore platform.

Maximus pondered the layout. Why go to the expense of constructing lengthy intakes when it was so much simpler to draw in surface water immediately contiguous with the OTEC plants?

One way or the other he would solve these mysteries.

But it was the girl riding a huge white dolphin that intrigued him the most. Fish One had only gotten a glimpse of her while reconnoitering the easternmost intake. This was only his second sighting of her, the first one displayed in a photograph taken from high altitude by satellite and provided by a telemetry expert from France. But the photo had been grainy and shot from a poor angle looking down. It had lacked the clarity and perspective the video was now revealing. The girl's long hair streamed back in a cloud of shimmering ebony as it caught the sunlight reaching into the depths, and a white wetsuit clung to her body, which appeared lean and lithe. Even with the dive mask partially obscuring her face, it was obvious she was an exquisite beauty. Here was the Dolphin Girl, his associate back in Haiti, was so eager to get his hands on.

Through bribes and monetary rewards over the last several months, he had gathered tidbits of information on her through a spectrum of Haitian informants, as did his associate. The compiled information had been thoroughly assessed by several top specialists to piece together a psychological profile of her character, which he found to be quite extraordinary if not impossible, assuming the evaluation was accurate.

Maximus replayed the recording, back-tracking the video once again. Two young children had accompanied her, a girl and boy, each riding a juvenile albino dolphin. Though difficult to tell, the children appeared to be seven or eight years old. This latest finding set off a chain reaction in his devious mind, and a plan quickly coalesced.

A caustic smile flooded Maximus' face as he continued to replay the short footage several more times. "Most interesting!" he said aloud, knowing that the table stakes in the zero-sum game had just risen sharply in his favor.

Chapter Five:
White Pox and Vigs

Destiny read the joy showing on the faces of both twins, her heart nearly melting with maternal stirrings. This was their third viewing of the hidden dolphin sanctuary.

"Can we see the new *thurentras*, mumsie?" Melody asked excitedly.

"Yes, can we, mum?" Troy Jacob chimed in, his enthusiasm matching his sister's.

The children's voices merged with the sound of water dripping monotonously in the expansive confines of the cavern, coming back at them in ebbing cacophonous echoes.

Destiny hesitated. She could see the children's excitement had infected their mounts, for both *Alpha* and *Omego* seemed to quiver in eager anticipation under them. Both the twins and their bond mates appeared totally unaffected by the danger they had been exposed to a short time earlier. If not for the pressure wave inhibitor each of them carried, including herself, the explosion might have caused them serious injury. With acts of sabotage plaguing the colony as of late, Jake had insisted she and the children wear them whenever they took to the sea.

"We'll pay them a visit in a little while," Destiny answered. "But you know as well as I that Granny has something to show us first."

"Aw, snails are so boring," Troy Jacob objected dolefully. "Why does she spend so much time studying them?"

A misty spray erupted from Hercules blowhole in disapproval, and Destiny patted him affectionately. "Because she thinks they may be the answer to restoring the coral reefs that are dying. The work she is doing is very important to the health of the planet."

"I guess," Troy Jacob conceded bleakly.

"Well I like snails," Melody announced haughtily.

Her brother frowned, giving her an admonishing look. "Snails are slow and slimy."

"You're slow and slimy!" Melody giggled playfully.

Troy Jacob's aquamarine eyes came alive with mischief, and Destiny was suddenly reminded of the boy's striking resemblance to his father. "Well, even a snail can beat you in a race. *My Alpha* is way faster than your *Omega*."

"Is not," Melody contested loftily. She looked down and caressed her bond mate lovingly. "We let you win the last race on purpose, didn't we my sweet darling." The juvenile albino beneath her continued to float quietly. "*Omega* didn't want *Alpha* to feel bad, and I didn't want you to sulk if you lost three times in a row."

A trace of petulance flashed briefly across Troy Jacob's face. He was not to be outdone. "Well, you're-"

Destiny jumped in quickly. "Insulting one another is not very nice," she reproved gently. The two of them could be a handful at times, and every so often she had to rein in their sportive banter. She knew they were very close and loved one another dearly, but unfortunately their naturally competitive natures knew no bounds. "Try to remember what uncle Jacob has taught you," she felt it necessary to add.

"You mean how being humble is a virtue," Troy Jacob grumbled.

Destiny smiled as only a proud mother could smile. "Yes, that and how all God's creatures have a purpose, even a snail."

Jacob had schooled the twins endlessly on the subject of ecology, and they well understood the impact a single organism could have on an ecosystem, particularly a coral reef, even one so seemingly lowly as a snail. The twins had absorbed his teachings with the avid curiosity of sagacious young minds, attaining a level of comprehension light years above other kids their age. They knew that coral reef ecosystems were normally nutrient-poor environments, a symptom of tropical waters in general and that these systems functioned much the same way as rainforests and wetlands did on land, recycling nutrients at a rapid rate. Though these marine habitats covered less than one percent of the

Earth's surface, they were home to twenty-five percent of all marine fish species. Nutrient producers such as plankton and seaweed, essentially plants that photosynthesize, were abundant in these sanctuaries of life and formed the base of the food chain, providing food for the bountiful small fish and other organisms, which in turn provided meals for larger animals.

Coral reefs were among the oldest ecosystems on earth and havens of phenomenal biodiversity in tropical seas, supporting more animal and plant life per unit area than any other marine habitat and generally accounting for thousands of species. A treasure trove of uncharted possibilities lay within this rich tapestry of biodiversity. Some scientists estimated that millions of species indigenous to coral reef habitats around the world were still yet to be found, and it was these undiscovered organisms that held potential value for alleviating human diseases. A plethora of drugs had already been derived from coral reef organisms as treatments for cancer, HIV, arthritis, bacterial infections, and viruses, with many more yet to be developed. This was one of the many goals the colony was focused on, finding new cures for diseases, but not just for those that afflicted humans. Beyond the human species and far more prevalent in nature, other ailments existed that had the potential of unraveling the delicate balance of life on a broader scale, and in so doing would negatively impact the entire planet. Of particular importance were the unique life forms endemic to the waters adjacent to Navassa Island. They held much promise for developing various cures for both human suffering and ailing marine environments, for the coral reefs abounding here were one of the most thriving and intact ecosystems in the Caribbean. Unfortunately, these same reefs had recently come under attack from another threat other than human sabotage.

Riding their bond mates with a fluid grace, Destiny and the twins made their way to the far side of the immense subterranean grotto, one of many that interlaced the limestone bedrock of Navassa Island. A trail of sparkling phosphorescence was left in their softly rippling wakes, the product of tiny microscopic organisms within the water. Agitated by the group's passage, they erupted like tiny starbursts before fading under the pale glow of soft green light that seemed to permeate every corner of the cavern, both above and below the water. The pervasive glow was yet another bioluminescent effect, produced by mossy lichen indigenous to the cavern. The lichen clung to the rock in many places, feeding on the limestone, and it highlighted the swirling lines of the massive structure over which they glided, a submerged edifice totally unnatural to its surroundings.

Reaching the far wall, the group slid beneath the surface and spiraled their way down through a winding circular tunnel with smooth walls until they leveled off and encroached upon a familiar archway, beyond which a moderately-sized chamber with a vaulted ceiling awaited them. Here the subdued greenish glow that had accompanied them through the passageway was replaced by brazen fluorescent lighting emanating from the roof above. The chamber was only partially filled with water of shallow depth and held breathable air. Several tabletops and shelves jutted above the water, all of them laden with a varied assortment of flasks, tubing, and sophisticated equipment. Other than the water pooled within the vaulted room, the place had the look of a conventional laboratory setting.

A woman lifted her head from the lens of a microscope, turning to greet them. "I'm glad you could come," Amphitrite announced, eyeing both the twins and Destiny with obvious pleasure.

Destiny stared back with mutual warmth and adulation. Despite their age difference, Amphitrite still displayed the youthful glow of a much younger woman, causing strangers to assume her to be Destiny's older sister rather than her mother. Even so, Destiny could not help wonder about the extraordinary abilities the woman who birthed her had once possessed. As Jacob had often said, the power of psychic healing defied scientific explanation.

Amphitrite had been a healer. With the help of Athena and the albinos, she had been able to cure the sick and injured with a simple touch. But upon regaining her memory, this inexplicable power had deserted her. Accurately prophesying events to come was another power Amphitrite had lost. Jacob had astutely reasoned that her inability to remember her past had somehow given her the power to glimpse the future, but that had been some years ago before her emotional reunion with Franklin. The fact that Amphitrite now had full memory of her former life seemed to support Jacob's prior conclusion. Ever since recapturing her original identity, she no longer possessed the enigma of precognition. As Harriet Grahm, she had been a successful marine zoologist, specializing in the study of coelenterates. Her husband, Dr. Franklin Grahm, another marine zoologist and perhaps the foremost authority on the planet when it came to dolphins, had been bereaved for many years thinking his wife, Harriet, had gone down with their beloved sloop, *Tursiops*, during a hurricane at sea. Pregnant with Destiny at the time, Harriet had survived with the help of a female bottlenose dolphin. But something incredible had happened to both woman and dolphin during the storm, bringing on extraordinary changes in each of them that would have profound and far-reaching effects as Destiny had come to fathom, setting off a chain of events that took them to Navassa Island and the building of Aquaria.

Suffering a severe case of amnesia and dehydration, Harriet Grahm had eventually been carried by the dolphin to a secluded cove along Haiti's western coastline. There Jacob had found them, nursing the woman back to health. Jacob soon discovered the woman had no remembrance of her past life, not even her name, and so he had begun calling her Amphitrite based on the circumstances of her arrival, which vaguely paralleled a similar event found in Greek mythology, for the myth portrayed Amphitrite as the Queen of the Sea and the wife of Poseidon, a regal goddess who had birthed Triton, the man-fish. An unusual bond had developed between Amphitrite and the creature who had rescued her, prompting Amphitrite to call the dolphin Athena. According to Greek legend, Athena was the favorite daughter of Zeus, king of the Olympians. To this day, Athena had continued on as Amphitrite's faithful companion and bond mate, always remaining close at hand to assist Amphitrite in all her endeavors.

A wistful nostalgia suddenly gripped Destiny as she recalled her earliest years. She had grown up in that hidden sanctuary Jacob called home, a wondrous haven untouched by the outside world, a place Jacob fondly referred to as *Gaia*. Sequestered in a land of ecological ruin, it had miraculously remained pristine and unpolluted, a tiny realm of vibrant multi-hued colors that pulsated with life. It was within its placid, warm waters where she had been dropped from her mother's womb at the same moment Athena had given birth to Natalie, for Athena had been gravid with calf. Destiny had learned to swim long before she could walk, and riding Natalie had come instinctually.

Natalie was the first of her kind to enter the planetary biosphere, an altogether new species of dolphin, endowed with albino skin and jointed prehensile appendages that approximated arms with hands similar to those of a primate. With a brain that exceeded human intelligence, Natalie had matured far more quickly than the average dolphin, successively mating with a string of ordinary male bottlenose and subsequently bearing either one or two calves each time she delivered, with the resulting progenies being either male or female, or consisting of mixed genders each time she bore twins. In procreating, she had bred two advanced strains of cetacean, some of them albinos like herself, and others that were a gray variation. All possessed an elevated intellect and a pair of hands at the terminus of arms that, when not in use, could retract and fold covertly into recesses beneath their pectoral fins. However, unlike their gray cousins, the albinos were generally bigger, spawned with an even greater muscularity and intelligence and the ability to converse in human languages. Strangely, albinos birthed by Natalie only mated with others of their kind, and with the exception of Hercules, invariably generated mixed genders in the set of albino twins they or their descendants in turn produced. But with both strains of the new breed, whether they be albino or gray, there was often little need for the acoustic communication commonly exhibited by cetaceans, for they relied primarily on telepathy for receiving and transmitting thoughts between each other and their bond mates.

The albino twins, Coral and Reef, were the first of Natalie's amazing offspring, followed two years later by Hermes and Aphrodite, another set of mixed gender albino twins. It was the union of Reef and Aphrodite that produced Hercules, and the subsequent union of Hermes and Coral that sprang forth Apollo and Artemis in the pod's earlier days, and Alpha and Omega a little over a year ago. Since birthing Natalie, Athena had also continued to mate, producing a succession of calves, but unlike Natalie, all were gray and did not have the ability to converse in human languages, though they were all born with the same unique forelimbs as the albinos. Athena, it seemed, could no longer breed any more albinos like her original progeny. Oddly enough, however, succeeding generations of grays originating from either Athena or Natalie were sometimes capable of birthing or siring an albino with the same traits as Natalie, even if they mated with a common bottlenose dolphin lacking those same attributes. Thetis was one such progeny of Athena's, who in turn had given birth to Achilles, currently the most athletic albino in the pod and the bond mate of Jake Javolyn, Destiny's husband. And with Phillipe yearning for an albino bond mate of his very own, Thetis had accommodated him by producing Perseus eleven months earlier. The pod had grown considerably over the last several years and now numbered in the hundreds.

As Destiny pondered these things, she thought about Jacob's views regarding these extraordinary life forms. Jacob believed the new breed had come into existence to show mankind the way, for he saw humanity as an utterly irrational species, totally unsuitable for responsible charge of the planet. A firm believer in the Gaia hypothesis, Jacob was convinced that humankind had brought such pressure to bear on nature that the life force behind creation had simply reacted by introducing a higher life form into the planetary ecosphere in order to save the world. Originally formulated by James Lovelock in 1972, the Gaia hypothesis was a highly controversial idea among ecologists, though it had slowly gained a foothold within scientific circles. It postulated that the entire Earth is alive and acts as a complete organism, possessing various self-regulating mechanisms for its survival. In keeping with the theory, Jacob contended that the Earth had brought on something new to counter man's destructive tendencies. At its core, the hypothesis states that life creates planetary conditions for its own purposes, essentially to suit itself. According to the theory, the Earth was a complex superorganism involving the interaction of the planet's biosphere, atmosphere, oceans, and lithosphere, a totality that constituted a feedback or cybernetic system seeking to optimize a physical and chemical environment conducive for life. So, while mankind, in all his combative, ego-oriented, divisive, exploitive, and technological madness, had brought all life on Earth to the brink of destruction, the emerging species was life embracing and sought to live in harmony with the dominant species, guiding it toward a collective change in its cultures, transforming its present temperament and showing it how to live in balance with the living world. In essence, the emerging species was an evolution of consciousness on the planet.

And both Jacob and Amphitrite were certain that a mysterious oblate jellyfish, a type of coelenterate never before catalogued, had triggered the arcane evolutionary process responsible for making the new breed possible. This same species of jellyfish had been the forerunner of the pumpkin-like, hydrogen belching *thurentra*, a hybrid life form that was a crossbreed of *holothuroidea* and the unknown coelenterate, produced by merging a sea cucumber with it. Through a horizontal transfer of portions of their genomes, an exchange of DNA had occurred between the two organisms to cause a most unusual mutation. And it was this mutation that had unexpectedly yielded the huge supply of precious metals and other elements, giving them the means to build Aquaria.

They knew that several varieties of *thurentra* were now in existence, and as far as they could tell, all had provided them with important elements and minerals that contributed immensely to the construction and operation of the colony. In some respects, a *thurentra* was comparable to both an undersea miner and ore processor. With hundreds of tentacles that extended thousands of feet into the Cayman Trench and reached the hydrothermal vents found four miles down, they had the ability to harvest and refine valuable elements and minerals spewing forth from these vents, pumping them up from the depths in a purified state. And while vast amounts of high-grade gold, platinum, magnesium oxide, and manganese were routinely made available to them for ongoing construction, it was the cold water the *thurentra* continually pumped up from the abyss that made the OTEC process workable. With Aquaria situated immediately above an area of sea with insufficient water depth, harvesting the ocean's inexhaustible supply of stored energy would otherwise have been impossible. Perched directly under the floating city were six *thurentra* of immense size that drew huge volumes of nutrient-rich cold water from the oceanic depths where dissolved nitrates and nitrites were plentiful. These particular organisms had been created by splicing the mysterious oblate jellyfish with the largest variety of sea cucumber Amphitrite and Jacob could find. With their taproot network of tentacles reaching far down into the nearby Cayman Trench, the water they brought up was forty degrees lower in temperature than the eighty-degree water at the surface. Aside from their ability to harvest certain types of metal, they also produced massive amounts of hydrogen gas. A byproduct common to all species of *thurentra* regardless of the particular metal they mined, the gas was continuously vented off by the strange organisms and collected by the colony.

Destiny took satisfaction in knowing the *thurentra* population had doubled since the day she had first let Jay Jay see them seven years earlier, for now there existed a total of fifty-two, with forty-six of the car-sized creatures roosting along the floor of the cavern. Of these, eight of them yielded gold and platinum, while thirty others provided a seemingly endless supply of magnesium in an oxide form better known as periclase. Polymetallic nodules primarily comprised of manganese and to a lesser degree aluminum were produced by the remaining eight *thurentra*.

As Jacob had explained to Destiny many years ago, magnesium and manganese played a critical role in the building of Aquaria, for these were the raw materials that formed the skeletal framework of the main structural components. Because magnesium in its pure form is soluble in sea water and will readily dissolve, it must be alloyed with small amounts of manganese and aluminum to keep it from dissolving. And though it was lighter than steel, it was comparable in strength. But rather than having to set up a mechanical manufacturing system in order to produce the alloy, the albinos had managed to bioengineer yet another hybrid organism that fed on the periclase and manganese nodules to excrete the needed alloy in an extruded form that resembled long strands of wire capable of conducting an electrical current.

In spite of all the benefits the *thurentra* population made possible, Destiny knew they could be quite dangerous to other organisms coming in direct contact with them, for they also acted as huge capacitors, storing electrical energy similar to the way certain types of eels did. This made her think back to the man she had discovered floating dead at the base of one of the cavern-dwelling *thurentra* years earlier, apparently one of Yeslam Raduyev's henchman during the pod's struggle with the radical Islamist and his allies. Nick Henderson, her father's surly and conspiring assistant, was another that had fallen victim to the hybrid's potentially lethal electrical charge, but he had survived only to be found dead a week later behind the cove's mystical waterfall where the dolphins had hidden their original cache of precious metals.

The thought of the cove brought back treasured memories, making Destiny suddenly long for its solitude and unmatched beauty. She had spent most of her life growing up there, sheltered and naïve about the true nature of the world that lay beyond. And though she had been basically happy and content, she sensed that something had been missing from her life. She had been especially aware of this whenever she ventured deep into the cave that existed behind the waterfall, cognizant of an inner voice beckoning her on. A portal lay within those darkened recesses, a time warp that somehow connected the past with the future, and it was within a dimly lit chamber located far back from the thunderous water where she had finally come to understand the actual meaning behind the murals that lay on the walls. It was there she and Jake had made love for the first time, and it was there the twins had been conceived, bringing her happiness to uncharted heights.

Destiny sighed contentedly. Yes, the cove was a special place, far different and removed from the colony. It was there Jacob and her mother had inadvertently created the first *thurentra* by dropping a sea cucumber onto the unknown jellyfish to see what would happen. And it was there that the resulting hybrid organism had begun bringing up huge amounts of precious metals from the oceanic depths once it had fully matured. But now there were two such organisms living within the cove's sheltered waters, and both continued to produce a staggering supply of gold and platinum using their prodigious tentacles to draw the valuable metals up from the deep.

Thurentras, it seemed, brought an additional benefit, one that directly affected the local marine environment. Corals and sponges, even those on the decline, quickly rebounded, becoming more robust and alive in the vicinity of these amazing creatures. This baffled Amphitrite and Jacob, for they were still unable to unravel the process that caused this.

The fact that *thurentras* were capable of reproducing themselves asexually had come as quite a surprise to the entire pod, for it was during the fourth year of a *thurentra*'s life cycle that a bulbous node would suddenly sprout from its leathery crown, growing rapidly within a matter of days as it swelled like an oblong balloon filling with air. Reaching the size of a ripe eggplant, it would suddenly break free and float to the surface, upon which it could be swept away by wind and current if it reached open water. This had happened with the first cove-dwelling *thurentra*, the oldest among these amazing organisms. It was slightly over two years earlier when Natalie had noticed the inflated node being taken out to sea with an outgoing tide very early one morning. But even before it reached the reef beyond the narrow inlet leading to the ocean, she had gently nudged it back into the cove's calm protected water, correctly deducing it would as yet be too immature to carry an electrical charge like the organism that had spawned it. Moving it to a pen where it could not escape, Amphitrite had kept a watchful eye to determine what new developments would take place, speculating that the small seedling would eventually rupture, releasing the hydrogen gas keeping it afloat. She had not been disappointed. In a matter of days, the sac burst, whereupon it sank to the cove's sandy bottom to anchor itself and begin to grow. Once alerted to this strange event, the pod took precautionary measures to capture all seedlings once they broke free. Carrying out such a task with the cavern-dwelling *thurentra* had been rather easy. This, however, had been far more difficult with the gigantic *thurentra* roosting beneath the floating city, for the seedlings as it turned out were the size of huge hot air balloons.

Amphitrite appeared not to notice Destiny's deep ruminations, though in times previous she would have sensed them immediately. Her attention was focused on the twins. "Both of you have seen what has been happening to the nearby reefs," she said.

"You mean the *white pox*," the twins chorused in unison.

Amphitrite beamed proudly. The twins were very perceptive and exceptionally smart for their age. "Yes, I'm talking about the white pox." She centered her gaze on Troy Jacob. "What can you tell me about this dreadful plague, Teejay?"

"It's very destructive to elkhorn corals," Troy Jacob chirped with alacrity.

Amphitrite nodded in agreement. "So how can you tell if the coral is infected?"

"It loses its brownish or yellowish color and turns white.

Amphitrite turned to the other sibling. "Can you tell me what causes it, Melody?"

"A germ that's very contagious to the elkhorn."

"What kind of germ?"

"It's called *Serratia marcescens*, a type of fecal enterobacterium."

Amphitrite looked pleased at Melody's perfect enunciation of a term that would have otherwise left most seven-year-olds tongue-tied. As usual, Jacob had taught the children well. She turned back to the boy. "Where does it come from, Teejay?"

"From human sewage."

"Yeech!" Melody blurted in mock horror, making her brother laugh. "That's disgusting," she quickly added. "We've been swimming through poop."

Amphitrite found no humor in the girl's antics. White pox was no laughing matter. It was a strange new menace that had joined the long list of woes that threatened corals in the world's oceans. A bacterium that was potentially deadly to humans was now killing off one of the most important reef-building corals in the Caribbean. It was a startling discovery because it was the first time ever that a human disease was found to kill an invertebrate. *Acropora palmata,* the scientific classification of elkhorn corals, was structurally complex and had a configuration that resembled the antlers of an elk, showing many large branches that provided habitats for a wide range of marine life. Compared to other corals, elkhorns were incredibly fast growing, but unfortunately had declined by almost ninety percent in the past fifteen years in Caribbean waters. Until recently, however, the elkhorn cover around Navassa had continued to thrive, remaining essentially unscathed by such ravages. But now, despite the salubrious benefits *thurentras* bestowed on the local marine environment, the white pox was threatening the survival of the Navassa elkhorns as well, for it had been brought into their midst by a carrier of the pathogen deadly to their health. A tiny snail called *Aesopus spiculus* had inexplicably found its way to Navassa in great numbers and spread the lethal bacterium to the *Acropora* corals, which were now dying off at an alarming rate.

"In actuality the water quality is quite good around Navassa thanks to the marvelous sewage treatment system incorporated into Aquaria's infrastructure," Amphitrite amended. "The bacterium seems to be confined to the elkhorns, so none of us have been exposed to human feces."

"So where's the sewage coming from?" Troy Jacob asked.

"We're still working on that," Amphitrite answered, "but we've been able to identify the culprit responsible for spreading the bacterium."

"Jacob told us a snail was spreading it," Melody said, continuing to sit astride Omega's back.

"That's right," Amphitrite concurred. She reached for a glass flask, holding it up so the twins could scrutinize its contents. A cluster of minute dark objects clung to the inside surface, each about one-tenth the size of a human thumbnail.

"I didn't know snails could be so puny," Troy Jacob decried. "Is that as big as they get?"

Amphitrite nodded. "We think we've found a way to remediate the damage these little creatures have caused."

Melody eyed the tiny snails with curiosity. "How?"

"By making a slight adjustment to their genetic structure."

"You've made a new type of snail!" exclaimed Teejay.

"Yes we have," Amphitrite concurred. "We spliced a gene from the brown algae found in these waters into the snail's genome. That particular gene is known to produce a potent compound used as a natural antibiotic to defend the algae against infection. Once this genetically modified snail makes contact with the elkhorns, it releases a secretion that kills off the white pox and renders the coral immune to further infection even if the coral is healthy and has not been contaminated by the bacterium."

"Wow!" blurted both siblings simultaneously.

"We made one more modification to the snail's genes, so there are actually two other benefits this new species brings," Amphitrite further explained. "The secretion it releases will kill the snails that carry the *Serratia marcescens* bacterium once they make contact with an immunized coral. The new snail also eats sewage and purifies the water, so not only are we going to release them into the Navassa ecosystem, we're also going to drop them into the drainage ditches and coastal waters back in Haiti."

This last declaration was a stark reminder to the children that Haiti was an ecological disaster. The impoverished Caribbean nation, poorest in the Western Hemisphere, had no sewage treatment facilities whatsoever. And although she could not prove it, Amphitrite was certain that the bacterium finding its way to Navassa via the *Aesopus spiculus* snail had originated in the polluted waters of Haiti.

"But you're going to need a gazillion of them," Melody was quick to point out.

"The modified snail reproduces exceptionally fast," said Amphitrite. "We've been breeding them for several weeks now and have several million ready to put to work. For starters, we'll release half of them into the local habitat, with the rest going to Haiti."

Troy Jacob eyed the genetically-modified snails within the flask thoughtfully. "Have you given them a name yet?"

"The new species is called *Aesopus vigoratus*."

Melody parroted the trailing word, appearing puzzled. "*Vigoratus*?" Her eyes suddenly lit up as she recalled Jacob's latest tutoring session. "Doesn't that mean 'healer' in Latin?"

Once again Amphitrite beamed proudly. "Yes, it does."

"Why don't we just call them 'Vigs'?" Troy Jacob suggested.

"If you like," Amphitrite replied.

"When are you going to send them to Haiti, Grandma?" Melody asked, her tone bubbling with sudden interest.

"The first batch will be delivered the day after tomorrow," Amphitrite answered. "We'll start with Port-au-Prince, seeding the harbor and drainage ditches with them."

Melody turned briskly on her mount to stare eagerly at her mother. "Can we go, Mom?" she petitioned anxiously. She looked to her brother for support. "Teejay and I really miss the cove. We haven't been there in over a year now and you promised we'd see it again real soon. We can stop there on the way back from Port-au-Prince."

Destiny hesitated. Even though eight years had now passed since the Cardoza incident, her beloved cove could still be a dangerous place, and the last thing she needed was to put her children in harm's way. In the intervening years, Rafael Cardoza and his thugs had made two additional forays aimed at pillaging the gold that lay hidden in the cove, only to be beaten back severely by the ingenious, though primitive security measures Jake had devised. Nevertheless, she could no longer ignore the inner voice beckoning her back to the place of her birth. Perhaps it was in response to the recurring lucid dream that had tormented her night after night in recent weeks. Jacob had told her long ago never to ignore her dreams, for they were often a warning that foreshadowed a disastrous future event that could be averted if appropriate preemptive steps were undertaken before it occurred. This particular dream might very well be one such precursor. It continued to gnaw away at her, invoking a deep-seated foreboding that lingered on the edge of her awareness, growing ever more ominous with each passing day until a yearning desire to revisit the cave's dark recesses had now become overpowering. Perhaps those timeless murals would give her a glimpse of things yet to come.

Destiny was abruptly jarred from her momentary reverie. "Please, please, can we Mom?" This time, it was Teejay who pleaded.

"But you have an identical cove right here in Aquaria," Destiny reminded him.

TJ frowned. "You know it's not the same. It's not even half as big as the one in Haiti."

"And the birds and butterflies are not real," Melody challenged.

Destiny hated it when they ganged up on her like this. But the twins were right, and she couldn't fault them for their yearning desire to revisit their birthplace. Even though the albinos had gone to great lengths in replicating the mystical sanctuary, the re-creation was nevertheless a scaled-down version of the real one. Constructed at Aquaria's epicenter, it formed the largest open area within the floating city and even displayed an artificial waterfall that cascaded down from a height of 230 feet in a series of plunging cataracts that duplicated the one back home. "It may be smaller but it's made to look just like the real one," she replied lamely, knowing it could never quite capture the ambiance of the true cove.

"But it doesn't even smell the same," TJ rejoined mournfully.

"And the rainbows are fake, too," Melody added.

"And it doesn't have any *thurentra*," TJ complained testily.

Without knowing why, Destiny suddenly caved, though it defied all reason within her. "A promise is a promise," she found herself saying despite her misgivings.

"So we'll be going then?" both twins pressed avidly, their mellifluous voices merging as one.

Destiny sighed in resignation, aware of Amphitrite's look of surprise. It was obvious her mother had not expected this. "Yes, we'll be going," she conceded. Swinging her gaze to Amphitrite, she asked, "Who will be supervising the seeding operation?"

"Zimbola, of course. He'll be taking the *Angel*."

Destiny nodded. Taking a trip back to the cove with the gentle giant assuaged her reservations. Other than Jake, Mat, or herself, she could think of no one better suited to protect her children.

Chapter Six: Cynical Views Explained

The reporter riveted her naturally inquisitive eyes on Jacob, still truly amazed at what she had witnessed earlier on.

"It appears you have no love for the UN," she stated pointedly.

Jacob shrugged. "We, in Aquaria, have no love of any organization or people who seek to impose their will on others."

"Not even if their will is focused on propagating a common good for all?"

"Like all ruling bodies and governments, the UN is comprised of greedy squabbling factions and individuals with hidden agendas usually aimed at amassing power and wealth."

"It's evident your view of the world is quite cynical," she replied. "Perhaps it clouds your perception of the democratic process, the merits of which you seem to reject. In spite of a few bad apples, wouldn't you agree that the UN establishes policy primarily through a majority vote of nations aimed at improving the world?"

"Majority rule is a noble idea, but unfortunately true democracy rarely exists, and in most cases is merely an illusion created to make the common man believe the fate of a nation resides in the hands of voters. The will of the people is rarely reflected in governments that espouse its virtues. As we know, elections can be and have been rigged by an unscrupulous minority, and in most cases can be bought if you have enough campaign funds to delude voters with a deluge of propaganda. But whether or not any of these things happen, the saddest thing of all with democracies is they do not last."

Surprise flashed briefly on the reporter's face. "Can you explain why?"

"Because the human failings of greed, complacency and apathy will eventually work their way into the system, and when that becomes sufficiently widespread the democracy will fail."

Jacob produced a gentle disarming smile, eager to erase the surprise that still lingered on the reporter's face.

"Have you ever heard of a Scottish history professor by the name of Alexander Tyler?"

"No."

"About the time America's original thirteen colonies adopted their new constitution in 1787, Alexander Tyler, a history professor at the University of Edinburgh, used the fall of the Athenian Republic some 2,000 years earlier as a prime example of why democracies cannot proliferate as a permanent form of government, for history demonstrates democracies are always temporary in nature. According to Tyler, once voters discover they can vote themselves generous gifts from the public treasury, the democracy will begin to crumble. From that moment on, the majority will always vote for the candidates who promise the most benefits, with the result that every democracy will eventually collapse due to loose and irresponsible fiscal policy. This is always followed by dictatorship."

"So what did Tyler discover about the longevity of democracies?" asked the reporter sardonically.

"Tyler's research revealed that the lifespan of the world's greatest democratic civilizations lasted two hundred years on average, with all of them progressing through the same cycle."

A trace of skepticism was now evident on the reporter's countenance. "All of them?"

"Yes. He found there to be eight evolutionary stages in all. It seems that all democracies spring from a culture of bondage, moving quickly to an environment of spiritual faith, which is the initial stage. From there, the spiritual faith garners momentum, progressing rather swiftly into a second stage of great courage in which the citizenry throws off the shackles of bondage to achieve liberty, which is the third stage. Both the French and American Revolutions are prime examples of the population attaining liberty from their oppressive government."

Jacob paused briefly to study the woman. "Would you like me to continue, or do you find the subject rather speculative and uninteresting?"

"Please go on."

"One only has to look at American history to prove what happens next. With their newfound freedom no longer hampered by an intrusive and overbearing government, the American people prospered greatly, moving rather quickly into a stage of abundance. Unfortunately, such abundance seems to have run its course as a result of overly restrictive governmental regulations and high taxation, the very things American colonists had rebelled against to launch their new nation. But it seems mainstream Americans have allowed this to happen by falling into a state of complacency, which is the next stage in the sequence. Coming off of that is a stage of widespread apathy, followed by dependency. And once a dependency on government sets in, a reemergence into bondage is only a step away, completing the cycle."

"The world has changed dramatically since Tyler's day," the reporter countered quickly. "Major advances in technology have changed our lives for the better. The United States continues to thrive well beyond this two-hundred-year time line."

"Has it? According to James Wilson, a contemporary professor at Hemline University's School of Law, the U.S. is now somewhere between the complacency and apathy stage, with some forty percent of the nation's population currently dependent on the government for its needs. Should its Congress grant amnesty and citizenship to the estimated twenty million aliens transgressing its borders illegally, he predicts the U.S. as we know it will cease to exist within the next five years."

"Do you honestly believe that will happen?"

"Yes. Judging from the leadership I've seen, America is being steered on a treacherous and unprecedented course toward socialism. It is quite evident its Constitution is being systematically dismantled. It would take draconian austerity measures to avert the impending collapse that is sure to come, but I doubt American legislators have the stomach to do this since it might become political suicide to do so."

The reporter offered no reply, eyeing Jacob curiously as her cameraman captured the moment on tape.

"But the heart of America's problem," Jacob went on, "lies within its monetary system."

"Isn't the American greenback the world's most stable currency?" rejoined the woman. "Financial markets abroad consider it to be the international reserve currency. Isn't the price of a barrel of oil measured against the U.S. dollar?"

"That is correct," said Jacob, "but it is inevitable the dollar will be replaced by another currency. The British pound was once the world's reserve currency before the greenback took over. Unfortunately, the U.S. dollar continues to be weakened by the debt-based monetary system that spawns it. Such a system basically extorts the American taxpayer by perpetuating an increasing national debt."

The reporter clearly looked stymied. "I'm not following you."

Jacob smiled knowingly. "It was the wish of America's founding fathers that the power to create and control money be in the hands of the Federal Congress and not in the hands of private bankers. They knew bankers could charge enormous amounts of interest and thereby impose their will on the people through control of the money supply. It was their belief that the citizens should share in the profits of the new nation. But they had to contend with private bankers who devised all kinds of trickery in an attempt to take control of America's money. A powerful European banker by the name of Mayer Anselm Rothschild once said, 'Permit me to issue and control the money of a nation, and I care not who makes its laws.' Bankers eventually got their way, and in 1913, the U.S. Congress passed the Federal Reserve Act. In doing this, the American government officially ceded its power to create money over to bankers."

"But the Federal Reserve is an agency of the U.S. government," the reporter contested adamantly.

Jacob held back the laughter wanting to escape his throat. "That is the misconception most people have. The Federal Reserve is a privately owned institution. The bankers purposely used the word 'Federal' to mislead the public. Their aim was to keep citizens ignorant of what was really going on."

"The United States seems to have prospered greatly during the last century," rebutted the reporter stubbornly. "What difference did it make whether its Congress or private bankers created the money supply?"

Jacob sighed deeply as if bearing the weight of the world. "For one thing, the U.S. Congress violated its Constitution when it enacted the Federal Reserve Act, for the Constitution specifically states that only Congress shall have the power to coin and regulate the nation's money supply."

"I still don't-"

Jacob quickly snuffed the reporter's obstinacy, eager to cleanse her ignorance. "U.S. dollars are issued in the form of Federal Reserve Notes, which are considered legal tender and the accepted medium of exchange the world over for goods or services produced. Unfortunately, it is debt-money."

"Meaning?"

"Meaning interest is being charged on every dollar created."

Jacob anticipated the mask of confusion clinging to the woman's face. "Would you like me to illustrate this point?"

"Please do."

"Suppose the U.S. government needs an additional billion dollars to cover its shortfall in tax revenues in order to continue financing its projects. Since it has already given away its sovereignty to simply print the money it needs, it must go to the Federal Reserve to get the shortfall. But the Fed does not just give away the money freely. It is willing to deliver one billion dollars to the U.S. government only in exchange for the government's agreement to pay it back with interest."

The woman felt truly naïve standing before Jacob. The man's outward grizzled appearance did not match the depth of his intellect. Though she was relatively untried and inexperienced as a news reporter, she was determined to make this assignment as interesting as possible.

"Having borrowers pay interest on money given them is common practice with financial institutions," she maintained mulishly. "It's the way of big business."

"So we are led to believe," Jacob muttered dryly. "But had the U.S. government retained its original authority to create legal tender rather than submit this power to a privately-owned agency, it would not have to pay interest on any money printed."

"I thought the U.S. Treasury Department printed the money."

This time Jacob could not restrain the small laugh escaping his lips. "No, I can assure you it does not. Whenever the U.S. Congress needs more money than it reaps in taxes, it authorizes the Treasury Department to print up the shortfall in promissory notes, which are then delivered to the Federal Reserve."

"Aren't promissory notes the same as money?" the reporter shot back. "Don't banks accept them as the equivalent of legal tender?"

Jacob's tone portrayed immense patience. "Promissory notes issued by the U.S. Treasury are actually U.S. bonds, which are not money. They are nothing more than the government's promise to pay back the funds it needs to run the country. Think of them as IOUs. A lender will not accept them unless there is an underlying confidence that the borrower will be able to pay back the loan. The drawback to this is that the borrower must pay back interest on top of the money borrowed. As a general rule, the amount of interest tacked on is dependent on just how much confidence the lender has in the borrower's ability to make good on the loan."

The reporter nodded in understanding. "Are you referring to the borrower's credit rating?"

"Yes. Currently, the U.S. holds a double-A-plus bond rating. It used to hold a triple-A rating, which is the best rating a borrower can have. But according to Standard and Poor, the credit of the U.S. has been downgraded since 2011, pushing global financial markets into uncharted territory. Even with the temporary fix of the Fed artificially holding down interest rates through a careless policy of monetary easing, the U.S. will eventually have to offer much higher interest rates on its bonds in order to sell them once the easing is lifted."

"Why do you see it as careless? Didn't this policy keep the American economy from collapsing?"

Jacob groped for the simplest explanation he could throw at her. "It is careless because the longer it is kept in place, the more it erodes the purchasing power of the dollar. The longer the program goes, the more sharply interest rates will spike once it is ended. Inflation will kick in and the price of everything will skyrocket. The American government will be forced to rely more heavily on the Fed if it is to keep running, borrowing more than ever before."

Jake noted the gleaning in the woman's eyes. "But the saddest thing of all," he continued, "is that money is created out of nothing."

The reporter's glimmer of comprehension abruptly faded. "You're losing me?"

"Let's go back to the billion dollars the U.S. government needs. In exchange for one billion dollars in Treasury bonds, the Federal Reserve will print one billion dollars in paper money as payment. The Fed's cost of printing up one billion dollars in paper greenbacks is nominal and will probably be less than a thousand dollars. The transaction, however, has indebted the American taxpayer to pay interest on the loan."

"I see your point," conceded the reporter.

"The process does not end there," added Jacob. "From that one-billion-dollar transaction, the Fed is now legally allowed to lend out another fifteen billion to other borrowers."

"Like who?"

"State and municipal governments, foreign countries, businesses, and individuals. Essentially any entity with a credit rating acceptable to the Fed."

"The reporter appeared to mull this. "Sounds as though money is being brought into existence by an institution that lacks the assets to support it."

Jacob grinned broadly, happy to see he was getting through to her. "It is! Bankers create money out of nothing simply by transcribing numbers in a ledger book and then giving out loans based on these numbers. Organizations and people who receive the loans can then write checks, which are backed by the numbers in the account ledgers of the bankers. But now the bankers can receive periodic payment on their loans with interest. It's all numbers, be it numbers in a ledger, on checks, or on dollar bills. Money that is not backed by real assets such as gold or silver is fiat in nature and holds no intrinsic value. It is actually nothing more than numbers on paper."

The reporter nodded again, her face fully mirroring this newfound enlightenment.

"It is a most diabolical scheme," avouched Jacob, eager to go on. "Using this process, many banks outside the Fed can legally lend out up to fifty times the amount of funds they have on deposit, essentially creating money out of nothing and then charging interest on it."

The woman's face suddenly clouded. "You make it sound as though paper money is worthless," she objected obstinately. "If people are willing to accept it as a medium of exchange, then it must nonetheless hold value and provide a basis of wealth."

With measured calmness, Jacob shook his head slowly. "True value lies in enterprise, innovation, and all the things produced through people's labors. Wealth is created by producers, not by redistributors of wealth like banks and governments, which do not create it. Paper money is merely a crude representation of wealth, and generally not an equitable one. Think of it as a rather abstract, inflated form of human energy. But it is not the money that is the actual problem, but the very system upon which it is based, for the system concentrates the collective energies of many into the hands of a few. The United States along with many other nations have been plunged into terrible and overwhelming debt since the implementation of the debt-money system. Following the passage of the Federal Reserve Act, the debt owed by the U.S. government has mushroomed to well over fifteen trillion dollars and continues of grow wildly out of control."

"So," said the woman, "aside from the greed, complacency, and apathy you contend has taken hold of the American people, you believe that runaway debt will be the biggest threat of all to the survival of the U.S.?"

"Most assuredly," affirmed Jacob. "When the Fed and banks create money through lending, they only bring into existence the principal amount loaned, not the interest that is tacked on. Money that was created as principal on a loan coming due in subsequent years must be used to pay interest coming due today. If all the loans throughout the world were called in on the same day, there would not be enough money in existence to cover all the interest coming due, so a portion of the borrowers would be in default. Since 1950, nominal debt in the U.S. has grown faster than the economy each year. The toll this debt takes on society has also risen in tandem with it mainly because more and more of the economy is going toward servicing the debt. That means a smaller percentage is available to produce and maintain the things that truly contribute to the country's standard of living. This has a direct impact on the nation's infrastructure, which is already being inadequately serviced and in decline. As this debt burden worsens, it is not inconceivable that bridges will start collapsing due to lack of maintenance."

"You paint a rather bleak and dismal picture," retorted the reporter. "But as I recall, U.S. debt has actually declined several times in the past, most recently in the late 1990s. So how can it be that the debt always keeps growing?"

Jacob noted a tinge of smugness in her tone. "When I speak of the national debt in the U.S., I am not only referring to that owed by the Federal government, but to the total sum owed by the American society as a whole, which also includes consumers and businesses, as well as state and local governments. In 1981 alone, U.S. Federal debt surpassed the one-trillion-dollar level and was growing exponentially. But state and local debt in combination with business and consumer debt exceeded six trillion, three times the value of all the land and buildings in America at the time. And in 2005, even though the Federal debt reached eight trillion, the total American debt had gone over forty-one trillion. Suffice it to say that an ever increasing amount of money must be borrowed to make good on the debt coming due."

The reporter just stared, unable to come up with a rebuttal, and Jacob seized the moment to drive home his point further.

"The American people have become tenants and debt slaves to the Federal Reserve and its agents in the land their forefathers conquered, for once a government borrows from a bank, it becomes servant to the lender and is no longer sovereign. Thomas Jefferson had warned about the consequences of such a thing happening, knowing that bankers could end up gaining secret control of the nation. And Woodrow Wilson, the very President under whose administration the Federal Reserve Act was enacted, rued the passage of the bill just before he died, stating that he had betrayed his country by allowing the actual reins of power to fall into the hands of a few dominant men. Enactment of the Act amounted to conquest of a nation without a shot being fired. Undoubtedly it was perhaps the most outrageous swindle in the history of mankind, for no matter who is elected to high office, the plutocracy that controls the Fed will seek to corrupt them by whatever means necessary, making many of them their agents in order to run the government from behind the scenes."

The reporter's response was immediate. "Your viewpoint reeks of conspiracy theory."

"So I've been told," Jacob relinquished airily before shaking his head adamantly. "But unless you can show me where I'm wrong, I still contend that the U.S. government is controlled by a shadowy cabal that is directly responsible for the decline of America and the capitalism which turned it into an economic giant, a decline based on greed, deception, and fraud. Make no mistake about it, these people wield enormous power, giving them the means to manipulate events not only in America but throughout the world. The UN intrusion you witnessed earlier is but a small example of this power. Here in Aquaria we have reason to believe they're making plans to overhaul the World Bank in order to dominate every nation on earth through the implementation of carbon taxes and military action to enforce them. Once this scheme is brought into play, the citizens of the world will be forcibly marched along a gradual path of economic servitude which will inevitably lead to absolute enslavement and unfettered oversight of every aspect of our existence by a one world government."

Jacob took a pause, deciding to add one more thing. "This plutocracy controls most of the mainstream news media and information centers in the westernized countries of the world, suppressing the truth and typically disseminating embellished and misleading news to suit their objectives. I seriously doubt this interview and what you captured on tape earlier on will ever be shown to the world in its entirety. Events will be doctored or cleverly altered to portray this colony in the most vile light possible."

With eyes widened in agitated shock, the reporter considered challenging the allegation, but from what she had seen from behind the scenes at the IBC, she suspected there to be partial truth in what the man before her was saying.

Deciding to ignore the remark, she approached the discussion from another angle. "Surely a man like you, who has apparently spent much time studying the shortcomings of America, must have a solution to its problems."

"To begin with, its Congress must regain its sovereignty by repealing the Federal Reserve Act and issuing legal currency that is debt-free. Unfortunately, John F. Kennedy had been in the process of doing this very thing before he was assassinated."

Jacob let the last sentence hang in the air so that the implication was clear.

"Are you implying that John Kennedy was murdered to keep the Federal Reserve Act from being repealed?"

"To rule out such a possibility would be illogical. The point I'm trying to make is that the power and motives of the people who stand to benefit the most from a debt-based monetary system should not be underestimated. These people are extremely ruthless and will go to any lengths to protect their interests. They will even instigate wars, financing opposing sides so that governments are forced to borrow for the sake of national defense. The death of thousands or even millions of people means nothing to them. In fact, they don't care which side wins as long as the countries involved are in debt to them. These people are responsible for much of the hunger, poverty, disease, and misery that exist in the world today."

The woman stared pensively, deciding which way to steer the interview. "So you believe all bankers are evil," she stated bluntly.

Jacob sighed. "Certainly not all. Most are merely naïve servants of a system they deem to be benign. They are unable to see the deep-rooted malignancy, nor the widespread harm it causes."

The reporter turned her gaze from Jacob, taking in her surroundings with assessing eyes. "Has debt been so unkind to this enterprise?" she asked appraisingly. "Surely you would never have been able to develop an operation of this magnitude without the assistance of bankers."

An enigmatic smile crossed Jacob's face. "Aquaria carries no debt burden whatsoever. It remains unhampered by financial liability of any kind."

The reporter's jaw dropped. "How is that possible?"

Jacob continued to smile. "What is produced here greatly exceeds Aquaria's consumption needs. You must remember that true wealth is really an excess of product over consumption. Every person living in this colony has a vested interest in its productivity. As such, their main concern is directed at minimizing the cost of goods and services they require for themselves."

"Are you saying everyone shares in the profits?"

Jacob nodded.

The implication was now clear to the reporter. "So it seems this community has embraced a culture that is quite socialistic in nature," she concluded. Her tone abruptly became admonishing. "Isn't that rather hypocritical, considering your negative view on where America is headed because of its recent leanings toward socialism?"

"Do not confuse this operation with socialism," Jacob said patiently. "The various forms of socialism this planet has seen during the last century have never worked, and for that matter, cannot work simply because it takes away an individual's desire to be productive. Under a socialistic system of government, citizens soon realize there is no incentive in working hard or starting a business when the bulk of their earnings will be redistributed to others who are basically non-productive by comparison. They quickly learn it is far more rewarding to enjoy the fruits of other people's labors rather than work. Most would rather sit idle than be a contributing member of society. Under socialism, entrepreneurs are penalized for their efforts while the non-producers are rewarded with a share of the wealth."

"Do all your adult residents work?" the reporter queried. She made it a point to keep her question explicit, having noticed numerous children at play within the complex.

"Yes, but not necessarily in the physical sense. Everyone has something to offer to make this operation a success. And those that can no longer work because they have become elderly and frail also contribute, imparting their wisdom to the young. In short, everyone is taken care of. Think of Aquaria as a super-organism, one that provides for the needs of the community inhabiting her, just as we provide for the needs of the cells in our bodies. Being essentially self-sufficient and autonomous, Aquaria yields all the things a human needs to live a comfortable life. We have more than a few laboratories devoted to making scientific advances and increasing productivity. Research and development of new technologies aimed at improving life on this planet is one of our primary objectives. Residents have their own living quarters. All food, power, lighting, and even clothing are derived from the sea. A medical center provides health care, and there are numerous forms of recreation and entertainment available to keep the inhabitants happy and content. And transportation costs within this city are virtually zero. Residents have none of the expenditures people normally have in land-based cities."

"What about taxes?" the reporter continued to probe tenaciously. She had read some of the material on Tursiops Worldwide on her way to the colony, discovering one particularly interesting fact. "Am I to understand this business enterprise pays no taxes of any kind?"

"That is correct. Our corporate charter is registered with the island nation of Anguilla, a tax-free haven."

"What about business overhead? It must be exceptionally expensive to operate a facility as large as this."

"Operating expenses as a percentage of revenues are relatively small. The costs associated with providing goods and services in this colony amount only to maintenance of the power-generating facilities and city infrastructure."

The reporter abruptly flashed a devious grin. "What if your residents want to travel abroad? What do they use for money?"

"All the people within this colony possess a savings account with credits to draw upon," Jacob replied blithely. "These credits can be exchanged for a legal tender of their choosing depending on their destination."

"Does anyone living here have financial problems?" asked the woman brusquely.

Jacob sensed she had to make a valiant effort at looking for any negative she could exploit, but he was now convinced it was all for show. "By tapping into the vast reservoirs of energy and nutrients stockpiled in the sea," he answered effusively, "we have liberated a flood-tide of the things vital to human sustenance. This translates into growing assets to be shared by all those who reside here. A bounty of all the necessities required for a stress-free and contented existence, including various forms of entertainment and medical treatment are freely available for everyone to enjoy. The only cost to each person is that they contribute something meaningful to the overall health of the operation. Poverty and financial hardship of any kind does not exist in Aquaria."

The reporter glanced at her watch and decided it was time to wrap up this portion of the interview. It was crucial she transmit the video segments to IBC headquarters immediately. From her point of view, she had so far been unable to unearth anything that would depict the colony as an environmental abuser. All her instincts told her that Jacob was being sincere in refuting Allotey's claim that Tursiops Worldwide was destroying the local ocean habitat.

She faced the camera, eliciting her best smile. "There you have it, friends. This is Amelia Amhurst of IBC News reporting from the floating city of Aquaria, the planet's first large-scale sea colony."

Chapter Seven:
The Reaper

Rafael Cardoza looked on, enjoying the first rumblings of amusement that rose up from his belly. The scream filling the air was exceptionally high-pitched and piercing, sounding like the shriek of a woman consumed by panic, and it was this that made him titter aloud.

Trapped within the cage, the man glanced back at the animal trying to get at him, unaware he had lost control of his own sphincter. Terrified, he spun his head around and pressed his face up against the bars, riveting Cardoza with wild, frenzied eyes.

As Cardoza watched, his mind reverted back to a similar event that had taken place several years earlier. Ever since then, he would always see the same scene unfold in his mind's eye. No matter who was being killed using this method, he would always see the same face and hear the same beseeching cries regardless of who was in the cage.

"You have to believe me!" the man pleaded, his quavering voice falling off to a crestfallen whimper. Looking back over his shoulder, he watched in horror as the gate came up a few more inches. Held at bay for the moment, the animal bellowed ferociously, a deafening, enervating rumble that quaked the air as it clawed and raked at the limited opening in frustrated rage. Tenaciously it tried to squeeze itself under the obstructing barrier that separated the two halves of the steel enclosure. Only a few more inches and it would get through.

With renewed vigor, the man gripped the bars, tugging and pushing with maddened strength, attempting to jam his pudgy body through the imprisoning steel. "I don't know where the gold is," he shouted in desperation. "Nick Henderson is the man you want."

Cardoza held up a hand, belaying the gate's rise. "Then you'll tell me where I can find him?"

"I keep telling you, I don't know." The words were screeched out like nails being dragged across a slate blackboard.

Cardoza's nose crinkled, the foul stench of McPherson's voiding bowels reaching out to assault him. "You do not deny you had gone to meet him, that he was to show you a stash of gold of considerable value?"

McPherson shot another quick glance behind him before shaking the bars savagely again. "He never showed. I went there to meet him, and he wasn't there. Why do you keep asking the same question?"

Cardoza grinned wolfishly, enjoying McPherson's torment. "If you went there to meet him, then I have to assume the gold must be hidden somewhere in that cove."

"Yes, yes," McPherson screamed. "Lemme outta here and I'll help you find it."

"Then you admit you know where it is?" Cardoza persisted. Though he had grilled McPherson again and again on this same point, he had to be certain the man was not holding back on anything.

McPherson's response came out in a strained gasp, as though he could not get enough air into his lungs. "It's somewhere in that cove… that's all I know." Beads of perspiration mingled with tears dribbled shamelessly down the man's ashen cheeks as he whipped his head around to take inventory of the beast again.

At sensing McPherson was close to fainting, Cardoza presented a face full of compassion. "I'll let you out on one condition." This was the part he loved best, giving victims the pretense of a last minute reprieve.

McPherson spun around, his eyes suddenly filled with hope. "Anything…anything," he stammered.

"I'll let you out," Cardoza repeated, "if you give me the names of the men who attacked me." The thought that he had been attacked by a force of unknown assailants infuriated him. He had been caught off guard back in that hideaway, losing five of his best men. And just when he was bringing in reinforcements to remedy the situation, the *Usurpar* had been holed by a pair of torpedoes. To his disbelief a sub had surfaced moments later, upon which two men had climbed out on deck. Adding insult to injury, they had fired a missile that had destroyed his luxury helicopter while it sat on the vessel's helipad, turning it into a raging inferno.

Wearily, McPherson fell to his knees, all sense of hope finally deserting him. "If I knew I would tell you," he sobbed.

Finally convinced there was no more information to be gained, Cardoza motioned the gatekeeper with a cruel, nodding smile, glad to put an end to the man's incessant whining, and in seconds there was nothing to keep the creature away from its intended prey.

McPherson cried out again, ever more shrilly this time, a piteous wail that sought to discourage the beast from attacking. But the big cat had not been fed in days, and it was ravenous with hunger. Cardoza had purchased the animal from a now defunct game preserve and made it a practice never to pamper the beast, wanting it to remain as feral and vicious as possible. At 550 pounds, the Bengal let out another throaty roar, displaying a set of fierce yellow fangs just before it leaped, and Walter McPherson's scream was abruptly silenced as the carnivore tore out his throat.

Cardoza watched as his pet feasted, fascinated by the look frozen on the man's face. Even death could not extinguish the utter terror that had animated the man's features only moments earlier. The eyes continued to bulge grotesquely in a wild-eyed stare, with mouth agape and lips drawn back in muted agony. They all carried the same look when terminated in this manner, but the face was not that of the naval captain he had executed back then. It belonged to another.

Satisfied for the moment, the Colombian drug lord turned away. He had murdered more than thirty victims using the tiger over the last several years, mostly underlings who cheated or stole from him, but also those who offended or failed him. The thrill of it, however, had gradually lost its luster, no longer producing the same level of excitement within him as it once had. But it did serve a useful purpose, he reminded himself.

Anxiously, Cardoza scanned the faces of the others privy to the scene, fifteen subordinates who worked for him. The apprehension he sought was evident in each face, though carefully masked in a show of contempt for the man just slain. And as always, they avoided making eye contact with him. Furtively, he shifted his gaze to the burly individual standing next to him, eager to gauge the Russian's reaction to the killing, and almost immediately he was both pleased and troubled by what he saw. Although he had invited Zinova here for another reason, he felt it prudent to show the man who he was dealing with. The execution served that purpose. It was a subtle yet stark reminder of how he dealt with those who failed him.

"Such is the fate of those who are careless with my product," Cardoza said, turning to Zinova. "This man lost several hundred pounds of cocaine to pirates at sea."

But as he scrutinized the Russian's face, Cardoza found himself growing increasingly irritated. It was not the reaction he had expected. Zinova continued to peer fixedly at the grisly sight as though aroused by the nakedness of a beautiful woman. He seemed completely oblivious to the implied threat.

All at once, several conflicting thoughts raced through Cardoza's mind. *He takes great pleasure in the spectacle of gruesome death, and that tells me he's right for the job. But he shows no fear at what happens to those who thwart me, and that could be a problem. A man without fear cannot be controlled.*

This last thought made Cardoza feel uneasy, and it suddenly occurred to him that Zinova might actually be many times more dangerous than the beast currently gorging itself within the cage. Men like Zinova were a rare breed, and he knew his plan would have little chance of succeeding without such a man. Having suffered a staggering loss amounting to nearly $300 million in uninsured damages eight years earlier, the value of Cardoza's vast holdings had been cut by nearly twenty-five percent. He had made it a practice to avoid insuring his ships and equipment. Underwriters were not about to make payment on a claim of this magnitude unless they first conducted an investigation. And an investigation had the potential of uncovering the true nature of his business, which would have made any claims null and void anyway.

Inwardly, Cardoza fumed. His tuna fleet had vanished without a trace, with all hands missing, including Pedro, his loyal and trusted nephew. The *San Carlo*, *San Pinto* and *San Diablo* were all gone, including their hidden cargo of heroin and cocaine bound for the U.S. The drugs alone had held a street value almost equal to the value of his fleet. And if that were not enough, replacing his custom-made copter had cost him an irksome $8 million, while repairing the damage to the *Usurpar* had set him back another $5 million. But now he was about to recoup those losses.

"You are fully prepared?" Cardoza asked. "Your team is assembled and in readiness?" He swung his gaze to the other two men accompanying Zinova. One was almost as big as the Russian and could have passed for his brother, a brute of a man with a bull neck who seemed to be just as fascinated with the shredded corpse in the cage as his boss. Zinova had introduced him as Drakov, though Cardoza had already forgotten his first name. The second man, however, cut a more striking figure. Though slightly smaller than Drakov, he displayed thick muscular arms that bulged from a sleeveless shirt. And while he carried an unsightly bulbous nose that jutted to one side of his angular, pugnacious face, it was his eyes that immediately caught an onlooker's attention. Cardoza had at first thought the man to be cross-eyed when he looked directly at him, but then he realized the folly of this impression. The man's eyes did not match. They were at odds with each other, with one blue and the other brown. But it was not these seemingly hideous attributes that made this man stand out from his associates. Rather it was the revulsion Cardoza sensed emanating from him. The execution he had witnessed held no allure for him, certainly nothing even remotely matching that of Zinova and Drakov. The man was clearly repulsed by what had just taken place.

Zinova paused to tear his gaze away from the captivating sight within the cage, the spell of it seemingly broken. "At midnight, we will set the trap." Abruptly, his eyes fell back on the mutilated body.

Cardoza held back a scowl, offering instead a casual nod. Zinova's aloof taciturn manner grated on him to no end, and it was becoming evident that the Russian had a definite tendency to avoid as little conversation as possible. Reputed to have killed more than 300 men, Zinova was a bear of a man, weighing close to 270 pounds and standing a head taller than Cardoza's five-foot-ten frame.

As Cardoza studied him, he was now certain all the things he had heard about the Russian were true. According to rumor, Karloff Zinova had been a major in the Spetsnaz, and Cardoza knew that Spetsnaz commandos had been the cream of the crop among Soviet combat troops during the Cold War, elite warriors comparable to U.S. Navy Seals in their training. Hand to hand combat was one of their specialties, and they were considered to be some of the best knife fighters in the world.

It was in Afghanistan where Zinova had initially earned his reputation as a killing machine, spreading fear through the ranks of the mujahideen. And it was the mujahideen who had begun referring to him as "The Devil's Reaper," in part because of the sickle displayed on the Soviet flag he represented, but mainly because of all the losses they had suffered in the bloody battles against him. But over time they had shortened the reference, simply calling him "The Reaper," and the name had stuck ever since. By the time the Soviets were ousted from the embattled country, Zinova had turned mercenary, offering his services to those who had the money to meet his exorbitant fee.

Cardoza couldn't help but wonder if Zinova was still the warrior he once was. In his estimation, "The Reaper" had to be well past his prime, with more than twenty years having transpired since Afghanistan and the fall of the Soviet empire.

Zinova withdrew his stare from the cage, impaling Cardoza with steely gray eyes. "You have the money?"

The drug lord glanced sharply at one of his lackeys, snapping his fingers pompously. The man immediately came forward, placing a small valise on a nearby table and opening the case.

"Four million now and the remainder once you successfully complete the mission," Cardoza said. "Would you like to count it?"

Stoically, Zinova closed the valise. "I don't think that will be necessary." Turning, he left with the money, his lieutenants on each side of him.

As Cardoza watched him go, he wondered if he had made the right choice in choosing this man for such a bold undertaking.

Chapter Eight: Bagpipes

Destiny awoke with a start, aware of her own gasping. The terrible vision still clung to her, lucidly lodged in her mind's eye. *Colossal, seemingly towering to the heavens, it loomed ever closer, a wall bearing incomprehensible destruction. Driven onward, it was an unstoppable juggernaut of gargantuan proportions, spawned by some unimaginable yet unknown force.*

Jake sat up drowsily, stirred from deep slumber by her erratic thrashing. He rubbed his eyes, brushing away the last tendrils of sleep before glancing at his wristwatch. It was just past 2:00 in the morning. Shifting his gaze to Destiny, it took him only a moment to perceive what was wrong. "It was that dream again, wasn't it?"

Destiny nodded, vestiges of dread continuing to haunt her. The same nightmare had been plaguing her sleep every night for the past several weeks now.

"It's just a dream," Jake consoled.

"There was something new in this one."

"Tell me about it."

Destiny sighed. "You sure you want to hear it? You look like you could use more sleep."

"Lay it on me!"

"There was an eagle in it this time. It was huge, easily the size of the *Angel*."

"That's one big bird."

"The twins were with me, and we were standing in darkness waiting for it. It was calling out to me, but I…" Destiny groped for words.

"Go on," Jake encouraged gently.

"It wanted us to climb on its back when it landed. I sensed it was evil and had no intention of doing so, but it said if I refused the consequences would be disastrous."

"So what did you do?"

"Since disastrous usually implies death and destruction, my options were pretty much limited. So, the children and I got on its back, and it flew up into the night sky. But then something happened to give me comfort and strength. You were suddenly there with us, and I knew we would all be okay. There was also someone else with you."

"Who?"

"I think it was Fernando."

"Fernando!?"

"Yes. Next thing I remember was the twins and I were on the *Angel* looking up as you and Fernando flew away. Fernando was holding onto a set of reins, controlling the eagle the way a rider controls a horse. Even though we were safe for the moment, we had to make some kind of arrangement with the Eagle Master."

"You mean Fernando?"

"No. I think it was someone else. The dream became jumbled at that point, but I vaguely remember us threatening the Eagle Master with some kind of action to keep him from murdering innocent people and bringing destruction on Aquaria."

"Can you recall what we threatened?"

Destiny shook her head in frustration. Both Jacob and her mother had taught her long ago never to ignore her dreams, for they often foreshadowed the approach of an undesirable event, one which could sometimes be averted if the correct action were taken. "I only know Aquaria was still in danger and could be destroyed."

She paused, trying hard to remember more. "At that point, the dream became confusing and hazy," she finally said. "It merged into the recurrent one I've been having over the past several weeks."

"It's still only a dream," Jake reiterated. "Most of the time they're meaningless."

Destiny arose from the bed, her comely young features marred by unsettling worry. "What if it's not?"

Jake stared up at her, knowing exactly what she meant. *Millions of people would die. Maybe hundreds of millions.* He was well familiar with Destiny's recurrent nightmare. She had told him about it the first time it had intruded its way into her dreams. "Then we'll stop it from happening!" he stated matter-of-factly.

"I don't know if that's possible anymore."

"You're not serious?"

Destiny let out a deep sigh, sitting back down next to Jake and looking into his eyes. "Something has happened to me, Jay Jay, something I can't explain." She hesitated, seeing the surprise registering on his face. He had become a believer and now she was failing him.

"You made a nuclear missile vanish into thin air," Jake reminded her. His tone was just short of incredulous.

"We all did that," she replied softly. "I was merely the lens that channeled the combined energy of all of us." She shook her head sadly. "But I seem to have lost this ability since that day. I don't think I'll be able to do something like that ever again."

"You have no way of knowing that."

"It's what I feel deep inside."

Jake had difficulty believing what he was hearing. Negative thinking was not a part of the girl he had come to love. "Have you discussed any of this with your mother?"

Destiny fidgeted uncomfortably, pulling her eyes from Jake's penetrating gaze. "Mother is not the same person she used to be, either. With the memory of her former life now fully restored, she no longer has visions of things to come."

"Maybe not now, but perhaps later."

"Jacob thinks she lost this ability when she regained her memory. He believes her previous failure at remembering her past somehow gave her the power to glimpse the future."

"Well you're still the same," Jake insisted, offering a big smile to lighten Destiny's dispirited mood, "a girl with a heart the size of Montana. Unlike your mother, you've always known who you truly are."

"Do I? Back at Navassa, I saw a side of myself I never knew existed, a side I'm not even sure I should be ashamed of. Had I been given a choice, I would have killed Raduyev in order to save you."

"But you didn't have to make that choice."

Destiny's manner hardened. "If ever I'm confronted with a choice like that again, then I wouldn't hesitate to do whatever it took to save you. The pod feels the same way."

"Hopefully, you'll never be faced with having to make such a choice."

Destiny had no desire to continue the discussion. Instinctually she knew that Jay Jay was the actual cause behind this change in her. In analyzing it, she could only conclude that falling in love could sometimes have unexpected consequences. It had affected her and the dolphins in a profound way, and some of the personality traits that defined Jake Javolyn had somehow infected the rest of them.

Or maybe they hadn't been infected at all. Maybe JJ's natural tendency to protect had inadvertently awakened something that lay dormant in each of them. Back at Navassa, JJ had killed twenty-three men including Raduyev in order to save her and prevent a monstrous plot from occurring, and the entire pod had learned a sobering lesson from that. In any event, they would no longer remain pacifists in the face of malice. They would now defend themselves and all those they loved. They would stand and fight, asserting their right to live. And in so doing they would truly be alive. Prior to Jay Jay coming into her life, a void had existed within her, though she had been basically happy. But now she truly felt alive, aware of the smoldering passion that burned deep within her.

Jake climbed out of bed and kissed Destiny lightly on the forehead.

"I'm taking the twins to Haiti," she decided to tell him. Up until this moment she still considered postponing the trip even though it would have greatly disappointed the twins, but now some gut instinct deep inside beckoned her on. More than ever now, she knew she had to visit the cave behind the cove's mystical waterfall without further delay, certain she would find the meaning of that relentless chilling dream. "We're going with Zimby."

Jake's jaw dropped, and he frowned in consternation. He had not expected this. "Why now?" he demanded curtly.

"Why not now?" she said quietly. "I promised I'd take them back to the cove for a short visit. Now's as good a time as any."

"No, it's not," Jake disagreed quixotically. "Things are beginning to heat up around here, and I can only imagine what the UN will be sending our way next."

"Exactly," Destiny acknowledged smoothly. "Maybe it's best the twins are out of harm's way."

Jake shook his head stubbornly. "I can't break away now. Jacob needs me here."

"I didn't ask you to come, now did I?" Destiny countered assertively. "Zimby will be there to protect us."

Jake pondered this before furthering his objection. Even though the colony had tactical defensive measures set up to counter most intrusive threats coming its way, he couldn't be absolutely certain they would be entirely effective. "Alright," he grudgingly conceded, "but what about Cardoza and his mob? You never know when he'll show up uninvited again."

"I would think he's learned his lesson by now. The cove's security system has already stopped him twice. He'd be a fool to try again."

"How can you be so sure of that? What if the system fails or he finds a way around it?" Jake's argument grew fierce. "Cardoza is like a ravenous lion with the scent of prey in his nostrils. The smell of gold is just too much for him to ignore even if he gets a bloody nose going after it. I still think it's far too risky."

"Danger, it seems, has become a way of life for us, Jay Jay," she pointed out pragmatically. "Whether you accept it or not, danger is forever going to be our companion, no matter where we go or what we do from here on out. This is the path we have chosen."

Jake opened his mouth to vehemently protest her logic, knowing how headstrong she could be once she had made up her mind on something. He remembered how she had struck out for Navassa Island with her mother and Bashir years earlier without him, brutally aware of the near-calamitous consequences of those actions had he not pursued her and intervened.

The discordant sound of ringing stopped the brewing words before they could escape Jake's lips. He picked up the phone in annoyance. "What is it?" he said gruffly.

"We have a problem, Jay Jay!" It was the voice of Ez, her tone sounding grave and concerned, and Jake's rising exasperation immediately thawed.

"What's wrong?" he asked apprehensively.

"A freighter may be under attack five miles south of us, but I have no way of confirming it." Ez went on quickly before Jake could interrupt. "Let me replay the transmission I intercepted and you be the judge."

A cacophony sounding like squelching bagpipes assaulted Jake's ear before a voice suddenly blurted," -being boarded by an unknown party. This is the *Southern Star.* Our ship has been boarded by-". Abruptly the distress call cut out, replaced once more by the stepped, distorted drone of bagpipes.

Jake digested this, detecting a trace of panic in the speaker's words. "Is that all you got, Ez?"

"Yes, Jay Jay. I tried hailing the *Southern Star* but there was no answer. My radar sensors indicate the ship is currently not under way. The disruption in the ship's radio transmission suggests that the broadcast was purposely being jammed. What actions do you recommend?"

"Have you alerted Mat about this?"

"Not yet. I thought it best to call you first."

Jake assessed the information thoughtfully before replying. He had to agree with Ez. Seal training had taught him the sound of bagpipes displacing a radio broadcast was often typical of deliberate jamming. And under the present circumstances it hinted strongly that the vessel was under attack by hijackers. "Inform Mat of the situation. Tell him I'm taking Achilles to check out the ship."

Jake put down the phone.

Chapter Nine: Hidden Booby Traps

The band of men moved through the rugged terrain with the stealth of phantoms. Under the cover of night, they had been airlifted by two heavily built rotary wing aircraft to a desolate stretch of beach along a minor headland jutting out into the sea. A map of Haiti's western coastline showed it to be the Devil's Horn. Located roughly 6.5 kilometers south of their objective, the area seemed the logical choice for launching their covert incursion.

The operation had been carefully planned using a set of aerial photographs provided by the man who had hired them, a notorious kingpin within the Colombian drug cartel. The photographs had revealed a beaten path that wound its way through the foothills just upland of their drop-off point. Had they followed the footpath to its terminus, it would have led to a small coastal village harboring a modest fleet of fishing boats. Oddly enough, the village did not exhibit the squalid, ramshackle conditions so typical of Haitian communities. It was orderly and clean, with all the structures and watercraft seemingly well kept. In fact, no sign of decay or garbage was evident anywhere. But it was not the village that held their interest. It was the sequestered cove bordering the trail to the south of the village.

Dawn was still hours away when Victor Belachek called a halt to their trek, a burly man with thick muscular arms and a bulbous lopsided nose dominating his bellicose face. He judged they had arrived at a point less than a kilometer from where the land fell steeply away. Unlike most of the terrain behind them, the photographs had shown a significant shift in the amount of vegetation covering this particular tract of land. Further back, the trail had traversed a largely defoliated landscape, only sporadically covered in low-lying brush. But where they now stood, he estimated they were just inside the tree line of a teeming rainforest. At least that was what the photos had indicated. As if to confirm this he scanned his surroundings only to be met with a pervading shroud of darkness.

Pulling a penlight from a pouch, he consulted the GPS unit he carried before checking his wristwatch. His face immediately clouded. Though they had arrived at the intended standby point, he noticed he was more than fifteen minutes late. A veteran of countless battles in Afghanistan and a former Spetsnaz operative, he hated falling behind schedule, always looking to carry out missions precisely as planned even though it would not matter in this case. Nevertheless, it made him wonder if he was getting too old for this sort of thing. After all, wasn't it he who had led his men this far, the one who had set the pace? And now they were going to attempt to penetrate a dense forest abundant with heavy undergrowth to reach their objective, this based on the feedback he had been given. He had been forewarned to be vigilant of booby traps set up along the way, perilous obstacles the drug lord's men had encountered during their last foray into this area. More than half of Cardoza's twenty man raiding party had been injured because of those hidden traps. They had stupidly tried to navigate these uncharted woods in total darkness, but he would not make that same mistake.

And while it was assumed those same obstacles would be no less dangerous during daylight hours, he would worry about that later, for right now he and his men had time to kill. Turning, he addressed the closest man in a whisper. "Pass the word for the men to hunker down and get some rest. Tell them to be ready to move at noon." This was part of the plan he and Zinova had meticulously crafted, a time when the sunlight would penetrate the forest canopy most effectively, a time when they would have a better chance at avoiding hidden traps.

With a hand resting idly on the stock of his assault rifle, Belachek stretched out on the damp ground, curiously wondering why Cardoza was so interested in taking control of the small basin beyond the forest.

The explosion of vivid radiance against the black void of hydrospace was dazzling as it streamed past. Whisked along by Achilles, Jake clung tightly to the albino's back, entranced by the flaring brilliance washing over him. Agitated by the pressure wave created by the dolphin's passage, thousands of microscopic, single-celled dinoflagellates erupted like miniature supernovas each second, sending out starbursts of bioluminescence that swirled and eddied around man and dolphin.

Jake focused his thoughts, pulling his attention from the mesmerizing light show. *How much further, Achilles?*

Achilles' answer resonated within Jake's head, a gentle puff that brushed up against his mind like a soundless whisper. *Just under a thousand meters, Jay Jay.*

Jake had grown used to the mind-link he shared with the dolphin, and now he sensed something else lingering within the midst of Achilles' thoughts.

What?

Destiny asks that you reconsider doing this, Jay Jay. She feels you are needlessly putting yourself in harm's way.

But you don't agree with her, do you? Jake knew he was reading Achilles correctly.

No, Jay Jay. Some things cannot be ignored, and this is one of them.

Satisfied, Jake shot off another thought. *Then we're in agreement and you know what I expect of you.*

Yes, Jay Jay.

Under the cover of darkness, the pair approached the freighter ten feet below the surface in the darkened sea. The moon had not yet risen, and the trail of sparkling bioluminescence left in their wake might be construed as nothing more than the footprint of a large oceanic predator by a vigilant observer aboard the large vessel. With the ship's engine currently at idle, Jake's task was simplified.

Another minute passed before Achilles slowed, and Jake opened the catch bag clipped to the belt girding his waist, aware of the ship's hull no more than three feet away. Unraveling the knotted nylon rope, he let the weighted end descend into the depths beneath him, allowing the line to extend to its full length. Sixty feet would be more than sufficient to achieve the goal he sought. Satisfied that the rope was untangled,

Jake handed the three-pronged grappling hook to Achilles who readily grasped it with one of his prehensile appendages. Abruptly, the dolphin swam off laterally into the darkness as Jake pulled the line back up, finally removing the 3-lb weight from the end of the rope and letting it fall into the depths. Taking two wraps of the line around his hand, Jake communicated his readiness to the albino.

You ready, Achilles?

Ready, Jay Jay.

Almost immediately, Jake felt the line go taut as it angled downward. Achilles would need sufficient depth in order to build enough speed to launch himself clear of the water. The line suddenly slackened, and Jake knew Achilles had reversed direction. He glimpsed a shadowy blur streak past trailed by a swirling wake of twinkling motes as Achilles leapt clear of the sea. Caught in the backwash of the dolphin's mighty tail fluke, Jake was momentarily tumbled backward before he steadied himself. In his mind's eye he espied what Achilles was seeing just before his bond mate hooked the grapple over the ship's railing and plunged back into the sea. As far as he could tell, the immediate area seemed to be clear of people.

Within seconds Achilles returned, and Jake slipped off his face mask, handing it over to his bond mate. The dolphin grasped it firmly in one of his prehensile appendages, taking momentary hold of Jake with the other.

Needless to say, do be careful, Jay Jay, Achilles thought uttered. *Try not to be reckless this time around.*

You just worry about your own hide, Jake was quick to admonish.

With powerful muscles in his arms and back, he hauled himself up the rope, using his feet to push off the freighter's starboard hull plates as he ascended. In moments, he reached the railing near the ship's stern and catapulted himself over it to land silent as a cat.

Strapped to his right thigh was the suppressed Heckler and Koch USP-9 submachine pistol he habitually carried in situations like this. The weapon was sheathed in a ballistic nylon holster that descended from the tactical utility belt fastened around his waist. The belt held five spare 15-round magazine clips. And riding Jake's right calf was his trusty K-bar combat knife, a tool that had saved him from certain death countless times.

Jake took in his surroundings with rapid fore and aft glances. Lights were strung out at 100 foot intervals along the ship's rail, trailing off toward the distant bow more than 900 feet away. He detected no movement against the backwash of feeble illumination they emitted. The vessel was an ultra-large cargo container ship with enormous carrying capacity, and Jake noted its unorthodox design. Whereas container ships commonly had a bridge situated amidships or close to the stern, this particular vessel had its bridge located near the bow, towering above it like the head of an enormous sea beast. Stacked five tiers high directly above him was a sheer vertical wall of steel intermodal cargo containers the size of trucks. Like most freighters in this contemporary class of ships, the *Southern Star's* deck was clogged with them, and Jake was quick to take advantage of a nearby narrow corridor, one of many set back between the towering rows. The deep shadow it afforded provided the cover he needed to check out his gear.

With practiced ease, he removed the USP-9 from its holster, pulling the waterproof plastic wrap from the weapon. Even after sea immersion, the submachine gun would normally fire, but the wrap was simply a precautionary measure designed to further reduce the possibility of a misfire. In being towed to the ship over a lengthy distance, he had been in the water far too long to discount the possibility of water seeping into the bullet casings and wetting the gunpowder. Dislodging the gun's magazine clip, he removed the first three rounds and held them close to his eyes in the limited light to make sure they were free of moisture. Satisfied, he replaced them and snapped the clip back into the gun's breech, making sure the firing mode was set on safety. Carefully he laid the weapon at his feet before pulling the spare clips one at a time from the utility belt, examining each for dryness before reinserting it back into its pocket and leaving the water-seal flap open for easy retrieval.

From the utility belt's largest sealed pocket, Jake pulled the final though perhaps most crucial piece of equipment in his arsenal. It was important it be kept dry, for any salt water clinging to its surface could severely attenuate its intended function. It was an exceptionally unusual device, and Ez had aptly named it "*The Cloaker*." The fabric comprising it was ultra-thin and felt extremely delicate to the touch, and Jake was continually amazed at how easily it deceived the senses, for in actuality it was incredibly tough and durable. When unfolded it resembled a loose-fitting cowl of crisscrossed webbing that allowed access to the utility belt and spare clips. It was surprisingly weighty in spite of its tissue paper thickness. Jake knew this was partly attributable to the gold and copper elements embedded in the semi-metallic material. Hurriedly he slipped it on, letting it drape to his feet and slipping the hood over his head before aligning the magnetic fasteners. Pulling a thin strand of wire from inside of the vest, he plugged the end into the tiny battery contained within the same pocket from which he had removed the cloaker. Thumbing the activation switch to "on," he listened for the faint telltale drone, a barely audible hum that quickly waned into silence. Satisfied that the system was now operational, he stooped and picked up the submachine gun, holstering it.

The garment would bestow him with the means to roam the ship unseen. Now activated, it could bend electromagnetic light waves in the visible range around the cloaked object, causing them to emerge on the other side as if they had passed through an empty volume of space. In the current situation, he would be the cloaked object, perpetuating an optical illusion to a vigilant observer that he was not there.

The cloaker was comprised of a highly sophisticated and intricate material forged in one of Aquaria's physics labs, another product resulting from Ez's engaging hobby of searching for new technological developments on the worldwide web. But obtaining this technology had not required hacking her way into a high-security computer system as she had done with the U.S. Department of Defense. She had found it in a paper published by a team of graduate students conducting experiments at a Duke University engineering research facility, discovering a highly complex set of algorithms that guided the design and fabrication of exotic complex materials known as *metamaterials*. Refining the technology further, she had developed an even more powerful algorithm that custom-designed a unique metamaterial with the specific cloaking characteristics Jake would require for clandestine excursions such as this.

Moving swiftly along the maze of corridors and tunnels provided by the stacked cargo containers, Jake worked his way toward the ship's bridge. It was simple logic to conclude that if the vessel were being hijacked, then that was where he would find the hijackers, at least the ones tasked with taking control of the vessel. For the most part, luck seemed to accompany him as he chose new directions where corridors intersected, generally managing to avoid taking a passageway that would lead to a dead end and usually guessing correctly. Only twice did he venture down a corridor which terminated abruptly, finding it blocked by the side of a steel container. Turning another corner, he suddenly came upon the port side gangway amidships, also finding it devoid of interlopers.

The mild ocean breeze that had been buffeting the vessel when he had first come aboard had now picked up a notch, and with the ship's engines continuing to run at idle, the vessel had swung around with its beam facing directly into the wind. A gibbous moon hung high overhead, casting a tenuous glow onto a slate-gray sea dimpled with building whitecaps. Swinging his gaze to the ship's bridge, he saw that the windows were awash in dazzling light emanating from the interior.

Gliding stealthily along the gangway, Jake froze in mid-stride as a shadow suddenly fell across one of the windows, a black silhouette against a backdrop of bright light. Someone was scrutinizing the freighter's aft deck from the elevated superstructure, and Jake had to restrain himself from darting back under cover, reminding himself that he was invisible to prying eyes, at least in theory. Beyond laboratory testing, this was his first actual use of the cloaker in a potentially dangerous situation, and he was having difficulty suppressing old habits by putting his unconditional trust in this new technology.

Like a ghostly sentinel, the figure held steady a moment longer before turning away, no longer obstructing the light cascading from the window. Jake took the opportunity to bolt forward abruptly, quickly closing the distance to the base of the bridge. And as he raced along, one fact in particular puzzled him. If the ship had been hijacked, the perpetrators had not come by sea. Of this he was certain. During hours of the night, a high state of security protocol was kept in place in the waters surrounding Aquaria, typically extending several miles beyond its outer perimeter. The pod always kept a few sentries roaming the sea around the colony, and had a band of pirates used a boat or even a submarine to board the freighter, the dolphins or their cetacean cousins would have detected it. Depending on the species of the spotter, such an occurrence would have been swiftly relayed either acoustically or telepathically, with the information ultimately reaching him. But that had not happened. On his approach to the freighter, Achilles had not detected any small vessels tethered to the *Southern Star*, nor anywhere in close proximity for that matter. That left only one conclusion, which was that the hijackers had come by air, if in fact the ship had actually been seized.

Jake quickly ruled out the use of parachutes by armed assailants to get aboard the ship. An air drop would have been much too risky, offering little room for error in the unpredictable and gusty winds that often sprang up at night over these waters. No. More likely they had rappelled down ropes from a hovering helicopter.

As if to add credence to Jake's speculations, the voice of his bond mate resounded in his head. Achilles was always keyed into his thoughts when the possibility of danger lurked close at hand, and Jake made it a practice to keep the mental link open under situations such as this though it could sometimes be distracting.

A helicopter has been detected probing Aquaria's air space, Jay Jay, the dolphin informed him. *Perhaps it has some connection with this occurrence.*

What size chopper? Jake shot back. *Any information will be helpful.*

The colony had highly sophisticated radar installations set up on the floating city and Navassa Island, and Ez was patched into these systems. Jake knew she would dig into her extensive data banks to match the chopper's profile with the make and model of rotary-wing aircraft currently probing Aquaria's airspace.

Achilles relayed Jake's query to another pod member closer to the city, who in turn emitted an acoustical dispatch which Ez was able to pick up through her underwater sensors. Had they relied solely on acoustics to send messages, communication would have been far too slow considering their present distance from Aquaria. Telepathic thought waves traveling at the speed of light greatly outpaced sound waves moving through water. Ez, however, was not capable of a direct mind link with the albinos and had to rely on acoustical transmissions for both receiving and sending information between her and the dolphins. Even so, this constraining hurdle was quickly overcome as the answer to Jake's query came back within seconds.

Ez says it's an Mi-35 Hind, JJ.

The reply stunned Jake. An Mi-35 Hind was a Russian-made aircraft and an upgraded version of its predecessor, the Mi-24, which had initially been deployed by the Soviets against the mujahideen guerrilla fighters in Afghanistan. Hinds were large, powerfully-built helicopters primarily designed for use as attack gunships, but they could also serve as low-capacity troop transports with room for eight passengers. The Mi-24 had been much feared by Afghan rebels, who had called it "*Shaitan-Arba*," Satan's Chariot. Hinds had been originally produced by the Mil Moscow Helicopter Plant and had been in operation since 1972, eventually finding their way into the military of thirty other nations. The profile of a Hind resembled that of a large insect, with the pilot and weapons operator seated in tandem, stepped cockpits under separate, individual canopies.

What disturbed Jake the most, however, were the armament systems these aircraft were capable of carrying. Very often they were outfitted with air-to-ground guided missiles and 23mm canon, but in his opinion their most potent weapon was the twin rapid-fire 12.7mm Yakushev-Borzov heavy machine guns housed in a pod that could be rotated under the chin bubble. Each gun was capable of unleashing a devastating amount of firepower, with the manufacturer boasting 4,500 rounds per minute. A remembrance of the electronic Gatling gun mounted to Sebastian Ortega's Bell helicopter suddenly invaded Jake's mind. Ortega had nearly destroyed his beloved North Sea trawler with the weapon before Jake had stopped him with the help of the albinos.

Jake put aside the thought, assessing other features he knew of the Hind. Housed within its sturdy frame were powerful twin engines that gave the aircraft the capacity to maneuver quickly in spite of the heavy loads incorporated into its design. It possessed a heavily armored body and nearly indestructible titanium rotor blades which could resist impacts from .50 caliber rounds from all angles. The cockpit was protected by ballistic-resistant windscreens and a titanium-armored tub. In short, a Hind was tough to bring down and could easily withstand the meager firepower Jake presently carried.

Nevertheless, Aquaria's defense system was quite capable of protecting the colony from an air assault if in fact that was the intention of the people aboard the Hind. As if to belay Jake's next thought, Achilles relayed another message.

Ez says the pilot of the Hind has issued a warning that if he's fired upon, the luxury liner Morning Vista will be destroyed.

Jake was immediately perplexed. The ship he was standing upon was a freighter, not a luxury liner, and the name of the vessel was the *Southern Star.* The warning didn't make sense.

Achilles quickly brought clarity to the conundrum. *The Morning Vista is another ship Ez has picked up on her radar, and she's currently within five miles of our present position, Jay Jay.*

If the Hind is brought down, how can it possibly destroy the Morning Vista? Jake snapped back. *They could be bluffing.*

Perhaps, Achilles offered, *but are you willing to gamble on the lives of innocents on such a possibility? Ez is trying to get more information from them to…*

The resonance in Jake's head ceased abruptly. *To do what?* Jake implored impatiently.

Hush, JJ! I'm receiving another message.

Jake waited anxiously, and the two seconds that transpired before Achilles came back seemed like an eternity.

Ez has detected a second Hind in the vicinity of Morning Vista. Need I say more?

The gloomy implication numbed Jake with dread and he stood frozen with indecision, his mind reeling with this sudden and unexpected revelation. Most modern luxury cruise ships were filled to capacity with passengers these days, and the *Morning Vista* might well be carrying thousands.

As if to add further gravity to this new development, Jake sensed a dark cloud descend upon him like the shock wave following a nuclear blast. He had felt it only once before when he had sought to rescue Destiny years earlier from the clutches of Ternier and Ortega, and the pure essence of it slammed into him with hurricane force. *What's wrong, Achilles?* Jake managed to utter, caught totally off guard by the sheer intensity of it.

Achilles had trouble gathering himself, and Jake had to prod him further.

A sorrowful wail bearing acute emotional distress resounded in Jake's head. *The pilot of the first Hind has given instructions and demands they be followed to the letter immediately and without negotiation… otherwise…*

Otherwise what, Achilles?

Otherwise everyone aboard the Morning Vista will be killed, the dolphin lamented miserably.

Jake felt the chilling despair of sweat creep over his body.

Achilles floundered despondently in trying to keep the link open, the magnitude of his emotion continuing to grow and on the verge of uncontrollable weeping. *The Hind is to land unharmed on Aquaria, at which time three of its residents will be standing by to board the aircraft.*

Please go on, Jake pleaded, afraid to hear what was to follow.

They have named the residents they seek.

Who? Jake demanded when Achilles hesitated yet again, unable to suppress the brooding premonition of disaster and tragedy rapidly taking hold of him.

Achilles' answer reverberated in Jake's skull like a shrill howl. *They refer to the Dolphin Girl and her children.*

Jake's response was like a lightning bolt of pure anger. *That is not an option! Tell Destiny I forbid it.*

Achilles remained silent, and Jake sensed the same steel barrier of frigid unresponsiveness he had experienced years earlier being erected. Destiny was now involved in the matter. There could be no doubt. Destiny was the focal point of the pod and its primary human interface. She was by far the purest of its human contingent and the only one among them who had access to all the Delphine minds, either singularly or in combination, whenever she chose. He knew she was in direct contact with Achilles at this moment and was purposely attempting to keep Jake from doing something foolish. She was going to keep him from engaging in this dilemma as much as possible, just as she had done when she had struck out for Navassa Island to confront Ternier long ago. She was urging Achilles to shut down the link the albino shared with

Jake. She, and she alone, would decide on the logical course of action to undertake.

The thought horrified Jake, and he screamed out in exasperation. "Do you hear me, Achilles? Don't shut me out!"

He realized he had physically shouted the question, failing to confine it to a mental query. Startled by his careless outburst, he glanced up sharply at the ship's bridge to see if anyone had heard him, and to his dismay he espied the same silhouette in the window as before. Someone was scrutinizing the rear deck as if in search of something. Abruptly he chastised himself for his own stupidity and irresponsible recklessness.

If not complied with, the Morning Vista will be destroyed, Achilles reminded him, this time sounding more in charge of his emotions.

Tell her under no circumstances is she to comply! Jake ordered shrilly, this time making a colossal effort to keep his response on a mental level.

There is yet another component to this unfavorable situation, Achilles warned insipidly. *The Morning Vista is not the only vessel they threaten destruction. If the lives of all those aboard the cruise ship are not enough of an incentive to meet their demand, then they will destroy the Kraken. Ez has it on her radar, and it is bearing directly at Aquaria on a northeast heading.*

This last bit of information hit Jake like a severe electric shock, and his mind staggered under the enormity of it. The Kraken was currently the largest crude carrier on the planet, able to carry slightly over one million barrels of oil in her immense hold. There was no way Ez could mistake the vessel's distinct and enormous profile, though it was a mystery why such a ship would be in these waters. The Kraken normally plied a route that carried it a safe distance north of Jamaica and Navassa Island as it made periodic runs between Mexico's Caya Arcas Terminal on the Yucatan Peninsula and the extensive oil refinery at the Port of Mayaguez in Puerto Rico while transporting huge volumes of low grade crude. As far as he knew, there was not a single port along the U.S. Gulf Coast or other areas of the Caribbean capable of accommodating a ship of such behemoth dimensions. The threat of an oil spill in the surrounding waters was one of the colony's biggest fears, for it had the potential of incurring irreversible damage to their budding enterprise. The fact that the Kraken was now south of Navassa didn't make sense.

For the first time in his life Jake felt completely helpless. It was as though he were bound hand and foot, both physically and mentally, in the face of such overwhelming odds. It was obvious the people the colony was up against had meticulously planned this operation so that there could be no doubt as to who the winner would be.

Tell Destiny not to board their chopper until I get back, Jake instructed dully, but he knew Destiny would not listen. His wife would not hesitate to put the lives of thousands and the very survival of Aquaria ahead of her own and those of their children. He knew her too well.

Destiny says to consider her dream, Achilles shot back, suddenly sounding hopeful. *She says there are parallels between the current situation and elements of her dream.*

Jake's mental outlook abruptly brightened. Yes, of course. Why hadn't he seen it? With lucid clarity, he suddenly knew what to do.

Chapter Ten: The Threat of Capsizing

The man scanned the ship's rear deck, searching for movement with the trained eye of a soldier. He could have sworn he had heard someone shout moments earlier, but perhaps it was nothing more than the passage of wind along the vessel's superstructure. Then again, he couldn't be certain. Though muffled, it had sounded like a guttural cry of deep anguish.

Still uncertain whether he had heard someone, he stepped away from the window quickly, not wanting to tempt fate. He was sure the material comprising the window's thick glass was made of a durable acrylic capable of stopping flying debris driven by gale force winds and crashing seas. Surely it could at least deflect rounds from a light firearm, maybe even a .44 magnum bullet, for he judged that a more powerful weapon would have been too cumbersome for a clandestine intruder to carry in an attempt to board the ship. Nevertheless, as a former member of the elite Soviet Spetsnaz, Vladimir Drakov knew it would be unwise to make that assumption. In any event, presenting himself as a target for more than a few seconds to a potential sniper, particularly one of Navy Seal caliber, would be foolhardy should the man they were baiting perceive him as foe. Standing in the window was only meant to be a lure.

For the second time in the last two minutes, Drakov spoke softly into his lip mike, speaking in Russian. "Have you located him, Sickle?"

The reply was curt and gruff, edged with frustration. "No, but I heard someone cry out."

So someone had shouted, after all. Deeply puzzled, Drakov couldn't understand why a former Seal would exercise such poor discipline. Seals were trained to infiltrate with absolute stealth. Maybe it was meant to be a distraction. Or maybe it was not the man they lay in wait for. A short time earlier, Sickle had spotted someone scale up the side of the vessel further back near the stern but had quickly lost sight of him. But one thing was for sure, which Drakov found strange. The intruder had not used a watercraft to reach the *Southern Star.*

"Hold your position!" Drakov ordered. "He'll show himself."

The trap had been carefully planned, with Zinova briefing the team thoroughly on how it would be executed. Hopefully they would be able to take Javolyn alive, but that was not their main objective. Their client had offered a substantial bounty on three others who were considered much more valuable.

Dolphin Girl. The term intrigued him. Zinova said the woman rode a huge white dolphin whenever she took to the sea, often accompanied by two young children, each of which also rode a dolphin. But the children's mounts were much smaller in size and were assumed to be juvenile versions of the same species of white dolphin bearing the woman, supposedly an undocumented breed with unique attributes. According to the intel Zinova had been given, it was presumed the Dolphin Girl was the children's mother and Javolyn their father. Aside from delivering the girl and her offspring into their client's hands, Cardoza had offered an additional bonus if Javolyn were brought to him still breathing. And the easiest way to do that would be to lure Javolyn to the *Southern Star* where he would be unable to protect his family and, more importantly, become easy prey.

Still, Drakov wondered if Javolyn had actually taken the bait. Perhaps it was someone else Sickle had seen come aboard. But Zinova had stressed that a man like Javolyn could not resist following up on the feigned distress call they had put out, especially if the call was made to appear as though it were purposely being suppressed by jamming. He knew a man like Javolyn would recognize the drone of bagpipes as a standard jamming technique. And with him not knowing for sure if the *Southern Star* had actually been hijacked, Zinova had predicted the ex-Navy Seal would seek access to the ship's helm to confirm whether or not that was true. He would not be able to stay away, for it was in his blood. A true warrior always spoiled for a fight.

Drakov glanced at his watch anxiously. This was taking far longer than he had anticipated. Come on, show yourself already! he willed angrily. Their planned timetable was rigid, and in another ten minutes Zinova would be returning to pick him up along with the remainder of his squad. Whoever it was that had come aboard was being extremely cautious.

Growing increasingly uneasy, Drakov stepped to the window again, once more trying to entice the intruder to the bridge. Sickle and two other team members were lying in wait near the base of the stairway leading to the bridge. The trap would be sprung using a tranquilizer dart, which Sickle had at the ready. It would render their prey unconscious within seconds.

Without warning, a sound of deep groaning resounded throughout the ship, and Drakov's first impulse was that the freighter had run aground. Almost immediately the deck shifted precariously underfoot as the vessel listed sharply to port. Thrown off balance, Drakov threw out a hand to steady himself. Swiveling his head, he cast alarmed eyes on the ship's skipper, who lay sprawled on the deck. "What is happening?" he demanded brusquely.

Captain Gleason struggled to regain his feet, gasping heavily as he hefted his corpulent bulk off the floor. Attired in dowdy khakis, he was a tall, stoop-shouldered, ungainly man with a short salt and pepper beard, deep-set eyes, and prominent wart dominating his nose. "Something hit us!" he blurted.

Drakov spoke curtly into his lip mike. "Sickle, report!" When no reply ensued, he repeated the command only to be met by silence. In annoyance, he checked the wiring on his headset. The last thing he needed was a communications malfunction.

Slowly the freighter began to roll back onto an even keel, and Drakov looked to the captain again. "What hit us?"

Gleason opened his mouth to speak, but was immediately rendered speechless as structural members within the vessel groaned again, harsher than before, almost as though the vessel were in agony. An ominous shuddering worked its way through the freighter as it canted sharply once more, this time to starboard.

Dumbstruck, Gleason realized the ship was in danger of capsizing if it listed another five degrees. Something was rocking the ship. A quick glance at the moonlit sea told him the water was not rough enough to cause this.

"What's going on?" stormed Drakov. He needed answers, and quickly. Time was running out.

"I don't know," Gleason yelled back in confusion. The last thing he needed was to lose the ship and its precious cargo. By his estimation, the *Southern Star* was close to top-heavy, stacked higher than normal with cargo containers, the uppermost ranks laden to capacity with tungsten ingots. Tungsten was an exceptionally heavy metal, close to three times heavier than iron per unit volume. Forecasts of extended balmy weather and relatively calm seas had induced him to exceed the usual safety margins in loading the ship. The risk would otherwise pay off handsomely, and his bonus would prove to be exceptional on this trip. But he hadn't planned on the latest instructions he had been issued, which had come unexpectedly hours earlier and ordered him to change course.

On paper the *Southern Star* was shown to be an asset of Ocean Transitions, Inc., an international maritime holding company, but the actual owner was Rafael Cardoza. Gleason knew he was a dead man if he blew this operation. His instructions were clear. He had to give these men his full cooperation and assistance in carrying out this operation.

Gleason turned to his helmsman, the only other person manning the bridge, a man of slight build and darting, sheepish eyes who clearly appeared shaken at this sudden turn of events. "Check the ship's sonar and tell me what you see?" he ordered shrilly. "And turn on all the hull cameras!"

With the *Southern Star* retrofitted with underwater cameras in combination with both vertical and side scan sonar, Gleason would be able to determine the cause of the problem. The ship had a total of six video cameras situated along the centerline of its keel, each camera fitted with a powerful floodlight and housed in a Plexiglas bubble set in the hull approximately every 130 feet. When activated the cameras could be rotated and moved up and down to view the surrounding water in their immediate area. The systems had been installed along with the twelve hidden compartments within the vessel's double hull shortly after Cardoza's purchase of the *Southern Star.* They were normally used to observe the loading and unloading of illegal contraband the ship routinely carried along with its legal cargo. With water taking up the remaining space in the secret compartments beneath the vessel's inner hull, police and coast guard dogs trained to sniff out drugs would be unable to detect the immense quantities of heroin and cocaine the *Southern Star* frequently transported.

Within moments of activating the systems, the helmsman's face turned ashen. "There's whales beneath us, hundreds of them," he cried out in fear. "They're all around us. The sea's swarming with them."

Listening to the exchange, Drakov furrowed his brows skeptically. "Whales are rocking the ship?"

Gleason staggered over to the console like a drunken sailor as he tried to compensate for the deck's worsening tilt. "That can't be the cause," he growled derisively, shoving the helmsman aside. "Even a hundred whales wouldn't be enough to…" Gleason abruptly went mute as his gaze fell on the video screen, his eyes immediately growing wide in disbelief and alarm.

Toggling the cameras one at a time, he could discern immense rotund shapes under the harsh glare of the floodlights. They were situated on each side of the ship, ranks of them just under and along the port and starboard bilge keels, enormous blunt heads pushing up against the hull plates like submarine bulldozers. The water was exceptionally clear, with underwater visibility easily exceeding 200 feet, allowing him to observe the cause of their predicament. Quickly rotating the cameras, he could see the tail flukes of the port rank working hard in unison as their combined strength imparted an axial moment to the vessel. As though of a single mind, the port rank stopped pushing all at once, and the ship began to right itself.

Almost level, the deck shifted again with frightening speed, and the freighter listed sharply back to port, this time more acutely than before.

Gleason kept a death grip on the console with one hand to keep from being thrown sideways. With the other hand he frantically worked the controls to the camera system, his eyes riveted to the screen. The starboard rank of behemoths were now driving their massive bulks against the hull, their tail flukes churning the sea with such force that he could actually distinguish cavitation wakes behind them.

Feeling his guts clench tightly, he found it difficult to believe what he was seeing. *Was it possible his eyes were deceiving him? Surely this couldn't be happening*. He had spent more than twenty years at sea, always having considered whales to be nothing more than big, dumb brutes incapable of the coordinated attack he was witnessing. Clearly visible to him were several species of whale he had learned to recognize during his many voyages. And while humpbacks and grays were most prevalent in the void beneath his vessel, he was surprised to see at least twenty blue whales among them. The sight unnerved him further, for blues were by far the largest and rarest breed of cetacean on the planet. He knew that adults normally carried 120 tons of body mass and grew to a length of about eighty feet, but he vividly remembered reading that the largest blue whale on record was a 94-foot female weighing 176 tons. The monsters he was seeing, however, appeared to be far larger in size, with body lengths exceeding 100 feet. Nearly driven to extinction by whalers of old, the number of blues worldwide had been slowly rebounding over the years. But to observe so many of these great leviathans in one place was highly improbable, if not altogether impossible. In concert, all of these beasts, blues, grays, and humpbacks, were purposely rocking his ship, using their combined sheer power and mass to increase the momentum of each roll forced upon it.

"God help us," he muttered inwardly. The whales were surely going to capsize the vessel if they continued their assault.

With foreboding dread, Gleason sensed the ice cold fingers of death draw closer. Even if he were to survive a capsizing, Cardoza would be unforgiving, for if the sea failed to take him, surely the Colombian's ravenous tiger would. Currently, the ship's twelve secret compartments were all filled to capacity with bundles of high-grade cocaine having a street value close to a billion dollars.

Gleason turned to the helmsman, shouting in panic. "Engage the engine and get us underway immediately!"

"What are you doing?" Drakov growled in dismay, stabilizing himself against a port bulkhead.

"We've got to shake those brutes off," Gleason shot back. "They're going to capsize the ship."

"The engine won't engage," the helmsman shrieked. "It shut down completely."

"That's not possible," Gleason countered, his dread continuing to mount. "Page engineering and find out-"

The order froze in his throat as the deck shifted violently back to starboard, nearly toppling him. Desperately he clawed at the control panel to keep from falling. A loud squeal suddenly assaulted his ears, and he immediately knew it was the sound of rending metal. Twisting his head around, he stared in horror out the aft window as the ship tilted precariously. The thing he had feared was beginning to happen. The upper tiers of cargo containers were beginning to tear loose from the interlocking pinions holding them in place.

Gleason found himself withdrawing inwardly from the turmoil engulfing his ship, almost as though he were a spectator watching a calamity unfold on the big screen in a movie theater. Maybe this was nothing more than a dream, he thought dazedly as the freighter continued to rock savagely, his fingers clinging tenaciously to the edge of the console. Vaguely he heard someone scream out in terror, perhaps his helmsman. Oddly, he felt an inexplicable calm begin to settle over him, and he found the sensation strange with death now so close at hand.

Chapter Eleven: Cloaked

Jake moved with utter stealth, totally invisible to predatory eyes. His suspicions that a trap had been set were all but confirmed with further news from Achilles. Using the Internet, Ez had resorted to her hacking skills to delve into the ownership of the *Southern Star*, wending her way through an intricate though devious maze of holding companies within holding companies.

The Southern Star is the property of Rafael Cardoza, Achilles had informed him. *It's obvious these people have purposely lured you here.*

Then I'm going to need a diversion to disrupt their scheme, Jake had replied.

Ez is way ahead of you and has formulated a plan, Jay Jay, Achilles had shot back. *Destiny has summoned the whales and they should be here momentarily.* Achilles elaborated further, providing additional details of what Ez had in mind.

Jake braced himself, fully prepared for the initial onslaught from the great leviathans as they began rocking the ship. The whales were indispensable members of the colony, providing the necessary brute power to move the enormous sea-grown modules into place during Aquaria's construction. Now they were serving another purpose.

Shadowy movement caught Jake's eye as he rounded a corner. In reaction to the ship's sudden radical list, a solitary head bobbed behind a packing crate situated near the foot of the stairs ascending to the bridge. Coincidental with the movement, something banged heavily not ten feet away, and Jake made out the forms of two others catching their balance. It was the logical place for an ambush.

Compensating for the anticipated motion of the shifting deck and placing his trust in the cloaker, Jake strode quickly, deciding to take out the lone figure lurking behind the crate. A minute earlier he had come upon a short length of steel bar, deciding it would make a handy weapon. Now hefting it behind his back to keep it shielded by his cloak of invisibility, he slipped up to the man with wraith-like precision and struck quickly. A dull thud resounded as the bar made contact with the man's head, and Jake grabbed his unconscious victim to keep him from falling heavily. Unexpectedly, something clattered to the deck, the sound partly deadened by the grating of tortured steel bulkheads as the freighter rolled sharply. In the dim light cascading from the bridge, Jake realized it was a tranquilizer pistol.

In less than a second, he assessed the situation. Though he noticed the man he had just kayoed was heavily armed, the intent of the ambush was not to kill. These men wanted a prisoner, plain and simple.

Reaching for the fallen pistol, Jake turned and faced the position where the other two men lurked. Another warning echoed in his brain with critical timing. *Prepare for a more severe counter roll,* Achilles cautioned him.

Offsetting his movement as though he were balancing on a rolling log, Jake closed the distance to the nearest ambusher as the ship groaned in protest again. The shadow before him seemed to stumble, thrown off balance by the lurching deck. In that instant Jake fired.

The dark figure reacted as though stung by a hornet, bringing up a hand to slap at the thing embedded in his neck. Jake followed with a sharp uppercut that buckled the man's knees. Crouched within arms distance, the man's partner rose to his feet, appearing confused at the reeling antics of his comrade. Jake took full advantage of this momentary lapse in vigilance, catching the second man with a vicious front kick to the groin. The second man's eyes snapped wide in dazed shock and bewilderment, then glazed over as a devastating right cross finished him off. Turning back to the sedated man, Jake saw him stagger on unsteady legs, then collapse completely in a fallen heap.

Jake tucked the dart gun into his utility belt and stared down at the two limp forms. The men wore military camos and were armed in the same manner as his first victim. Each of them was outfitted with a lip mike and carried a submachine gun, utility belt with spare clips, grenades, and other lethal paraphernalia. Undoubtedly mercenaries, he surmised. Studying the immediate area, he noticed something else. Lying atop an oil drum lashed to the deck were two rolls of heavy duty duct tape, apparently set aside by these men in preparation for binding their intended prisoner.

The harsh sound of rending steel told him cargo containers were beginning to tear loose, and he realized time was running out. Hurriedly he grabbed one of the rolls of tape as the ship shuddered from bow to stern. Working quickly, he trussed up the last man he had rendered unconscious before moving over to the first. Each was bound in the same fashion, hands to feet behind their backs. The task was made all the more difficult by the rocking ship, which continued to list more severely each time it counter-rolled. He did not bother with the sedated man, assuming that the drug, whatever it was, would keep the man comatose for several hours. He then applied tape over their mouths lest they regain consciousness and yell out a warning to whoever lay in wait up on the bridge. Stripping all three men of their weaponry including their utility belts, he was about to toss all of it into the sea but stopped short as Achilles broke into his thoughts.

Ez says you're going to need those, Jay Jay. The dolphin quickly explained why.

The fact that Achilles could follow these happenings through Jake's mind's eye came as no surprise. He had grown used to it.

An idea suddenly came to Jake, and he rummaged through the utility belt of the tranquilized mercenary, almost immediately discovering what he had hoped to find. But there was only one, a spare sedation dart. Pulling the tranquilizer pistol from his belt, he loaded it, knowing it would come in handy.

Satisfied with his work, Jake took stock of his surroundings one more time to be sure there were no other potential assailants lurking about, fairly certain that no more than four men would have been assigned to the freighter for this mission of abduction. Shifting his gaze to the bridge, he stared up at the light streaming from the aft window, knowing there was unfinished business to attend to.

Moving with the grace of a tightrope walker, Jake managed to keep his balance as the deck teetered jerkily underfoot. The stairs leading to the bridge were only a few feet away, and he grabbed the railing just as the ship shuddered ponderously as it rolled back the other way. He held on tight as the vessel leaned so steeply that the ocean rose up to breach the port side scuppers. The screech of abrading metal assaulted his ears, and he caught a glimpse of nearby cargo containers beginning to shift.

Jake summoned Achilles. *Tell the whales to ease up a tad or they'll capsize her. I'm going to need prisoners.*

I'm way ahead of you, Achilles replied. *They know overturning the ship is not in their best interest. Even if they don't capsize her, should any of those containers come loose and fall into the sea, they could get injured. Ez checked out her cargo manifest. She's top-heavy, Jay Jay. The uppermost containers are filled with tungsten ingots. Not a very wise thing for a ship's captain to do.*

Jake broke off the chatter and climbed the stairs as the ship continued to rock to and fro, but now with a subtle difference in the severity of each roll. The harsh screech of rending steel abated slightly as he climbed higher. In moments he reached the top landing and peered through the doorway window. Only three men manned the bridge, with two of them clinging to the control console in obvious fright. The third man, a harsh looking individual, did not share the fear the others exhibited. Rather he appeared both annoyed and confused by what was taking place. He was armed with a submachine gun and outfitted in the same fashion as the mercenaries Jake had subdued minutes earlier.

Have our friends give the vessel a final rock, Jake instructed Achilles. *I've got one more unfriendly to take out.*

A wicked tremor suddenly shook the ship and Jake used the disturbance to open the door. One of the men at the console cried out in panic as the vessel listed acutely once again. Jake paid him no mind. He was focused entirely on the armed mercenary who held fast to the frame of the aft window, the man's automatic weapon slung over a shoulder. In an instant Jake was on him, coming up from behind and snaking an arm around his throat. A rear naked choke was always dependable in subduing an opponent, and he was a master at applying it.

Jake let out a labored grunt. The man was an ox, big and powerful, generously endowed with thick layers of rock-hard muscle in his back and shoulders. Added to this was a thick bull neck that made constriction of the carotid artery or windpipe difficult. It was as if he were attempting to choke out a tree.

The man reacted swiftly. A set of strong stubby fingers rose up to pry unmercifully under Jake's forearm to break the hold. Jake held on tenaciously, locking the hand of his encircling arm onto the biceps of his other arm and squeezing with all his strength. His opponent fought hard, twisting and turning before stumbling to the canted deck. Jake remained stubbornly clamped to the man's back, managing to get his legs wrapped around the man's torso in a figure-four grapevine for additional leverage. A few more seconds elapsed before the man went limp. To be sure his victim wasn't feigning unconsciousness, Jake held fast a moment longer before releasing the hold. By this time the ship had come back close to an even keel, listing only slightly to starboard due to shifted cargo.

Rising to his feet, Jake shed his cloaker. Gleason became aware of him, appearing startled at this sudden intrusion, but his eyes widened in alarm as Jake pulled his machine pistol from its holster and leveled it at him.

"Move so much as an inch and I'll turn both of you into shark chum," he said.

Gleason froze, as did his helmsman. Terror was clearly etched on his face as his eyes fell on Drakov's inert form. He had perceived Drakov as ruggedly tough and unbeatable, a man you didn't dare cross. But the individual now menacing him was obviously tougher, a person who would have no scruples whatsoever at carrying out his threat.

Jake re-holstered his weapon. Judging from the cowed expressions the other two men wore, he decided they would not be a problem. Reaching into a pocket, he removed the second roll of duct tape his would-be abductors had left on the drum. Within a minute he had the unconscious mercenary thoroughly bound. Just as he completed the final wrap, the man abruptly stirred. Jake rolled him onto his side, and as he did so, the man squirmed furiously.

Jake shoved the barrel of his weapon into the man's throat with brutal force. "Who sent you?" he demanded.

Drakov continued to struggle, blinking away the last vestiges of his short-lived oblivion. Murderous wrath consumed his face as his gaze focused on the man constraining him.

"Who sent you?" Jake repeated.

"Go to hell!" Drakov spat.

"My guess is that you and your buddies once served in the Russian army and now offer your services to the highest bidder," Jake opined, judging from the commando's heavy Ukrainian accent. "You work for Rafael Cardoza, don't you?"

Drakov continued to glare back, his eyes offering nothing but hatred.

Jake prodded Drakov harder, jamming his weapon with savage force into the commando's throat. It infuriated him to no end that this man was part of a plot to kidnap Destiny and the twins.

Drakov wheezed harshly, eyes bulging and beginning to turn blue as he strained to get air through his constricted windpipe.

Jake eased up on the pressure at the sound of an approaching whirlybird. He turned his eyes to the man he assumed was the ship's captain. "Do you have radio contact with the Hind?"

Gleason stared back blankly. "The who?" he asked dumbly.

"The chopper coming toward us," Jake stated gruffly. "Are you able to contact them?"

The captain nodded resignedly. "Yes." He started to say more, but the ship's radio suddenly came alive. His vessel was being hailed.

"This is the Reaper, come in *Southern Star*." Though spoken in English, the voice behind the words reeked of a Russian heritage.

Gleason stood at abeyance, looking to Jake for instructions.

"Answer them!" Jake commanded through clenched teeth. "But if you alert them in any way as to what's going on here, I'll kill you where you stand."

Gleason acknowledged the threat, his eyes clearly mirroring his fear. Turning back to the console, he keyed the mike. "This is the *Southern Star*," he replied.

"Is everything in readiness?" the disembodied voice asked.

Gleason hesitated. He looked back at Jake nervously.

Jake thought quickly. "Tell him yes."

When Gleason complied, the voice on the radio suddenly sounded suspicious. "Put my team leader on."

"Tell him there was a problem, that he's preparing the package at this moment," Jake said hurriedly, pushing his weapon forcefully into Drakov's throat once again to keep him from screaming out a warning.

Gleason did as instructed.

The voice came back again, still sounding leery. "I tried calling him. Why does he not answer?"

"Tell him his radio is not working," ordered Jake.

Gleason keyed the mike again. "His radio got damaged."

Just as the captain finished speaking, the door to the bridge opened without anyone appearing.

"About time you showed up," Jake muttered.

Mat Daniels suddenly materialized as if out of thin air, followed by Bashir an instant later as their cloakers deactivated. Mat glanced over at Gleason and the helmsman before setting his gaze on the bound captive at Jake's feet. "Judging from the way you handled things, I'd say you performed quite admirably without us," he said with a humorous grin.

"I hope you have our pilot in tow," Jake said.

"He's here. He's down on the deck with his IPhone. Ez is giving him a last minute crash course in the operation of a Hind. Unfortunately, we have another guest as well." For emphasis, Mat gestured toward the doorway as a familiar face appeared.

Jake's jaw dropped in horror. "Are you crazy, Phillipe?" he admonished angrily. He turned his ire back on Mat, glowering at him as if he were insane.

"Don't look at me," Mat protested. "I didn't bring him. He showed up on his own, apparently using that dolphin of his for transportation."

Phillipe held Jake's stone-faced gaze, staring back unwavering and defiant. "You're going to need help."

Achilles immediately interceded. *The boy's right, Jay Jay. You need four walking bodies to bring this plan to fruition, otherwise you risk raising the suspicions of the bad guys that something is wrong.*

Peeved as he was, Jake couldn't fault Achilles' logic. They would have to use Maskers to get aboard the Hind, and to use a Masker effectively, you had to use a living, breathing person. A Masker was yet another of Ez's inventions, a small device a user wore on their wrist. It employed a hologram technology similar to the one Ez used to project her image. The features of any persona could be programmed into them in order to deceive an observer, and since Achilles had seen images of the mercenaries Jake had subdued through the mental link they shared, he had telepathically relayed them to others of his kind close to Aquaria where speak-see audio transmissions of those images were picked up by Ez from the surrounding waters.

Begrudgingly, Jake turned back to Mat. "How many Maskers did you bring?" he asked bleakly, expecting to hear they'd still be short one."

Mat held up a canvas bag. "Relax, good buddy. I make it a point to always carry a spare knowing how twitchy some of these gizmos can get. Let's hope they all work."

Before Jake could say anything else, Achilles intruded his way into his thoughts again.

Jay Jay, we have a new development which may prove indispensable to remediating the multiple threats confronting us. Ez thinks you can use it to make a deal.

Jake's mind raced. Destiny's description of her latest dream came flooding back, a portion of which echoed lucidly in his head: "Even though we were safe, we had to make some kind of arrangement with the Eagle Master."

Are you implying we have a bargaining chip? Jake asked, his hope beginning to soar.

Yes. This ship has hidden compartments in the hull that are only accessible from below water.

How do you know that?

As you humans are so fond of saying when resorting to logic, I connected the dots. There are cameras situated along the keel and Rafael Cardoza is a notorious drug lord. There had to be a reason for emplacing those cameras in such an unlikely area, so I had Apollo scan the hull with the DBT he was still carrying. The info was sent to Ez for processing, and it revealed twelve sizable compartments, all filled with cocaine.

An idea abruptly came to Jake. *Was Ez able to determine its total worth?*

Yes, based on the latest DEA statistics and the estimated quantity, she computes its street value at zero point nine seven billion dollars, give or take a million.

Jake addressed the captain. "I assume this vessel is equipped with a satellite phone," he said.

Gleason hesitated, seeming to weigh how he would respond to the question, but gave a half-hearted nod as the barrel of Jake's weapon came up to bear on him again.

"Well I suggest you use it to contact your boss."

"What do you want me to tell him?"

Jake produced a devious smile. "Tell him to call off his dogs or this ship will be sent to the bottom."

Chapter Twelve: Commandeering the Hind

Zinova mulled Gleason's words, deep in thought as he sat at the controls of the Hind. Radios occasionally malfunctioned on missions, so nothing to get overly concerned about. Perhaps Javolyn had been far more difficult to capture than anticipated, causing Drakov's radio to get damaged in the process. In any event, he had no reason to doubt Drakov had not succeeded in getting the job done. Drakov was his second in command and the most reliable member of his team of professional mercenaries. Like himself, Drakov had once served in Spetsnaz and had been under his command in Afghanistan.

Gleason's voice suddenly sounded in Zinova's ears, snapping him out of these thoughts. "Your team is standing by at the helipad for extraction," the captain informed him.

Zinova swung the Hind around, making one more complete pass around the freighter with the chopper's powerful spotlight kept on the vessel to make sure nothing was amiss. In his profession, one could never be too cautious. A highly skilled pilot, he brought the Hind to a hover forty feet from the landing pad perched directly over the ship's bridge, a modest structure barely big enough to accommodate the Russian-built aircraft.

Holding his position, Zinova made no effort to land as yet, instead directing the beam of the spotlight on several men making their way up the helipad steps.

"Keep your guns at the ready!" Zinova ordered his weapons operator seated forward of him. "Everyone, stay alert!" he instructed the other two men stationed behind him in the fuselage.

Zinova swiveled the spotlight a few more degrees, and under the harsh glare he watched as the two lead men carried a third man while two others followed behind. The last man looked up, and Zinova could clearly see it was Drakov. Nevertheless, he continued to study the small group for several more seconds, wanting to be sure everything was as it should be. One by one, he recognized the faces of the remainder of his four-man squad as they climbed higher. Bringing his eyes to bear on the man being carried, he looked upon the unconscious countenance of the person Cardoza had sought, a ruggedly handsome face belonging to someone who had killed several of the drug lord's men. It was obvious the face belonged to Javolyn, the face of a warrior. There was no mistaking the resemblance, for Cardoza had provided him with photographs of the former Navy Seal.

Satisfied that the mission had gone as planned, Zinova edged the aircraft forward and lowered the landing gear. As the Hind settled, he craned his head around to observe the figures as they came aboard. His eyes were then drawn to the girl sitting passively on a rear seat, her arms enfolding a child on each side of her. Her beauty was stunning, and he had trouble tearing his gaze away. Strangely, she seemed unaffected by the sight of her husband's inert form as it was hauled aboard.

Distracted for the moment, Zinova was totally unprepared for what ensued next. As one of the rear crewmen leaned out to lend a hand, Javolyn suddenly came alive, gripping the crewman's arm and yanking hard. The crewman lost his footing, stumbling through the side door and falling onto the helipad deck. The man was immediately knocked flat as one of Drakov's team kicked him squarely in the solar plexus. Another kick, executed like a bolt of lightning from the same team member, disabled him completely as he tried to rise back on his feet. Almost simultaneously, the butt of a weapon slammed with vicious impact into the face of the second crewman, but before Zinova fully grasped the situation, a machine pistol was jammed forcefully into the side of his neck. Zinova blinked in confusion before realizing it was Javolyn who held the weapon.

"Get outta the seat!" Javolyn said in a guttural hiss, his voice carrying above the roar of the rotors.

Zinova hesitated, his mind reeling with this sudden turn of events, but before he could even weigh his options Javolyn tore off his flight helmet and grabbed him by the hair, making him wince in pain.

"Unless you want to stop breathing, I recommend you give up this seat," Javolyn growled.

Zinova unbuckled his safety belt, contemplating whether he should put up a fight, but Jake yanked him brutally by the hair, forcing his bearlike frame from the seat and walking him backward with the gun still held to his neck.

Sitting forward of Zinova's position, the head of the weapons operator turned to investigate the commotion. Drakov rushed forward, firing the remaining dart from the tranquilizer pistol. The operator lifted a quivering arm to pull out the thing lodged in his cheek, only to slump forward an instant later as the potent drug took effect.

Drakov turned to another team member following on his heels, and as if on cue, both seemed to undergo a weird transformation. Their clothing and features appeared to expand and contract before changing completely, morphing into new personas. With his Masker now turned off, Mat Daniels tossed aside the dart pistol and removed the slack body from the weapons control chair, hauling it backward to clear the way for Fernando, who took over the seat.

"You sure you're up to flying this thing?" Mat found it necessary to ask, shouting out the question to be heard above the whine of the rotors as he stripped the flight helmet from the weapons operator.

A grim smile lit Fernando's face as his eyes roved over the controls. "If it has rotary wings I can fly it," he replied confidently. "Of course, a little guidance from Ez also helps."

Mat handed him the flight helmet, watching curiously as Fernando slipped it on and buckled himself in. "I always thought the pilot's seat was behind weapons control on a Hind. Are you certain you're in the right seat?"

Fernando began running his hands lightly over the controls to get the feel of them. "A Hind is somewhat similar in some respects to the Cobra gunships used in Vietnam," he explained briskly. "The co-pilot sits forward and below the pilot, but also serves to engage the weapons systems. I can both fly this bird and fire the weapons from here."

"Well, then, good luck and you have my most profound blessings," Mat said, moving back to join Jake, who had vacated the chopper with his prisoner held close.

"Get down with your chest to the deck and your hands behind your head," Jake ordered Zinova.

With Mat and Phillipe now assisting Jake, Zinova was hastily prodded to the deck and quickly bound hand and foot with a spool of thick cord Mat had brought with him. The two unconscious crewmen along with the weapons operator were then laid out beside Zinova and subsequently bound in a similar manner.

Mat glanced over at Phillipe admiringly. "Very impressive with those kicks." A wealth of heartfelt praise was evident in his tone. He looked down at the mercenary Phillipe had kayoed. "Those lessons seem to be paying off."

"I have good teachers," Phillipe replied, referring to the rigorous training Jake and Mat routinely put him through.

"Your father would have been proud of you," Mat persisted. "He was quite a martial artist himself."

"I just hope I can measure up to being half the man he was."

Mat patted his cheek affectionately. "I don't think that's gonna be a problem for you, kid."

Turning, Mat scrutinized the twins clinging to their father's legs as he embraced Destiny fiercely. "Hate to intrude on this family gathering," he finally interrupted, "but we're not out of the woods yet."

Jake nodded in agreement just as Achilles gave him another mental nudge.

Jay Jay, Zimby has arrived and will pick up Destiny and the children on the ship's starboard side near the bow where there is a boarding ladder.

Jake shot a look to the water below him. The *Angel* was just pulling abreast of the freighter.

Destiny stared up at Jake questioningly, and he knew she had also heard Achilles. "You're not coming with us?" she said. There was resignation in her voice and a sudden outpouring of trepidation in her eyes.

Jake shook his head. "I want you and the twins to head for the cove. I've given it more thought and decided it's probably safer there than in Aquaria right now."

Destiny's face clouded in sadness and a glimmer of tears began to show. "They're never going to leave us alone, are they?"

"It's the way of the world," Jake muttered stoically. The essence behind the words she had uttered hours earlier chimed in the back of his head. Danger had in fact become a way of life for them and was forever going to be their companion, for this was the path they had chosen. She had spoken those words pragmatically, bravely, but was she really cut out for coping with this sort of thing?

Destiny nuzzled her face into Jake's chest. "I'm so afraid for you, Jay Jay. I never want to lose you."

Jake held her tight, aware that she was far too pure in rectitude to be subjected to the growing violence now aimed at them. "I warned you long ago it was going to be like this from the beginning, didn't I? Trying to make the world a better place always brings on the hyenas. They'll keep coming until they learn it's no longer in their interests to do so."

"Stay safe!" Destiny implored, unable to hold back the tears. She reached up and kissed him passionately before pulling away and walking to the edge of the platform.

Jake knelt quickly and hugged the twins tenderly. "Be good and do what your mother tells you," he said.

"We will, dadoo," they chorused in unison, hugging him fiercely before scurrying over to Destiny. With a final wave, they descended the stairs.

Jake rose and turned to Mat. "The ball's now in Cardoza's hands. It's up to him to call off the Kraken. Stay here and scuttle the freighter if he refuses. I'll go with Fernando. With any luck, we'll bring down the other Hind before it can carry out their threat on the *Morning Vista*."

Jake turned to climb aboard the Hind, but Mat grabbed his arm with a powerful grip. "Don't do anything foolish."

A ripple of amusement suddenly flashed across Jake's somber expression. "Hey, I'm not the one doing the flying."

Mat kept his expression stern. "Try using discretion this time. You keep prodding the devil and he's gonna stick that pitchfork where the sun don't shine."

"So you keep telling me."

At that moment, Bashir came bounding up the stairs. He had disappeared following the ouster of the Hind crew, but now he was returning with something carried on his shoulder and breathing heavily from the exertion. "Take this!" he urged. Seeing the look of surprise on Jake's face, he added, "Just in case you might need it."

Jake took the object and nodded gratefully, but as he turned to leave, Mat stopped him again. Mat's demeanor remained serious. "Don't get yourself killed," he growled. "Remember, there's a subtle difference between compulsive valor and unavoidable discretion."

"Nag, nag, nag," Jake shot back as he yanked his arm free and boarded the Hind. Nodding to Fernando, he gave a vigorous thumbs-up, prompting him to get going. Jerkily, the Hind rose, climbing erratically before stabilizing as Fernando got the feel of the controls.

Looking down, Jake spotted Hector assisting Destiny and the twins as they climbed aboard the *Avenging Angel*. He kept his gaze locked on them as the Hind gained height and distance from the freighter, their arms waving wildly at him as they looked up at the departing aircraft.

The satellite phone seemed to chirp with an exaggerated urgency, a distinct sound that identified the caller. In annoyance, Maximus opened the channel. "This had better be important," he hissed. Even though his and the caller's phone were encrypted so that all communication was indecipherable to potentially prying ears, his policy was to limit calls over the air waves.

"Call off your ship!" the voice on the other end blurted frantically.

"Why should I do that?" Maximus replied calmly. He hated it whenever his people lost their cool, but the answer that came back was more than he expected.

"They threaten to sink her."

"Sink who?"

Rafael Cardoza ignored the question, ranting on in panic. "I've suffered enough losses over the last few years and I'm not going to sit back while a major investment slips into the deep. Call off your ship!"

Maximus raised his voice angrily to cut off Cardoza's next screaming outburst. "Calm yourself and tell me what happened."

"Javolyn has somehow turned the tables on us and taken control of my ship. He says he'll sink it unless the Kraken changes its present course and veers away from Aquaria."

A broader picture of what Cardoza was telling him abruptly came together, and Maximus knew the plan had backfired, at least a portion of it. "I thought you said these Russians were infallible, the best in the business."

Cardoza was suddenly silent on the other end, scornfully reminded that it was he who had recommended the Reaper's services.

Sitting at the observation console in the bridge of his mega-yacht, Maximus scanned the radar screen. The blip was still there not five miles away, flying donuts above a much larger object. Another blip suddenly appeared on the screen, slowly closing the distance with the first blip.

"Is Javolyn still aboard the *Star*?" Maximus asked apprehensively.

"I don't know. The *Star's* captain won't respond to any questions. He's no doubt a hostage being held at gunpoint and told what to say." Cardoza paused, then lost his composure again. "Are you going to put a stop to this?"

"Do you actually think I'd destroy the largest ship on the planet?" Maximus reprimanded coldly. Like Cardoza, he had no real intentions of sacrificing one of his assets, particularly since it carried more than just crude. Making the opposition believe it was going to be used as a battering ram or a vehicle of massive pollution was merely a bluff. Using its sheer size as an intimidation ploy should be enough to get what he wanted. He needed Navassa healthy and thriving, for it harbored those incredible dolphins. He could use those creatures. They represented a sizable labor force capable of building things below the ocean surface, and he had only to stretch his imagination to envision other useful and profitable endeavors they could be used for. But the girl was the key to controlling them. All the intelligence he had so far been able to gather on them pointed to that one conclusion. With the girl and her children in his custody, he would gain control of the island and Aquaria along with it.

"I've always given you my full cooperation," Cardoza replied, trying hard but unable to suppress the pleading edge creeping into his tone. "But now I need yours. Help me get my ship back."

Maximus eyed the radar monitor suspiciously. The second blip was now closer to the first. "What do you suggest?"

"Alvarez! Send Alvarez!"

Maximus pondered the appeal skeptically, recalling what had happened earlier. With Allotey leading the way, Alvarez and his men had fled the colony like a herd of gazelle spooked by the scent of lions in the air. Nevertheless, even with their usefulness now in doubt, it was his only available option to pacify Cardoza, whom he still needed.

Making a snap decision, Maximus capitulated. "Alright, you can have Alvarez. He's currently in Kingston, so it shouldn't take long for him to reach your vessel."

"You won't regret this," said Cardoza, relief clearly evident in his voice.

"Now tell me," Maximus went on smoothly, "is everything proceeding as scheduled?"

"Yes."

"What about the doctor?"

"He will arrive by private jet tomorrow."

"Good," Maximus said, continuing to monitor the radar. "But there's a change in plans. I want you to commence the operation forty-eight hours ahead of schedule."

A moment of hesitation ensued before Cardoza responded. "The remaining shipment has not yet arrived," he objected wearily. "Without it, we will fall short of what is needed."

"Where is it?" Maximus snapped.

"On my ship."

Maximus frowned darkly, none too pleased with what he was hearing. "After Alvarez takes back the Star, do whatever is necessary to get that shipment quickly," he instructed adamantly.

"Why the change in schedule?"

"Do not question me, just make sure it gets done!"

Ending the link, Maximus cast a sour gaze on the screen as the radar blips began to merge. Thumbing the intercom, he paged his chief technician.

A moment passed before an obsequious voice tense with nervousness answered. "Osgood here."

"Launch the drone," Maximus ordered.

Osgood hesitated as if mulling a question. "I'll get it airborne right away, Mr. Maximus. What's the target?"

"You'll find out quick enough," Maximus barked. "I'm coming down now to man the controls." A wicked smile transposed his face as he made for the door.

Chapter Thirteen: Unknown Attacker

Donning the helmet he had stripped from the pilot and plugging the wire connection into the radio console, Jake sat down heavily in the pilot's chair and stared intently ahead. The moon had arisen, and under its subdued glow the sea below appeared like an endless sheet of gray slate with no whitecaps in evidence.

"Can you hear me, Fernando?" he asked.

"Loud and clear," Fernando answered.

"Let's hope we see them before they see us. What have you got for weaponry?"

"Looks like twin rapid-fire machine guns in the chin turret and a guided missile system."

"Are they operational?"

"I think so. My guess is the machine guns fire seven point six-two rounds and the rocket pods are loaded with thirty millimeter rockets."

Jake had noticed one of the rocket pods just before boarding the aircraft. He had also caught a glimpse of the twin barrels jutting from the chin turret. "Which are you going to use?"

"I'm better with guns," Fernando stated glumly. "The problem with Hinds is they're tough to bring down. All their vital parts are armored with titanium shields, which make them close to invincible against the relatively small caliber rounds this baby can deliver. If push comes to shove, the rockets may prove more effective, though I don't have much experience with them, I'm afraid."

Jake was about to offer encouragement, but something below in the distance caught his eye. "Thirty degrees right at one o'clock," he shouted. "Do you see it?"

Fernando took a moment to spot the object before responding. "Got it!" Banking the chopper slightly right, he brought them on a new heading.

"The other Hind's got to be close by," Jake cautioned.

"How do we know if that ship's the *Morning Vista*?" Fernando said.

"Cruise ships are generally the only vessels you'll find at sea lit up like a Christmas tree. She's the *Morning Vista*, all right."

Jake scanned the night sky above the ship in search of the other chopper. "Chances are the other Hind's running without her lights, so finding her might be a problem," Jake grumbled.

"No it won't," Fernando replied flatly. "This bird's equipped with radar." His voice suddenly quickened. "And I do believe we've located her sister."

"Where?"

"Look at the small screen on the upper right side of your panel. The blip on the bottom shows her."

Jake saw it immediately. "So much for catching them by surprise," he uttered dismally. "If we have radar, I have to assume they do, too."

A voice suddenly sounded on the radio, and it wasn't Fernando's.

"Barsuk v Jnec, Irihodit' nazad."

"Can you speak Russian, Fernando?" Jake queried hopefully. "I think they're hailing us."

"Sorry, but Russian ain't my thing."

"Barsuk v Jnec, Irihodit' nazad," the voice repeated, now with an urgent, strident edge.

"Jnec zdes'," another voice suddenly blurted over the radio sounding different from the first.

Jake's puzzlement was immediately held at bay as Achilles called out to him from the sea below, translating what was being said. *The last transmission you heard is Ez,* Achilles rapidly explained in that compressed fashion typical of their mental link. *She's answering the pilot of the other Hind, who is hailing you with the words Badger to Reaper, come back. She replied, Reaper here. She monitored the voice of the pilot you subdued earlier and is mimicking his signature tonal qualities to lull the other pilot closer.*

"That's Ez you're hearing," Jake informed Fernando. "She's baiting the other Hind closer by answering in the voice of this chopper's former pilot. Let them get really close and then open up with the guns. Just make sure the ship below us isn't in the line of fire."

"Leave the rest to me," Fernando shot back, his tone reflecting confidence.

With growing anxiety, Jake listened to the conversation taking place in Russian between Ez and Badger, the exchange sounding terse and incomprehensible to him as Achilles stopped translating. He held his breath as the other Hind suddenly loomed into view, a dark shadow within the night sky.

Jake was pressed down into his seat as Fernando banked the chopper hard, coming about to follow on Badger's tail. The other Hind held steady before him for a brief moment before Fernando let loose with the guns. A broken laser beam of red tracer rounds rushed out, slamming into the aft section of the targeted aircraft like a swarm of angry hornets. A firestorm of sparks flew in all directions as lethal projectiles found their mark against the Hind's titanium tail rotor.

Almost immediately, a din of panicked Russian vitriol erupted painfully in Jake's ears as Badger cried out in protest. He was again pushed forcefully into his seat as Fernando fought to stay glued to the Hind as it suddenly broke left and dove for the ocean.

"Damn!" Fernando griped in frustration. "These babies are tougher than I thought. I hit his rotor squarely and the rounds just bounced off."

"Stay on him and try again!" Jake encouraged.

"This guy's good," Fernando yelled back, continuing to bank sharply as Badger corkscrewed lower. "I'll be lucky to get another shot."

"How about taking him broadside?" Jake suggested.

"Just keeping on him is tough enough," Fernando gasped, fighting to talk as the punishing G-force laid siege to his body.

Jake wondered if Fernando was up to the task. Air combat was a young man's game. Even though Fernando had been around helicopters for the major portion of his life and had served in the military as an aviation mechanic during the Vietnam War, he was now well into his sixties.

"Hold still, you bastard!" Fernando groaned testily. "I don't want to kill you, I just want to put you into the drink."

Jake watched as Badger suddenly leveled off, then broke right. He realized they were less than fifty feet above the sea and that the *Morning Vista* lay directly before them. It was obvious Badger was making a beeline directly at the cruise ship, now less than a thousand feet away.

"Hold your fire!" Jake shouted curtly. He knew that if Fernando used the guns now, he risked hitting the vessel with stray rounds.

"Don't you think I know that?" Fernando snapped back in exasperation. "He's a crafty sum bitch."

Jake held his breath, unsure if Badger would retaliate by carrying out the original threat on the cruise ship. Helpless to do anything, he could only stare as the Hind held steady before them, a tempting though forbidden target as it bore straight for the ship.

Fernando fought against the ever present danger of target fixation, a spell that had often claimed the lives of pilots since the first days of aerial combat. Target fixation could cause a pilot to become focused so intently on their quarry that awareness of other obstacles and hazards diminished. Collisions with impediments like the side of a mountain sometimes resulted when a pursuing pilot failed to anticipate a darting move by an elusive target. He knew Badger had to either veer away or pull up at the last possible second to avoid crashing into the ship. He had to stay tight on the Hind's tail. If he pulled away or gave up the chase entirely, he would leave himself open to a potential counterattack. And if his reflexes were too slow, it might very well be him and Jake that ended up like squashed bugs on the side of the vessel.

Jake braced himself as Badger's ship suddenly sprang skyward as if yanked by a huge bungee cord stretched to its limit and on the rebound. Fernando followed, grunting loudly against the strain of gravity as their Hind's powerful engines catapulted them up and over the *Morning Vista's* superstructure with less than ten feet to spare.

Shooting a glance out the side window, Jake espied several passengers on an upper deck stare up in terror at this sudden intrusion on their peaceful interlude. Weightlessness immediately caught up with him as Fernando dipped the Hind back toward the water, still hot on Badger's tail. Skimming just above the sea, Badger zigzagged back and forth, making his copter as difficult a target as possible, all the while spewing a torrent of incomprehensible invectives over the radio. Dogged in his pursuit, Fernando mimicked Badger's every move, keeping a ready finger on the trigger for an opportune shot. But just as he was on the verge of unleashing another salvo, Badger abruptly leapt skyward again.

Jake felt as though he were on an exhilarating roller coaster ride at an amusement park, but there was nothing amusing about this ride. A brutal G-force abruptly accosted him as Fernando banked savagely to starboard, and he realized their quarry was no longer in front of them. In that instant he glimpsed the flash of green tracers seemingly coming straight at him before streaking past. Another second elapsed before something dark and fleeting zipped by, and had Jake blinked he would have missed it altogether due to its incredible rate of speed.

"What just happened?" Jake shouted in dismay, feeling the Hind under him dart back to port.

"We're being attacked!" Fernando yelled back. "Look at your radar! Another aircraft just fired on us."

Jake shot a look at the screen, immediately seeing what Fernando described. A tiny blip moved rapidly across the monitor. Achilles quickly interceded to bring structure to Jake's jumbled thoughts. *JJ, you are under attack by what appears to be an unmanned drone,* his bond mate informed him. *Ez has run a thermal scan on it and found it to contain no pilot. She measures its velocity at more than Mach three.*

Where did it come from? Jake asked.

From under the sea. Ez detected it as soon as it launched from the water. Achilles' composure began to crack. *She's got a radar lock on it at this moment and says it's coming around on your six.*

The resonance of Achilles thoughts suddenly shrilled, and Jake felt his bond mate's trepidation as though it were a living thing. *I am now conjoined with the entire pod, JJ. We will attempt to predict the intentions of this unknown attacker.*

A sense of urgency suddenly gripped Jake like the talons of an eagle as Achilles shrieked out a prophetic warning. *Break right, break right.*

Without any hesitation, Jake grabbed the cyclic stick in front of him and jerked it harshly right, completely overpowering Fernando's light touch on the controls. The crush of gravity pressed in on him like an iron fist as the chopper swung acutely to starboard. This time a missile shot past the Hind's port side, missing it by inches. Jake lost sight of it as the Hind veered away.

"Sorry about that, Fernando," Jake apologized.

"No apologies necessary," Fernando croaked harshly, barely squeezing out the words. He stopped speaking momentarily to draw in breath. "You probably saved our hides, at least for the moment. Whoever's firing at us has supersonic capability."

"That whoever is a drone with no pilot," Jake rejoined brusquely.

"How can you tell?"

"Achilles informed me."

Fernando continued to take the Hind through a series of evasive maneuvers. Though the Hind had a speed way below their attacker, its lower velocity gave it far greater maneuverability. "Well you're wrong about a pilot," he corrected.

"What do you mean?"

"Someone's got to be controlling that thing."

Another shrill alarm went off in Jake's head. This time he was told to break left. Once again he grabbed the stick, yanking it hard to port. The Hind responded almost instantly, its forward inertia at odds with the excessive centripetal force brutally imposed on it. Another missile streaked past as the punishing crush of gravity returned with a vengeance.

Put the Hind into the water, JJ, and we'll rescue you, Achilles pleaded. *You don't have a chance against that thing.*

Jake weighed the merits of Achilles' suggestion. With the entire pod linked up mentally, it sometimes gave them the power of precognition, enabling them to glimpse the future and take the necessary steps to avoid an undesirable outcome. He had often referred to this power as a 'super-mind' capability. On several occasions in the past he had observed this amazing ability, and he vividly remembered his first encounter with it years earlier. One of the albinos had made an incredible leap from the water to intercept and snatch a grenade meant for his beloved boat, tossing it out of harm's way before it exploded. In doing this, the dolphin had to have had advance knowledge of the grenade's precise trajectory, for it would have needed to dive deep to gather sufficient speed for its leap without tracking the grenade by sight. Determining its launch point and timing its jump from the water further complicated the feat, which would otherwise have been altogether impossible without this foreknowledge. But in spite of the advantage this ability gave them, he also knew the future was often too shrouded in mist for the pod's super-mind to consistently see what calamity could potentially happen and take the correct action to avert it. Jacob had explained it to him and called the phenomenon 'backward causality', a theory that contends the precognition experience unleashes a powerful psychokinetic energy that brings the desired future to pass. Therefore, it was only a matter of time before the unknown assailant remotely flying the drone scored a hit. Whether their Hind could withstand a direct missile strike because of its heavy armor was only a matter of speculation. This is what Achilles was telling him.

I have an idea, Achilles, Jake replied, suddenly energized by a sudden thought.

I see it clearly, JJ. Please hurry. The drone is coming around for another pass. It will be on you in twelve seconds.

Jake spoke quickly. "Fernando, I need you to slow this bird down and present our friend with a profile."

Fernando's reaction was as expected. "Are you nuts?"

"You'll have to trust me on this," Jake urged gruffly. "There's no time to explain."

"I guess I've lived long enough," Fernando grumbled mournfully. "It was nice knowing you, my friend."

Jake unbuckled himself from the seat and scrambled into the passenger cabin. Already he could feel their airspeed plummeting as Fernando flared the main rotor. To keep from being thrown forward, Jake had to grab hold of whatever was available to steady himself. The thing

Bashir had given him just before he had embarked on this crazy stunt was still where he had placed it, wedged between two seats. Pulling it free, he hefted it to his shoulder and braced a leg against one of the seats as the Hind came to a near hover and rotated ninety degrees. The tube-like object he held had hand grips and closely resembled a bazooka, yet another product of the albino ingenuity.

Something barely visible caught his eye, a seemingly insignificant black dot against the pale twilight of dawn. It swelled rapidly, coming straight at him with blinding speed, a bird of prey homing in for the kill.

Jake held steadfast, a montage of conflicting thoughts racing through his head, wondering if he should have taken Achilles' advice, asking himself why he always insisted on playing such foolhardy odds. Mats admonishing words came back to haunt him, and it was as though his friend were speaking at this moment. *How many times must I remind you, good buddy, that there's a subtle difference between compulsive valor and unavoidable discretion.*

Jake held his breath and squeezed the trigger, suddenly besieged by the possibility he would never again hold Destiny and the twins in his arms.

Chapter Fourteen: Dizzying Vertigo

Maximus sneered caustically as he eyed the target on a three-dimensional display. At full magnification, he could view his quarry as though it were less than a hundred feet in front of him. For reasons unknown, the Hind had given up its elusive and erratic maneuvers, so effective that he was beginning to believe its pilot was psychic, eerily anticipating his every move. But now the Hind was his for the taking, a virtual sitting duck that would be easy to obliterate. In spite of its titanium armor, he knew it could not possibly withstand simultaneous hits from his two remaining missiles. Easing back on the throttle, he slowed his attack speed by one-half as he guided the drone toward the target. This time he would not miss.

With his thumb poised eagerly over the launch trigger, something suddenly coalesced on the screen before him. The thing snaked and twisted without form, coming alive with a full spectrum of dazzling color against the heralding light of dawn. It took Maximus another second before he realized what he was seeing, and by then it was too late. Overcome with dizzying vertigo, he felt the bile rise in his throat as uncontrollable nausea engulfed him. With mouth parted wide, a stream of vomit spewed copiously from between his lips as though from a broken sewer pipe under enormous strain. A pain like nothing he had ever before experienced knifed through his brain, a blinding, searing agony so intense that it made him feel as though he had been cast into the deepest part of hell itself.

Standing further back from the screen, Osgood was only vaguely aware of his boss' seizure as Maximus collapsed to the floor and filled the room with a piercing scream. All the angst and depression churning his guts moments earlier was suddenly gone, replaced by a sense of breathtaking euphoria and happiness as he fixated a trancelike stare on the monitor. Unable to pull his eyes away, he became oblivious of the room around him. In stark contrast, Maximus squirmed and writhed in a pool of vomit, clutching his cranium as though to contain skull fragments from erupting in all directions.

Osgood felt whole again, continuing to savor the afterglow of the thing he had witnessed as it disappeared from sight. With Maximus' guiding hand no longer on the joystick, the drone veered away from the Hind and plunged for the sea as though it were a sea eagle sensing prey on the water below. Another second passed before it burst into a thousand fragments as it collided with the water at twice the speed of sound.

Jake released the trigger on the bazooka-like device, breathing a sigh of relief as he looked down. Under the lightening sky of dawn, he was able to discern wreckage from the drone scattered over more than five acres of ocean surface. His gambit had paid off beyond his expectations. The albino art had strange effects on people, and the extent to which a person fell victim to those effects depended on a person's core nature. Symptoms ranged from mild to severe, with a small percentage of viewers remaining unaffected at all. The symptoms, however, were normally temporary in duration and usually faded within a short length of time once the art was no longer visible to the onlooker. Some people became violently ill, while others experienced various degrees of nirvana.

Jake was one of those who fell into the latter class, as did all human members of the colony. But it was the dark mentalities that could be made ill just by looking at these cryptic artistic expressions, and the extent of their illness always depended on the level of their innate malevolent dispositions. It was this that he had counted on, an inherently sociopathic mind at the controls of the drone. And while two-dimensional representations of these bizarre creations were certainly effective, holographic projections were far more powerful in the way they affected an individual.

A glimpse of the dolphin art was always profoundly calming to Jake, and even more so when it was displayed three-dimensionally. In aiming the holographic projector at the approaching drone, his eyes were automatically drawn to the vision it invoked. As Jacob had explained on more than one occasion, the intertwining abstract lines pulsing with multi-colored light held mysterious qualities that did something to the human psyche, bordering on the hypnotic. On some deep esoteric level incomprehensible to human awareness, the brain was able to interpret the meaning of the convoluted symbolism subconsciously. And in doing so, it somehow found a way to bring a person's true essence to the surface, forcing them to feel it on both physiological and emotional levels. People who were basically decent at heart often experienced euphoria, while people who walked a fine line between good and evil usually felt nothing. But people who were essentially wicked would invariably become physically ill. Thus, the dolphin art was quite literally capable of bringing humans to the doorsteps of heaven, the void of purgatory, or the brink of hell depending on their deep-seated psychological traits.

This knowledge made Jake's thoughts wander back to the prison in Port-au-Prince when he, Mat, and Zimbola had helped Destiny rescue her mother, Jacob, and the Baptistes from the clutches of Henri Ternier and Erzulie. It was there Ternier and his acolytes were brought to savage though temporary illness by a conjured hologram of one of Achilles' enigmatic creations. With Destiny and Amphitrite mentally linked to the conjoined pod mind, they had managed to bring forth the vision for all in the prison to view, including the inmates and guards. Images of the rapturous looks of those unjustly imprisoned and the contorted facial expressions of others collapsed and writhing in extreme agony were firmly etched in Jake's memory, with Ternier seemingly suffering as though his head were about to explode. Through some telekinetic miracle, the doors to all the holding cells had magically sprung open, with more than half of the inmates in rhapsodized stupors filing unhurriedly out into the streets. Joyful and feeling as though he were floating on air, Jake had ambled dazedly among the slowly milling crowd, all the while letting Destiny lead him from the prison by the hand until his blissful condition began to subside.

Still warm and content from his exposure to the hologram, Jake pondered what had just happened. It had taken little more than a second for the art to work its magic, suggesting that their attacker was quite iniquitous. The drone had simply nose-dived into the sea, and this told him its pilot must have been hit by an acute seizure to lose control of the aircraft so quickly.

Preoccupied with this evaluation, Jake was totally unprepared for what happened next. The Hind was suddenly jolted by a heavy impact that nearly sent him flying out the open doorway. Only his quick reflexes saved him as he flung out a hand to grab a stanchion. With his body fully extended and hanging precariously from the cabin, his gaze fell on a dark shadow as it zipped past overhead.

"We've been hit!" Fernando bellowed sharply.

Jake managed to get another hand on the stanchion, fighting hard to pull himself back into the cabin. He realized he had completely forgotten about Badger, and he berated himself unmercifully for letting the hologram stifle his alertness.

The chopper had listed over, rapidly gathering speed, and he had to shout at the top of his lungs to be heard above the rush of wind that swept into the fuselage with gale force intensity. "How bad?"

"We're going in!" Fernando screamed back. "Hold on!"

The Hind's powerful turbines screeched out in protest, the sound growing to a raucous wail that was painful to the ears. It was obvious to Jake the engines were severely damaged and no longer had the power to keep the chopper aloft.

Fernando had also forgotten about Badger. Like Jake, his vigilance had also been corrupted, having been caught in the hologram's soothing spell. But now fully awakened from its rapturous effects, he went to work swiftly. Taking the pitch out of the main rotor, he let the Hind drop toward the water with the aerodynamic characteristics of a brick approximating free fall. The cyclic fought him as he tried to take the aircraft out of its sideways plunge, and he could tell the hydraulically powered controls were beginning to fail. With considerable effort, he managed to bring the Hind back on an even keel with its nose pointing down in a steep glide.

Jake was familiar with the maneuver and held on tight, his bowels feeling as though they were climbing into his chest with the rapid descent. Fernando was going to soften their crash landing by auto-rotating the bird in. He would conserve the momentum of the main rotor as much as possible until they were close to the water and then flare up the nose as he threw maximum pitch into the blades to slow the chopper's vertical descent.

At a height of fifty feet above the sea Fernando barely managed to level the Hind off, using all his strength to pull back on the stick and the collective simultaneously. The Hind responded sluggishly, slowing as though in annoyance as the nose rose up begrudgingly. At that moment the hydraulics failed completely and the controls locked up.

"Brace yourself!" Fernando yelled.

The warning was unnecessary. Jake increased his grip on the stanchion, knowing this was going to be a severe impact as the sea loomed up far too swiftly. Something slammed into the side of his head with brutal force, and a kaleidoscope of bursting colors swirled before him. Another instant passed, and he had the sensation he was being drawn into a bottomless black hole at the center of the galaxy.

Badger followed the stricken Hind down, watching lugubriously as it sent up a towering spray upon impact with the water. Shooting it down gave him no satisfaction, for he had grown especially fond of these helicopters since joining up with Zinova. In his opinion, Hinds were in a class second to none among rotary wing aircraft. They were quite unique and difficult to replace on the international market. Undoubtedly, the Reaper would be more than displeased at losing one of his prized assets, that is, assuming he were still alive.

Bringing his own Hind to a hover, Badger scrutinized Zinova's chopper as it wallowed in the waves and began to sink. The destruction of such a valuable piece of hardware made him feel as though he were losing a close friend, and as it began to disappear from view, he replayed in his mind the recent course of events that had led up to this moment.

He had caught sight of the approaching aircraft a full two seconds before it swept in at blinding speed, seemingly coming straight at him. In a knee-jerk reaction, he had banked hard right to avoid a possible collision. Executing another series of complex evasive maneuvers, he had used all his piloting skill to steer well clear of both this new intruder and the pursuing Hind. Periodic glances at his radar screen had told him that he was no longer under attack. At seeing no imminent danger, he had swung his chopper around in a wide arc. Directly ahead, Zinova's Hind had slowed to a near hover, and in the sea below he had espied remnants of what he assumed to be the other aircraft. Another look at his radar confirmed the existence of only one blip in the surrounding sky.

Greatly puzzled, he had tried to make sense of his commander's unexplained attack and the downed intruder, but then his copilot and weapons operator had brought immediate light to the riddle.

"It's Javolyn!" his copilot had yelled over the intercom, his tone ringing with stark amazement. "He has taken Zinova's copter."

Thrown off balance by such a ridiculous assertion, he had found it necessary to question the claim. "Are you certain, Ivan?"

"It's him, I tell you," Ivan growled back testily. "I can see him clearly in the open doorway."

Badger had known at once that his copilot had seen an enhanced view of Zinova's Hind on his telescopic ranging screen. Zinova had briefed the team carefully on this operation, providing all his men with photos of the people they had been hired to capture. But Javolyn, the former Navy Seal, had somehow found a way to turn the tables on the Reaper and had commandeered his ship. That thought alone had been difficult for him to accept, for he had never known the Reaper to be beaten by anyone.

Throwing a surge of power into the main rotor, he had headed directly at the other Hind, coming up quickly on it from behind. "Blow him out of the sky!" he had ordered the copilot.

With the element of surprise on his side, Badger had watched as the copilot unleashed two air-to-air missiles in succession that caught the Hind squarely on its engines' exhaust.

Badger dropped these thoughts as the downed Hind rolled over and slipped into the depths, her chin bubble bobbing to the surface one last time before disappearing completely. Continuing to hover, he suddenly became aware of something in the water below. Narrowing his eyes, he realized a body had floated to the surface. "Look to your left!" he instructed Ivan. "Do you see it?"

"It might be Javolyn," came back the reply.

Badger studied the sea, gauging the swells. Doesn't look too bad, he thought? Perhaps they could salvage something from this. Making a quick decision, he issued an order. "Ivan, get back there and retrieve him. I'll bring us lower."

"He's floating face down. How do we know it's him?" retorted Ivan, his tone conveying he was not so eager to carry out the command.

Badger gritted his teeth. Sometimes his copilot could be quite difficult to deal with. If not for the fact he was deadly with the weapon systems, he would have asked Zinova to replace him long ago. "Do as I tell you!" he roared harshly.

Ivan unbuckled himself and stomped irately to the rear, glaring impudently at Badger as he passed. "I hope you know what you're doing," he grumbled in annoyance. "A rogue wave could swamp us and then we'd be out two Hinds, not to mention food for sharks."

Badger brought the Hind lower, careful to keep the belly of the fuselage just above the water. The sea had calmed considerably, with wave heights averaging no more than a half meter in his estimation.

"Bring us right another meter," Ivan shouted. "He's just beyond my reach."

Badger sidled the Hind a tad sideways, judging that he had positioned the chopper correctly.

"Good!" Ivan yelled. "Keep her steady."

Badger craned his head around to watch as Ivan lowered the folding retractable steps and grabbed a length of rope from a storage box. Prudently, Ivan put on a harness and clipped on a safety strap that would prevent him from falling into the water. Tethered securely to a bulkhead, the strap would also provide him with leverage as he leaned out to grab hold of the body.

"Let me know when you have him," Badger yelled back impatiently. He turned his head forward to watch for any change in sea conditions, setting his eyes on the horizon as a reference point to hold the chopper in an unwavering hover. The chopper was so low that it seemed to him as though it was floating rather than hovering. The cruise ship he had been prepared to attack upon Zinova's command lay in the distance at one o'clock.

Ivan moved down the steps slowly, careful not to lose his balance. Planting his feet firmly on the lowest step, he let out an obscene curse as his boots were suddenly awash from a small wave. Leaning out, he managed to get a hand on the body bobbing idly before him. He quickly realized it was the shorty neoprene wetsuit the man wore that had kept him afloat. Cautiously he pulled him closer, prepared to fend off an attack, for it was possible the man could be playing possum and was purposely luring him in. But the blood clouding the water quickly allayed his fears. The sea in the immediate area ran red with it. It seeped from a deep gash marring the man's left temple. Lifting the head clear of the water, he scrutinized the face.

Smiling devilishly, Ivan raised his voice to be heard above the deafening cyclonic rotor wash as it blasted the water into frenzied agitation. "It's Javolyn, all right," he shouted proudly, trumpeting out the words as though it was he who had decided to retrieve the body.

"Hurry it up!" Badger yelled back irritably. "What's taking you so long?" Being this close to the water made him edgy.

As far as Ivan could tell, Javolyn appeared dead. This was further substantiated when he placed a thumb over the man's carotid artery and was unable to detect a pulse. Securing the rope around Javolyn's torso just under the armpits, he climbed back into the cabin.

Badger craned his head around again. "Is he secure yet?" he asked hotly.

"Give me a sec to tie off the rope."

Badger was anxious to get going. And while delivering Javolyn's remains to Cardoza held a high priority, rescuing Zinova was even more important. Assuming he were still alive, there was a good chance he was being held captive aboard the *Southern Star.*

Ivan shouted again. "I've got him slung like a side of mutton. You want me to pull him in?"

An idea began to take root in Badger's mind. Maybe he could make a trade: Javolyn for Zinova. The fact that Javolyn was dead would not matter, for Zinova's captors wouldn't know that. He wanted the offered trade to be obvious, but he also figured the sight would keep the captors from firing upon the Hind. "No, leave him hanging," he ordered. "Get back up front."

Badger held the hover long enough for Ivan to reclaim his seat in the weapons' bubble. Seeing that his copilot was ready, he put pitch into the main rotor and felt the Hind begin to rise. Something thumped heavily behind him, and the airframe abruptly shuddered as though a heavy load were suddenly imposed on it. The chopper yawed stiffly, its nose coming around to starboard, and he knew at once it was struggling to gain altitude.

Perplexed, Badger craned his head around the side of the seat to look for the cause. His eyes immediately went wide with shock. A dolphin rested on the cabin floor, a large white dolphin with its tail jutting out the open doorway. Extending outward from the creature's body was a set of grasping appendages, and held within its right appendage was a length of rope that trailed behind and out the doorway. The dolphin turned its head briefly to stare at him, and in those black orbs he sensed a deep abiding intelligence.

The dolphin turned its head again, this time seemingly studying the closed door on the opposite side of the cabin. Using its free appendage, it reached up to grasp the door latch and slide the door open. Another moment passed as Badger continued to stare transfixed, not trusting his eyes as the creature reached over to pull its considerable bulk through the opposite doorway and fall back into the sea.

Still stunned, Badger's eyes fell on the rope as it slid snakelike across the cabin floor, coming in one door and out the other, pulled along by the creature that held it. Something banged loudly against the lip of the doorway through which the dolphin had entered, and he caught a fleeting look of a large shackle tied to the rope. It bounced haphazardly into the cabin before flying out the opposite door. Attached to it was a steel cable at least one-inch-thick, and he suddenly realized what that cable represented. The thought sent a heavy jolt of fear coursing down his spine, and it galvanized him into putting maximum pitch into the rotor blades. With the full power of the turbines behind the blades, the Hind began to rise again. A quick glance at the altimeter showed fifteen meters, then twenty.

Badger spun his head to look aft again. The cable was still there, moving rapidly across the cabin floor in a rasping slither. What he was witnessing couldn't be real, he told himself. Things like this just didn't happen.

With mounting dread, he snapped his eyes forward again. The Hind was still climbing, just passing the thirty-meter mark. And then his dread turned to full-blown fear as the chopper's upward progress was suddenly halted. The abrupt stoppage jarred him to the bone as he came up short against his shoulder straps, but they saved him from being catapulted into the cockpit roof.

As if from far away, he heard Ivan yell out angrily to demand what was wrong, but he had no time to for explanations. Swiveling his head, he saw the cable was now stationary and taut as a bowstring. In desperation, he pulled harder on the collective in hopes of breaking the cable's tenacious hold, but the collective was as far as it would go. With the engines screaming, the Hind swung pendulously from side to side, fighting insanely to overcome the thing keeping it from going any higher.

Looking out the port window, Badger espied the cable stretching to the water, aware that its angle was rapidly changing. It was slicing through the sea, moving out laterally from the vertical. Glancing out the starboard window, he saw the same thing happening. The ends of the cable were being pulled in opposite directions. Horrified, he looked at the altimeter. The Hind was dropping.

Sweating profusely and with pounding heart, Badger looked off to his left again. Where the cable cut through the water, a huge dark shape easily forty meters in length breached the surface. His first thought was that it was a submarine, but then he saw the spray of rising mist that spewed from it, and he realized it was a whale spouting. Girthing its head was some kind of a harness, and shackled to the harness he discerned the end of the cable. Glancing out the opposite window, he spotted another whale. The whales were working in concert, inexorably pulling the Hind down.

This isn't real, he tried to convince himself. *Wake up you dumb Ukrainian!* he admonished, hoping this impossible predicament would simply vanish. Do you hear me? Wake up, it's only a dream! he screamed inwardly. But the sight would not go away.

Badger closed his eyes and braced himself as the sea rose up to claim the Hind. The airframe bucked severely as it met the water, then tilted sideways just enough for the main rotor to catch the surface. The abrupt impact with the aqueous medium was too much for the rotor shaft to bear, causing it to buckle and send a brutal shock wave that carried into the turbines to tear them apart. Almost immediately the blades stopped spinning and the fuselage began to flood.

Unbuckling himself quickly, Badger made for the storage compartments further back where the life vests and inflatable life raft were kept. Ivan was right behind him, cursing up a storm. "You crashed us," he accused angrily.

Badger was too stupefied to reply, instead noticing that Javolyn's lifeless body bobbed aimlessly in the waves just off to one side of the floundering aircraft, still tethered to the rope Ivan had looped around him. Three white dolphins suddenly broke the surface and rushed forward, one of them removing the knife strapped to Javolyn's calf and cutting the line holding him. The same dolphin turned to lock eyes with Badger for one brief moment, and in a sudden flash of perception, Badger knew those eyes belonged to the same creature that had entered the Hind minutes earlier.

Ivan pushed past him furiously, pulling the inflatable raft from its place of storage and yanking the inflation cord. As the raft inflated with an audible hiss, he turned back to eye Badger with derision. "What's the matter with you?" he scolded heatedly, seemingly unaware of the dolphins. "Can't you see we're sinking?"

"Didn't you see?" Badger uttered lethargically, still mesmerized. "They have hands."

"Have you lost your mind?" Ivan shot back. "Snap out of it!" He didn't have a clue as to what Badger was talking about. Up until the Hind was stopped dead in its climb, he had been checking out the readouts on the weapons systems. After that he had turned to berate Badger for his inept flying. He hadn't witnessed any of the things Badger had seen.

Turning, Ivan pulled the fully inflated raft toward him by its tethering line, but as he did so, the dolphin Badger had been eyeing slapped the water brutally with its tail to send a blast of water into the faces of both men, momentarily blinding them.

Wiping the water from his eyes, Ivan felt the tethering line go taut and fly from his fingers. Regaining his sight, he realized the raft was moving away. In desperation he dove forward with outstretched arms to retrieve their best chance of survival, but his fingers merely grazed the wet rubber as he fell headlong into the water. Surfacing quickly, he looked on in disbelief as the raft drew rapidly away, moving as though under its own volition. Stroking wildly, he made an effort to swim after it but soon discovered the attempt was futile. Exhausted and coughing up water he finally gave up the chase, gulping air into heaving lungs and staring dazedly as he watched the raft drift farther away. Treading water clumsily, he was suddenly aware that it was being towed by dolphins. Struggling to stay afloat, it occurred to him he had forgotten to don a life jacket, and he immediately spun around to go back to the Hind to get one before it sank. He was not a strong swimmer and he knew Badger couldn't swim at all.

Ivan glanced around apprehensively, a spasm of panic knifing sharply through him as he scanned the surrounding water. The chopper and Badger were now gone. The thought that had been haunting him ever since Badger had brought the Hind close to the water suddenly grew to monstrous proportions, for one of his biggest fears was sharks.

Amelia Amhurst awoke with a start, finding herself sitting upright and breathing sharply. Realizing where she was, she let out a deep sigh of relief, then leaned back to rest her head on the soft pillow once more. To her surprise, she discovered she had been weeping in her sleep, for her cheeks were wet, dampened by tears of anguish. Remnants of the nightmare still clung to her like prickly burrs from a thorn bush, and with a cautious dread she tried to make sense of it before it faded completely like most of her dreams.

She had been standing on one of the exterior esplanades gracing the colony's central structure, gazing in fascination at the thing hanging high in the heavens. It glowed with a vibrant luminosity in the midst of a pale dawn, a vision of morphing color and writhing motion. The sight had instilled an exhilarating tranquility within her, and she had intuitively perceived it as a harbinger of limitless promise. Transfixed, she had basked in its spell, reveling in the rapturous joy it gave her. But her bliss was soon shattered. An immense cloud had appeared on the horizon, bringing with it such intense gloom that it swallowed everything before it in an inky blackness. The darkness came on with the swiftness of a fanged predator, making her tremble in trepidation. It swelled larger, seething with an unseen yet unmistakable malevolence, poised to engulf the thing that signified the final bastion of hope and her along with it. Horrified by its destructive intent, she had sought escape, but her legs failed her. Suddenly there were people all around, hordes of them, running in frenzied madness. Gaunt and emaciated, they cried out in terror at the horrid blackness bearing down on them, their bellies distended with starvation, their clothes tattered and ragged. Tripping and stumbling along, she sobbed ruefully at her lack of courage, finally falling in the midst of the stampede. Fearing she would get trampled, she brought her knees to her chest, shielding her head with her arms as her lungs heaved with exhaustion. With the ebony darkness crushing in on her, she let out a final piercing scream, vaguely cognizant of the pulsing light. Almost abruptly, she found purchase in the reality where she now lay.

She closed her eyes, then opened them again, taking in the room surrounding her. Idly she let her gaze wander to the wall opposite the bed. An unusual oil painting hung there, and she remembered seeing others of a similar though varying composition in those portions of the city Jacob had allowed her to see. What was she looking at? Describing it was ineffable, for no words could adequately convey its motif. Though she knew it was an illusion, starbursts of differing color seemed to spring forth from it if she stared at it too long. A jumble of lines appeared to twist and interlace without end, seemingly dwindling to points far off in space. They left behind wakes of serene happiness that rippled outward to wash over her. She had gone to sleep staring at the artwork, suddenly aware that the vision in the dream had been conjured from what lay on the canvas. Though the latter portion of the dream had disturbed her, she realized the debilitating blackness had failed to extinguish the light, for it had continued to flicker with a measured cadence just before she awoke.

Unable to sleep any longer, she arose and moved to the balcony to take in the early morning vista. The view was stunning, bordering on the surrealistic, and she gasped at the sheer beauty of it. A heavy fogbank blanketed the waters surrounding the central structure, the mist glistening with a soft magenta glow as it stifled rays from the red solar disk ascending just above the horizon. Her room faced the north, giving her an elevated panorama of Navassa Island.

Jacob had been very cordial, inviting her and her cameraman to an overnight stay, providing them both with lodging in the highest level of the city. She had readily accepted, eager to learn more about the facility.

She was still awed by what she had seen the previous day following the incident with the UN delegation when Jacob had given her and her cameraman a guided tour of the city. Though the facility was still under construction, she had been astounded by the interior architecture, which seemed to be unconstrained and infinitely more graceful than the rigid dictates of cubic geometry common to most land-based structures built by man.

What she had observed was suggestive of the natural free-flowing lines on the exterior of a seashell, leaving her truly spellbound. It was a fantasyland of endless wonder. The interior spaces were laid out with smoothly curving walls, floors, and ceilings, which gently rose and fell like swells in a rolling sea. A seemingly endless mix of lofts and galleries abounded. These overlooked serene pools, fountains, and cascading waterfalls in public areas, with numerous open stairways, ramps, and escalators making them reachable from a network of interlaced walkways and decks, many of them terraced, winding their way around rising pillars and beneath arching bridges. A definite biological look characterized everything, as if designed by some alien, unearthly intelligence that sought to mesmerize the beholder, and it was this intrinsic organic design that influenced all aspects of Aquaria's internal appearance. Lighting was recessed and indirect, suffusing the hallways and corridors with a soothing glow. Oyster whites, coral pinks, nautilus tans and other subdued hues came together in a kaleidoscope of color that was punctuated by startling splashes of scarlet, daffodil yellows, cobalt blues, and iridescent greens, with the varying tinctures merging and streaking like oil paints in an artist's palette prior to fully mixing. Built into the walls in many places on levels above the sea were thick panes and bubbles of glass, behind which swam multitudes of exotic fish among brilliant corals and anemones of flaming ruby, opal, and magenta, further enlivening the interior domain of the city.

And then she recalled the area at the heart of the central structure that had truly stunned her. It was by far the largest open space inside the facility she had so far seen, an enormous amphitheatre with tiered walls that rose up better than 250 feet from an elongated lagoon of placid water. Spilling down from a height close to the ceiling along the far side was a roaring waterfall that plunged along a series of cataracts, sending up spray and mist as it met the water in the lagoon. She had stood along a walkway that overlooked the water at a level midway up in the vast chamber, giving her a panoramic view of the open space. Bordering the water on one side was a white sandy beach sporadically adorned with palm trees, and set back from the water were three thatch roofed dwellings in close proximity to each other. The tiered walls were rife with leafy flora, and growing from the ledges was an abundance of various types of fruit-bearing trees and flowering bushes in an explosion of vivid hues. Flitting among them were hordes of multi-colored tropical birds and butterflies representing a variety of species. Looking above she had taken in the roof of the structure, amazed by the way it mimicked an azure sky, and seemingly floating within it was a brightly lit globe made to resemble the sun. It bathed everything beneath it in a dazzling wash of grandeur light that accentuated the mix of colors blanketing the artificial setting. But the most striking feature of all was the rainbow that hung above the base of the falls. The view had taken her breath away, for it was as though she had been transported to a surrealistic chasm that existed on a faraway planet. The combined effect caressed the eyes and fondled the spirit.

"This is incredible," she had remembered saying to Jacob. "But aren't you afraid those exotic birds and butterflies will escape to other parts of the city. There's so many."

Jacob had smiled arcanely. "They're not real. What you are seeing are holograms, three-dimensional images produced by the interplay of laser light projected at various frequencies."

"So I'm looking at an illusion," she had remarked in disbelief.

"Not entirely. With the exception of the fauna, sky, sun, and rainbow, everything you see before you is comprised of real objects. While the birds and butterflies are optical illusions, the trees and plants are actually alive. All the other components such as the sky and rainbow are artificial, ingeniously combined to make the setting before you appear real."

Something high up had caught her eyes. "What are those?" she had asked, pointing to one side of the artificial sun. A portion of the sky had winked out to reveal a rapidly dilating opening in the roof where several objects snaked down like the arms of an octopus, each wrapped around the trunk of an enormous tree. She had perceived the arms as being segmented, gradually tapering down from a thickness the size of an average man's waist to the girth of a ship's hawser.

Jacob had taken a moment to study her expression, and in retrospect she knew he had seen the look of an awe-stricken child seeing something wondrous for the very first time. "We call them 'The Tentacles'," he had answered with an amused grin. "They function much the way cranes you often see used for constructing skyscrapers in land-based cities, but these are far more versatile and structurally sophisticated. They have played a big part in the building of this city and are capable of lifting enormous loads."

She had watched as the root ball of the tree was lowered into a hole situated on a wide ledge midway up on the far side of the chasm. To her it had seemed impossible that the arms could still support such a heavy load while extended at such an oblique angle. While the first three tentacles maintained their hold on the tree to keep it vertical, two more tentacles, each tipped with a claw-like bucket the size of a pickup truck, had meandered down from the roof opening to dump soil around the root ball and bury it. Taking only seconds to do this, the buckets had then closed and tamped down the soil to compact it around the base of the tree. In moments all five tentacles had retracted back into the ceiling.

She had continued to stare as the circular opening contracted to disappear completely, after which the full canopy of an azure sky came back into view. "Who controls those things?" she had asked. She had then gone on to query him about how they were able to move so fluidly and quickly without an operator having a direct line of sight in order to manipulate them so skillfully.

When Jacob answered, she had sensed he was holding something back. "Oh, there's an operator, all right," he had explained a little too cryptically, and from his mien he seemed to be deciding how much information he should offer. After a pause, he said, "The operator uses hidden cameras positioned along the ledges and located near the tip of the tentacles as points of reference for moving things."

Satisfied with the condensed explanation for the moment, she had directed her gaze back to the newly planted tree. "What kind of tree is that?" she had said. "I've never seen one like it."

Jacob had responded quickly. "It is called a mapou tree. Once it fully matures it will have doubled in size. There are some Haitians who believe such trees to possess ancestral spirits and mystical powers."

His reply had made her turn to study him curiously. Such a statement had seemed totally incongruous with Jacob's erudite persona. "Are you one of those believers?" she could not help but ask.

Jacob had suddenly appeared contemplative. The question had seemed to dredge up a profound experience stored deep in his memory, and had she been able to read his thoughts at that moment, she would have seen what had taken place on that fateful night back near the tiny coastal village where he had grown up. She would have felt his horror and astonishment as he tried to pull Amphitrite's hand away from the giant mapou tree used by the locals for what he considered to be ridiculous animistic rituals. She would have discovered the unleashing of an unimaginable psychokinetic force capable of enormous destruction. She would have known that had he not witnessed it with his own eyes he would never have believed such a thing was possible. She would have been privy to a seemingly implausible event where the earth had fissured to evoke a colossal landslide that had destroyed a convoy of Tonton Makout coming to destroy the village and all its residents.

She remembered the thin smile that had eventually come upon Jacob's face after she had asked the question, and had she been able to assess the inner workings of his mind then and there, she would have gleaned some of the teachings his deceased grandmother had tried to instill in him prior to that epiphanic event. She would also have learned how he had so stubbornly refuted them in those days. Had she been able to glimpse those resurrected memories of his, she would have understood exactly what he meant when he had finally responded to her curiosity. "Superstition often springs from occurrences that cannot be adequately explained by science, yet we should not close our minds to these things," he had simply said. "Let me just say that anything is possible in the limited four-dimensional subspace to which our minds are naturally attuned."

Amelia broke from these recollections, suddenly aware of where she was. The red solar disk of the dawn sun had risen a few more degrees as she stood on the balcony high up in Aquaria. With difficulty, she pulled her gaze from the majestic beauty that stretched away before her. Turning, her eyes were immediately drawn to the enigmatic artwork hanging on the room's back wall. All at once she felt herself plummeting, and a rush of images went flashing by. Intuitively she knew what she was seeing. It was the memories that one simple question had evoked in Jacob's thoughts. And now she was grasping the full context of it. She was seeing the causation, the total spectrum of events that had led to the building of the magnificent structure upon which she now stood.

The moment passed quickly, and once again she found herself on the balcony, staring down in mesmeric wonder of the cottony fog bank still clinging gently to the surrounding sea. Already thin wispy vapors were wafting up and away as rays from the sun slowly lifted the thick enshrouding mist.

With enhanced insight, Amelia drifted back into deep musings as she stared unseeing at the island in the distance. The tour Jacob had given her continued to dominate her thoughts, and she recalled something else he had said, that Aquaria was basically a floating island founded upon clusters of buoyant cells which supported various components of the complex. Directly under the central surface structure, each cell acted as the base of a tower that interlocked with other towers. These towers were surrounded by sprawling lagoons and containment ponds used for inciting intensive algae growth and producing a glut of products from the sea.

The primary structural components of Aquaria were modular, with each module being hexagonal in shape, allowing it to abut snugly to neighboring modules with no wasted space. All modules were fabricated in the sea by a unique and revolutionary manufacturing process, molded by their designers and tailored to the physical and psychological needs of their human occupants. The starting modules forming the initial ring, six in all, were all identical and by far the largest, each having a vertical height of 1,300 feet and a horizontal width of 600 feet. Encircling the seed module, they comprised the highest platform. Following the completion of this ring of modules, the next ring was added, all having the same hexagonal width of 600 feet, but with a lesser height than the starting ring. The heights of succeeding rings gradually diminished as the city sprawled outward, growing much like a flower extending its petals. As Jacob had further explained, the primary components of the central surface structure extended five rings out and were now complete, giving the array the configuration of a squat mountain with an apex soaring 550 feet above sea level. Construction of the entire complex, however, was still ongoing and would not be finished for another year. Once completed, it would become home to 100,000 people, a tenfold increase over its current population of 10,000 residents.

The number had surprised her. "Won't that be a bit overcrowded?" she had questioned dubiously.

Jacob had patiently taken the time to point out that unlike conventional cubicle architecture where huge spaces go unused, the free-form approach to interior design allowed for a much more efficient use of space. "Think of Aquaria as an organism rather than a structure," he had emphasized, stressing that the guiding philosophy in its construction was to engineer the space itself to insure the comfort of its denizens. "A living environment that is intimately connected to the people it shelters," he had gone on to say.

He had shown her artistic renderings of what the floating facility would look like when construction finally ended. A protective mounded breakwater designed to absorb 75-foot storm waves would surround the complex. With an overall diameter of 5.8 miles in the shape of a hexagon, the twenty-fifth and final ring of modules would serve to support the breakwater, providing additional open space for gardens, hydroponic greenhouses, and pavilions. It would shield an arrangement of containment ponds on its lee side from the occasional onslaughts of an often unpredictable and moody sea, allowing for white sandy beaches to grace its outside periphery and providing a calm environment for additional beaches and recreational areas along the perimeter of the central surface structure.

As she pondered everything she had seen, she realized aesthetics was the overriding motif in the marine colony's design. Not only did it personify the city's inner layout, but it would dominate the facility's entire outer surface once completed, with park-like settings planned for many locations.

With Jacob having directed her gaze from a lofty vantage point on Aquaria's uppermost platform, she had clearly seen that the breakwater was now complete on four of the six sides that would eventually encompass the complex, with those still missing being the southeastern and southern borders. Sitting atop and running along the inside of these barriers were areas set aside for orchards and the cultivation of hydroponically grown crops in extensive multi-tiered greenhouses, providing fruits and vegetables to supplement the diet of the inhabitants. Winding among them were pathways that led to residential pavilions reserved for those who would prefer living on or near the beach rather than in one of the apartments in the central structure.

But it was the sprawling containment ponds that had captivated her interest. They extended nearly one and a half miles, reaching from the beaches bordering the central edifice to the areas of cultivation situated along the lee side of the newly constructed breakwater. She contemplated her first unobstructed view of them. When she had gotten her initial glimpse of the colony during her inbound flight, they had not been visible from the air, veiled by an obstructing cottony cloud that hid everything but the greater portion of the central structure. Assailed by a scorching tropical sun, however, the thick vaporous mist had finally evaporated, leaving every area of the complex exposed to the naked eye.

According to Jacob, the containment ponds were Aquaria's primary source of exported produce, projected to account for seventy-seven percent of its revenues once the complex was fully operational. Within the ponds currently operational, huge quantities of blue-green algae were being harvested, triggered into explosive growth by the cold, nitrogen-rich water brought up from the deep ocean abyss, some of which became food for animals low on the food chain, those being shrimp, crabs, lobsters, abalone, and a variety of shellfish, with specific ponds set aside for each species. Scrap waste protein from processing these lower animal life forms was then used to spawn teeming populations of high-value fish such as tuna, mackerel, herring, and cod.

Mouth agape, she had taken it all in, bedazzled by what lay before her. "This facility is huge," she had acknowledged reverently.

"Yes," Jacob had nodded in agreement. "Even at this stage of construction, Aquaria is by far the largest floating structure ever built. When completed, the sum total weight of all her components will exceed slightly more than eight point four million tons."

"It's unbelievable," she had murmured breathlessly, speaking more to herself rather than Jacob.

Continuing to linger on the central structure's upper platform, Jacob had swept his arms wide as if embracing the vast panorama stretching away toward the horizon. "We managed to build all this with minimal dependence on outside inputs, mainly using what the ocean provided," he had proclaimed proudly.

"But how is that possible?" she had asked, her mind reeling in a sea of unanswered questions.

Jacob had turned to look her full in the face, his countenance coming alive with the enthusiasm of one eager to teach. "The concept is rather simple," he had replied bemusedly. "We grow most of the components that make up this facility."

She had simply stared, searching his eyes for possible signs of insanity, but was unable to find any. Her cameraman had caught his uttered explanation on tape, and she had taken the time to review it in stark wonder.

"All of the primary structures were accreted from seawater," Jacob had gone on to elucidate. "Structurally, they possess the same characteristics as reinforced concrete, but are actually stronger and lighter than conventional concrete. In some respects, the accretion process is similar to the way the shell of a mollusk is formed. Only two ingredients are needed to do this, these being calcium carbonate and an electrically conductive metal in the form of rebar or a wire mesh. The metal acts as a skeletal framework and is assembled to give a particular structure its intended shape. Magnesium, alloyed with small amounts of manganese and aluminum, is the metal we use. This metal has a tensile strength comparable to that of steel, though it is much lighter in weight. All of the constituents we require are abundant in seawater and can be extracted out of solution rather easily. By applying an electric current to the framework, the calcium carbonate is forced out of solution to bond electrochemically to the charged metal, forming a cement-like coating over the skeleton. The electricity, of course, is supplied by our OTEC power-generating facility at the center of this complex."

Amelia broke from these thoughts, suddenly aware that she had wandered into the apartment's bathroom. Looking at her reflection in the mirror, she wondered if she truly knew the person staring back. For the first time since joining the IBC, she felt out of place working under the banner of the media giant. Something did not sit right about the organization. Had she been ignoring her gut instinct all along? Had her ambition so blinded her that she refused to acknowledge the peculiarities of the company? Could it be that the IBC was violating the primary principles of sound journalism, established for the sole purpose of deceiving the hoi polloi of nations and molding public opinion to conform to the wishes of a shadowy group lurking behind the scenes? Jacob had indicated the interview would ultimately be distorted to cast Aquaria in an unfavorable light, and she had not refuted it. By doctoring facts and putting various spins on events through shrewd editing, the IBC could easily mislead the masses. With heartfelt conviction she realized she would betray herself if she continued to abet an organization controlled by ruthless and corrupt people bent on propagating lies.

One thing was for sure now. She would do whatever she could to keep the IBC from besmirching the image of something so wondrous as Aquaria.

Chapter Fifteen: Economic Collapse on the Horizon

Achilles was distraught with anguish as he sent a silent call of distress to Destiny. *Please come,* he cried. *We need you! Jay Jay needs you!*

Destiny's response was immediate. *What's wrong?*

Reading her reply, Achilles could tell she was braced for bad news. *JJ is severely injured with head trauma and may be dying,* he informed her. *I can barely detect a pulse within him. Fernando has also been injured, but only slightly.*

I'm on my way, Destiny answered without hesitation, and Achilles knew at once her anguish surpassed his own.

It was still early in the morning on day two of her visit to Aquaria, and Amelia had more reporting to do. But now she would try to help the colony rather than abet the people she worked for. Jacob had graciously agreed to take time out of his busy schedule and continue with the interview, revealing still more about Aquaria and their objectives.

Strolling casually along a red brick pathway that wound its way through one of the many vibrant gardens situated atop the southern breakwater, she stared up into the Haitian's craggy face as her cameraman walked backward in front of them, his camera focused on their conversation.

"So you're convinced the United States and Europe are in decline," she said.

Jacob nodded grimly. "As I've pointed out, both have been led down the road to socialism, and history has already shown us such ideology does not work, for it ultimately erodes a nation from within. I have no doubts both the U.S. and Europe are headed for a fiscal cliff."

"You also believe Aquaria will be unaffected if this happens," Amelia replied, echoing another of Jacob's convictions.

Jacob's face remained solemn. "Yes, our colony is autonomous and self-sufficient. Though our system here tends to mimic the principles of capitalism, it is untainted by the greed that has ruined other nations."

"And you claim the Federal Reserve is exacerbating this problem for the Americans," Amelia added, continuing to recap the main points Jacob had hit upon earlier.

"For the first ninety-nine years of its life, the Fed had no accountability to the United States government. It was not audited by the U.S. Congress, nor was it legally bound to do so. It produced no books, nor did it file annual statements or show balance sheets to anyone outside its domain. As such, it was an unrestricted money monopoly. Only until recently was it audited, and that was only a partial audit under the Federal Reserve Transparency Act passed by Congress in two-thousand twelve. What was uncovered was truly shocking."

"What was that?"

"For one, over a three-year period beginning in two thousand seven, it provided more than sixteen trillion dollars in covert financial assistance to some of the largest financial institutions and corporations in the United States and throughout the world. It knew a disastrous market meltdown was on the horizon. And while this was initially taking place, the Fed's chairman and the U.S. Treasury Secretary kept assuring everyone that the bubbles brewing in the marketplace were merely a hiccup and that the fundamentals were still strong. They lied to the American people while alerting members of Congress to restructure their financial portfolios so as to avoid getting hurt like the typical citizen when the market did crash."

"But one would think propping up the market was a good thing," Amelia said. "Didn't it keep the world economy from collapsing completely?"

"It gave the illusion of stabilizing the system to make it appear as if everything would quickly rebound to a robust state of health. In reality it did nothing to improve the ailing economy or the unemployment situation that ensued. By creating vast sums of essentially worthless paper currency via its printing presses, it injected massive amounts of liquidity into the financial institutions at zero interest, requiring them to buy equities, but only after world markets faltered."

"What if they refused to buy equities?" Amelia interjected quizzically.

"Then no loans would be forthcoming," Jacob clarified. "That was the Fed's underlying stipulation for providing such cheap money. As I said, the loans were interest-free, so the banks really had no qualms about complying with such a simple requirement. In fact, many of them bought back their own stock with the money."

"Are you certain of this requirement?"

"One only has to evaluate the facts objectively to understand why such cheap money was issued."

"What was the Fed's motive in doing this?"

"Generally speaking, equity markets the world over have always been looked upon as barometers of economic health. By providing a deluge of money into them, stock indexes were once again driven back to high though artificial levels, especially with many corporations taking advantage of this by repurchasing their own stock. This deceived the average investor as to the actual underlying strength of the market."

"Sounds like a house of cards," Amelia offered.

"And a very fragile one at that," Jacob agreed, "one that can come crashing down again at the slightest sign of economic uncertainty. Keep in mind that the Fed can call in those cheap loans any time it chooses, causing a reverse scenario in which all the banking institutions are forced to dump their equities. By holding short market positions through advance notice from the Fed, vast amounts of investor wealth can be periodically siphoned off into the hands of these super-rich elitists. This accounts for most of the boom-bust cycles you often see in the markets. The elite make it a habit of manufacturing scenarios that can cause markets to go into free-fall, and it is these events from which they always profit."

Amelia fought to subdue the naïve, wide-eyed expression wanting to dominate her face. Winning the battle, she prodded him further, subtly attempting to highlight the enlightenment Jacob was providing. "You had mentioned earlier that America's founding fathers had warned against such banking monopolies."

Jacob stopped and stared out to sea through an opening in a nearby stand of peach trees. A ship could be seen in the distance. The subtle frown that came to his face did not escape Amelia's notice before he launched into another discourse.

"Presidents Thomas Jefferson, James Madison, and Andrew Jackson all argued that the Republic and its Constitution were always vulnerable to the dangers of the so-called money power, which in essence were elitist bankers who were always seeking to gain a monopoly over the issuance of currency long before the establishment of the Fed. Jefferson himself believed that the issuing power of money should be strictly in the hands of Congress and the people to whom it belongs, further insisting that such power should never be issued to bankers. To him, the banking institutions were more dangerous to liberty than standing armies."

"You also had insinuated that bankers were responsible for creating socialism," Amelia said. "Can you explain what you meant by that?"

A shrewd smile came to Jacob's face. "Did you know that Karl Marx was actually commissioned to write his voluminous works on communism?" he said, choosing to skirt the question for the moment.

Amelia's manner reflected ignorance on the subject, but she sought to use it to solidify Jacob's argument wherever it was headed. "I had always been under the impression he wrote it to express concern for those downtrodden by the rich."

This elicited an amused chuckle from Jacob. "Marx was one of the evillest people to ever walk the earth, and by his own admission professed to have given his soul to the Devil. He hated God, and his chief aim was the destruction of all religion. This intense hatred is thoroughly embedded in his writings, the Manifesto."

Jacob's expression altered into one of sadness. "Greed, not altruism, was the primary motivating force behind Marx's Manifesto, much of which was proven to have been plagiarized from the work of an obscure social ideologue named Victor Considerant more than twenty years earlier. And scholars have shown some of it was actually modeled after the doctrines and philosophies maintained by the Egyptian Pharaohs for governing the masses."

"Then who paid him to write it?" Amelia pressed.

Jacob plucked a beautiful red rose from a nearby bush and casually sniffed it before replying. "Elitist bankers in Germany and America paid him."

Jacob anticipated Amelia's look of surprise, and he smiled knowingly. "Sounds illogical, doesn't it, for why would rich and powerful people pay someone to create an ideology to agitate the lower classes into armed revolt where society is turned upside down? Nevertheless, it is a well-documented fact many historical scholars have brought to light over the last hundred years. At its core, Marxism was and still is an elitist scheme for consolidating power, plain and simple. It has nothing to do with relieving the misery of the poor or advancing mankind to a higher state of social awareness. It is a device concocted purely for the exploitation of man by a very small and privileged minority, with supremacy of the elite as its main objective."

Amelia continued to keep an expression of stark amazement etched on her face for the sake of the camera, but under the surface she was clearly in Jacob's corner now, fully captivated by his erudite manner. "I always thought Marxism favored the working class and sought to do the opposite, to stop the exploitation of the poor by the upper class."

"Absolutely not," Jacob said. "The proletariat fell victim to this new ideology with its promise of wealth distribution. It did not favor the proletariat at all, and it certainly did not favor the bourgeoisie, which was targeted for elimination and the confiscation of their assets. It was simply a blueprint for the takeover of political and economic power by a relatively tiny elite minority who were bent on snatching the wealth of the middle class."

"So it was all a pretense, a plot to stir the have-nots into armed revolution," Amelia parroted.

"Yes, in nineteen seventeen it triggered the Bolshevik Revolution in Russia," Jacob went on. "It was class warfare at its worst. Marx looked upon the proletariat as little more than stupid cattle, using their jealousy and envy of the bourgeoisie to enforce a hell on earth where fear, suffering, terror, and treason ruled supreme. Under Lenin's reign, blood flowed like a river with close to two million people being murdered merely for their anti-socialistic thinking."

"But why would these elitists put their own fortunes at risk by instigating such a revolt?" Amelia said. "Couldn't such a scheme have backfired?"

"No, because these people groomed and financed Lenin to lead the revolution. Lenin was merely a puppet. He carried out their directives, ensuring they remained unscathed from the ensuing turmoil."

"You mentioned that Marx wanted to bring down religion," Amelia said. "What was his motive?"

"He was a practicing Satanist. He hated anything that gave reverence to God."

"Are you saying he actually worshipped the Devil."

"Most assuredly. The strange part is, he grew up in a Christian family, and early in life confessed Jesus Christ as his Savior. He knew Scripture well. But over time he underwent a transformation, choosing to side with the Devil. Writing the Manifesto seems to have reinforced this shift, for Communist doctrine clearly and consistently preaches atheism, which is a denial of God's existence. Marxism is a godless philosophy. This in itself shows Marx was a fraud. He did not practice what he preached, since a Satanist cannot be an atheist."

"Why is that?" Amelia interposed quickly, appearing more confused than ever.

"Using theological reasoning, if there is a Heaven, then there must be a Hell. Choosing to take sides with the Devil means going against God. Believing in one implies a belief in the other. Therefore, a true atheist would not have believed in the existence of Satan."

"I see your point," Amelia acquiesced thoughtfully.

Jacob smiled with satisfaction, enjoying the way his historical revelations were getting through to her. But he was not yet ready to drop the subject, proceeding to enlarge upon it further.

"Marx fancied himself as a poet, and I have to admit he was quite good at it. He had an exceptional flair for revealing his true nature within his lyrics, some of which reflected the full measure of his wickedness. Not only did his poems profess a succinct hatred for God, they also conveyed his loathing of mankind in general, since according to Scripture, all human beings were created in the image of God."

"It appears you have studied Marx quite extensively," Amelia said, impressed by Jacob's knowledge of the man. But she needed more for the camera, undeterred that her efforts might be in vain, for once the videos reached IBC headquarters, it was almost a certainty that this segment of the interview would be edited out. For some inexplicable reason, though, she had still been unsuccessful in sending clips of earlier tapings.

"Can you quote any examples of his poetry?" Amelia asked eagerly, somehow perceiving he could.

Fulfilling such a request came easily to Jacob, for he had been blessed with an eidetic mind. He could recall everything he had ever seen, heard or read in exact detail.

"This one personifies his contempt for humanity," Jacob said, launching into a verbatim quote of a Marx poem:

"…Yet I have power within my youthful arms

to clench and crush you with tempestuous force,

while for us both the abyss yawns in darkness.

You will sink down and I shall follow laughing,

whispering in your ears Descend,

Come with me, friend."

Amelia looked horrified. "My God!" she uttered.

"Here is another of his verse that may shock you," Jacob intoned somberly:

"With disdain I will throw my gauntlet

full in the face of the world,

and see the collapse of this pygmy giant

whose fall will not stifle my ardor.

Then will I wander godlike and victorious
through the ruins of the world,
and giving my words an active force,
I will feel equal to the creator."

Amelia stared, momentarily stunned by the sheer impact of the words. "What an incredibly perverse individual."

"Yes," Jacob concurred. "Marx was a monster, and his Manifesto inflamed the minds of the proletariat as though they were all possessed by the same demons that drove him. But this much is clear, communism was created by elitists as an antithesis to Western capitalism, devised to produce a system that gave them ultimate power. Through the mechanism of controlled change by controlled conflict, they sought to achieve a New World Order where they would reign supreme. What's more, there is a wealth of information to prove these people were members of the Illuminist Freemasons. To this day this cabal still exists."

"Are you referring to the Illuminati?" Amelia chirped in astonishment.

"Yes."

"I thought they were a thing of the past, that they died off long ago."

"That's what they would like the world to believe, but I can assure you they are still around and stronger than ever. When Marx was writing the Manifesto, a highly select body of secret initiates within the Illuminati financed him. They called themselves the League of Twelve Just Men."

"It sounds strange that they would consider themselves just," Amelia said.

Jacob's expression soured momentarily, then turned stoic. "Unfortunately, evil people rarely see themselves as evil. Most of them actually believe they are doing humanity a service. They think the masses are too stupid to run the world in a responsible manner. And while these financial elites are the actual culprits in creating most of the ills that continue to plague the globe, they are emerging from the economic wreckage more powerful than ever before. Even worse, they are dictating the terms of their own enrichment to servile governments throughout the planet."

Jacob stopped walking, bringing his gaze to bear seaward once more through another opening in the orchard's thriving foliage. He remained mute for several seconds as he studied the same ship that drew his attention minutes earlier, and sensing that something was wrong, Amelia refrained from intruding on the pronounced contemplation that suddenly took hold of him.

Seeming to dismiss the vessel, Jacob turned to face the camera again, though he seemed distracted. Continuing with the interview, he said, "We, in Aquaria, believe the state of the world is more precarious than ever, that..."

The cell phone Jacob carried rang curtly, cutting off the next leg of his confabulation. The sound it emitted told him the incoming call was of a priority nature, one that demanded an immediate response. "Pardon the interruption," he apologized, turning his back to Amelia and her cameraman.

"What is it, Ez?" he uttered softly, holding the phone snugly to his ear.

"It appears there is a strike force looking to take back the *Southern Star*," Ez informed him. "From your present location, you can see the ship. Look to the sky above it."

Jacob lifted his eyes, quickly locating close to a dozen objects plummeting toward the freighter. An aircraft could be seen higher up. "Are you able to identify them?" he asked.

"I assume them to be the same UN team sent here yesterday judging from the aircraft insignia and configuration. Mat has already been alerted."

Jacob's spirits abruptly plunged at a speed nearly equal to the mercenaries hurtling toward the vessel, and he found himself suddenly pining for the quiet life he had abandoned in order to undertake the building of Aquaria. Almost as quickly he chastised himself for entertaining this thought. A dereliction of his calling was beyond consideration. He had made his decision long ago, and he knew he would rather die than deviate from the path he had chosen to follow. To fortify his resolution as he often did, he reminded himself of a quote from Edmund Burke, a famous Irish statesman: '*The only thing necessary for the triumph of evil is for good men to do nothing.*'

"Thank you, Ez," Jacob said wearily. "Please keep me apprised of developments."

Jacob mulled the situation with trepidation. Mat's contingent would be outnumbered three to one, and Phillipe's safety weighed heavily on his mind. With deep resignation, he turned back to Amelia. "Unfortunately there are pressing matters that demand my attention. Hopefully we'll be able to pick up on this interview later this afternoon. In the meantime, feel free to roam the facility at your leisure."

Amelia nodded, watching as Jacob turned and walked away. Redirecting her gaze, she espied the lone ship several miles distant. It was then she caught sight of the descending skydivers, their chutes deploying one by one as they sought to alight on the vessel. Gesturing frantically, she signaled her cameraman to capture the event on video. But her cameraman was already recording the event.

Mat looked at Bashir, still finding it strange that the man standing before him had once been a member of Al Qaeda. But after working with him for the past several years now, he had come to trust him implicitly. Through some inexplicable means, Destiny and Amphitrite had found a way to bring out the good in him. And there had been a wealth of it. Like a suppressed geyser that could no longer be contained, it had all come gushing out. Not only were they able to correct his severe physical injury, they had also been able to heal his psychological and emotional impairments as well.

"Put this on!" Mat commanded, offering Bashir his cloaker. Unfortunately, all they had among them were two.

"I respectfully decline," Bashir replied stoically. "It fits you better."

The Palestinian's response did not come as a surprise, for Mat knew Bashir would readily put the lives of others ahead of his own.

Glancing behind him once again, Mat espied the descending paratroopers. They had executed a seemingly perfect HALO – High Altitude Low Opening – a classic military aerial maneuver, dropping like meteors to an altitude of perhaps 500 feet before deploying their chutes. From that alone he could tell these were crack troops, making him believe this was not going to be an easy fight regardless of a few advantages he had at his disposal. Already he could see the lead commando flaring his chute sharply in an attempt to alight on top of a cargo container situated 900 feet away near the ship's stern.

Mat turned quickly to Kalid, Bashir's second and another former Islamic radical. Like Bashir, Kalid had dropped his allegiance to Al Qaeda long ago, devoting himself entirely to the establishment of Aquaria. He knew it was because both men looked upon Destiny and her mother as nothing less than angels sent to earth by Allah to change the world forever. Their belief was unshakable, and their loyalty to the colony was without question. No words, no matter how logically put forth, would ever shake them of this belief. They were committed and would defend the colony and its inhabitants with their very lives if necessary.

"Then I offer it to you, Kalid," Mat uttered in frustration. He had no time to haggle, watching as several more chutes flared. The wind had shifted just enough to keep the Chilean commandos from landing closer to the bow. As best he could tell, conditions were working in his favor at the moment. Unless members of the strike force wanted to drop into the sea, they were forced to settle for the ship's stern.

Kalid eyed the cloaker with contempt. "I also decline," he spat disdainfully.

"Suit yourself," Mat said irritably, "but don't tell me later you should have accepted after a bullet takes your head off."

"I don't think that would be possible," Phillipe joked nervously, doing his utmost to inject levity into a darkening situation.

Mat scrutinized the lad closely. In spite of all the training he and Jake had given him, and in spite of his commendable performance in his combat debut a short time earlier, Phillipe was still green. And should anything happen to Phillipe while under his watch, he knew Jake would be unforgiving.

"The way I see it," Mat opined briskly, looking to all three men, "we can either stay and fight or make a hasty retreat in the sub."

He shot a quick glance through a port side window, looking down at the water, but failed to spot anything. *Allah's Sword* remained on standby, lurking submerged somewhere in hailing distance of the ship. The sub was once captained by Raduyev, the nefarious Al Qaeda operative, but had since fallen into the hands of the Aquarians mainly due to Bashir's unwavering loyalty to the colony. At the moment it was being piloted by Abdel, a former Yemeni freighter captain who had lost an arm when his ship had been sunk by Sebastian Ortega. After Abdel's life had been saved by the pod in the aftermath of that event, Abdel had since become another devoted disciple of Tursiops and its objectives. With the exception of Phillipe, Mat's team had reached the *Southern Star* via the submarine.

Bashir spoke up quickly. "We must stay and fight. This ship is the only insurance we have to keep Aquaria from being destroyed." For emphasis, he pointed in the direction of the enormous tanker, its superstructure now just barely visible in the distance as it made its way over the horizon. In another minute, the ship would be out of sight. "If we give this ship back to them, it is possible the Kraken may return."

Mat looked at Kalid, reading the same conviction in his face as well.

"I'm with Bashir," Phillipe said when Mat turned to him.

Mat noted the worry on Phillipe's face, but he knew it had nothing to do with personal safety. It was evident Phillipe was thinking about Jake. Two hours earlier, Perseus, Phillipe's bond mate, had informed the lad about Jake's misfortune. And while Jake's injury was life threatening, there was nothing any of them could do to help. But Jake was in good hands. He was currently in Destiny's care aboard the *Angel*.

"All right then, it's settled," Mat growled, keeping stern eyes on Phillipe. "But you make sure you keep your cloaker activated at all times."

"But I have a Masker," Phillipe objected sourly.

"No buts," Mat retorted adamantly. "Either wear the cloaker or you're out of the fight."

Phillipe nodded grimly. Wearing the cloaker Jake had left behind would make up for his inexperience in a firefight.

Mat pulled out his cell phone and lifted it to his mouth. "I need a new program, Ez. Send me-"

"I'm way ahead of you," Ez interrupted. "It's already in your Maskers. I advise you to test them first. You're right on the edge of their receiving range."

Mat grabbed Bashir's wrist, touching a button on the device strapped to it. Almost at once, Bashir's image underwent a transformation. He did the same thing with Kalid's, with each one producing the desired illusion. Each Masker was outfitted with a receiver, enabling it to be reprogrammed from a remote location as circumstances dictated.

Mat completed the test by touching the button on his own device. "How do I look?" he said, seeking feedback from the others.

"Mean and ruthless," Phillipe opined. "At least I have an idea what we'll be going up against," he quickly added.

Mat nodded, then looked at Bashir and Kalid for their assessments.

"Very ugly," Bashir quipped.

"And very arrogant," Kalid answered distastefully.

Satisfied, Mat lifted the cell phone to his lips again. "All the units seem to be working just fine, Ez."

"That's good," Ez replied, "but I strongly advise each of you to use Option Two on your units before-"

"Bye, Ez," Mat interceded, cutting her off and stuffing the phone into a pocket. Try as he might, he had never felt comfortable talking to a computer, particularly since it always seemed to be one step ahead of him.

Chapter Sixteen: Jake's Life Hangs in the Balance

Captain Francisco Alvarez unstrapped himself from the harness, letting the chute flutter off into the sea. He was eager for a fight. He and his men had been unbearably humiliated at the hands of the colonists, taking flight like a panicked mob fleeing a swarm of stinging wasps. But now he would take his revenge against these insignificant vermin, looking forward to using the corvo slung at his side. Crouched low and gently caressing the haft of the weapon, he watched as his commandos swooped down one by one to land on other cargo containers abutting his own.

Alvarez considered the little information he had been given. Allotey had told him the freighter had been hijacked by a small strike force that had come from Aquaria. He was to take back the vessel, freeing the ship's captain and crew, including a man called Zinova and his associates, assuming any of them were still alive. Based on Allotey's assessment of the situation, it was surmised they were all being held hostage.

Using hand signals, Alvarez instructed his men to fan out and make their way forward. During the pre-mission briefing, his orders had been explicit. Their primary objective was to take back control of the ship's bridge. Aside from capturing two of the hijackers, they were to crush all opposition without mercy. Yes, taking two prisoners would be sufficient to give him satisfaction. The thought caused him to run his fingers along the scabbard sheathing of his corvo as he moved cautiously between rows of cargo containers. His men were good at this sort of thing, surely the best in the world, and he had no doubts they would get the job done.

He had read the dossiers on both of the former Navy Seals that ran Aquaria's security and he was not impressed by what was revealed. He and his men were far better warriors than any Navy Seal. As he mulled this, Javolyn's face loomed up in the forefront of his mind, an image of haughty defiance and audacious insolence. The man had seemed totally unconcerned with the authority Allotey represented, plainly displaying an open disrespect of Alvarez and his men.

A short burst of gunfire broke out somewhere off to his right, the sound muffled by the intervening barriers of cargo containers. It was obvious at least one of his men was already engaging the hijackers. Several more bursts rang out as Alvarez continued to make his way forward. Then all was quiet.

Alvarez crept around a bend, Javolyn's image continuing to mock him. He would get his revenge, slicing with the corvo to carve that impudence right off his face. The sound of movement directly ahead caused him to stop and remain perfectly still. His finger tightened on the trigger of his Uzi, primed and ready to squeeze off a salvo, but he failed to see anything.

Letting out a slow breath, he advanced a few more feet, fully prepared for a skirmish. A burst of blinding color suddenly appeared in front of him, swirling and whipping like monstrous tentacles caught in a powerful eddy. They lashed out to coil around his brain before he could even think to react, bombarding it with sizzling motes that snaked and interlaced before stretching to the boundless reaches of space. Staggered by the sheer intensity of it, he felt the inside of his skull being scorched as a surge of scalding bile rose up in his throat. Frozen in its grip, a sickness unlike anything he had ever experienced engulfed him. Closing his eyes tightly to escape the sight, he lay on his back convulsing uncontrollably and regurgitating his last meal. With his mind teetering on the edge of sanity, he barely managed to grasp what was happening.

Using all his will to guide a trembling hand, Alvarez managed to lift the cup shielding the tiny syringe strapped snuggly to his right thigh. With his remaining strength, he slapped down on the plunger. A potent mix of dextroamphetamine and a non-hallucinogenic LSD derivative was immediately injected into his femoral artery. He normally refrained from resorting to the use of drugs, but he had been warned about this strange debilitating weapon the colonists used to keep spies from breaching their facility, a type of visual display that made intruders ill upon looking at it. He had been told these displays were placed in key sectors of Aquaria and came in the form of paintings with an abstract motif. He had scoffed at the idea, unable to accept the notion that a two or three dimensional rendering of art could make him sick simply by looking at it. Nevertheless, Allotey had been firm, insisting Alvarez and his men be prepared for such a possibility. And while they had all been outfitted with the syringes during their visit to the colony, he had seen no reason for him and his men to use them unless it became absolutely necessary. His suffering now, however, was infinitely many times worse than what he had experienced back there.

Alvarez felt his sickness suddenly ease as the drug took effect, and from somewhere nearby the sound of gunfire invaded his awareness, a short staccato burst followed by a rasping grunt. Cautiously he opened his eyes, prepared to close them again, but the vision was now gone.

An eerie quiet descended as he rose on unsteady feet, and he realized the corridor was empty. Feeling his strength quickly rebounding, he sidled around the corner of a cargo container. The crumpled body of one of his men lay before him, and crouched over it was Allotey, who appeared to be binding his man with plastic tie wraps.

Dumbstruck, Alvarez was momentarily speechless. "How did you get here?" he managed to utter. Allotey had not accompanied his team. The man had no military training and certainly didn't have the skills to perform a HALO jump to reach the *Southern Star* as did Alvarez and his men.

Startled, Allotey stood, turning slowly to face him.

"How?" Alvarez demanded, his voice rising in confusion.

Allotey's austere persona suddenly morphed, starting at the eyes. A tangled mass of lights sprang forth from them, rapidly expanding to engulf the UN envoy. In an instant, an explosion of color gushed forward, reaching once again for the Chilean commando.

Alvarez reeled, a sense of vertigo taking hold of him. But the cocktail of drugs flowing through his veins gave him the means to resist, and he did not become incapacitated like before. Though disoriented, he managed to level his weapon and squeeze off a burst, unsure exactly where to aim. Sparks erupted close by, and he realized he was being fired upon as a barrage of bullets collided with the side of a nearby cargo container. In reaction, he dove low, tucking in his shoulder and executing a forward roll to avoid being hit. Springing back to his feet with the agility of a cat, he scrambled around a corner. Ricocheting rounds buzzed over his head like maddened bees seeking to sting as he raced along an empty corridor. With his mind spinning in turmoil over these inane happenings, his only option was to escape.

Kalid was still conscious when Mat found him slumped in a pool of blood. He was bleeding profusely from a bullet wound in his lower left thigh. Using two plastic ties strung together, Mat applied a makeshift tourniquet to stem the loss of blood.

"I don't understand what went wrong," Kalid gasped.

"What do you mean?" Mat whispered back, cinching the ties tightly above the wound.

Kalid grimaced, fending off the pain before answering. "At first the hologram worked, then it did not."

"Looks like it worked just fine," Mat muttered. He glanced around cautiously to take a quick inventory of his surroundings before dropping his eyes to the commando Kalid had subdued. The man had stopped retching and lay eyeing his captors dazedly.

"No… you don't understand," Kalid stammered back, having trouble getting his thoughts in order. "There was another."

"Another?" Mat looked around apprehensively a second time, wondering if he should reactivate his cloaker.

Kalid nodded. For emphasis, he stared at the bound commando. "This man was the second."

"Was this man the one who shot you?"

Kalid shook his head torpidly. He had lost a lot of blood and was on the verge of blacking out. "I used the hologram on another."

"Are you saying it had no effect on him?"

"It did at first. He became very sick." Kalid indicated the subdued commando. "But while I was busy with this one, the other one was back on his feet. I tried using the hologram again, but it no longer worked on him."

Kalid's rambling suddenly became clear. "So he shot you?" Mat said.

"Yes…I returned fire, but I don't know if I hit him."

"Which way did he go?"

"That way."

Mat looked in the direction Kalid indicated, his mind struggling to analyze this strange twist. As far as he knew, the use of Option Two was infallible in bringing down bad guys. Recovering from exposure to it generally took several minutes, and re-exposure should have been just as debilitating, if not more so. But somehow the commando had regrouped and managed to fight back.

Unlike Kalid, Mat refrained from using Option Two. The hologram's calming effects made him too lethargic to be effective in battle. But he knew Kalid would try to avoid killing whenever possible. And strangely, Kalid was able to function efficaciously while resorting to Option Two.

A warrior mentality was in Mat's blood, and he had no issues about taking out an adversary by more conventional methods whenever the situation called for it, even if it meant killing. At this moment, these mercenaries were the enemy, and you neutralized the enemy without speculating on their core natures. Whether they were morally good or evil made no difference. Already he had taken down three commandos using his stealth capability. In each case, he had dispatched an unsuspecting foe using the steel bar he carried, crashing it down with brutal force. He had left each of them unconscious or possibly dead, trussed up in a manner similar to the way Kalid had bound his own captive. Phillipe was also contributing, for Mat had seen two others drop in a heap, their assailant remaining invisible. That meant six others still roamed the ship, assuming Bashir had not subdued any of them.

Mat was pressed to make a decision. He couldn't leave Kalid, and yet he could not let the ship fall into the hands of the remaining commandos.

Without further thought he shed his cloaker.

"What are you doing?" Kalid asked wearily.

Mat pulled Kalid to his feet and leaned him against a cargo container. "Put this on!" he ordered.

"No!"

Kalid's injured leg began to buckle and Mat grabbed him harshly to keep him from falling back down. "Do as I say, damn it!"

Kalid resisted feebly as Mat forced the cloaker around his body and activated it. Roughly, he moved him to a nearby recess between two containers and shoved him in. He had no time to be gentle. Quickly, he retrieved Kalid's weapon and placed it under the cloaker, satisfied that both man and weapon appeared invisible.

"Stay put until I get back," Mat snapped. Without waiting for a reply, he initiated his Masker and made his way forward toward the bridge.

Destiny held back tears as she eyed Jake's prostrate form. With his head swathed thickly in gauze wraps, he lay quietly in the bed he always used aboard the *Angel*, appearing to sleep peacefully.

"Can you hear me, my darling?" she said softly. She held his hand and lifted it to her lips, kissing it tenderly. Unable to stifle the heartache, a tear welled up and trickled down her cheek. "Please forgive me for failing you. The power has left me."

Hercules' thoughts suddenly merged with her own. *Do not blame yourself. The power has left us all. We have changed.*

Destiny's mind churned with memories of earlier times. Healing catastrophic injuries, though difficult, had once been possible for the pod to achieve. On such occasions, she had always acted as the lens through which the others focused their mental energies. Adding her own considerable potency to the flux, the net effect had been miraculous to those worthy of being cured. As a result, torn or distressed flesh had mended quickly, with the greatest amount of healing usually taking a matter of minutes rather than weeks. But restoring a living creature to normal health would inevitably take a toll on her, sometimes leaving her physically drained.

A small sob escaped Destiny's lips out of frustration. All she had been able to accomplish was stabilize Jake's head trauma. She had managed to stop the brain hemorrhage, which Achilles had been able to discern using ultrasonic sound emissions to scan the injury. That was all. The power to actually heal had completely deserted her.

And so had her once dependable power of precognition. Her latest dream had proved that. It had only been partially accurate. It had never hinted that Jake might be severely injured, that he might die while dealing with the Eagle Master. To her, Jake had always seemed invincible. If not for the prompt intervention of Achilles, Hermes, and Aphrodite in reaching the crash scene, Jake would have surely perished. Thankfully they had been able to summon two blue whales from Aquaria, less than three miles away. The whales had been preparing to tow a breakwater module into place and were already fully outfitted with harnesses and towing cables.

A deep voice rumbled mournfully, interrupting Destiny's thoughts. "How is he?"

Destiny looked up to see Zimbola looming over her. With his exceedingly large frame, he had to stoop down to keep his head from hitting the cabin ceiling.

"Stable for the time being." Destiny turned back to gaze through the porthole just above the bed. The soft undulations of the waves flowing past did nothing to improve her anxiety. "How much farther to the cove?"

"A little under an hour." The big Jamaican paused, his features solemn as he stared down at Jake. "You sure you don't want me to turn around?"

Destiny sighed deeply, still struggling to hold back a flood of tears. She had to stay strong. "I can't be sure of anything anymore, Zimby."

Zimbola nodded resignedly. He knew she was making a hard decision, for Jake's life might very well hang in the balance by not putting him on life support in one of Aquaria's state of the art medical facilities. But circumstances were rapidly heating up. Just a short time earlier while the crown of Aquaria's central tower was still in sight, Ez had apprised both of them of a brewing raid on the colony she was able to decode by hacking into a secure UN channel. Military forces were currently being mobilized to take over the floating city, and Jake, along with other colony leaders, were to be taken into custody.

"Where are the twins?" Destiny asked.

"Up in the pilot house with Fernando and Hector."

Fernando had fared much better than Jake during the crash, having been strapped securely into the copilot seat. He would have gone down with the Hind if not for the intervention of Hermes, who had gotten him out as the chopper was falling into the depths.

"If only Big D were operational," Destiny said.

"Yes," Zimbola concurred. He looked down at Jake again. Though he rarely showed emotion, his eyes were misty. "It is most unfortunate."

Destiny felt the ire building within her, ambivalent to the repulsion it should have induced prior to the birth of the twins.

You must remain calm, Hercules warned. *Anger is our enemy. It has infected us all. If we let it grow any stronger, it will place JJ beyond our reach.*

Destiny took in a deep breath, doing her best to quell the rising tempest within her. Up until that moment with Ternier and Raduyev so long ago, anger had been an unfamiliar emotion.

Mat spotted two commandos preparing to ascend to the bridge just as a kaleidoscope of intertwining color flashed at the top of the stairs. Not wanting his reactions to be dulled, he avoided looking at it, keeping his gaze locked on the enemy. One of the men shouted, then let loose with a burst of automatic fire, directing it up into the eruption of light.

Almost immediately, Mat realized Kalid's assertion to be true. Option Two was not working. No doubt Bashir was up there resorting to its use, for Mat had instructed him to hold the bridge. To save him, Mat had no choice but to use deadly force.

Without giving it another thought, he leveled his weapon and opened up on both commandos from behind. One man went down instantly, but the other managed to whirl, his body jerking spasmodically as he absorbed a spray of rounds, his Uzi continuing to spit out a hail of bullets haphazardly in all directions. Mat poured the remainder of his clip into him, amazed at the man's tenacity and durability. Abruptly his hands went numb as a random bullet slammed into his weapon and sent it flying from his grasp.

Mat stared dazedly. The second man had stopped firing and now lay sprawled on the deck. Regaining his senses, Mat reached for his fallen weapon, his fingers still tingling. He saw that the receiver for the magazine was gouged, the place where the bullet had struck. Pulling hard on the clip, he quickly discovered it would not come out. His assault rifle was useless.

"Do not move, swine!" a voice suddenly snarled from behind in thickly accented English.

Mat froze. He had to remind himself he was no longer wearing the cloaker.

"Do not turn around, otherwise you will be shot," the voice commanded gruffly. "Kneel down and place your hands behind your head."

Mat hesitated just long enough to glimpse the bridge. No help would be coming from that quarter, it seemed. The hologram had vanished and there was no sign of Bashir.

"Do it or die!" the voice hissed.

Mat placed his hands behind his head, but refrained from kneeling. It was a long-shot gamble, but his ploy was simple, and that was to rile the assailant standing behind him. Taking a prisoner, it seemed, held a high priority with this man, otherwise he would already be dead.

"Get on your knees!" The tone was more belligerent this time.

Using the man's voice as a gauge, Mat judged where his unseen foe stood. He continued to stand, ignoring the dictate. His only chance at survival was to remain standing.

"I said on your knees!" the man screamed in frustration.

The thing Mat hoped for came quickly. A gun muzzle prodded him harshly in the back. He had noted all the commandos carried an Uzi, a relatively short-barreled weapon. That meant his assailant would be just where he needed, and that was up close and personal.

Timing his move, Mat spun slightly off to one side with lightning quickness, catching the man squarely on the bridge of the nose with a raised elbow and sweeping his legs out from under him. It was a move he had practiced incessantly ever since learning it in the Seals, but this was actually the first time he had ever had an opportunity to use it.

Though stunned, the man squeezed hard on the Uzi trigger, but Mat had already deflected the barrel with the edge of his hand just enough to avoid being hit. The barrel felt like a hot poker as it discharged, but he ignored the pain as he got a firm grip on it. With his opponent momentarily blinded by the initial blow, Mat delivered half a dozen hammer-fists to the commando's face, turning it to a bloody pulp. Ripping the Uzi from his hands, Mat stood and stomped down hard with the heel of his boot, crushing that portion of the man's face left unprotected by his helmet. The commando went limp instantly, either dead or severely comatose.

A hand touched Mat's shoulder, and he spun around, ready to engage another foe, but there was no one there.

"Easy, Mat, it's me." Phillipe's persona suddenly materialized.

Mat looked around quickly, taking stock of the immediate area, then shoved Phillipe off to one side, a place of partial concealment behind some stacked crates. "What the hell are you doing?" he admonished harshly. "Turn your cloaker back on."

Phillipe's image winked out. "I think Bashir was hit."

Mat peeked around the side of a crate to survey the bridge, but there was no one in sight. "What makes you say that?"

"I saw him fall when these men opened fire on him."

Mat dropped his gaze to the three men he had taken out. They were still visible from his vantage point. "You get any more than the two I saw?"

"No," Phillipe's disembodied voice answered. "I saw no others."

Mat nodded, keeping a wary eye on his surroundings. "Then by my count, there's three left lurking about."

"Where's Kalid?" Phillipe asked.

"Out of the fight. He caught one in the leg, so I gave him my cloaker."

Poking his head around the crate, Mat espied the bridge again. "I've got to get up there."

"I'll go," Phillipe offered.

With a hand still on Phillipe's shoulder, Mat felt him begin to move. "When cows fly," he growled softly, yanking him back.

"But they can't see me," Phillipe protested.

"Forget it!"

"Then take my cloaker."

"Not an option. Jake would have my hide if anything happened to you under my watch."

"But-"

"End of discussion."

Mat risked another glimpse of the bridge, but all was quiet. "Stay here and be ready to give me cover fire in case all hell breaks loose. Don't try using the hologram, because it no longer seems to work on these clowns."

"Yes, I noticed." Phillipe grabbed Mat's arm before he could bolt for the stairs. "Is it possible some of these men are basically good? Are they not soldiers just following orders?"

"Anything's possible, kid, but I seriously doubt it. From what Ez has told me, Allotey and Alvarez have been responsible for the murder of innocents while working for the UN. I can only conclude that the men following them are just as bad."

"Then how is it possible they are unaffected by the hologram?"

Mat shook his head. "I wish I knew the answer, but right now we've got to get them before they get us."

That said, Mat pulled Phillipe's hand from his arm. Still holding the Uzi he had confiscated, he raced over to the last commando he had neutralized, pulling several spare magazine clips from the man's utility belt as well as a fragmentation grenade that hung conspicuously from it. Reloading the Uzi, he stuffed the remaining clips and grenade into the pouches of his own belt, all the while keeping a sharp eye on the bridge above.

Taking a deep breath, he leapt for the stairs. The adrenaline was already flowing swiftly in his veins, giving his legs added spring as he surged up the steps two at a time. The discussion he had just had with Phillipe hung in the back of his mind, and with an effort, he cast it aside. He was a warrior, and in the heat of battle a warrior did not try to analyze the enemy's moral rectitude, for to do so could get one killed.

Alvarez had come upon five of his men soon after his as yet unexplainable engagement with Allotey, ordering each of them to inject themselves with the drug cocktail. One man, the newest member of his team, was reluctant to follow the command, and Alvarez was forced to use harsher persuasion to make him obey, pointing his Uzi in a threatening manner.

Satisfied, Alvarez divided up his men, leaving three of them to take the ship's bridge from the outside while he and two others would use a more covert route to reach the helm. Just prior to this mission, he had been shown plans of the freighter and knew where to go. Finding the hatch, he sought near the bow, he and his men lifted the cover and climbed down a set of rungs that took them well below decks. After that, he led his team along a series of corridors before locating a circular stairwell that accessed ten decks above, the highest being the helm.

Reaching the top landing, Alvarez sidled up to the door that gave way to the bridge, craning his head around cautiously to view what lay on the other side of the door's small round window. He immediately drew his head back as a bout of gunfire suddenly erupted. The sound was muffled by the steel walls that surrounded him, but the distinct pinging of ricocheting rounds told him the bridge was being assaulted. More gunfire joined in, and then all was abruptly silent.

Alvarez risked another peek through the glass. A dark smile came to his face when he saw what lay beyond, and he shoved the door open with savage force. The bearded man that slumped against a far wall glanced lethargically at the sudden intrusion, apparently too weak or dazed to move. He was cupping a head wound that was bleeding profusely. Only one other person manned the bridge, a skinny, nervous looking individual who stood at the ship's controls, most likely the helmsman.

The helmsman turned ashen as Alvarez and his two subordinates stormed into the room.

Alvarez stepped close to the wounded man and kicked away the AK-47 that lay next to him. The man's hand fell away listlessly from the wound as his body sagged to the floor. Alvarez had seen enough battle casualties to know the injury was not a fatal one. From the look of it, a bullet had grazed the man's head, cutting a deep furrow across the scalp and possibly fracturing the skull.

The helmsman yelled out in pain and fright as one of the commandos grabbed him roughly by the arm and twisted it.

"Leave him and secure the bridge wings!" Alvarez ordered his men. He would need the helmsman to steer the ship.

One commando immediately scrambled for the larboard wing while the other let go of the helmsman and raced for the starboard side. Perched on the bridge wings, each man would have a commanding vantage of what lay below.

Alvarez pulled a pair of handcuffs from his utility belt and shoved the hijacker onto his stomach. An object strapped to the man's left wrist prevented one of the cuffs from being applied. Hastily he removed it, wondering what purpose it served. Putting it aside, he clicked the cuff into place, squeezing it tight enough to restrict the flow of blood. He was aching to use the corvo, but unfortunately his captive had lapsed into unconsciousness.

In annoyance, Alvarez flipped him onto his back and slapped his face several times to rouse him, but to no avail. The man was out cold. Needing answers, he looked over at the helmsman. "Where is your captain?"

"I…I don't know," the helmsman stammered. He appeared terrified.

Alvarez kept his face hard, though he smiled inwardly. He enjoyed invoking fear in others. "Tell me what you do know," he commanded in a foreboding tone. It was a voice he had perfected to instill trepidation.

The reply came out in a squeal not much different from a barnyard pig sent to the slaughterhouse. "They took him and the others below."

Alvarez was about to interrogate the man further when a single shot resounded outside. A quick glance through a port window showed the man he had stationed there stagger back from the overlook. The commando spun, looking back at him with lifeless eyes before collapsing. His lower jaw was gone, blown clean off.

Hunkering to one side of the port wing door, Alvarez nudged it open a crack to shout out a warning. "I have one of your men. Any attempt to come up here will be his death sentence."

Alvarez shut the door, looking behind him at the sound of footsteps. The other commando was scampering across the bridge to join him.

"Get back there!" Alvarez screamed. "Do you want them to come up behind us?"

The commando pulled up short, then ran back to cover the starboard door.

Alvarez assessed the developing situation, wondering if only one man remained under his command. If true, the odds had changed dramatically. It was something he had never anticipated.

Turning back to the helmsman, Alvarez posed a question. "Is your radio working?"

When the helmsman nodded, Alvarez issued a set of instructions to be carried out, all the while keeping vigilance of the port side bridge wing beyond the glass. He had only to wait less than a minute when the helmsman's radio transmission was answered. His pockmarked face broke out in a sinister grin when he heard the reply.

Phillipe spotted the movement on the larboard bridge wing immediately, seeing the commando lean over the bulwark to pick off Mat as he raced up the stairs. He had been prepared for such a possibility, and sighting accurately on the man's exposed face had required only a slight adjustment in his weapon's alignment.

Both Jay Jay and Mat had trained him well in handling firearms, spending several hours each week with him at Aquaria's firing range. The fact that he possessed remarkable eyesight, a trait inherited from his father, further enhanced his advancing skill as a marksman, and he had soon amazed his teachers with his shooting precision. But this was the first time he would actually fire at another human being, and he had only an inkling of a second to reconsider squeezing the trigger. Any delay on his part could result in Mat's demise.

Abruptly, the weapon bucked as though it had a mind of its own, catching Phillipe by surprise as a single round spewed forth. He clearly saw the target's head jerk back, disappearing from sight altogether. In that moment he knew it was a killing shot, and the thought saddened him. No matter how he rationalized it, he realized killing repulsed him.

The thoughts of Perseus reverberated in one corner of his mind. *Do not chastise yourself. You did what was necessary at the moment.*

I wish there had been another way, Phillipe rued.

Sometimes that is not possible.

Yes, Phillipe wanted to believe, his eyes continuing to scan the bridge wing as Mat climbed higher. Only one flight of steps needed to be ascended for Mat to reach the top, but Phillipe saw Mat suddenly pull up short. A voice rang out loud enough to be heard even from where Phillipe was positioned.

Inform the others Bashir has been taken prisoner, Phillipe advised Perseus, the thought dropping his spirits still lower. Bashir was like a brother to him, a kind and gregarious brother.

Perseus' response was equally downcast. *It has already been done.*

With an effort, Phillipe forced himself not to dwell on what he had just done, pondering their current situation instead. According to Mat, there should only be two commandos left, but with Bashir being held hostage, their opposition had the upper hand.

Perseus invaded his thoughts again. *I hate to be the bearer of more bad news, Phillipe, but Ez has just learned the mobilization of additional UN forces to the colony is proceeding much quicker than originally anticipated.*

How long? Phillipe replied.

Ez calculates twenty-four hours. Perseus followed up with more disturbing news. *Ez has intercepted a communique originating from this ship. Reinforcements have been requested and will arrive within the hour.*

This news unsettled Phillipe further, and he glanced briefly at Mat, who still remained one flight of stairs short of the bridge wing landing.

Currently lacking a bond mate of his own, Mat would not be privy to this newfound information.

Rising from his hunkered position, Phillipe headed for the stairs, relaying another thought to Perseus. *Mat must be told of this.*

Hunkered down on the staircase leading to the ship's bridge, Mat searched the sky. There was still no sign of the UN reinforcements Phillipe had apprised him about. He was at his rope's end, knowing time was running out. With Bashir's life hanging in the balance by the two remaining Chilean commandos, he didn't dare engage them.

"Seems we're at an impasse," Mat lamented.

"Maybe not," Phillipe said, purposely letting the statement hang to wet Mat's curiosity.

Mat turned to eye him, but with Phillipe's cloaker currently turned on, his young protégé remained invisible. "I'm listening."

"Ez managed to get hold of the ship's plans and relayed them to Perseus. Perseus knows an alternate route that can take us to the bridge. He'll guide us."

Mat shook his head. "Your plan is flawed, kid. More than likely they'll have the access door either locked or barricaded. Even with your invisibility, once that door begins to open the bullets will start flying."

"That's only part of the plan. Ez says she will take care of the rest."

Mat groaned inwardly, not fond of the idea that Ez was once again calling the shots. Ez was essentially a machine, and machines were not infallible. "What scheme has she come up with this time," he grumbled.

"I'll tell you on the way," Phillipe's disembodied voice answered. "Just follow me."

Mat felt a hand grip his shoulder, and begrudgingly he let himself be guided down the stairway.

Chapter Seventeen: Compromised

The familiar coastline rose up, haloed with silver and orange incandescence by the morning sun rising behind it. With the tide still high and only a mild sea breeze to deal with, Zimbola piloted the *Angel* smoothly into the tight opening in the barrier reef. The opening afforded only inches of clearance on both sides of the vessel, and had the water been lower, passage through it would have been impossible for the North Sea trawler. But with a small group of albino dolphins delineating the channel, Zimbola was able to avoid tearing open the vessel's keel on the jagged coral that thrived below the surface. And though he had traversed this precarious passage numerous times in the past, always guided by the dolphins, he nevertheless felt uneasy doing it.

Once through, Zimbola breathed a sigh of relief, giving thanks to Agwe, the Haitian sea god. Swinging the vessel ninety degrees to port, he skirted the craggy escarpments lining the shore. He was quite versed in the landscape's deceptiveness, for he knew the coastline would appear quite impenetrable to a person less familiar with its nuances. This, however, was an illusion, made even more so by a slight modification they had made to the shoreline.

Reaching for a small electronic device resembling a television remote, he leaned from the cabin and aimed it forward of the boat before thumbing one of the buttons. Almost immediately a huge section of rock began to rise upward, revealing an opening behind it. With deftness, he angled the craft into a cleft barely wide enough to accommodate it. Once his stern was clear, he activated the device again, causing the same formation of rock to slide back into its original position. A look at the backside of the rock showed it to be nothing more than a Hollywood prop, a false façade constructed of fiberglass and wood made to appear like part of the escarpment dominating the shore. This was something Jay Jay and the dolphins had designed and built as a precautionary measure in keeping interlopers out. Other security measures had been emplaced as well.

Rocky bluffs rose high on each side as Zimbola guided the *Angel* along a narrow waterway. Like the channel through the reef, the inlet provided the vessel only minimal clearance as it plodded slowly ahead. The Jamaican glanced up, waving in greeting at two men stationed atop the bluffs, one to a side. They manned camouflaged pillboxes that had been installed to repel attackers. They were denizens of the nearby village of Malique, part of a larger security force hired on to safeguard the inlet and what lay beyond.

Zimbola checked his watch, knowing a change of guard occurred every twelve hours. In another twenty minutes, the guard would be rotated. Continuing down the channel, he turned the wheel a few degrees to negotiate a slight dogleg in the waterway, which finally gave way to a sheltered basin of gin-clear water. It was a sequestered cove set in a gorge with steeply tiered sides that funneled down to the water from high above, giving it the shape of a crudely shaped though elongated amphitheatre.

Standing on the *Angel's* bow, both children stared in wonder at the incredible vista, a home away from home. The view was spectacular, appearing like something out of a fairytale. Like their mother and many of the dolphins, this was where they had been born, the place Jacob referred to as Gaia, a place they and the others affectionately called *The Cove*.

The eyes of the children were immediately drawn to the basin's far end. A natural spring gushed forth from the highest point along the rim, sending a plume of whitewater cascading down in a series of cataracts before making its longest and final plunge to the pristine water below. At such a distance, the waterfall roared soothingly, sending up a swirling mist that often displayed a rainbow when exposed to sunlight. With the sun still below the basin's rim, much of the vista was cast in shade. But even the shade could not subdue the explosion of color that abounded. It was a mecca alive with flora and fauna. A seemingly countless assortment of fruit-bearing trees and flowering shrubs in full bloom hugged narrow terraces set in the tiered slopes, and flitting among the lush vegetation were throngs of multi-colored songbirds and butterflies representing numerous species. A white sandy beach studded with palm trees ran along two-thirds of the water's edge, finally ending at the base of the falls. And nestled along one rocky alcove set back from the beach were three thatched structures that further adorned the panorama, the one on the left being built just prior to the birth of the twins.

Unable to constrain themselves a moment longer, both children leapt gleefully from the *Angel's* prow. They were immediately joined by their bond mates, Alpha and Omega, who whisked them off toward the falls.

"Children, wait!" Zimbola shouted from the wheelhouse, but from experience he knew it was an effort in futility trying to keep them aboard the vessel a second longer. A rare smile broke his features as he watched them race away. It was a game they often played to see who could reach the falls first. He was glad to see them frolic like this. Seeing their father in his present condition had made them uncharacteristically morose during the last few hours.

Standing at his side, Hector spoke up. "My money's on Melody this time."

"With those two, it is foolish to bet," Zimbola replied, knowing races such as this usually end in a tie.

Hector climbed down from the wheelhouse and moved forward toward the bow as Zimbola reversed the trawler's variable pitch prop. Grabbing a long gaffing pole, he stood at the ready as the 65-foot vessel eased to a stop where the cove was widest. In one smooth motion, he hooked the mooring ring they had installed years earlier, quickly connecting a shackle to the ring with a practiced hand. Pulling slack out of the mooring chain, he tugged sharply on it to make sure the one ton mooring block was firmly embedded in the sandy bottom.

Satisfied that the vessel was now secure, a sense of pride took hold of him. He had grown to love the *Angel.* And while he had to admit she was not a comely looking craft, he saw resilience in every battered inch of her, a seaworthy vessel that dripped with character. Like both her owners, those being Jay Jay and Zimbola, she was tough, durable, and reliable, a boat you could always depend on. As he reflected on these things, he considered her name. Though they all referred to her as the

Angel, it wasn't her full name. Not the name painted on her stern in big block letters.

AVENGING ANGEL.

Hector had mulled this strange contradiction whenever he looked upon her with the same adoration as he was doing now, always coming to the same conclusion. The name fully mirrored Jay Jay's dual nature. It implied a strong sense of justice, a live and let live attitude that sought to keep those he cared for safe from peril. With those around him unthreatened and out of harm's way, his friend and boss was basically a Teddy Bear at heart, generous to a fault. But menace those he loved in any way, and he was capable of becoming a holy terror without mercy, risking life and limb in a near reckless manner in order to protect them.

Hector dropped these thoughts, looking up to scan the upper elevations of the chasm and waving. Sentries had come out of their positions of concealment. There were four of them waving back, each manning a strategically located station separated from the others and set up to defend both the cove and the airspace above. He knew all these men. They were locals who had been carefully screened and found to be good, trustworthy people. They were fully committed, heart and soul, to the grand scheme concocted by Jacob and the pod. They would not fall victim to greed or be tempted by the secrets the cove held. And most of all, they looked upon Destiny and her mother as though they were goddesses. He had no doubts they would fight to the death on their behalf.

Hector smiled, remembering the last two attempts Cardoza and his ruffians had made on this place following the establishment of security measures, with each attempt ending in a dismal failure. He knew the lure of gold made men do crazy things, but with the Colombian drug lord it was an obsession, and he was convinced Cardoza would try again.

Making his way to the stern, Hector saw Destiny emerge from the rear cabin, a vision of stunning loveliness in spite of the troubled look on her face. So beautiful, he thought, and yet she has no awareness of her own physical beauty. It was an innocent thought, devoid of lust, for he viewed the inner beauty that dwelled deep within her to be her most alluring quality. It radiated outward to touch all those around her like warm rays of the sun, and it was this that made him adore her. She was the perfect match for Jay Jay, a man unlike other men.

Destiny turned to face him with damp eyes. "I'll be going ashore, Hector. Please stay with Jay Jay."

Hector nodded, feeling her pain. "Jay Jay is tough. If anyone can survive such an injury, it will be Jay Jay."

Destiny turned quickly and dove for the water, not wanting Hector to see the tears spilling from her eyes. She was immediately joined by Hercules, who carried her in the direction of the falls.

Hector watched her go, suddenly aware that Zimbola and Fernando had also come out on deck to see her off.

"What is she doing?" Fernando asked.

"She looks for answers," Zimbola said. Though he had never climbed behind the falls, he had an inkling of what lay up there.

Mat and Phillipe made their way through the *Southern Star's* interior, locating the stairwell that led up to the helm. Reaching the door that accessed the bridge, Mat risked a peek through the door's Plexiglas window. A quick glance was all he needed to assess the situation.

Off to one side, Bashir lay unconscious, bound hand and foot. Crouched next to him with a shoulder to the port wing door was Alvarez. The remaining commando guarded the starboard wing door, and standing frozen at the helm was a skinny individual who appeared terrified.

Mat ducked down just as Alvarez whipped his head around to take stock of the access door. In that fleeting moment of surveillance, he could tell Alvarez was rattled. Certainly, that would make sense with ten of his men now out of the fight. The captain's head was in constant motion, swiveling back and forth nervously to take darting glances through the bridge windows in all directions. He was taking inventory of everything around him, especially the skies as he looked anxiously for the arrival of reinforcements.

Mat tested the door latch, surprised that it moved. Hefting the grenade he had taken from the last mercenary, he handed it to Phillipe. "You ready?" he asked.

Phillipe nodded, seemingly eager to get on with this. With the assistance of Ez, they had worked out a plan with only a slim chance of success at saving Bashir, but with UN reinforcements on the way, they dared not delay any longer.

A low buzzing came to their ears, the sound quickly growing louder. Mat risked another peek through the door's window. Alvarez was looking upward, his attention drawn to the source of the sound.

In that instant the ship listed precariously to starboard, but Mat was prepared as the deck tilted sharply underfoot. Flinging the door open, he lurched into the room and let loose with the Uzi, throwing a hail of rounds at the commando stationed at the starboard wing door. That was his immediate option, since he risked hitting Bashir had he fired directly at Alvarez. Completely caught off guard by the combination of distractions, the commando went down before he could even level his weapon. But even before he fell, Mat dove for cover behind a nearby console, taking away any opportunity for Alvarez to have a target.

Scooting through the door right behind Mat, Phillipe tossed the grenade toward Alvarez, who had lost his balance by the sudden roll of the ship. Almost at once, the ship swung back onto an even keel, and as it did so, the Chilean captain's eyes widened in horror at seeing the grenade bouncing across the floor. In a flash he was on his feet, ripping open the nearby door like a madman and scrambling out onto the port side bridge wing.

With his cloaker turned on, Phillipe remained invisible. He raced for the same door, bringing his weapon to bear on the back of his fleeing quarry, but some deep seated inhibition kept him from pulling back on the trigger. In that brief moment of inner conflict, Alvarez scrambled down the stairs, disappearing from sight.

Phillipe was nearly knocked down as Mat crashed into his unseen form. "You're letting him get away," Mat yelled, shoving past and giving chase. Bounding for the stairs, Mat stopped short of the first step, pointing his weapon below and firing. A shower of sparks kicked up as ricocheting rounds pinged harshly but harmlessly off steel. Alvarez was already past the next landing down, effectively shielded from the volley.

Frustrated, Mat turned to look back at Phillipe. "Get Bashir to the chopper!"

Phillipe deactivated his cloaker to become visible again. "Where are you going?"

"I've got to get Kalid."

"We'll wait for you."

Mat glanced upward to scan the sky. "There's no time, and besides, the chopper can only hold four," he lied hurriedly, knowing it could actually carry five. "I'll have Abdel pick us up. Now get going."

"But… "

"Do as I say, this is not open to discussion."

Before Phillipe could protest further, Mat vanished down the stairs.

Destiny stopped working her way up the craggy escarpment momentarily to make sure the twins were not following. They still sat astride their bond mates at the base of the falls where she had left them. Nevertheless, there was no mistaking the inquisitiveness in their eyes as they gazed back at her, their minds at wonder with what lay up there. Ever since they could walk, she had forbidden them from ever going behind the falls. She had made it clear that the place was strictly off limits. But deep down she knew it was only a matter of time before their curiosity got the better of them, ultimately making them disobey. After all, how could she expect them to obey such a mandate when she herself had gone against her own mother's wishes on this same issue at an early age. Behind the falls lurked unexplained mystery. Within its darkened recesses lay a strange intangible power that beckoned her every so often as it was doing now. But it had been quite some time since she had last come here. Jay Jay had been with her during that visit.

She smiled fondly at the memory. In the deepest recess of this place was where the twins had been conceived.

Climbing higher, she pulled herself onto a stone ledge that wound behind the plunging water. The roar was deafening. Staying focused, she dug fingers and toes into small cracks and crevices within the moss covered rock to keep from slipping. Though the climb was difficult and treacherous, she had done it many times before, ascending fairly quickly. Rounding a bend, she entered the cave, letting her eyes adjust to the semi-darkness before reaching for the flashlight tied to her waist and turning it on.

The cave widened as she went further back, and once again she noted the familiar array of artifacts lining the base of both walls as she passed. She held the flashlight low to avoid looking at the repugnant displays situated above the artifacts. A montage of murals covered the sides of the cavern. They had been painted by an unknown artist from ages past, and elaborately depicted within those murals were horrific atrocities inflicted on the Tainos by bearded men clad in armor. The Tainos had been a gentle and giving people native to Hispanola, but they had been quickly enslaved and nearly wiped out by arriving Europeans who hungered for gold.

The scenes within the murals had shocked her the first time she had laid eyes on them. Growing up in a place filled with wondrous beauty and sheltered from the outside world, she was unprepared to acknowledge a side of the human species she never knew existed until that moment. The paintings captured a broad range of abject human suffering and death quite explicitly, with frightening portrayals of starvation and emaciation on exhibit. Natives being used for slave labor were subjected to the lash and being hung by the neck. These along with decapitations and other grisly sights had been too much for her naïve young mind to bear, and seeing such abominations for the first time had caused tears to flow unabated down her cheeks. Thereafter, she had avoided looking upon them whenever she ventured into the cave.

Such depictions had been the primary reason for making this place off limits to the children, for they revealed too many inhumane horrors she considered unhealthy for young minds.

Destiny moved deeper into the grotto. The cave narrowed just beyond the last of the dispiriting murals, and a jumble of fallen rock came under the flashlight's glare. Stepping carefully between some boulders, she slipped sideways into a fissure before ascending a series of steps that had been carved into the rock. The stairway rose steeply a short distance, and in moments she emerged into the center of a large chamber. Like the steps, the chamber had also been chiseled out of solid rock, for it was much too smooth and uniform in configuration to have been formed naturally. With a height of twelve feet from floor to ceiling, it formed a perfect square, twenty feet to a side. This was where she and Jay Jay had made love the very first time.

The roar of the falls had faded to a soft susurration where she now stood. With eyes lowered and the flashlight pointed down, she took a deep breath, preparing herself for whatever might be revealed, for she knew this place was much more than a room sculpted from solid rock. It was a portal.

Feeling ready, she aimed the flashlight at one of the walls. A small gasp escaped her throat at what she saw. The painting overlaying the wall had changed. It no longer showed her pregnant mother in a storm tossed sea as she clung to the dorsal fin of the gray bottlenose dolphin that had saved her. She remembered every detail of that old mural, for it had accurately depicted an actual event in her mother's life. The dolphin was Athena, who was to become her mother's bond mate. The bodies of both had been severely welted, the result of coming into contact with strange oblate jellyfish. It was this happening that had ultimately set the stage for the emergence of the new breed and the building of Aquaria, or so they all believed.

But now the scene was gone, replaced by one of Jake taking on Colonel Ternier's small army of thugs at Navassa Island. Under the glow of a bonfire burning eerily at the base of the lighthouse, he stood fast, a look of grim determination etched on his face as he mowed down fifteen men with the assault weapon held firmly in his hands. This was a side of her husband she had learned to accept, for had he not turned into a killing machine on that dreadful night, she would surely have perished at the hands of Erzulie, Ternier's vengeful mother.

Destiny studied the mural a moment longer before illuminating the wall immediately to the left. That painting had also changed. It no longer showed her mother tenderly cradling an infant in her arms while standing waist-deep in water. The baby had been Destiny. The cove's waterfall had been displayed in the background, serenely gushing whitewater as Athena floated next to her with a newborn calf of her own, having given birth at the same moment as her mother. The calf had been Natalie, the very first of her marvelous species.

But instead of showing these things, the mural overlaying the entire wall showed a majestic panorama of Aquaria in its present state viewed from afar. It was partly shrouded in mist, and arched directly over it was a rare sight. It was a perfect representation of the double rainbow bridge she and the twins had witnessed just prior to visiting her mother in the subterranean cavern on Navassa. Behind it lay Navassa Island with the old lighthouse visible. East of the island in the mural's upper right corner was an enormous oil tanker, which she suspected to be the Kraken, judging from its relative size and configuration. One final aspect caught her eye. A luxury mega-yacht lurked in the foreground in the lower left corner. It seemed to resemble quite distinctly a vessel they had passed on their way to the cove.

Eager to scrutinize the next wall, she turned to her left, no longer expecting to view the small pod of albino dolphins plowing through the sea, six of them surrounding her and Hercules in a hexagon formation. In its place was a rendering of the Russian Hind being inexorably pulled into the sea by two blue whales, Jay Jay's body dangling limply from its fuselage as it strained to stay aloft.

Destiny pondered the first three murals, each portraying an event that had already transpired. The renderings they had replaced had also depicted events that had previously occurred when she had first come upon them years earlier. Back then, the fourth wall had shown her something that had not yet taken place, and that had shown Jay Jay on his waverunner as he gave chase to Ortega's helicopter, firing upon it with his Stoner. Based on the sequence of previous displays, it stood to reason that the fourth wall would also portray a future event.

Taking a deep breath, she braced herself in preparation for what was to be revealed. Tears immediately welled up in her eyes, but they were not tears of anguish. They were tears of joy.

The mural showed an underwater scene. Centered within it was Jay Jay, seemingly fully recovered as he rode Achilles. She and the twins were shown a short distance away, each astride their own bond mate as they kept pace with him. Below them was a coral reef teeming with life, and directly ahead was a broad dark hole situated beneath an overhang blanketed with anemones and red sponge. Intruding its way into one side of the hole was the transparent access tube that connected with the offshore berthing platform. She knew the place well. It was a section of reef abutting the entrance to the subterranean dolphin sanctuary that lay hidden below the Navassa lighthouse.

She knew she was viewing something that had not previously occurred. Two items within the scene told her this. Strapped to Jay Jay's right thigh was the USP-9 submachine pistol he routinely wore whenever imminent danger was close at hand. She could not recall him ever wearing it during prior visits to the cavern. Secondly, a hail of ropey white spumes appeared to reach for them from above. She recognized what those spumes represented. The water was being peppered with a hail of bullets, but the liquid medium was making their lethal velocities ineffectual, causing the rounds to quickly slow and sink harmlessly away. Someone was giving chase and shooting at them from the surface.

An odd sound suddenly caught Destiny's attention, making her stiffen. Someone was summoning her. The voice was barely audible, touching the surrounding air in a soft sibilant whisper, but there was no mistaking its meaning.

"*Destiny!*" it called.

Glancing around sharply, she looked for the caller, unsure if she had imagined it. The thought that it was a mental cue evoked by one of the dolphins was abruptly dismissed as the voice summoned her again, this time more lucidly.

"*Destiny!*" it repeated.

She became aware of the background hiss of the falls, its low susurration now rising in volume, and instinctively she knew the plunging water was the source of the voice. The mysterious presence that dwelled within this strange domain was calling to her.

"You must believe in yourself, my child. Do not lose faith, for you are still the person you have always been."

"Please show yourself!" Destiny petitioned.

"Look upon the wall before you and I will reveal myself!" the voice instructed.

Destiny heeded the command, not surprised to see the mural change before her eyes. A vision of Esmerelda slowly took form, her face alive with compassion.

"You have helped us before," Destiny said. "Can you help us again?"

"All that you need lies within you," Esmerelda answered. *"You must never stop believing in yourself."*

"It is as though the entire world is against us," Destiny deplored helplessly.

Esmerelda spread her arms wide. A vision of the earth as seen from space abruptly materialized behind her. *"Do not mistake the unfolding of recent events to be caused by the aggregate of humanity. What you have so far witnessed is part of a specific predetermined plan enacted by a small band of powerful brokers acting behind closed doors. These brokers are ruled by a puppet master of immense wealth who is answerable to no one and seeks to destroy Aquaria and all it stands for. He chooses and controls many international leaders to carry out his nefarious goals, much of which is aimed at manipulating the global economy in order to amass more power and wealth."*

"How do we overcome that?"

Esmerelda smiled benevolently, a halo of stardust surrounding her face. *"By believing, my child. You must simply believe."*

"A dream continues to plague me each night," Destiny bewailed. "It reveals a great dark force bearing down on Aquaria. It blocks out the sun and appears to be unstoppable."

"Yes, I know, my child. It is an enormous sea monster controlled by the puppet master. But like all entities of a dark nature, they risk being destroyed by the very evil they spawn."

Destiny let out a frustrated sigh. "I have been compromised. My powers have been corrupted through my own doing. Without them, believing in anything seems futile."

Esmerelda shook her head. *"You deceive yourself, child. Your unconditional love for those around you has made you even stronger. It is a source of great power. It binds all of you together and is the foundation of unblemished faith."*

Destiny continued to feel dispirited. "All we have strived for is lost. It is difficult to hope for something that is no longer possible."

Esmerelda continued to smile, remaining resolute. *"Have faith. Hope is something not seen. You must have patience and steadfastness, continuing to believe with all your being until the belief is physically manifested. Once you possess it, all is possible."*

Destiny felt strangely lifted by Esmerelda's words, though pessimism still plagued her. "I'll try," was all she could think to say.

"There is no try. Maintain a singleness of heart, never letting negative thoughts take charge of you, for such thoughts will bring on fear and doubt. Faith and fear will always be at war, so you must choose one or the other. But the choice is simple when you realize faith will always overcome fear."

Destiny took pause to dwell on the words. She had led a sheltered life growing up in the cove, relatively unaffected by the outside world with all its problems. But the arrival of Jay Jay had introduced a new set of circumstances into her life, with a growing sense of fear being one of them. She had feared for the pod, for Jay Jay, for her children, for everyone she loved. And she feared for Aquaria. She had fallen victim to this primitive though intrinsic human emotion, letting it take control of her reality. She saw it clearly now, recognizing its damaging influence, yet she still had trouble letting it go.

"If only I had your conviction," she found herself saying.

"You must cleanse your mind of the fear that shackles it," Esmerelda stressed. *"Once you do this, you will realize you are a spiritual being with incredible powers. Only then will you fully understand that you and all those you love are deathless souls having a physical experience. Like those magnificent creatures to whom you are forever linked, you were brought into this world to fulfill a profound purpose. Just believe in yourself and all that you wish for will follow."*

"I wish you were still here with us," Destiny said wistfully.

Esmerelda's face lit up in an enigmatic grin. *"Oh, but I am, child. As long as you keep me in your heart, I will always be with you."* The grin turned solemn and she turned her broad face as if to espy something in the distance. *"Danger approaches. You must hurry."*

Before Destiny could voice a question, Esmerelda spoke again. "*I see mismatched orbs coming your way. If the cove is to remain unscarred from the ravages of man, those orbs must not be terminated.*"

Destiny wrapped her mind around the riddle, trying to make sense of it, but Esmerelda had more to add. "*There is one more thing. Someone you once knew will return to help fight against the forces that seek to destroy Aquaria.*"

"Who?"

"*You must be strong, child, as I ask you to look above.*"

Destiny aimed her flashlight at the roof of the chamber and gazed upward, her heart beating wildly at what she saw. The word that left her lips came out in a startled cry. "No!"

"No!" she repeated, bringing her eyes back to Esmerelda, but Esmerelda was now gone.

Chapter Eighteen:
T-Crystals

Without knowing why, Harriet Grahm was suddenly drawn to a few crystals lying atop a workbench. These were what she and the dolphins had nicknamed T-crystals. There were four of them, each about two inches in height in the shape of a four-sided pyramid. Seconds earlier they had begun to pulsate once again, shedding excess energy in the form of violet light. But this time the light was even more intense than before, and the frequency had increased. Puzzled, she stared in contemplation, wondering what was causing them to react like this. Without immersion in a marine environment the crystals should have remained dormant. These were some of the latest crystals brought up from a depth of 950 feet by Hermes a few hours ago, retrieved near the base of one of the gargantuan *thurentra* directly beneath the floating city. Every so often these same *thurentra* produced a few of them that were all identical, emulating the way their smaller cousins specialized in producing a product of their own. The crystals were peculiar in the way they acted. They absorbed sound waves and tended to distort sonar originating from a submarine or other prying object from getting a clear picture of the immense organisms that provided nitrogen-rich cold water to Aquaria's OTEC generators. Crystals like these could be grown larger and made to function as power inducers. All you needed was to run saline water over them and they gathered in the energy the water held, seemingly able to amplify that energy many times over before unleashing it. The larger the crystal, the more power it would provide. The albinos had theorized the crystals operated on a principle of quantum entanglement, claiming their extraordinary molecular lattices were attuned to a higher dimension and able to pick up vibrations where energy was either subtle or readily available. Up to now, every test she and the dolphins had run on these extraordinary gems had proved unsuccessful, thus their precise molecular composition had remained a mystery. That particular fact was unimportant to her, however, for like the new breed of dolphin and *thurentra*, she believed T-crystals were yet another gift provided by the living planetary system called Gaia.

Though she had trouble understanding the principle, she knew these crystals had so far been put to good use. The albinos had incorporated them into the hydrodrive that provided *Johnnie* its incredible thrust. They were also the primary components in the PWIs - Pressure Wave Inhibitors – the dolphins had developed once the mysterious explosions started occurring on the nearby reefs. Unfortunately, these same crystals could be a bit twitchy and sometimes did strange things just as they were doing right now, and she suspected the four crystals that lay before her were picking up the anxiety she felt.

Staring a few moments longer at the crystals, she grabbed two of them, pocketing them in a pouch strapped to her waist. Why she needed them she could not explain, but she knew they were destined for some arcane purpose.

Working in her lab deep under Navassa Island, Harriet knew something was wrong hours earlier. It was a budding sense of approaching disaster. But it had been Athena that brought form and substance to her mounting dread on the mental link they shared. Jake's dire predicament had been relayed over the pod's telepathic network, ultimately reaching her through Athena. It was then that she had been besieged by a strange notion.

Without hesitation, she contacted Ez via the facility intercom. "Ez, I need you to turn off the pumps to Big D."

Ez answered immediately, though she sounded puzzled. "Is there a problem?"

"No problem," Harriet said. "I only need them off for a few minutes at most. Please open the hatch. I'll explain later."

"As you wish," Ez said.

Riding Athena down to the lowest level of the submerged structure, Harriet saw the hatch was already open. With the flow of hundreds of tons of seawater that was moving every second now halted, she and Athena were able to safely enter the large chamber, and a moment later they floated before a set of massive crystals. Spaced equidistantly, six of them formed a hexagonal ring that surrounded a seventh crystal. Each of the crystals comprising the hexagon was in the shape of a four-sided pyramid that was equal in size to its neighbors. Unlike the crystals that ringed it, however, the center crystal was three times larger in volume and formed a perfect three-sided pyramid. A subdued violet glow emanated from the outer pyramids, while the center pyramid emitted a soothing crimson light.

It was the albinos that had theorized and constructed this configuration of crystals, certain they would eventually interact to become a promising source of enormous power. These, too, had been harvested from the deep-lying *thurentra* by Hermes when construction of Aquaria was in its infancy, and like Aquaria, they had grown progressively larger as the floating city had mushroomed in size.

Harriet stared transfixed at the center crystal before leaving her mount and swimming above it. So far, this was the only one of its kind produced by the huge *thurentra*, a three-sided pyramid brought up from depth. Like the four crystals on her workbench, it had also started out small. Tentatively, she placed a hand on its apex, finding it warm to the touch. The reaction she had hoped for did not come. Disappointed, she withdrew her hand. She knew all the crystals were still growing and had not yet reached the size the colony would need. Feeling helpless, she was suddenly struck by another notion, and straddling Athena once again, she left the chamber and headed for the structure's outer perimeter, requesting that Athena take her to one of the gold-harvesting *thurentra*.

Closing her thoughts to her bond mate, she hovered off to one side of the pumpkin-like organism, and before Athena could intervene, extended an arm to make contact with it. Unlike her daughter, she did not possess Destiny's ability to withstand a severe electric charge, let alone store it. She knew she was risking her life, for the electrical discharge of a *thurentra* could be fatal.

Something flashed before her eyes, and she felt her heart catch in her chest before an acute sense of vertigo set in. The disorientation passed quickly, supplanted by a distant memory that flooded her consciousness. Overwhelmed by the sheer intensity of it, she found herself back in that tumultuous sea, waves toppling all around her. Without warning, a sheer mountain of water crashed down to drag her under, tumbling her into those luminous searing tentacles she well remembered. All at once her body stiffened as the burning fires of hell took hold of her.

Another moment passed before the vision faded, leaving her staring off into space. Vaguely she felt Athena under her. Something was happening to her, something she couldn't explain. She only knew she had to get back to Aquaria with all the speed she could muster.

Alvarez was nowhere to be seen as Mat reached the main deck at the bottom of the stairs. Nevertheless, he ducked down behind a stack of crates and took in his surroundings with extreme vigilance. It suddenly occurred to him that he should have taken Phillipe's cloaker, but in his haste he had not thought to do so.

One thing made him smile, however, and that was Alvarez falling for one of the oldest tricks in modern times of war. Thinking the grenade was armed and ready to explode, the Chilean captain had bolted from the bridge like a gazelle running for its life with a cheetah hot on its tail. But Mat had taken the time to disarm it on his way to the helm, carefully unscrewing the detonator and removing it. Two other diversions had also contributed to the ruse, and that was the perfectly timed arrival of the helicopter in unison with the whales rocking the ship. With begrudging respect, he had to give Ez her due, for her plan had succeeded admirably.

Mat moved cautiously, making his way further astern and wondering if Phillipe was up to the task of carrying Bashir up another flight of steps to the helipad situated directly over the bridge. Abruptly he chastised himself. The youth was in exceptional physical condition, well endowed with a muscular physique made all the more powerful by daily weight training sessions and cardiovascular workouts involving running and biking along Aquaria's promenades and breakwaters.

As if to allay his concerns, Mat heard the buzz of the chopper gain strength. Looking up, he caught a fleeting glimpse of the Bell Ranger swing out over the water as it lifted off, its pilot astutely choosing the starboard side of the vessel for a departure. Since Alvarez had fled to the ship's larboard side, it was only logical the starboard sector would present less risk in drawing fire. And he knew the pilot would not have taken off unless both Bashir and Phillipe were aboard.

Mat suddenly halted as he listened to the drone of the chopper. Something was not quite right. Instead of the sound receding, it rose in volume. A narrow opening between two containers gave him a clue as to what was happening. Instead of taking a flight path directly back to Aquaria, the aircraft had circled back and was now on a heading that would take it to the Haitian coast.

Mat had no time to mull this unanticipated circumstance, though he had an inkling as to the reason. He was simply thankful that Phillipe and Bashir were now off the freighter. Moving swiftly, he found the darkened niche where he had left Kalid, calling out in a whisper before exposing himself to the opening. "It's me, Kalid. Don't shoot!"

Kalid answered, though he sounded weak. "I hear you."

Mat entered the niche. "Turn off your cloaker!"

Kalid's form materialized, and Mat could see his condition had deteriorated since he had left him. "What happened?" Kalid asked.

"Save your strength," Mat murmured, "we're getting off the ship."

Mat pulled out his cell phone, bringing it to his lips and speaking quietly. "Ez, do you read me?"

"Loud and clear," Ez responded.

"Is Abdel still standing by?"

"Yes, Mat."

"Have him pick us up amidships on the freighter's port side."

Mat had only to wait a few seconds before Ez came back. "He's on the way. ETA is three minutes twenty-two seconds."

"Thanks, Ez." Mat stopped short of re-pocketing the phone as Ez's voice came back again. "Perseus tells me there's no ladder at that location."

Mat checked his wristwatch, gauging the time. "We'll have to jump."

"My sensors are picking up another aircraft approaching your position. More than likely it carries the UN reinforcements requested by Alvarez."

"How long?"

"Assuming no unanticipated factors throwing off my calculations, you should be on your way out of there just before they set down on the ship."

Mat continued to monitor the time, counting off the seconds. "By the way, Ez, why is our chopper heading toward Haiti?"

Ez's reply confirmed Mat's own appraisal. "Her pilot believes she will have a better chance of reviving Bashir if she goes there."

Mat nodded absently. "Does this ship present a danger to Aquaria on its present course of drift?"

"No," said Ez. "Even if the wind changes direction, the whales will keep it well away."

Mat thought about how he had been able to disable the *Southern Star's* engines. He had used the T-BEMP Generator carried aboard the sub, a device developed by the dolphins. T-BEMP stood for Tight Beam Electromagnetic Pulse, and the generator that emitted it was capable of frying the electronic circuitry that operated the ship's engines. And with its engines now inoperable, the freighter was a drifting hulk.

With that last thought, Mat poked his head out of the niche to make sure Alvarez was not lurking about. Turning, he checked his watch again before eyeing Kalid. "Okay, partner, time for a hasty retreat," he said, hauling the injured man to his feet and supporting him.

Awkwardly, he half-carried him down a corridor that opened up at the ship's rail. Just as Ez had estimated, the sub rose above the water at the predicted time.

Kalid grimaced as Mat helped him over the rail. "After you, my friend," Mat uttered, giving him a smile of encouragement.

Kalid looked down with his back to the railing, not liking the drop to which he would subject himself. He was fearful of heights and the water was fifty feet below him.

"Look, there's dolphins down there waiting to help you," Mat urged.

Just as he finished saying that, something parted Mat's hair a split second before a burst of gunfire reached his ears. Whipping his head around, he glimpsed movement along the ship's rail 100 meters forward of where he now stood. He immediately recognized Alvarez.

"Go!" Mat yelled, giving Kalid a violent shove and sending him plummeting to the water with arms flailing.

Another burst ensued, and an enfilade of rounds zinged off a cargo container further astern. Mat spun, letting loose with a volley of his own and emptying the clip. He fired high, knowing the Uzi he held had limited range. Rounds sparked close to his target, and he saw Alvarez duck back between containers. Since Alvarez also carried the same type of weapon, he knew his adversary's sallies would lack sufficient accuracy from where he was positioned.

Mat ripped out the Uzi's spent clip and replaced it, glancing down at the water as he did so. An albino had Kalid in its grasp and had brought him to the side of the sub's small conning tower. Sluggishly, Kalid climbed the rungs. Someone poked their head above the hatch and reached out to haul Kalid in headfirst, and Mat saw that it was Samuel, a strapping Haitian youth two years younger than Phillipe.

Still at distance, Alvarez poked his head from the side of a container, prepared to fire again, but Mat held him at bay, squeezing off another withering burst and emptying the clip. Seeing Alvarez withdraw his head, Mat shifted his gaze to the sub once more. Kalid's feet disappeared down the hatch, and a moment later Samuel's upper torso reemerged.

Mat yelled at the top of his lungs. "Get the sub away from the ship!" Frantically, he waved an arm to warn him away.

Samuel seemed to understand, nodding before lowering his head to shout down into the sub to relay the command to Abdel at the controls. Rounds began peppering the water around the sub, some of them pinging off its steel hull and causing Samuel to vanish from view. Abruptly a hand snaked up to swing the hatch closed, and all too slowly the sub began to move. Seconds passed as it gained speed alongside the freighter's hull, taking on a heading toward Alvarez's position before veering away. Sparks flew as more rounds collided with its conning tower, but otherwise had little effect.

Mat reloaded the Uzi with his remaining clip, pointing the weapon in his foe's direction and firing until it was spent. Throwing down the firearm, he immediately vaulted over the rail, aware that one of the grays was there to assist him as he splashed harshly into the sea. Grabbing the dolphin's dorsal fin, he was whisked below the surface and away from the ship.

At a safe distance, the gray resurfaced. Mat inhaled deeply, continuing to hold on as the dolphin caught up with the sub, now a quarter mile from the *Southern Star* with its engine at idle and only its conning tower jutting above the water. Once aboard the sub, Mat glanced up to espy at least twenty chutes flaring open as additional blue helmeted troops descended toward the ship. Mat battened down the hatch to the conning tower, glad to be off the freighter, but contemplating his next course of action.

Jake found himself scaling a steep precipice, groping about for handholds on the craggy surface. A shadowy gloom lay all about him and only a pinpoint of light directly above gave him a sense of orientation.

"Your cause is lost," someone close by mocked. "You will fail just as we did."

Jake knew that voice. Looking below, he saw Yeslam Raduyev clinging to the rock. He discerned other forms climbing up from the void, and instinctively he knew who they were. Colonel Ternier and Erzulie were following, and next to them he sensed Sebastian Ortega.

"You are going to die!" they chorused with sadistic glee.

Jake saw Erzulie's arm lash out as she hurled something, and he caught sight of a cobra rising up, its jaws opening wide to sink deadly fangs into him. Lethargy suddenly immobilized him, and he felt too weak to bat it away before it could land.

A hand abruptly shot out to snare the snake before it could strike, and Jake knew it was not his own hand that had saved him. Surprised, he looked to his right to see Amphitrite holding fast to a crevice beside him, the snake writhing wildly as she clutched it just behind the head.

Amphitrite gave him a comforting glance before turning her gaze below. "You cannot hurt him," she said in a calm but resolute voice. "Be gone you vile witch!" Effortlessly, she flung the cobra back down. Erzulie screamed hideously, letting go of the rock and tumbling into the void as the cobra tore into her neck.

"Get him!" Ortega raged, taking charge to rally the others.

Jake tried to scramble higher, but his arms felt numb.

"I've got your back, good buddy. Just keep going and pay no attention to these bastards."

Jake looked to his left, amazed to see Myers next to him. Myers gave him a reassuring smile, appearing to enjoy the prospect of a good fight the way he always did. As Raduyev reached for Jake's ankle, Myers stomped down hard with a heel, catching the Chechen square in the face. The blow reopened the old wound marring Raduyev's cheek, causing a small fountain of blood to spurt. The Chechen stubbornly held fast to a niche in the rock, glaring up at Myers with utter hatred. Myers kicked down again, and this time Raduyev let out a harsh grunt before falling away into the blackness.

With equal dispatch, Myers did the same to both Ternier and Ortega, and Jake saw them plummet, their screams trailing away.

Jake felt a modicum of strength flowing into his arms and he pulled himself higher. Suddenly aware that Myers was not following, he stopped and looked down. "You coming?" he asked.

Myers grinned. "Sorry Jake, but you know that's not possible." He looked above to glimpse the pinpoint of light. "Now get going, you big lummox. Others await you!"

Jake started to climb, but Myers called to him again. "And Jake…"

"Yes."

"Thanks for keeping your promise. Phillipe has grown into a fine young man."

"He came from good stock," Jake replied.

"Take care of yourself, buddy, and don't be reckless like I was."

With that said, Myers' image began to fade before disappearing completely.

"I'll try," Jake muttered sadly, feeling the loss of his friend all over again.

Climbing higher, Jake realized Amphitrite was no longer with him as well, but he heard another voice, though it was still far away. "Hurry!" it beckoned.

Jake suddenly felt lethargic again as he strived for the light. "I don't think I can make it," he answered back weakly. He felt his remaining strength rapidly ebbing. Speaking was becoming difficult now, and his arms and fingers were starting to give out.

Yes, you can, a familiar presence encouraged.

Jake felt Achilles catch him just as he lost his grip on the rock.

Hold onto me, Achilles instructed.

"My strength is gone," Jake gasped.

Draw strength from me and hold on.

"Then you won't be able to make the climb," Jake objected feebly.

Others are channeling their energies to you, Achilles replied.

Jake felt a sudden surge of energy flow into him. With renewed strength, he gripped the leading edge of Achilles' pectoral fins, holding on tight as the dolphin used its powerful prehensile extensions to haul them up the craggy wall, hastening their ascent. In moments the pinpoint of light expanded and brightened, and Jake became aware that he was hearing more than one voice.

"Jay Jay!"

The combined sound conveyed urgency, echoing off into the void. An arm extended from the light, reaching down for him and pulling him up.

Jake opened his eyes to find Destiny withdrawing her lips from his. He discovered he was immersed in water, buoyed up by Achilles and three other dolphins.

"Thank god you're back with us again," she cried. Her cheeks were streaked with tears and she appeared physically drained.

"I saw your mother," Jake said. "She helped me. And so did Myers."

Troy Jacob and Melody were suddenly hugging him fiercely. "We were so worried," they chirped in unison, "but Mum and the dolphins were able to make the cut on your head disappear." Melody placed a hand on his temple, running her fingers across it. "See, it's almost gone."

Jake looked at Destiny. "What happened?"

"Your helicopter was shot down and you suffered a severe concussion." Destiny studied him quizzically. "You don't remember?"

A montage of fleeting images abruptly flashed before him, and he saw the ocean rising up at him all over again. "Fernando was with me." The thought caused him to go rigid. "Did he…"

"See for yourself." Destiny looked up to indicate the man leaning over the *Angel's* swim platform.

"You okay, Jay Jay?" Fernando asked, obviously happy to see his friend fully revived.

"Think so," Jake said, noticing Zimbola and Hector also looking down at him. A broad, uncharacteristic smile plastered the big Jamaican's face.

"Let's get you out of the water," Zimby suggested.

Jake extended a hand and Zimby pulled him from the water with little effort.

The sound of gunfire suddenly erupted from high above, making Jake look up. "What's going on?" he asked.

The smile Zimbola had been carrying was now gone, replaced with a weighty graveness. "We've come under attack!" he exclaimed, looking to Jake for guidance.

At precisely 12 noon, Victor Belachek got the men moving. As planned, they spread out into four separate three-man squads to engage the bunkers set up along the rim of the basin. And while the bunkers were well concealed, he knew exactly where they were located. But to reach the bunkers, they had to either avoid or disarm booby traps they were sure to encounter along the way.

Leading two men, Belachek kept his eyes warily peeled for trip wires. With the need for caution, the going was painfully slow, made all the more difficult by dense foliage that acted to effectively camouflage thin strands of wire. If disturbed with additional tension, they could trigger a variety of mayhem designed to injure or kill. Not falling victim to them would be a daunting challenge. Nevertheless, he and his men were seasoned professionals and would be up to the task, particularly since their last mission had been on a similar assignment in the jungles of Colombia. Cardoza had also paid them well for that engagement, hiring Zinova and his band to eliminate factions of a competing drug lord. Memories of the mission gave Belachek a small measure of satisfaction, for they had disarmed at least two dozen well concealed IEDs on their way to raiding and setting in flames a cocaine plantation. During the fight they had lost only one man while wiping out a security force nearly four times greater than their own. By the time the raid ended, they had counted fifty-nine kills. And though he enjoyed the thrill of victory, killing did not give him pleasure. This made him wonder if perhaps he was losing his taste for battle. Perhaps he was getting too old for this type of work. Unfortunately, it was the only trade he knew.

Low crawling forward and carefully pushing aside a cluster of fern leaves, Belachek came upon his first trap of the day. As expected, it was a trip wire strung to a height of six inches above the forest floor. Swiveling his head, he looked first right, then left, failing to see where the wire ended. Pulling a small wire cutter from his utility belt, he snipped through the thin strand. Tracing one of the wires to the base of a tree located five meters off to the side, he saw what the wire would have released. A spiked boulder attached to a rope was suspended precariously to swing down on an unsuspecting interloper. Following the other end of the wire, he discerned a similar device perched high up, though it was not easily recognized unless one were looking for it. Each boulder was small, no more than twelve centimeters in diameter in his estimation, with short spikes designed to inflict shallow stab wounds. He could tell this type of trap was meant to injure rather than kill, with the aim of discouraging further encroachment into this forest.

Belachek took a moment to consult his GPS unit again. He was now within forty meters of his target, and that was the bunker closest to the falls. Already he could hear the soft hiss of the plunging water. Based on the intel he had been given, he would only have to neutralize the lone sentry manning that bunker.

Turning, Belachek looked back at the strapping young man following on his heels. Alex Trekov, a recent addition to Zinova's mercenaries at

Belachek's urging and currently the youngest and least experienced among them, was brushing leaves aside, intent on uncovering something he had come upon. Belachek had eagerly taken him under his wing, deciding to mentor him in the art of covert military tactics.

"What did you find?" Belachek whispered.

The lad's eyes were wide with amazement. "I think it's gold!"

"Don't touch it!" Belachek ordered, knowing it might be a lure. Booby traps were often baited to attract the unwary. Picking up the bait could easily detonate a bomb.

Shiny metal glinted brightly under a shaft of sunlight reaching the forest floor. Pulling a bush knife from his belt, Belachek gently prodded the soil around the object before pushing the blade deeper to probe under it. He had to make certain it was not a spring-loaded land mine. If it was, lifting the metal would trigger it.

Satisfied that nothing lay hidden beneath it, Belachek pulled the metal from the soil to examine it more fully, hefting it as he did so. As Alex had said, it appeared to be a bar of gold, probably more than eight kilograms in his estimation. A quick mental calculation told him he was holding more than $350,000 in his hand, assuming it truly was pure gold and not something made to look like the precious metal. Tungsten plated with a thin layer of gold, he knew, was sometimes used to make counterfeit ingots. With a unit weight that closely matched that of gold, tungsten was ideal for counterfeiting such a valuable commodity.

Alex stared at the metal's smooth, polished surface as though mesmerized. "Is it gold?" he asked excitedly, his voice loud enough to be heard by alert ears lurking in the bush.

Belachek scowled, bringing a finger to his lips. He hated careless outbursts when stealth was needed. "Keep it down!" he admonished, whispering out the command. He scrutinized the gleaming metal, trying to make sense of this strange find. *So, this is why Cardoza wants us to gain possession of this place,* he reasoned. *There's probably a lot more of this to be had once we neutralize those bunkers.*

"Well is it?" Alex persisted, his question still above a whisper.

Belachek noted the hunger in his protégé's eyes, knowing what the sight of so much wealth was doing to him. Like himself, Trekov had come from a poverty-stricken family back in the Ukraine. And though they were well paid to carry out missions like this, the idea that they could possibly walk away from this with so much more was an intriguing thought.

"Maybe," Belachek answered, desperately wanting to believe it was not a fake. Oddly, it displayed no markings stamped into it. A small cache of gold ingots had been looted during the raid on the cocaine plantation, and he remembered seeing the percent purity, weight, and batch number stamped into them. That find had been quickly appropriated by Zinova, claiming it would be needed for the upkeep of his Hinds.

A rustling of leaves made both men look behind them. Dimitrei's head poked through the foliage, his eyes immediately falling on the gold Belachek held.

"Is that what I think it is?" he queried, his expression alive with greed.

Belachek placed the ingot back on the ground. "We'll come back for this later." Turning, he started to crawl toward the sound of the falls.

"Like hell we will," Alex grumbled, scooping up the metal and attempting to cram it into an already stuffed pouch.

"Leave it!" Belachek ordered. "It will slow you down."

Alex looked back at him, and Belachek saw something in his eyes he had never seen before. Though subtle, it was rebellion.

"I'll be fine," Alex insisted, removing some protein bars from the pouch and replacing them with the ingot.

"That gets split three ways," Dimitrei declared. "The others don't have to know."

"Maybe we'll find more once we reach our objective," Belachek reconciled soothingly, recognizing what the scent of gold was doing to these men. It was important he pacify them quickly, otherwise the mission would be lost. "Now stay focused and we'll address this later," he said sternly.

Belachek crawled forward again, searching the ground before him appraisingly. Over the next ten meters he failed to come across a single trip wire or trap of any kind, but something else caught his eye. It was more gold. Assuming it was genuine, three more bars of it lay strewn directly in front of him as though dropped by careless hands. But these were much larger than the ingot Alex carried, maybe three times larger in the form of bricks.

Fighting back the temptation engulfing him, Belachek used his bush knife to probe the soil surrounding the nearest brick. Finding nothing suspicious, he tried lifting the brick from a prone position, but quickly rose to his knees for more leverage. It was heavy, gauging it to be more than twenty-four kilograms in weight. Like the ingot Alex carried, it had no identifying marks stamped into it. Based on the current price of gold on world markets, he knew he might be holding slightly better than a million dollars in his hand, with twice that amount still on the ground. Three point three million so far discovered, with the possibility of finding more. But that assumed it was bona fide.

Belachek was suddenly aware that Alex and Dimitrei were now hunkered down beside him. Their images reflected off the mirror-like finish of the brick he held, and in their eyes he detected a mix of awe and avarice.

"We're rich!" Dimitrei blurted. His tone was giddy. Before Belachek could stop him, he reached for one of the other bricks.

Instinctively, Belachek tackled Alex, slamming him to the ground and shielding him with his body. He was too seasoned a professional to assume the next brick was safe to pick up. His instincts proved correct.

Something sprang laterally from adjacent foliage, pivoting around in a blinding blur of motion. Dimitrei dropped the gold and let out a shrill howl of pain as the thing slammed into his side. Belachek saw it was a wooden plank studded with small, pointed dowels, several of which were firmly embedded in Dimitrei's hip.

"You fool!" Belachek chastised. He knew all element of surprise was probably lost now. Jumping to his feet, he yanked the plank free, noting that several of the dowels had come loose and were still lodged in the man's flesh. Already a heavy stain of blood was spreading out from the puncture wounds.

Dimitrei tried to get to his feet, but immediately fell back down, writhing in agony. Belachek could see he would be useless in a fight.

Grabbing Alex by the wrist, Belachek pulled him low. "Stay down and follow me!" he ordered. "We've got to rush that bunker. Chances are they already know we're here."

"What about Dimitrei?" Alex asked in confusion.

"Leave him! We'll come back for him later."

Belachek began low crawling swiftly, hearing the heavy breathing of his protégé right behind him. More gold bricks lay in his path, but he ignored them. Avoiding them completely, he looked behind him to make sure Alex was doing the same. He had to stay focused, keeping vigilant for more trip wires, but strange as it seemed, he did not encounter a single one. The falls were much closer now, letting out a soft pervading rumble, and he wondered if it might have drowned out Dimitrei's cry of pain.

The possibility of this was immediately dismissed when a piercing scream suddenly cut through the forest off to his right, overlaying the sound of tumbling water. Inwardly he cursed, knowing full well one of the men in the adjacent team had also fallen victim to the enticement of gold. *Damn fools!*

A staccato burst from a light assault weapon immediately ensued, and the realization that the plan had completely unraveled hit home. Abruptly, a much heavier machine gun barked back in reply, and he knew the defenders of this place were now fully alerted to their presence.

Hurriedly, Belacheck pulled out his GPS and got a bearing on the bunker he had to neutralize, seeing he was within eight meters of it. The sound of the firefight had now escalated, with more distant firearms coming alive. A full-fledged battle was now underway.

Belachek checked his watch, aware that time was running out. Only fifteen more minutes remained for his unit to take out these bunkers. Yanking the pin from one of the two smoke grenades he carried, he held down the spoon and looked back over his shoulder, expecting to see Alex hunkered down behind him. But Alex had disappeared.

At that moment, the heavy machine gun emplacement from the nearby bunker opened up, sending a torrent of rounds skimming just above his head. Had he been standing, he would have been killed instantly. The barrage was deafening, and foliage all around him disintegrated as the slugs tore into the jungle. The gunner was raking the forest, swinging the weapon back and forth haphazardly.

Still clutching the smoke grenade, Belachek hugged the ground. Caught in the grip of indecision, he considered backtracking to locate Alex. *Damn him!* he raged inwardly. Though he was no novice to the unpredictability that often accompanied firefights, he had never faced chaos to the degree he was now experiencing.

Belachek's ears perked at the sound of another scream, nearly drowned out by the jackhammer roar of the heavy weapon. It had come from the woods directly behind him. A second later the big gun cut out.

Groping the ground where he had dropped the pin to the smoke grenade, Belachek retrieved it, reinserting it back in the device. Quickly, he low crawled back the way he had come. Four meters back he found Alex. The lad lay unmoving with his face to the ground. The bricks of gold they had last encountered were next to him. A pool of blood was slowly gathering under him.

Belachek froze, staring in horror. *No, not this!* he mourned. The thing he had dreaded most had finally come to pass. Gently, he turned Alex over to see where he had been hit. Blood gushed from a hole in his abdomen.

Withdrawing a packet from a pocket, Belachek sprinkled sulfur powder on the injury before applying a gauze compress to stem the bleeding. Hurriedly, he dressed the wound, wrapping it tight with the compress in place. The firefight escalated as he did this, with the din of small arms and heavy machine guns drumming the air in the distance.

Alex opened his eyes to stare up at him. "You probably think I'm a poor excuse for a soldier?" he uttered weakly.

Belachek ignored the question, checking his watch instead. "The choppers will arrive in another five minutes," he said, barely managing to remain stoic as a flood of emotion filled his guts. "Just hold on and we'll get you out of here."

Alex looked ashen, as though every ounce of blood had drained from his face. "Why do you care about me so much?" he asked.

Belachek could see he was fading fast. "Just hold on," he repeated, knowing there was no more time for questions.

Turning, he looked back in the direction of the bunker just as the heavy machine gun let loose again. The jungle all around him was being sprayed with bullets, wreaking havoc on the thick vegetation and pelting him with tree branches and splintered wood.

Belachek ducked lower, suddenly overcome by a vast emptiness. The realization that he had led a meaningless life came back to haunt him yet again. No, it was worse than meaningless. He had let himself fall into a pit of moral decay. The truth tormented him like an open sore, with all the depraved things he had done throughout his existence coming to bear on his soul. Oh how he longed to escape from it.

Redemption! The word clung to his thoughts like a thorn buried deep in his flesh. If only he could carry out one redemptive deed, then he might be free.

Consumed with self-loathing, he began crawling toward the bunker. He would have only one chance at saving Alex, even if it meant losing his life trying.

Chapter Nineteen: Defending the Cove

Jake felt his strength rapidly returning as he buckled himself into the harness. The harness connected to an electrically-powered winch system that would take him to the top of the gorge. He had installed it several months earlier for emergencies such as this. It was located at the steepest and highest part of the basin, a near vertical ascent of 320 feet next to the falls.

Zimbola handed him the latest firearm Jake had purchased through the Haitian arms dealer he occasionally used back in Port-au-Prince. It was a gas-operated 12-gauge shotgun with a detachable drum magazine. The magazine currently held thirty-two shells of double-ought buckshot, but the gun could also fire frag-12 rounds that would explode on impact. Called the "Sledgehammer," the weapon was ideally suited for close quarter combat in dense jungle environments. When fired, it had a near-zero recoil with almost no muzzle climb. It had two firing modes – semi and automatic. Having stainless steel components, it required no cleaning or lubrication.

An idea came to Jake and he looked to Destiny. "I need you to stay on the phone." For emphasis, he glanced toward the intercom off to the right side of the winch. It interfaced directly with all four bunkers.

Destiny nodded in understanding.

"Hit the button!" Jake shouted, the sound of sporadic gunfire from high above now gaining in intensity.

"Wait!" Destiny cried. She reached in and gave him a fierce kiss before pulling away. "Please be careful."

Jake gave her an ironic smile. "Aren't I always?!" Swiveling his head, he looked back at Zimbola. "Hit it!"

Abruptly, the cable went taut and Jake felt himself being whisked rapidly upward. Reaching the top in thirty seconds, he unbuckled himself and ducked down on a small outcropping of limestone, taking quick inventory of his surroundings. The discharge of heavy weapons and small arms fire cracked the air in the distance, but with the sound muffled by heavy vegetation, he knew the source of the gunfire would be much closer than perceived. As if to confirm this, something mimicking an enraged bee buzzed past his head.

Reflexively, Jake hugged the ground as several more rounds zipped by, some of them zinging off the rock and kicking up small plumes of dust. This was immediately followed by a deafening barrage from a much heavier weapon almost on top of him.

Jake glanced to his left, knowing from where the sound emanated. A seemingly impenetrable barrier of trees and underbrush stood less than thirty feet away, and barely visible along the edge of it was a tiny little fortress comprised of sandbags and earth. It was armed with twin .50 caliber machine guns. Someone inside was returning fire at unseen attackers.

Jake jumped to his feet and scrambled for the bunker, leaping into a small rear opening that allowed access. A thin wiry individual manning the gun from a swivel seat glanced back, surprised at this unexpected intrusion. A relieved grin broke out on the man's face at seeing Jake.

"Give me an update!" Jake yelled, his ears still ringing from the discharging weapon.

Jimenez swung his head around to keep vigilance of the woods beyond the gun port. "All the bunkers are being attacked simultaneously."

"Has that been confirmed?" Jake asked, noting that Jimenez was not wearing his headphones. He had made it a priority to install a wire network that allowed all four bunkers to communicate with one another.

Jimenez nodded vigorously. "The attackers seem to know exactly where each bunker is situated."

"How do you know?"

"I heard someone cry out from the woods in front of me. So did Maurice. He believes a raiding party has stumbled into the traps you set. He started taking fire right after that. When he returned fire, all hell broke out."

Jimenez let loose with another barrage, swinging the twins through a thirty-degree arc and shredding more foliage a short distance away.

Jake weighed the implications. Maurice was in Bunker Number 2, two bunkers away. From the sound of the battle, he could tell the attackers were armed with only light assault weapons. Coming by way of land to engage the fortified bunkers, carrying heavier weaponry would have been cumbersome and impractical. They had relied instead on stealth to slip up quietly and take out each of the bunkers. Obviously these people had taken great pains to plan the operation, but unfortunately for them it was not going the way they had envisioned it.

This was a subject Ez had breached several months earlier. She had predicted that a rich man like Cardoza would have the right connections to use satellite reconnaissance as a means of pinpointing the location of all the bunkers, and this would have occurred during a change of guard when the men manning those bunkers were most visible along the rim of the basin.

Those fortifications with their armaments had been completed in the nick of time, for they had been indispensable in opposing Cardoza and his henchmen on his last two attempts to take the cove. The first of these attempts had been clumsy, and he had several more of his valuable assets badly damaged on that occasion. Using two large whirlybirds loaded with a small army of thugs, he had attacked by air, failing miserably in the process. Flying into a storm of withering fire coming from multiple positions, both aircraft had proved to be no match for the twin fifties, which could be elevated by eighty-five degrees to shoot upward, and it didn't take long to send them buzzing off into the sunset billowing dense trails of smoke. With each gun having a maximum effective range of 2,000 yards and a firing rate of 550 rounds per minute, all four gun emplacements were capable of sending out a total of seventy-three rounds each second in combination.

Cardoza's last attempt at taking the cove had also proved equally clumsy when he had tried to come in by land in the middle of the night. With most of his men stumbling into an array of hidden traps, the bunkers had hardly been needed to fend off that foray.

But Jake had no illusions about the continued effectiveness of these security measures. While they proved to work against inept thugs, they would be crude and rudimentary at best against more capable troops. He knew a man like Cardoza would not give up easily, and Ez had surmised the drug lord would ultimately hire on professional soldiers to do his dirty work, men who were well trained at avoiding booby traps and taking out concealed gun emplacements. To counter such a possibility, Jake had planted bars of gold in the surrounding forest, some rigged with springboard contraptions armed with spiked dowels. He had anticipated the sight of so much gold would cause encroachers to become sloppy.

Upgrading the cove's security with more sophisticated state-of-the-art measures had been on the planning table for some time now, but Jake had been far too busy with the building of Aquaria to turn a set of Ez-created designs into working prototypes.

Jake heard something pop a short distance away, and he immediately knew what had caused that sound. This was quickly confirmed when the smell of potassium nitrate began to permeate the air. Within seconds, a heavy green mist billowed forth to engulf the bunker, cutting down visibility.

"Stay alert!" Jake cautioned. "They're using smoke to screen their approach. I want you to hold your fire for the time being." Abruptly, he sprang for the exit.

"What are you doing?" Jimenez asked.

Jake spoke quickly without looking back. "Keeping the fox away from the hen house."

Outside the bunker, the smoke was thick. Jake stayed low, slithering along the ground where the haze was thinnest. The thought that he still hadn't rigged Claymore mines around the bunkers nagged away at him, for this would have been an appropriate time to use them. He had put in an order for a supply of them two months earlier through the same black market arms dealer from whom he had purchased the fifties, making him wonder if the requisition had been filled by now. Nevertheless, he had one other measure in reserve.

Like a blind man, Jake groped his way along the sandbags forming the side of the bunker. The bunker was a simple four-sided fortification without a roof, though it had tree limbs and freshly cut leaves laid atop the bags to camouflage it from above. The overhead cover could easily be pushed aside to fend off an aerial assault using the fifties. But a fragmentation grenade lobbed on top of it could easily take out the gunner. Jake's immediate objective was to keep this from happening.

An odd vision suddenly came to Jake, flashing in his mind's eye like a group of neon signs. Bunkers two, three and four were also bathed in smoke, but lurking within the thick haze were men he could clearly see. It was as though he were viewing three screens at once on a closed-circuit television system set up for monitoring security, and at this moment they were in striking distance.

Jake had no time to ponder this strange perception. Without hesitation, he fired off a mental directive to his bond mate. Achilles came back a second later. *Destiny has relayed your message.*

Jake felt the shock waves pass underfoot as the detcord exploded. This was the measure he had in reserve. Detcord was flexible plastic tubing filled with PETN - pentrite. He had installed lengths of it fifteen feet out in front of each bunker in a crude semi-circle, overlaying it with stones and gravel to act as shrapnel when the cord detonated. The end result would be almost as effective as Claymore mines.

Another vision flashed briefly within Jake's thoughts, and he counted four fallen men. Two of them lay sprawled along the perimeter of bunker two, while bunkers one and three showed one each.

Jake moved to the corner of the tiny fortress, gaining a position to the right side of the gun port. Craning his head around the side, he stopped and waited, pointing the shotgun out in front of him. Wanting to conserve his ammunition, he had set the weapon on semi-automatic.

A slight breeze had sprung up, and from the feel of it on his face he could tell it was causing the smoke to drift across the front of the bunker from left to right. Sensing rather than hearing movement, he kept his trigger finger poised in readiness.

The thing he had anticipated occurred only seconds later. A dark shadow rose up out of the haze on the opposite side of the gun port. The "Sledgehammer" barely bucked as Jake unleashed a single shot.

He was firing at close quarters and the possibility of missing his target was zero. Without hesitation he fired again, keeping his body hunkered behind the corner of the bunker.

The shadow teetered forward, brushing past and toppling over. Jake extended an arm and prodded it cautiously with the barrel of the shotgun. It took him less than a second to grasp the situation, and he realized he had been tricked. It was not the form of a man that lay on the ground but that of a tree branch heavy with leaves.

Knowing he had given his position away, Jake rolled to his right, seeking the protection of a large tree he knew was located ten feet away. Muzzle flashes erupted within the gloom, accompanied by the deafening clatter of a light machine gun. Bullets ripped through his clothing but failed to connect with any flesh. Bolting wildly, he stumbled into the tree trunk, taking refuge behind it. Flashes continued to spark in the haze behind him, and he felt the impact of rounds tearing into the timber that shielded him from the onslaught.

Timing a reply, Jake leaned out from behind the tree the instant his attacker stopped firing, pulling back on the "Sledgehammer" trigger and squeezing off five rounds in rapid succession.

A cry of pain suddenly cleaved the air, and Jake was sure he had scored a hit on the unseen attacker. Hugging the ground, he circled wide looking to flank his adversary. Visibility was quickly improving. Carried off by the breeze, the smoke was beginning to thin.

Within moments Jake came upon a dark splotch marring a small cluster of leaves. Testing it with his fingers, he knew it was blood. Creeping forward, he found another splotch, heavier than the previous one. His foe seemed to be retreating, leaving a growing trail of blood in his wake. Doggedly, Jake continued to follow, the sporadic sound of both heavy and light machine gun fire hanging in the background. In moments he came upon something on the ground before him. It was a Kalashnikov AK-104 assault rifle, a compact, modernized version of the ubiquitous AK-47. Obviously the foe he was hunting had discarded the weapon, too weak to carry it any further.

By now the smoke had cleared completely, and Jake espied movement behind some ferns. Creeping up slowly, he discerned two men in a small clearing, one of them on his knees and cradling the other in his arms. Both men were smeared with blood, with the one doing the holding seemingly unconcerned with the battle raging in the distance. This had to be the adversary he had tracked.

Jake held his position, studying the scene with a critical eye. Another AK-104 lay on the ground near both men, and three of the gold bars he had planted littered the forest floor next to them. And while he saw that the spiked plank had been sprung, he didn't think it had caused the injury of the man being held. Blood trickled from his open mouth, a sure sign of internal hemorrhaging, and the bandage girthing his belly was soaked red. The man holding him looked sad, almost apologetic, and Jake suddenly found himself overcome with emotion. All at once the memory of Tora Bora came flooding back, for he had held a dying Myers in the same manner.

The man Jake had wounded abruptly sagged, coming to rest beside the comrade he had been cradling. Jake scanned the foliage all around him, looking for movement but failed to detect any. Bringing his eyes back to the men, he moved into the clearing and knelt beside them.

Still conscious, his adversary stared up at him as though he had anticipated his arrival. Instead of the hate Jake had expected to see, the man's expression conveyed something altogether different. It was the look of a man resigned to his fate, a man not defeated by Jake but by a life spent walking the wrong path. That was what Jake read in his eyes, eyes set in a face that bespoke of countless battles and vanquished foes. Strangely, Jake had the odd sensation this man was looking to atone for the sins he had committed.

And then Jake noticed something peculiar. The eyes did not match. One was brown and the other blue.

Almost at once, Achilles' presence resonated within his thoughts. *JJ, you must not let this man die.*

Why?

Destiny believes this man will play a key role in the Cove's salvation.

Puzzled by this, Jake did not try to question Destiny's instincts. He decided he would do his best to honor her request.

"You are Jake Javolyn," the man stated languidly. The words were enunciated with thick overtones that suggested a Russian or Ukrainian lineage.

"How do you know my name?" Jake asked.

"There is… no time to explain," Belachek uttered, fighting back the pain of his injuries.

Jake noted the cause. Blood oozed slowly from his right shoulder and the left side of his rib cage. Double-ought buckshot could wreak havoc on the human body at close range, and he suspected the underlying bone in both locations was shattered.

Belachek got control of his pain. "If you agree to save my son, I can stop the carnage."

Jake eyed the other man who lay seemingly dead. "This is your son?"

"Yes."

Jake reached down and placed a finger on the man's neck. Though barely perceptible, he felt a pulse. "This madness must end right now if you want my help," he said. "How do you propose to end it?"

"I am the leader of this madness," Belachek replied weakly. With difficulty he groped for a portable radio attached to his harness.

Jake grabbed his wrist. The radio might actually be a concealed suicide device designed to kill all three of them.

Belachek stared up at him with those mismatched eyes, a silent plea held within them. "Though we may be enemies, we are brothers in war," he said softly. "As one warrior to another, you have my word I will not harm you."

Jake relaxed his grip. "Cardoza hired you, didn't he?"

Belachek's eyes went wide, looking past Javolyn at something behind him. Jake whirled to espy a dark form loom over him, unable to swing the Sledgehammer around in time.

The man sneaking up on him abruptly froze, dropping the knife he had been holding. An expression of disbelief and horror consumed his face as both his hands rose up to clutch the metal shaft embedded deeply in his throat. Gurgling horribly, he stumbled off to one side before falling face-first to the ground, his legs twitching spasmodically. Several blood-encrusted dowels jutted from the man's right hip.

Jake whipped his head back around to stare at the mercenary leader, prepared to fend off an attack. The haft of a ballistic knife was held in the man's hand.

Belachek managed a small smile. "I never liked him."

"You're Spetsnaz!" Jake said. A student of war, he knew Spetsnaz agents were notorious for using these spring-loaded weapons, which launched the blade contained within them like a missile.

Belachek's smile turned to a grimace as another bout of pain engulfed him. "If you please," he gasped. "Lift the radio to my lips. I don't have much strength left."

Jake accommodated the request, depressing the transmit button and holding it down as Belachek issued a set of commands in a language he didn't understand.

If you're still linked to me, Achilles, maybe you can tell me what he's saying, Jake petitioned, knowing all the albinos were multilingual.

He speaks in the Russian tongue, JJ, and is ordering his troops to fall back to the staging area.

You're sure of this?

The umbrage Jake detected in his bond mate swept in on him like a gust of arctic wind. *Does a whale defecate in the sea?* Achilles replied sarcastically.

Smart ass!

Within moments the sound of small arms fire began to die off, though sporadic bursts from the heavier guns continued.

Jake focused his thoughts yet again. *Achilles, have Destiny instruct the bunkers to cease firing.*

It took another minute for the twin fifties in bunkers two, three, and four to cut out entirely, and Jake knew they had heeded Destiny's request.

Belachek spoke into the radio again, and Achilles translated. *JJ, he's trying to make contact with Reaper and Badger.*

Shortly after recovering from his coma, Jake had been apprised of Badger's fate.

A look of bewilderment contorted the Ukrainian's face when Jake pulled the radio away. "Your friends won't be coming," he said. "Both Hinds have been destroyed."

Belachek had weakened further and his tone reflected it. "If that is true, then why am I hearing a helicopter?"

Jake's ears perked. Though subtle, the sound of rotary blades churning the air hung in the background.

What's happening, Achilles?

Help is on the way, JJ. The chopper you hear is one of ours.

Jake was perplexed. Aside from Fernando, who was still down in the cove, there were only three other members of Tursiops capable of piloting a helicopter, and two of them were currently away on business.

Who's piloting it?

You'll find out soon enough, Achilles replied. *Stay put, they're coming back your way to lend assistance.*

Jake listened as the sound of the whirlybird diminished, perceiving it had landed on the outcropping of limestone abutting Jimenez's bunker. Looking back down, he saw that the mercenary leader was now unconscious.

Another minute passed before leaves parted on one side of the clearing, and Jake saw Zimbola emerge from the underbrush. A petite woman followed on his heels, appearing far younger than her years would suggest.

Jake had known Destiny's mother had been learning to fly a helicopter, taking lessons from Fernando, and was proving herself to be a capable pilot. But as he studied her expression, he was suddenly reminded of a woman he had met only briefly in the past. This was not the Harriet Grahm he had come to know so well over the last several years. Some inner sense he could not explain told him this, something arcane and beyond the scope of scientific explanation. Here was the essence that had led to the building of Aquaria.

The mental presence of Achilles reverberated in Jake's head. *Yes, JJ, Amphitrite is back with us again.*

In spite of mounting pressures, Jacob felt it necessary to summon Amelia to his office. "For your own safety, you should leave this facility now," he advised.

Amelia saw the troubled look on his weathered face, a countenance that seemed to bear the weight of the world. Obviously something dark was quickly approaching, reminding her of the nightmare she had experienced the night before.

"What troubles you?"

Jacob sighed wearily. "A UN task force is being mobilized to take control of Aquaria. It's going to be far larger than the one you witnessed yesterday."

"How do you know?"

Jacob studied her for one brief moment, looking for signs of deception but only seeing naïve innocence. "Ez," he said, "replay the news broadcast you picked up this morning."

Puzzled, Amelia glanced around the room, searching for the person Jacob had addressed. Her eyes came to rest on the far wall, the place where Jacob seemed to be focused. Completely covering it was a sprawling view of Aquaria's lagoons and containment ponds stretching off to the north, with Navassa Island hanging further out amid cobalt blue waters. The panorama was picturesque and breathtaking, and her initial impression was that it was a photograph taken from the highest point on the facility's central structure. But subtle movement within the scene told her otherwise, for a cable car was slowly traversing the tramway toward the offshore platform where a small ship was pulling alongside to berth. It suddenly occurred to her she was watching a real-time video display on a flat screen TV at least fifteen feet wide and ten feet tall.

An expression of stunned amazement crossed her face as the screen changed over to a news bulletin. She was watching herself in high definition, standing on the same promenade deck when she had first arrived at the colony. But the perspective was all wrong. Navassa Island and a sparkling blue sea should have been visible in the background, not the bare white wall that dominated the space behind her.

"This is Amelia Amhurst of IBC News, reporting to you live from Aquaria, the world's first large scale sea colony." The smile she had presented to her audience changed as she spoke, slowly turning glum.

"A little known international corporation called Tursiops Worldwide is the builder of this colony, which is located adjacent to Navassa Island, a tiny Caribbean isle that lies midway between Jamaica and Haiti. In 1998, the island and the waters surrounding it fell under the administrative jurisdiction of the U.S. Fish and Wildlife Service, which declared it a National Wildlife Refuge. Such protection was deemed necessary since the submerged coral shelf adjacent to the island was discovered to be one of the most intact and thriving ecosystems in the Caribbean. The island itself has a distinctive biodiversity, providing a home to various plants and animals found nowhere else in the world, one of them being a rare iguana previously thought to be extinct."

A series of videos flashed across the screen as she said this showing aerial views of the island and stunning underwater scenes. Species of animals and plants endemic to the habitat were also shown, including the rare Navassa Island iguana.

"These are examples of what this area of the world used to look like, a habitat untouched and unspoiled by the ravages of man. But through a lease agreement with Tursiops Worldwide, this locale became the site for constructing what amounts to an enormous floating city. One of the conditions of the lease was that this habitat was to be left unharmed."

Amelia saw herself fill the screen again, and she cringed at the look she had given the camera as she listened to herself speak. It was a look designed to please her superiors. Seeing it now, she felt ashamed. "Unfortunately, that was not in the cards. Reports coming from undisclosed sources had indicated extreme ecological abuses taking place within these waters, compelling this news channel to investigate."

She remembered uttering those exact words, there was no denying it.

The scene immediately shifted, and what followed made her jaw drop. Recordings taken from the helicopter prior to landing had been doctored. The clear, pristine water she had witnessed girthing Navassa was shown to be roiled with a milky white sediment. It intruded its way into the containment ponds and lagoons, extending out to the city's central structure and beyond. Randomly interspersed atop the clouded sea were heavy oil slicks. They appeared ebony black and reflected sunlight like polished anthracite.

"As can be seen in these videos, this once healthy and thriving habitat is systematically being destroyed by oil spills and the dumping of other contaminants into these previously undisturbed waters, churning them up and turning them into what amounts to be a massive cesspool. Aside from this despicable and unsightly pollution, it is highly probable the seafood products Aquaria sells so cheaply on world markets is highly tainted with toxins that makes them unsuitable for human consumption."

The news item continued. "Compounding these abuses, it is rumored that the operation is emitting enormous amounts of nitrous oxide into the atmosphere." As she said this, another scene showed dense vaporous clouds being emitted from the facility's superstructure, drifting high into the sky and dispersing into the atmosphere. "Nitrous oxide is highly destructive to the earth's protective ozone layer," she went on to say. "This gas is three hundred times more powerful than carbon dioxide in causing a greenhouse effect. It is believed the phosphates the colony routinely mines on Navassa Island are the cause of this since phosphates favor the formation of a purer form of nitrous oxide."

Amelia's eyes went wide with horror. That was the claim of the UN envoy, Malikai Allotey, made to look as though she had spoken them herself. And while she was not in these incriminating scenes, her voice had been carefully dubbed in to describe what the camera was showing. Though it sounded like her, she had never uttered the wordage that had accompanied those images nor what she was hearing now.

"As is evident from what we've documented, the people running this colony have little regard for the coral reef habitat that surrounds Navassa Island, putting profits well ahead of any concern for the environment."

Outrage took hold of Amelia as more lies ensued, and she began to tremble from the sheer blatancy of them.

"Using explosives for carrying out their operations, Tursiops is systematically destroying a delicate ecosystem that was once unblemished and unpolluted." As if to prove the statement's accuracy, the scene shifted yet again to display the towering geyser her cameraman had captured.

The scene was replaced by another, this one showing the arrival of a helicopter with a United Nations logo. Dubbed in again was Amelia's voice, though she had never voiced what her ears were hearing.

"Having gotten wind of these atrocities, the World Ecological Affairs Council, a newly formed branch of the United Nations, sent in a fact-finding team to determine if they were true. But unfortunately, the team was met with hostility and sent running for their lives. As is evident from the video, a security force stationed at the facility used flame throwers to drive them from the city."

Amelia was appalled by the sight of flames licking out at members of the UN team as they scrambled for the safety of their helicopter to escape, an event that had been meticulously altered with an overlay of special effects.

Adding insult to injury, another scene came to dominate the screen. It showed images of paratroopers landing on the ship she had seen during her last interview with Jacob. Amelia's disembodied voice followed.

"As if to further antagonize the international community, elements of Aquaria have reputedly hijacked the *Southern Star*, a container ship that ventured within close proximity to the floating city. In reaction to this, the United Nations sent in a military force to take back the vessel. Though unconfirmed, it is speculated that the hijackers sought to take control of the ship's cargo of tungsten, a metal that is used in the manufacture of counterfeit gold bars. Rumors have arisen that Tursiops was able to finance the construction of Aquaria by using gold as a trade barter. If this is true, international vendors supplying equipment and goods to Tursiops may discover they took possession of worthless metal in consummating the deals."

The image of the hijacked freighter was suddenly replaced by one of the United Nations General Assembly showing speakers in heated debates.

Amelia's voice droned on. "As a consequence of Aquaria's transgressions, an emergency meeting of the UN has been called to order to decide ownership of Navassa Island, which has been contested for over two hundred years. The Republic of Haiti has disputed sovereignty of this tiny island since 1801, claiming the United States illegally took possession of it under the Guano Act for the purpose of mining *guano*, a natural occurring fertilizer. As a result of this meeting, the United States has graciously accepted the General Assembly's overwhelming unanimous vote to concede sovereignty of this tiny territory back to its rightful owner, that being Haiti. Subsequent to this action, a UN task force is being mobilized to take control of both the island and the adjoining floating city."

Jacob turned off the TV as an image of Amelia followed to end the news bulletin. He knew that no other fabrications would be forthcoming.

Amelia felt dizzy, her mind reeling with what she had seen. It occurred to her that one particular item had been deleted from the newscast, and that was the alleged indiscretions of Allotey and Alvarez as announced by the Haitian woman called Ez. Jacob had been right. The people she worked for had carefully edited the news clips captured by her cameraman, purposely photo shopping them to flagrantly vilify Aquaria in the worst possible light.

Amelia could not bring herself to look at Jacob. "I want you to know I never said most of the things you heard, nor did I have anything to do with their editing," she said shamefully.

Jacob's reply was soft. "I know."

His tone made her turn to face him, and in his eyes she could find no recrimination. Only kindness lingered there. "What are you going to do?" she found it necessary to ask.

"The same thing any living organism does when its survival is placed in jeopardy."

The statement and all that it implied horrified Amelia. "You can't win. If you fight back, you'll put this facility and all those on it at risk." Strangely, she did not fear for herself as she said this. Even so, she was compelled to dissuade Jacob from doing anything rash.

Jacob stared back with a calm demeanor. "I never said I expected to win."

"People might die, is that what you want?"

Jacob noted the wetness that was quickly gathering in her hazel eyes. Strangely, her show of compassion made him want to reach out to comfort her. "I never want to see anyone die," he said soothingly, "not even those who deserve it."

"Then why resist?"

Jacob produced a gentle smile. "Because to submit would reflect a sense of fear on our part, and we will not cave to intimidation by bullies."

"Are you at least going to evacuate the colonists?"

"The possibility of an attack was discussed with the populace long ago. You must understand that the majority of Aquarians are of Haitian heritage. As former members of an impoverished society, they would rather die than go back to the life they once had. And while I don't normally make it a practice to speak for everyone who lives here, I believe there is not one person among us who would refrain from giving up their life if they thought doing so might save Aquaria."

Amelia merely stared back in admiration of his conviction.

Jacob felt it necessary to add more. "If we do nothing, then we will be subjecting ourselves to the chains of tyranny. Only by resisting will we truly be free, even if it means dying."

As he said this, the words of Plato, one of history's great philosophers, resonated within him to strengthen his resolve: *"The price of apathy towards public affairs is to be ruled by evil men."* He often used the philosophies of noble men to reinforce his own convictions, and under the present circumstances those words could not have rung truer to life.

Chapter Twenty: Psychokinetic Healing

Amelia rode one of the twenty high speed elevators that serviced Aquaria's central structure, taking it down to the facility's main level. She was furious. Her cameraman had been deceitful, purposely lying. Eric Bolder had previously told her he had been unable to transmit the news clips they had recorded to IBC headquarters.

"Wireless transmission is not always reliable in remote locations, and this place is definitely off the beaten path," Bolder had explained. "We'll most likely have to hand-deliver the recordings once we finish this assignment."

Something was definitely amiss here, and she was going to get to the bottom of it. Upon leaving Jacob's office, she had gone directly to Bolder's suite, which was across the hall from her own. Failing to find him there, she figured she might locate him on the helipad where the IBC chopper sat. Aside from serving as her cameraman, Bolder was a licensed pilot and had flown them out to the colony.

Making her way to the helipad, she was again amazed by the facility's sprawling immensity. By contrast, she saw very few people along the way, but as she passed them they greeted her with welcoming smiles. Jacob had said there were currently 10,000 residents dwelling within Aquaria, with living space designed to accommodate a population of 100,000 once the floating city was completed. He had made it a point that even with that many people, the colony's efficient use of interior and exterior space would prevent the type of congestion often seen within the world's largest urban centers.

Each face Amelia came upon appeared to radiate the same thing, and that was contentment and joy. Looks of discomfort and irritability typically displayed by milling crowds in the cities back home were entirely absent. If left alone by the international community, these people would never go hungry or cold. Poverty would become a thing of the past. They would never lack for anything because Aquaria would take care of all their needs.

Amelia loved this place, moved all the more by the ubiquitous art that flourished among the city's incredible interior architecture. Oil paintings and holographic projections of it were everywhere, each one different and yet eliciting the same feeling of ecstasy within her. Within this wondrous place her spirit was free.

Reaching the helipad, she came around the side of the aircraft and stopped short. Bolder was leaning over something in the chopper's rear compartment, unaware of her presence. He looked ill, and as if to confirm this, a puddle of vomit lay close to his feet. Held within his hand was a syringe, its needle embedded in his thigh. He was breathing deeply, rapidly, as though he were under great physical duress, and as she watched she could see the distress engulfing him suddenly abate. Within moments, his breathing normalized.

Offended by the sight, she spoke without thinking. "What are you doing?"

Bolder spun as though he were a child caught by his mother raiding the cookie jar.

"You're a druggie!" Amelia accused, shocked by what she was seeing.

"No...no! Bolder stuttered with embarrassment. "You have it all wrong. I have to take this to treat my affliction. I have health issues."

Amelia eyed the syringe suspiciously. "What issues?"

"A few years ago I contracted Hepatitis C. This drug keeps it under control."

Amelia stood mute for several seconds, collecting her thoughts. It was then she realized Bolder had never looked quite right ever since arriving here. Now that she thought about it, he had appeared especially queasy while filming the central structure's interior.

"Okay, I'll accept that," she said, "but why did you tell me you were unable to send the recordings when, in fact, you had already done so?"

Bolder's beseeching demeanor suddenly shifted, becoming petulant. "At the time, something was interfering with the transmission, but I kept trying anyway and finally it got through. What's the problem?"

"Did you know they were aired?"

A look of surprise transcended Bolder's face. "Already! That's fantastic. Maybe there'll be a nice bonus in it for us."

"Did you also know those recordings were intentionally altered to criminalize the people working here?"

Bolder shrugged. "So what. In this business it happens all the time. Things are often taken out of context to add drama to an event. You better learn to accept that if you want to advance your career."

Amelia felt it necessary to scream to get through his obstinate manner. "The company went way beyond the context thing. The recordings were overlaid with special effects. They purposely doctored them to vilify this colony. They showed the surrounding water to be polluted with oil and the UN team being chased away with flame throwers."

"My job is to record events on camera and yours is to provide commentary, nothing more," Bolder grumbled. "What the editors do with it is their business."

"They added commentary I never said," Amelia objected hotly. "They dubbed in words using my voice."

"Cry me a river, Amhurst, you're breaking my heart."

Amelia's jaw dropped in disbelief. "I'm stunned you find a deception of this magnitude to be so morally acceptable."

Bolder smiled mockingly. "Sweetheart, the only thing acceptable to me is my paycheck. I do what they pay me to do, no questions asked."

"Then I guess you'll be earning it. A UN task force is on its way to take control of this city."

"That doesn't surprise me."

"These people are being unfairly persecuted," Amelia decried, totally offended by his callous tone. "The truth needs to come out."

Bolder chuckled. "What truth!? Pardon the pun, but this whole operation smells fishy."

"What are you insinuating?"

"Just look around you, Amhurst. Where do you suppose these people got the financing to build this palatial complex? My guess is that it cost several billion to construct it, not to mention the enormous architectural and engineering fees to design it. Have you noticed that most of the people working here come from Haiti?"

"So?"

Bolder shook his head, still grinning. "Don't you get it? Haiti is one of the poorest nations on earth. No lending institution in their right mind would have been foolish enough to fork over billions to a people who obviously had no collateral."

Amelia riposted quickly. "You heard the interview. Jacob said Aquaria carried no debt burden whatsoever due to its exceptional profitability."

"Precisely my point. They obviously needed seed money to get this operation started, so where did it come from?"

Amelia groped for an answer. "Someone must have believed in their vision enough to risk backing them."

Bolder shook his head again, this time with a sneer. "Wrong! The planners must have been involved in some incredibly lucrative illegal activities to get them started."

"Like what?"

"How about drug running for one." Bolder's smile broadened at seeing the look of horror on her face.

"No way!"

"Oh, yeah," he shot back, nodding annoyingly as he said it. "Four years ago I was on assignment in Port-au-Prince investigating the massive corruption that exists there among Haitian officials, including their limited and inadequate police force. Most of them are easily bribed and on the payroll of drug lords to turn a blind eye to their activities, which makes Haiti an ideal staging area for huge transshipments of cocaine and heroin headed for the U.S. and Western Europe."

When Amelia refused to comment, Bolder tossed out another idea. "Or how about scamming their way into an operation of this size."

"Scam? What do you mean by that?"

"Instead of using money to buy materials and equipment, or for that matter, services, they used gold. Only it was counterfeit."

Amelia's eyes widened. "Then you did see the newscast."

"I don't know what you're talking about."

"The newscast implied the very same thing you just mentioned, speculating that fake gold may have been used to pay for the construction."

For one brief moment, Bolder seemed to be thrown off guard, though he still held that insufferable smile. "I did not see the newscast."

"If that is true, then I have to assume you knew about this allegation before we got here. Could it be that someone at IBC headquarters clued you in on what they were planning to do with the fruits of our labor?"

"You're one loony broad if you believe that."

Amelia cast her gaze in the direction of the freighter still visible in the distance. "That ship is called the *Southern Star*, and according to the newscast, is carrying a large payload of tungsten. The newscast claimed those skydivers you recorded dropping down on it were a UN strike force sent to take it back from hijackers coming from this city. It inferred the Aquarians needed the metal to make counterfeit gold."

Turning back to face Bolder, she looked him in the eye. "Did you have advance notice that event was going to take place?"

Bolder let out a small laugh, and to Amelia, it sounded a tad forced. "You're crazy, Amhurst!"

"You think so. You seemed to know exactly where to point the camera at the time of the incident."

"You're letting your imagination run wild. I saw the skydivers at the same time you did, so I carried out the job I'm paid to do, and that's to document any event potentially relevant to this investigation. But I can tell you one thing, I can easily believe that ship was hijacked by these people."

"You can?"

"This colony is still under construction, which means they still require massive amounts of material and equipment they can't get from the ocean. I'm talking about items that must be retrofitted to the sea-grown structures to make this facility fully operational. Perhaps they need to fabricate more counterfeit gold to pay for it and that ship carries the very metal that will make it possible."

"You know what I believe, Bolder?"

"Tell me!"

"I believe these colonists are purposely being framed and that you're collaborating with the people setting them up."

"Believe what you want, Amhurst, but we've got a job to do. If a UN task force is on its way, there's going to be plenty of stuff for us to document, not to mention the hefty bonuses we'll be getting."

Amelia was growing tired of the patronizing grin plastered on his face. "The people here are not going to give this place up without a fight. Perhaps it's time you left."

Bolder's grin faded to a squinty-eyed scowl. "It sounds like you wouldn't be coming with me if I did."

This time it was Amelia's turn to smile. "Your astute perception is to be congratulated. I'm through working for slimeballs. I'll not abet them again."

Victor Belachek found himself running. A debilitating pain consumed him, slowly gnawing away at his remaining strength to make the effort seem like he was plodding through a muddy swamp. Nevertheless, he kept pushing himself forward, desperately wanting to escape the familiar though unshakable presence chasing after him. Afraid he might stumble, he risked a peak over his shoulder to glimpse his pursuer, only to see himself. Try as he might, he could not get away.

But then something odd happened. The ground under his feet suddenly firmed, and he felt himself moving faster. Glimpsing back, he saw himself begin to recede.

"He's coming around," he heard a faraway voice say.

All at once the pain lifted as though a deeply rooted spike had been plucked from his body, and the pleasing scent of jasmine drifted in on him. Disoriented and confused, he opened his eyes to find himself immersed in water, kept afloat by…

Belachek started, thrashing about wildly as he realized he was surrounded by several finned creatures.

Hands gripped both his arms, clamping down with shocking power to restrain him. That same voice rang out again, this time up close. "Easy there, fella!" it said. But the voice did not belong to the one immobilizing him.

Javolyn stood above him, perched on the stern platform of a large boat. "I think you can pull him from the water, Zimby."

An arm thick with muscle reached down to grasp him just above the elbow and heft him effortlessly from the water. The arm belonged to a hulking black giant standing next to Javolyn.

"Lie down!" Javolyn ordered as the giant deposited him on the platform. "You're still healing. Give it a few more minutes and you should be good as new."

Dazedly, Belachek stared up at him searchingly, trying to recall how he had gotten here. It took only a moment before images of the battle descended on him, and with that remembrance he reached up to explore the massive wounds that should have killed him. He was stunned to find no shattered bone or torn flesh.

"It's touch and go on this one," Belachek heard someone else mutter. This time it was a woman's voice. Her tone was weary, as though a great strain were imposed on her.

Still lying on his back, Belachek rolled his head to one side to observe two women in the water. They were administering to Alex, who was being buoyed up by those same finned creatures. It was then he realized he was looking at several white dolphins, the largest one nearly the size of an orca.

"Some people are not receptive to psychokinetic healing," the same voice uttered.

Psychokinetic. He knew what the word implied. The KGB had performed countless experiments on the subject, and as a young man, he had been one of their guinea pigs.

Belachek saw it was the older of the two who had spoken, though both appeared young and could have passed for sisters.

"You must save him!" Belachek groaned, starting to rise. "He is my only son."

Javolyn pushed him back down. "They're doing everything they can."

A flood of emotion rushed in to take hold of Belachek, spilling onto his tongue. "I have to make things right," he cried, closing his eyes tightly to hold back an eruption of tears. "I was a terrible father. He was two when I deserted him. After his mother was killed in a car crash, I left him at an orphanage. I could not bear the responsibility of having to raise a child by myself. I…"

Belachek caught himself, suddenly aware that he had never bared his soul to anyone. The fact that he was doing it now, and no less to strangers, was totally alien to him. Nevertheless, this newfound experience felt cleansing, as though great gouts of puss were being purged from his body.

They must have done something to me, he thought, something I cannot explain.

"Grab hold of the hand before you and let go of your feelings," the older woman urged. "It will help us help your son."

Belachek somehow sensed what she was asking of him, and unashamedly he opened his eyes to release a gush of tears. But the hand he expected to hold was not human, though it had what resembled five digits with an opposable thumb. The hand was large and dwarfed his own as he reached out without fear to clutch it. It belonged to the largest dolphin, which had extended an arm from under a pectoral fin. He noticed the creature had its snout pushed up against Alex, as did the other dolphins.

An anxious moment passed before the older woman let out a deep sigh. "It's working!" she suddenly cried, her tone reflecting the depth of emotion gripping Belachek. "His pulse grows stronger."

"Will he live?" Belachek asked.

"Yes," the woman replied. "Your son will live."

Chapter Twenty-one: Cardoza's Lair

Belachek asked, "Your children?" as he rested in a foldup beach chair Hector had set out for him on the *Angel's* bow. Though he was recovering rapidly, he needed fresh air, and the sights and pleasing aromas wafting within the cove both fascinated and refreshed him. Intrigued, he watched the playful antics of two young children riding smaller versions of the strange white dolphins that had assisted in healing his injuries. At the moment they were racing each other across the cove's limpid waters, goading each other on and bantering back and forth with gleeful shouts of wild abandon.

"Yes," Jake said, "but sometimes they can be a handful."

"You are a lucky man, Jake Javolyn. You have balance in your life, two beautiful children and a kind, compassionate wife. You are surrounded by people who love you."

Jake said nothing, somewhat taken back by Belachek's open display of wistfulness.

Belachek inhaled deeply, enjoying the sweet smell of jasmine and wild flowers before letting out a prolonged sigh. "I am indebted to you."

"Yes you are," Jake replied. "And now I'm going to request payment."

"What do you wish of me?"

"Cardoza has been a thorn in our side for a long time. We need you to show us the way into his lair, to point out his weaknesses."

Belachek sat quietly, lifting his head to admire the tiered sides of the chasm. "Do you seek revenge?"

"No, not revenge. This man is a threat to my family and must be destroyed. He leaves me no choice but to go after him on his own turf. If

I don't do that, sooner or later he's going to succeed with his nefarious schemes. Will you help us?"

Belachek held back an answer, turning to study Jake with those mismatched eyes. "Yes, I'll help you," he finally said. "Get me some paper and a pencil."

Driven by an unquenchable desire to gain more riches, Senator Brent Van Heflin had made hasty arrangements to go on an overseas trip shortly after his meeting with Truman Hearthwatch. Using the same private charter service he always flew, he boarded the luxurious Lear Jet 35 at 10:00 a.m. two days later at Dulles International Airport.

At $6,500 an hour, the service was going to be exceptionally expensive. Time spent in the air for round trip passage plus the standby time while the plane sat on the tarmac awaiting his return could easily exceed $150,000 in his estimation. Nevertheless, it was not going to cost him one dime of his own money, and this brought a smile to his jowl-draped face. The trip would be fully paid for at taxpayers' expense, falling under the guise of a fact-finding mission.

As Chairman of the Senate's Science and Technology Committee, Van Heflin had a legitimate claim for undertaking the mission. He had arranged for an impromptu meeting with the Haitian Minister of Agriculture to discuss why stockpiles of crop seeds generously donated by the Plagiarius Corporation were being destroyed by peasant farmers. But he already knew the why. The meeting was scheduled to take place in Port-au-Prince the following day, and the thought of having to land in the slum-ridden and earthquake ravaged city repulsed him. But today he would take care of a more pressing matter in the coastal town of Tiburon. And while he knew this trip would not garner much scrutiny from the press, it was actually a cover to carry out business of a personal nature.

Tiburon. The senator mulled the word, rolling it silently off his tongue. Pronounced *Tee-byoo-ron*, it meant 'shark' in Spanish. He thought it a befitting name for the place, particularly since it epitomized the powerful landowner who resided on its outskirts. Located near the western tip of the country's southern peninsula, the town was one of the oldest, and for that matter, one of the least despoiled in Haiti.

Looking out the window adjacent to his seat, Van Heflin viewed the panorama below him as the Lear began its descent. With the exception of partial defoliation and erosion marring rugged terrain farther inland, the landscape in this region exhibited a subtle, almost idyllic beauty. Along the coast, thin strips of white sandy beaches edged by thick clusters of palm trees contrasted sharply with the steeply rising hills of greenery abutting them. The beauty turned spectacular as the plane dropped over the Bay of Anse-Milieu at the entrance to the town and aligned with the private runway on a neatly laid out and sprawling plot of land paralleling the shore.

Though he had seen the place once before, he could not suppress the ardor gripping him as he gawked in awe for the second time around. Zipping by beneath him were lush, well-tended gardens of varying color that gave way to an imposing castle-like fortress of turreted walls. The structure was massive. Originally built by the Spaniards, with adjuncts and auxiliary features added later on by the French, the fortification sat majestically overlooking the deep-water bay. Surrounding it was a 50-foot-wide moat of slate gray water, giving the structure a distinctive medieval aura.

During his prior visit, its landlord had made it a point to tell him what he had stocked the moat with, but Van Heflin had seen the fins cleaving its surface and the sizable bodies carrying those fins, making him shudder involuntarily. He had learned that they were tiger sharks, and he had counted at least two dozen of them patrolling the encircling canal, with not one of them less than twelve feet in length in his estimation. He had also learned that the moat was constantly recharged with fresh seawater pulled up from the bay and was filtered by a buried intake pipeline and pumping system that kept the marine carnivores healthy. Another buried pipeline discharged the oxygen depleted water back into the sea.

As the Lear swept past, he saw that the drawbridge spanning the moat was in the down position, with the portcullis behind it fully exposed and open. Where the fortress faced the sea, the land dropped steeply from the edge of the moat, falling to a shoreline littered with outcroppings of gray rock. From there a long pier, perhaps 300 feet in length, extended out into the bay. A paved road connected the pier to the fortification, winding its way up the slope through a series of meandering turns.

Another sight caught his eyes, one he truly coveted. Sitting at anchor amid the bay's indigo and teal blue waters just offshore of the stronghold was an enormous luxury yacht nearly the size of a cruise ship. The place was indeed a paradise. Such amenities he'd like for himself once he left politics, but right now he dared not flaunt such wealth for fear of what it could do to his senatorial image.

In moments the jet settled down on the runway, and the senator unbuckled himself as it taxied to a stop. Hefting his considerable bulk from the leather seat, he arose and smiled lasciviously at the attractive stewardess as she unlatched the cabin door and lowered the steps for him to exit. On the in-bound flight she had performed to his satisfaction in the small but plush sleeping quarters situated at the rear of the plane, and he discovered he was already looking forward to another bout with her on the return trip.

Sweat beaded quickly on his brow as he exposed himself to the hot, muggy climate, so shockingly different from the air-conditioned confines of the aircraft. Eager to escape the stifling heat, anger abruptly welled up in him at seeing no one there to meet him. He hated to sweat. Impatiently, he checked his watch. Fuming in silence, he wondered why there was no one here to pick him up. His pilot had radioed ahead, giving an accurate ETA. As he waited for a vehicle to arrive, perspiration quickly dampened his clothing, and he wondered if he should go back inside the Lear until someone showed.

The senator stared in the direction of an enormous hangar set at the end of the tarmac farthest away from the fortress. Several men were engaged in unloading a truck, and a forklift could be seen moving toward the hangar. It rumbled softly, carrying a pallet full of crates as it disappeared beyond the hangar doors. Idly he watched as it reappeared and headed back toward the truck to pick up another pallet.

A car suddenly appeared at the opposite end of the runway, coming from the direction of the fortress. It was a late model SUV, all white to reflect the heat, and as soon as it pulled alongside him, Van Heflin impatiently opened the front passenger door and sat down heavily on the cool seat, now fully bathed in his own sweat.

"What took you so long?" the senator grumbled.

The swarthy individual in the driver's seat appeared uncomfortable. "Why have you come a week early?" he asked nervously, glancing in the rear view mirror to look back at the fortress. "Cardoza was not expecting you so soon. He is in a terrible mood."

The senator studied him appraisingly. The driver was one of Cardoza's lackeys, the same individual who had picked him up the last time he had paid a visit to this place, a person of little significance within the drug king's organization, but a useful one nevertheless. Van Heflin had felt it prudent to recruit him as a paid informant during his prior trip. He made it a policy to keep tabs on all his associates, and the practice sometimes yielded invaluable information.

"What's bothering him?" the senator demanded.

The driver's worrisome expression suddenly dissolved, replaced by a sly, toothy grin with one of his incisors missing. "My boy keeps asking me for a pony, but unfortunately I cannot afford to buy him one," he said.

Van Heflin held back his annoyance and reached into a pocket. "Rico, did anyone ever tell you that avarice is sinful?" Taking three crisp $100 bills from his wallet, he handed them to the driver. It felt strange for him to do this, for he was usually the one on the receiving end of deals involving graft.

Rico eyed the wallet wolfishly, seeing it was stuffed with bills. "Ponies are expensive here in Haiti," he declared gruffly.

Reluctantly, the senator withdrew two additional hundred dollar denominations from the billfold, handing them over.

"And, of course, a saddle will be needed if my boy is to ride the pony."

The senator gritted his teeth, pulling out another $300 and shoving it roughly into Rico's extended hand.

Seemingly satisfied, Rico pocketed the money quickly, continuing to let the car sit at idle. "One of Cardoza's ships has been hijacked," he finally offered.

"Tell me something I don't already know," Van Heflin growled petulantly. "The ship was taken back yesterday."

Rico nodded. "Yes, but the engines are not working and Cardoza has sent another of his ships to tow it back to port."

This was something Van Heflin hadn't known. Mulling this tidbit of information, he asked another question. "What else can you tell me?"

"The doctor and Allotey are here," Rico said, checking his rear view mirror again.

The senator's eyebrows rose up in surprise. He already knew about the doctor, but Allotey was the last person he expected to find meeting Cardoza. "Allotey you say?! Why's he here?"

"I don't know."

"When did the doctor arrive?"

"Yesterday."

"I hear the blight is not working," Van Heflin stated. "Is this true?"

Rico nodded again. "So far, there have been no crop failures, and this only adds to Cardoza's bad mood."

Van Heflin digested this, finding it strange. By all rights, non-hybrid food plants should have no resistance to the exceptionally virulent blight that had been purposely unleashed on Haitian food crops, particularly those indigenous to the country's soil and climate. The blight had been released four months earlier and should have sabotaged crops by now. Something was going on here that didn't make sense.

"Anything else?" Van Heflin asked.

"I must warn you to be very careful around Cardoza today. He is like an enraged beast. A raid he had planned did not go well."

"Where was this raid and what was its objective?"

"He hired Russian mercenaries to take control of some land near Malique."

"Malique? Where is that?"

"It is a small fishing village located between Gonaives and Saint-Marc up north."

Something vague bobbed up in Van Heflin's memory. What was it? He wrapped his mind around the thread of it, dredging it from the subconscious depths so that its full context came to the surface. All at once, the conversation he had had with Hearthwatch came flooding back, and with sudden clarity, he remembered. Emmanuel Baptiste, the CEO of Tursiops Worldwide, was from Malique.

"What was so important that he had to send mercenaries?" he asked.

"I hear talk that something very valuable lays hidden there. But it is well guarded. Each time he has tried to take it ended in failure."

The senator kept his face composed, though it was tough suppressing the grin wanting to light his features. Now he was getting somewhere. "You didn't by any chance hear mention of gold in that place, did you?"

Rico's eyes widened with alarm. "Cardoza would feed me to his tiger if he knew I told you."

"So these rumors of gold are not just hearsay," Van Heflin proclaimed smugly.

The driver swiveled his head around to look back at the fortress. "We better go now or Cardoza will become suspicious why we're taking so long." Having said that, he put the SUV in gear and turned it in the direction of Cardoza's lair.

Chapter Twenty-two: Ravenous Sharks

Senator Brent Van Heflin was not intimidated by Rafael Cardoza's ire, though it pulsed from him in intermittent waves. One moment he'd speak in a level, eloquent voice, then openly display his displeasure at something said in a show of uncontained fury. None of his henchmen dared to look at him when this occurred, knowing full well what could happen, and the three hooligans standing with their backs to one wall kept their eyes averted. In spite of Rico's warning, the senator knew Cardoza would not direct his rage at him, for both he and the notorious drug baron were on the same team, indispensable members of a cabal controlled by the most powerful man on the planet, a man even more ruthless and unforgiving than Cardoza, that being Malcolm Maximus.

Sitting at a sprawling conference table, Van Heflin took pause to study one of the men situated across from him. It was evident Malikai Allotey was clearly cowed by Cardoza's outbursts.

"You and your Chilean cohorts are clumsy and useless," Cardoza accused, glaring at the Libyan with contemptuous, smoldering eyes. "Twice you failed us."

Allotey squirmed. He looked around at the others in a bid for support. His normally prim, hubristic air was completely absent. "Unanticipated circumstances arose that were beyond our control," he protested, almost wailing out the words. "You have your ship back."

The Special Envoy to the UN seemed to wither further under Cardoza's unwavering baleful stare, and he dropped his eyes to the table, refraining from adding more.

Cardoza kept scalding eyes fastened on him for a sustained moment before turning to the senator. "I assume your earlier than expected arrival concerns the blight."

Van Heflin gave a nod, sitting regally with self-importance and feeling immune to Cardoza's belligerence. "Why has this supposedly highly toxic Morior strain failed to work accordingly?"

"If I knew the answer, you would be the first to know."

"But you're in charge of Plagiarius' Caribbean branch," the senator stated bluntly. "Isn't it your business to know?"

Cardoza's eyes immediately flared, and Van Heflin wondered if he had overstepped his bounds. A pulsing silence filled the room, and he became aware of the shocked, open-mouthed stares of the other occupants impinging on him. On his way to the conference table, he had been led down a seemingly endless series of stone steps that eventually terminated in a musty, dimly lit corridor with rows of cast iron doors on each side of it. He had surmised it was an ancient dungeon, though he couldn't be sure if any of the cells went unused, for only darkness lay beyond the barred rectangular grills set in the doors. A mildly foul odor permeated the air as he passed, making him crinkle his nose.

The dungeon connected with another chamber, and within its gloomy confines he recognized an assortment of implements he had only seen in history books and museums, their intended functions all too obvious. A rack with rollers, chains, and leather straps sat ominously to one side along with other devices, and hanging on the dank walls were various instruments, their very appearance somehow conveying terror. It was a medieval torture chamber, and it adjoined the anteroom room where he now sat.

As Van Heflin pondered these things, he fully understood why Cardoza had selected this room for the meeting instead of the one used during his first visit to this place. It had been purposely used to induce fear in those in attendance. The first meeting had taken place several levels higher within the fortress, making guests feel at ease with the magnificent panoramic views beyond the glass windows.

But down here there were no windows, not the kind that offered vistas that would put a visitor at ease, though there was a glass partition that covered an entire wall directly across from where the senator sat.

A chill ran up his spine as a huge shadow drifted slowly past within the murky water on the opposite side of the glass.

Van Heflin's abrupt discomfort did not escape Cardoza's notice, and the drug lord suddenly grinned smugly. "I see my creatures fascinate you," he said, turning to watch as another shadow coasted past, this one even larger than the one that had preceded it.

The senator judiciously diverted the conversation to cool Cardoza's impending wrath. Even that smug smile could not hide the violent flames that burned deeply in his eyes, flames Van Heflin had carelessly ignited by the insult, and he knew the man could lay into him at any moment. "I assume they're all tigers?" he found himself saying.

"Not all," Cardoza grunted. "I've added one more since your last visit."

Van Heflin kept his gaze on the glass, avoiding Cardoza's eyes. "And what would that be?"

Just as he uttered the question, the glass went darker, dwarfed by something on the other side that spanned the partition end to end. As it passed, it blocked out the meager sunlight filtering down through the murky water.

"You just saw her, a female great white two inches shy of twenty-three feet. With great whites, the females tend to grow bigger than the males. This one weighs more than three tons. I call her Scylla. Are you familiar with that name?"

"No."

"The name originates from Greek mythology. Scylla was a beautiful woman turned into a monster with three rows of razor-sharp teeth."

"Where did you get it?"

"Same place as all the others. Sharks often end up in the nets of my fishing vessels, and my crews are instructed to keep the biggest ones alive and deliver them here. They know not to bring me anything smaller than a twelve footer."

"But you seem to prefer tigers. Why is that?"

"Their teeth are the nastiest, much more destructive than that of a white. Even a raking slash with them can tear a man open."

As Cardoza said this, something bumped heavily against the partition, startling the senator. An ebony black orb the size of a coffee cup pressed up against the glass, seemingly drawn to the light within the room. The orb appeared to fixate briefly on Van Heflin before drawing back, and the massive body to which it was attached turned to face the glass head on. A gaping mouth edged with serrated triangular teeth tested its surface."

"I believe Scylla regards you as a potential meal, senator," Cardoza declared, his eyes suddenly cold and foreboding as he elicited an ominous grin.

Van Heflin pivoted in his chair, attempting to mask the shudder that swept through him. He was especially fearful of sharks and generally avoided swimming in the ocean. The thought of predatory sharks lurking in the moat made him feel uneasy, but that white monster absolutely terrified him. Only the glass partition was keeping it from entering the room, and he wondered if it was actually capable of withstanding a charge from the 3-ton beast.

Cardoza was about to add something else, enjoying the trepidation he had instilled in the senator, but the door to the room suddenly flew open and another of his lackeys scurried in.

"What is it?" Cardoza yelled, scowling fiercely at being denied his moment to torment.

The man turned ashen, nervously handing him a phone. "You have a call, sir."

Cardoza snatched it from his hand and brought it to his ear. The violence etched on his countenance slowly receded as he listened intently, and after a minute he placed the phone back in the lackey's hands. Eager to get away, the lackey quickly left the room.

Seemingly caught up in deep thought, Cardoza brought only peevish eyes to bear back on the senator, the previous rage held within them moments earlier now reduced to a simmer.

"Our agenda has been stepped up," Cardoza said. "The arms shipment is due to arrive here tomorrow."

"When did this happen and why wasn't I informed?" Van Heflin asked, taken back by this sudden change in plans.

"Our Supreme Leader made the decision yesterday." Cardoza studied the senator critically. "Perhaps you would like to discuss it with him face to face?"

Van Heflin's jaw parted in surprise, but before he could voice a question of his own, the door to the chamber opened again, and two men walked in. The first man gave the impression of a bulldozer paving the way for the man behind him. An oversized navy blue blazer could not hide his heavily muscled shoulders that spanned more than half the width of the 6-foot-wide doorway, and he was forced to duck his head to keep from hitting it on the upper frame. Sporting a close-cropped crew cut of blond hair, he surveyed the room as if issuing a silent challenge to everyone within it. But there was no mistaking that the second man was the leader.

The senator recognized Malcolm Maximus immediately, who he knew never went anywhere without Swensen, his hulking Nordic bodyguard. Maximus stood a head shorter than his counterpart and carried an austere, aristocratic bearing, impeccably dressed in a gray pinstripe suit that was precisely tailored to his medium-size body. His gaze was sharp and stern as he took in those seated. Though he was well into his sixties, he lit the room with an ice cold aura of supreme authority.

Without hesitation, Maximus moved to the customary place of leadership at the head of the table and seated himself, with Swensen taking up an imposing position behind his chair. It was then that Van Heflin understood why Cardoza had not occupied that chair himself.

Maximus made a show of darting his eyes to each of the four faces at the table before singling out Van Heflin. "I'm rather surprised to see you here, senator," he said in that same halting, raspy voice Van Heflin had heard so many times before, mostly over the phone in coded Latin. "I would think you would have more pressing duties stateside."

Van Heflin cleared his throat, suddenly besieged with nervousness. "Things are moving ahead as necessary."

"You think so?" Maximus said. His tone was derogatory, his eyes flaming with scorn. "Then why is it little headway has so far taken place with these annoying colonists?"

"Certainly you've already heard," Van Heflin replied in a flustered voice, desperately trying to produce a placating smile. "My government is abiding by the UN's decision to concede Navassa Island over to Haiti. Once the final paperwork of concession is signed by our President, any lease agreements it has with Tursiops will become null and void. These colonists will have no choice but to vacate the island."

"What if they insist on staying?" Maximus growled. "Have you forgotten that most of these colonists are Haitian? It is almost a certainty the current Haitian government will allow them to remain and continue fostering their operation. As it is, Tursiops has been providing a significant amount of its resources to help in rebuilding Haiti, and those firmly entrenched in the power structure here are showing far more friendliness toward them than we had expected."

"But a military strike force is being mobilized by the UN to evict and incarcerate them," Van Heflin was quick to point out. "Using the media to our advantage, we've effectively stigmatized them into looking like rogue eco-pirates."

"It won't be enough," Maximus snapped. "At most, UN intervention may prove to be a temporary setback to their operations. Unless there is a change in this country's governing administration, the odds of gaining complete control of their enterprise will be uncertain. Over the past year, the CEO of Tursiops, a Haitian national by the name of Emmanuel Baptiste, has made numerous overtures to the Haitian Ministry of Agriculture, providing large shipments of natural fertilizer to peasant farmers free of charge. The fertilizer is mined on Navassa Island and seems to have doubled, if not tripled, crop yields, particularly the maize they grow here."

"Then maybe we should end this problem by having the UN task force destroy Aquaria altogether," the senator exclaimed impulsively. As soon as he said it, he realized it was a foolish option. If any gold was kept in the floating city, it might very well end up in the briny depths.

"Your judgement disappoints me, senator!" Maximus scolded heatedly. "I don't want it destroyed. I want that city. I want that island. I want to take complete control of their entire project, lock, stock, and barrel, including those strange white beasts helping to build it. Already I've learned this Baptiste character is currently in negotiations with the Haitian government to construct a massive automobile manufacturing facility that will produce eco-friendly cars at incredibly low cost to be shipped all over the world. Apparently these colonists have designed cars to run strictly on hydrogen, most of which will be supplied by Tursiops. On top of that, these people are seeking approval from the Haitian Ministry to build several power-generating facilities that will also run exclusively on the hydrogen they produce, and Baptiste has offered to supply it free of charge. On a global scale, they're also providing this same expertise to other nations that rely on oil and coal to power their electric plants, converting them to run on hydrogen. Should these things become fully implemented, the standard of living in Haiti is going to rise exponentially with all the jobs that will become available."

Van Heflin grew increasingly edgy at the severity of the lecture being laid upon him, and he risked a fleeting glance at Swensen's towering form standing behind Maximus. The Nordic giant's eyes bore into him like swords.

"We can't let that happen," Maximus went on, his anger suddenly cooling. "That is why we will have no choice but to accelerate our agenda." Turning, he looked over at Cardoza. "Rafael, give these men a brief summary of the plan," he commanded.

Cardoza spoke gravely. "Once the arms are fully distributed to our constituents in the key cities, our paid agitators will incite the population into the widespread rebellion needed for a government takeover."

Maximus narrowed his eyes, setting them on Van Heflin again. "Let me be clear about this, senator, we'll be relying on your congressional influence to keep your government from interfering in this manufactured coup."

"Certainly, you'll have my full cooperation. But without crop failures and the ensuing food shortages to incentivize the masses, how are your agitators going to incite the peasants into armed revolt? I hear sixty percent of the population derives their income through employment with the farming co-opts, and so far the blight has failed to work."

Maximus set his gaze on the only member of the group who had so far not spoken. Dr. Herbert Ermstine was completely bald, short, obese, and bespectacled. With his dark skin, he could have easily been mistaken for a Haitian, though he was actually born in Nigeria. He had arrived the previous day to attend this meeting, flown in on Plagiarius' private jet. Nearing seventy years of age, he had once served as the Haitian Minister of Foreign Affairs under "Baby Doc" Duvalier. Currently, he was the leading scientist at Chemtectics International, a subsidiary of Plagiarius, performing most of his work in Africa. He was the man Maximus had groomed to head Haiti's government once the coup took place.

"Do you have any theories why the blight failed, doctor?"

Ermstine appeared tired, still getting over the jet lag that continued to plague him. "Yes. It is probable that something in the fertilizer coming from Tursiops makes the crops resistant. But only through extensive testing will we be able to determine exactly what that something is."

"How long would this testing take?" Maximus demanded.

"It could take months."

Maximus nodded, seemingly unconcerned with the doctor's assessment. "This is another reason why the Aquaria project must be stopped as quickly as possible, senator. We have to end those shipments of fertilizer once and for all, otherwise they might start sending it to other parts of the globe, and that would be a major impediment to our plans."

Maximus leaned back in his padded chair and looked at Cardoza. "Rafael, tell the senator how we plan to trigger a revolt."

A demonic grin came to Cardoza's face. "We are going to contaminate farmland with a specially formulated herbicide capable of killing all native food plants."

"Your Morior chemical was supposed to do that," Van Heflin said, knowing that the meaning of the moniker was a Latin word for '*withering away*.' "What makes you think this new compound will prove any better?"

Cardoza continued to smile. "It is ten times more lethal than the Morior. The Morior's primary component consisted of metalaxyl, a potent fungicide that should have been deadly to food crops grown here when delivered in the high concentrations we used. But this new compound, called *Sterilis*, is different, one you might categorize as a highly toxic defoliant."

"You mean like the Agent Orange defoliant used in Vietnam?" Van Heflin asked.

"It carries some of those dioxin properties, yes, but the chemical makeup has been altered to make it even more destructive than that used in Vietnam. Once deployed, it will only take two days for food crops to die, bringing on the required widespread unemployment and social unrest. Our agitators will worsen the problem further by stirring public emotions into a frenzy."

Van Heflin appeared skeptical. "And how do you propose to disperse it?"

"The same way we dispersed the Morior compound. We will use the same fleet of unmanned drones retrofitted with aerosol sprayers. Just as before, they will be specially programmed to spray targeted tracts of farmland and fly only under the cover of darkness."

Van Heflin thought about the defoliant name. Cardoza had called it Sterilis. In Latin it stood for barren or useless, implying it would turn crop fields barren and render them useless, at least for a time. He realized it was a most adequate description.

"But what are the long term effects of this new compound?" he interjected again.

Cardoza shrugged indifferently as if such a consideration were of no significance. "There will be a sustained period where nothing will be able to grow once it gets into the soil, not even our hybrid seeds."

"Do you know how long?" Van Heflin pressed. He needed to know, aware of all the headaches that could come his way in having to deal with the problem later on. Strapped with the task of appropriating funds for the Haiti Watershed Initiative for Natural Environmental Resources, he would be forced to give a show of looking for a solution to a problem that couldn't be fixed.

"Have you thought about the consequences of doing this? You may inadvertently invoke a permanent state of political upheaval in a nation already beleaguered with economic and social instability."

Van Heflin looked to Dr. Ermstine to see how he was reacting to this, but he could see from his expression that he was unperturbed. "Even if we do gain control of the government, it may prove to be short-lived," he found it necessary to add.

"The defoliant will eventually biodegrade," Ermstine offered, yawning somnolently as soon as he said it. "But it will take at least three years before even our hybrid seeds will be able to take root in the soil."

"This you know for sure?" Van Heflin asked.

"Yes."

"Then without massive international aid, the population may very well be on the doorstep of starvation by then," Van Heflin pointed out. "Are you willing to deal with all the turmoil and strife that will ensue?"

Ermstine let out a slight titter, and the senator became aware of a sardonic smirk on Cardoza's face as well. "It's all part of the agenda," Ermstine stated smugly. "The Haitian population has gotten much too big, and many of them are nothing more than useless eaters. A prolonged famine will be needed to reduce their numbers. The defoliant is also designed to kill off substantial portions of the masses once it gets into the water supply since it is quite deadly to animal life as well as plants. But eventually the hybrid seeds so painstakingly developed by Plagiarius will grow in the toxic soil while crop varieties that have suitably adapted to local conditions over many generations will not, and by then we will have accomplished our goals."

Van Heflin frowned. "Are these the same seeds the farmers have been burning?"

"Yes," Ermstine said, yawning expansively this time, revealing a set of unusually large, ivory white teeth. "Once the defoliant biodegrades below a critical level, these seeds will be able to withstand the toxicity that remains. As a matter of fact, at lower concentrations the defoliant was developed specifically to react in sympathy with the chemical coating the seeds."

"Are you referring to the Omicron Seven compound?"

"Yes."

Van Heflin looked to Cardoza again. "These farmers are obviously onto the threat these seeds pose. Do we know how they learned of this?"

The smile dominating the drug lord's face abruptly died. "My sources believe someone representing Tursiops alerted them." The smile reasserted itself. "But once we destroy their crops, we will spread a rumor that it was caused by the fertilizer provided by the colonists."

Van Heflin produced a smile of his own, nodding in admiration at the utter simplicity of the ploy. It was yet another way to discredit and vilify the Tursiops organization. And using media participation to expand the fabrication, they would twist the knife even deeper into the scandalous wound they had already inflicted against the colony. The entire world would be screaming for Aquaria heads.

The senator knew what Omicron-7 actually contained. Aside from his role as Chairman of the Senate Science and Technology Committee, it was his business to know that it was a concoction of high levels of *mancozeb, thiram* and *maxim XL*, not to mention a few other nefarious compounds. It was a dangerous mixture of fungicides and herbicides so toxic that it exceeded acceptable levels put out by the EPA, and according to international law, should have been illegal to use.

But Plagiarius had seen opportunity following the earthquake that had hammered Port-au-Prince and its outlying regions in 2010. The earthquake had been catastrophic, destroying nearly 100,000 homes and injuring 30,000 people. It had claimed 1,000 lives, leaving most of the city in rubble and causing an estimated $8 billion in damages. With farmers having insufficient quantities of seeds for planting, Plagiarius had stepped in to provide assistance, benevolently donating over 500 tons of seeds to Haitian farmers at its own expense. But Plagiarius had profited anyway. Money for the seeds had actually been appropriated by Congress through a last minute earmark cleverly and discreetly slipped into a bill by Van Heflin, allowing Plagiarius to be paid for its show of generosity, nevertheless. The donated seeds, however, were hybrid varieties of maize and various types of vegetables, genetically modified to withstand the toxicity of the chemicals coating them. From all outward signs, the project's aim was to triple food production for the poverty-stricken Haitian people. Rigged by Van Heflin to appear like a humanitarian gesture by a concerned U.S. Congress, the project was actually a pretext to carry out something sinister. It was a test run to determine the destructive effects of the corporation's Morior blight on native crops before releasing it to other parts of the globe. In addition, it was to assess the special immunity of the hybrid plants against the blight more fully, which would essentially destroy all planetary food crops lacking the genetic makeup of the hybrids. Once the world was forced to rely on Plagiarius as a sole source provider of these seeds, the company stood to make untold mega-fortunes by jacking up the price of this essential commodity to stratospheric levels. And by virtue of that, the wealth of every man at the table would increase multiple times more, with Maximus and Cardoza making off with the largest shares by far.

Through extensive lobbying in Washington, Plagiarius held huge prestige as a government contractor. With no less than thirty-five former Federal employees on its payroll, most of them having previously served as congressional members and high ranking bureaucrats, it was relatively easy for the biotech giant to get what it wanted. This was further ensured by virtue of a Supreme Court judge currently sitting on the bench who had once represented Plagiarius as a defense lawyer over various lawsuits involving pollution. And recent passage of the latest Agricultural Appropriations Bill by congress had a provision that effectively stripped Federal courts of the authority to halt the planting of genetically modified seeds even if they posed a health risk. The provision was a rider written by Plagiarius lawyers and covertly inserted in the bill by none other than Van Heflin at the last minute, by-passing the usual review by Agriculture and Judiciary Committees. In essence, it made Plagiarius immune to lawsuits involving health issues.

In spite of the way Plagiarius would promote the use of its patented seed products, and in spite of their ability to withstand the blight, the hybrids had several shortcomings with which the senator was intimately familiar. They needed more water to grow, and fresh water was scarce in Haiti. They also required more fertilizer. And while they would provide twice the normal yield of most non-hybrids following their planting, the yields would plummet dismally after the first generation, since seeds from the resulting crops had little potency. This was a plus for Plagiarius because it would cause farmers to rely strictly on the company for a never ending supply of seeds.

Use of the seeds even without the blight presented a dangerous problem. When planted near or alongside indigenous food crops with open-pollination, the resulting plants would invariably hybridize, ultimately diluting the gene pool of plants that had adapted to the local environment.

"The wisdom of your scheme is to be congratulated," Van Heflin said, looking at Cardoza with as much admiration as he could muster.

"Blaming crop failures on the Tursiops fertilizer is a brilliant stroke of genius."

Pausing momentarily, he could see the praise had the desired effect, for Cardoza seemed to puff up like a peacock. "When do you plan on releasing the defoliant?"

"Tomorrow at midnight," Cardoza said. "We have already stockpiled over six hundred canisters of Sterilis, storing them within the hangar you saw at the end of my runway. The last batch is scheduled to arrive later tonight along with the first of our arms shipment."

Van Heflin nodded, a genuine smile coming to his face. In spite of a few setbacks to their agenda, the staged deceptions and manipulations had so far worked to their advantage with surprising success. They were on the verge of accomplishing great things, and his hunger to enrich himself further suddenly gathered strength to gnaw away at him like a ravenous beast. With the UN now having voted unanimously in favor of ceding Navassa Island back to Haiti, it was imperative he breach the rumor of gold with utmost delicacy, knowing the greed of the men surrounding him surpassed his own.

"Perhaps now's the time to discuss another matter which has come to my attention." The senator stopped speaking to let the statement hang in the air. He sensed all eyes locked on him, waiting for him to continue.

Maximus broke the silence. "Which is?"

"It concerns the financing of Aquaria. To build such an immense facility must have cost billions, yet I am unable to uncover any sources of financing for its construction."

"I've found the same dead end," Maximus concurred.

Van Heflin pressed on, having gone too far now to turn back. "I've heard rumors about how they've been able to obtain the extensive amounts of equipment and materials going into the facility."

"Get to the point!" Maximus grumbled, checking the time on his Emperador Temple wristwatch. Studded with over 1,200 diamonds it was the world's most expensive watch.

The senator espied the timepiece with envy. "I hear they've bartered with gold."

Van Heflin set his gaze on Maximus as he said this, seeing only the impassive stare of a seasoned poker player. In Cardoza, however, he detected something analogous to a fidget, ever so slight.

"Now assuming the rumor is true, where do you suppose these poor, economically depressed Haitians got it? Based on an estimate of the facility's sheer size and scope, a minimum of twelve thousand tons of high grade gold would have been needed to build it."

A cynical smile broke out on Maximus' face. "So this is the reason for your early arrival," he rasped. "You smell gold and you want some of it."

The senator looked around the table. Allotey was practically drooling over the thought of so much gold, his eyes alive with avarice. Ermstine ran his tongue along his thick lips as though actually tasting the precious metal. Cardoza, however, stared back at him with murder in his eyes.

Van Heflin was not to be deterred. He wanted his rightful share. "These people must have it stored someplace," he said. "The question is, where?"

Maximus sat up straighter in his chair, a regal king presiding over his court. "If this gold does exist, I'm sure we'll find out where soon enough," he stated, seemingly eager to end this trivial matter.

"The floating city or the nearby island are the most likely places where it's stored," the senator persisted. "If it's discovered by UN troops once the facility is taken, there's no telling how much of it will disappear."

Van Heflin looked sharply at Allotey as he said this. The Libyan appeared indignant. "It's important we make sure that doesn't happen," he added.

Maximus eyed him curiously. "What do you suggest?"

"I think it would be prudent that at least two of us be there to inspect the facility immediately after it's secured."

Van Heflin knew the only ones among them that would have a valid reason for being at Aquaria following UN intervention were Allotey and himself, for certainly it would appear highly suspect if Ermstine, Cardoza or Maximus showed up. Ermstine had to keep a rather low profile until the coup had actually taken place, and that would be after Tursiops was ousted from the colony. Maximus and Cardoza, on the other hand, had to remain in the shadows. But he, himself, could easily come up with an excuse for being there. As head of the senatorial Science and Technology Committee, he would pull the necessary strings to be on hand to tour the facility once it was in UN hands, feigning an interest in the innovative technology Aquaria used. Of course he'd have to get the antidote Hearthwatch had told him about in order to counter the debilitating effects of the strange art he would surely be exposed to once he ventured into the floating city.

Maximus sneered, then laughed. "You know very well that would be you and Malikai." He riveted the senator with a searing look. "Let me be perfectly clear about what I told you before. You'll be needed stateside to use every ounce of influence you can exert in keeping your government from interfering in this coup. Is that understood?"

Van Heflin nodded staidly, having anticipated such a reaction. "You'll have my full support and cooperation," he replied.

Maximus turned to Allotey. "I will expect a full accounting of whatever your troops find." He let the statement's underlying threat linger a moment longer before going on. "I will expect you to make sure any caches of gold are fully secured until we can come up with a plan to remove it." Suddenly remembering what a glimpse of the holographic art had done to him, a sour expression came to his face. "And make sure all the troops are injected with the drug before entering the city this time."

Allotey shot a nervous glance to Swensen's hulking form hovering behind Maximus. "Of course," he stammered obsequiously, "but how do we deal with the weapon they used against us? The heat was unbearable. All the men felt like they were on fire. Using the drug would have made no difference."

Maximus thought back to what Allotey had conveyed to him following the incident, and he was now quite sure of the weapon used once he had filled in the missing pieces. Through his vast web of informants, he had learned about the breach into the supposedly secure U.S. DOD computer system. Someone had hacked their way into the ADS 2 file months ago and made off with the weapon specs, and that someone had to have been an employee of Tursiops. And while it was obvious they had advanced the technology another step, he would be fully prepared this time around.

"They hit you with non-lethal microwaves," Maximus commented, "but we'll have measures in place to counter them upon your arrival."

Noting the inquisitive look clinging to Allotey's face, Maximus stopped him before he could pose any more questions. "The details of the invasion plan are still being worked out, so there is no point in discussing it further. All will be provided you just prior to the mission."

The senator broke the silence that descended on the room, now taking full advantage of Maximus' unforeseen presence at this meeting. With him here, it would be safe to bring up one last point. "If gold does exist, and I'm almost certain that it does, there may be one other place where it's stored."

Maximus frowned in annoyance. "Where?"

"Somewhere near Malique." Van Heflin risked a darting glance at Cardoza. The drug lord's eyes were like two burning cauldrons, the flames harbored within them now fully stoked and nearing a flashpoint.

"Never heard of it."

"It's a small fishing village near Gonaives up north. The head of Tursiops is from Malique."

"Once the coup is accomplished, we can investigate such a possibility," Maximus conceded.

Van Heflin could no longer hold back his innate greed. He had gone too far now to stop himself from stepping over the threshold. "I assume we will all get a share of whatever's found," he said.

Maximus grinned without warmth. "Your insatiable hunger for riches never ceases to amaze me, Brent. But as you well know, spoils are divided according to rank and privilege within *The Order*. I shouldn't have to remind you this policy was established by our forbearers long before you were born."

The senator grimaced inwardly. Though he was not privy to all the components that comprised this shadowy hierarchy, he had learned enough over the years that a loosely knit conglomeration of individuals and groups formed the gears of its machinery, including various foundations, private think tanks, union chiefs, political action committees, and other front groups. But then again, as far as he knew, Maximus was the one that held the ultimate rank and privilege, the

Supreme Leader who sat at the top of the pyramid. And Maximus had the power to circumvent the rules, dispersing the booty as he saw fit.

"Besides," Maximus went on in a sudden change of voice, "you're going to be quite busy over the next several years, more so than you've ever been, and it will be crucial your career suffers no scandalous setbacks."

The statement puzzled the senator. Maximus was grinning like a fox, his manner noticeably less rigid. "I'm always busy," Van Heflin muttered defensively, "and I've always managed to stay one step ahead of scandals."

"It will be different this time," Maximus persisted emphatically. "Making a run at the Oval Office will put you in a whole new limelight."

A dead silence immediately descended, and Van Heflin could feel every eye in the room scrutinizing him as though he were a newly discovered life form. Truly stunned, he studied Maximus closely to see if this was some kind of joke, but he knew Maximus never joked.

"*The Order* has decided to back you as a nominee for the U.S. presidency," Maximus clarified, his demeanor abruptly becoming serious again. "You'll have unlimited funds to support your campaign. With your unblemished senatorial record and a mainstream media fully endorsing your run, you should have no trouble getting elected."

Van Heflin remained speechless, too overcome with excitement to say anything for the moment. This was totally unexpected. The presidency was something he had always wanted, but a thing much like a forbidden fruit. Unless the gods granted it, he dared not reach for it. And Maximus was certainly a god. But then again, he was a Bonesman, and having entered the esteemed though semi-clandestine ranks of the Skull and Bones at Yale years earlier, he realized with striking clarity that he had been bred and groomed to be President all along.

But as the senator thought about it, it suddenly dawned on him there would be a problem, and he voiced his concern. "But how can I run? It's already past the deadline to get on the primary ticket, and the presidential election is only months away."

"Let me worry about that," Maximus affirmed with a dark smile. "For what I have planned, there won't be any election in November. By then, martial law will be in effect and the election will be suspended for at least another six months, which will leave us ample time between now and then to get you on the slate and prepare you for the ensuing debates that are sure to focus on preventing another catastrophe that led to imposition of martial law in the first place."

Maximus held back from offering more, letting the statement hang for several more seconds before going on. "We'll strategize your campaign once the coup here in Haiti is accomplished."

Checking his wristwatch, Maximus rose from his chair and placed his knuckles on the table. "Gentlemen," he rasped, "I will expect each of you to carry out your part so that our objectives can be reached. Failure is not an option." Without another word, he turned and strode briskly for the massive cast iron door that sealed off the room and separated it from the torture chamber. The door was as old as the fortress and creaked on rusty hinges as one of Cardoza's men swung it outward to let him pass. Swensen swept the room with an ominous gaze before following.

As soon as the door closed, Cardoza addressed the others, smiling expansively as he spoke. "Too bad our leader could not stay for the entertainment I have planned."

An alarm immediately sounded in Van Heflin's head. There was something sinister in Cardoza's tone. "What kind of entertainment?" he asked suspiciously.

Cardoza ignored the question. "If you gentlemen will follow me," he said, rising and heading unceremoniously for the door.

Begrudgingly, the senator arose, making sure to trail behind the other men in the procession, including Cardoza's hooligans who showed no enthusiasm as they trudged along. Except for Ermstine, everyone appeared glum. As they ambled through the dungeon, he noticed a door to one of the holding cells had been left wide open. He found this odd since it had been closed on his way down here. Slowing his pace, he became aware of the horrible stink hanging in the air. When he had passed this way before, only a mild odor had accosted him, but with the cell's door now fully open, the immediate area reeked. Repulsed but curious, he stopped and peered into the cell's dark interior. Though it was impossible to tell, it appeared to be unoccupied, but he knew someone had been defecating within its confines, and recently at that.

Eager to get away from the stench, he quickened his step to catch up with the others. It was a long walk as they retraced their way along the same dimly lit corridors and stone steps as before. Eventually they left the main keep and came to an outer courtyard within the fortress. It was open to only a sliver of sky, surrounded by massive ramparts, battlements and turreted towers looming overhead, and was the first area visitors encountered after entering the stronghold through the gatehouse.

Once again, Van Heflin found himself marveling over the layout of the fortification, so seemingly impregnable to attack. Recessed into an inner wall of the main keep was a long cage the size of a ship's cargo container, and within the cage was Cardoza's pet Bengal tiger. The cage was situated on the keep's south side, well back from the gatehouse which lay along the western quarter of the fortress.

At seeing the procession of men, the huge beast rose to its feet and began pacing back and forth, setting fierce yellow eyes on the procession. Through information provided by Rico during his previous visit, the senator knew why the drug lord kept the tiger, and once again he noted the barred gate within the cage that separated the pen into two halves. It was then that he wondered if the entertainment Cardoza had spoken of involved the carnivore. But Cardoza ignored his pet, continuing on and rounding a corner, eventually leading everyone to the gatehouse that gave way to the portcullis overlooking the moat. Even before Van Heflin reached the drawbridge, he heard the pleading wail of a man in great distress.

Van Heflin was startled to see Rico dangling by the wrists. He was attached to a rope that wound through a pulley situated at the end of a thick wooden pole. The pole was slowly being extended horizontally from an opening in the fortress wall thirty feet from the side of the bridge. Rico was completely naked, and the senator saw that his thighs had been slashed, smeared red with copious amounts of blood dribbling down to his ankles and dropping to the gray water filling the moat. Already he could see fins racing back and forth directly below.

Cardoza turned to face his entourage, his eyes singling out Van Heflin. "This man betrayed me, and I will not tolerate betrayal."

Van Heflin watched as the tip of the pole was advanced to the middle of the canal, unaware that his legs were quaking. Rico struggled violently, his eyes opened wide and following the mass of fins skittering wildly along the surface beneath him.

The head of a man poked from the opening in the wall from which the pole extended, looking to Cardoza.

"Lower him slowly," Cardoza shouted. "I do not want my guests to be disappointed." He turned and motioned to someone beyond the group of onlookers. "Bring the prisoner to the edge of the bridge," he commanded.

Van Heflin swung around to observe a man being escorted onto the drawbridge by two of Cardoza's ruffians, one on each side. The senator studied him briefly, guessing he was in his early sixties, though it was hard to tell because of the grime smudging his face. He was wearing tattered clothing, soiled as though he had been forced to lie in filth. This was further confirmed by the offensive odor wafting off him. He appeared forlorn and pathetic as he was led to the middle of the bridge and forced to stand overlooking the water. Not really caring why the man had been led here, Van Heflin brought his eyes back to the main event.

Rico let out a bloodcurdling cry that caused hackles to rise along the senator's neck. Inch by inch, he was lowered, his legs kicking wildly, the water's surface now churned fiercely from the horde of predators massed together and competing savagely for a share of him.

"I have been loyal to you," Rico screamed, blood from his wounded thighs flowing more acutely from his intense exertions. The water had now turned red with it. "Please, Rafael, do not do this," he begged.

Cardoza smiled sadistically. "I have been monitoring you, Rico. You have no compunctions about revealing my affairs to anyone willing to pay even a meager sum to obtain that information." As he said this, he turned to stare at the senator.

Van Heflin looked away, unwilling to meet the drug lord's eyes, suddenly unsure if his own life was in jeopardy. *No, that was not possible*, he told himself. *Maximus needs me. Maximus would have Cardoza's head if anything happened to so vital a member of The Order.* For one indecisive moment, he considered walking away from the horrifying scene, but to his own surprise he could not bring himself to look away, overcome with fascination. He discovered he was awakening to a side of himself he never knew existed.

Cardoza studied the senator in annoyance. This was not quite the reaction he should be seeing. Van Heflin appeared to be enjoying himself, thrilled by the prospect of grisly death. Nevertheless, he hoped the sight would be burned into Van Heflin's memory as a harsh reminder never to meddle in his affairs again. The bug he had planted in the SUV had served its purpose, and Cardoza had heard every word of the conversation between Rico and the senator.

Cardoza turned back to take in Rico's torment. Using the tiger to appease his anger no longer had the same luster it once had, but he suddenly found himself enthralled by this new form of revenge. No one outside his immediate clan of henchmen was supposed to have knowledge of the gold, not even Maximus. He had taken great pains to keep it a secret, even after the raid on the cove had ended in failure. Eager to stay abreast of the mission, he had purposely diverted one of his tuna trawlers, the *San Pedro*, from its duties and had stationed it just off the coast in close proximity to the cove he so desperately wanted, staying in close contact with the ship's captain using an encrypted satellite phone. The ship's crew had stood by an inordinate amount of time awaiting the return of Zinova's choppers, but when no Hinds showed up, the trawler had steamed down the coast where it had chanced upon what was left of the raiding party. Only six men had remained, one of them so badly wounded that he was not expected to live, and their leader, the one with the mismatched eyes, had not been one of them. Upon Cardoza's orders, the *San Pedro* had dispatched a boat ashore to retrieve the survivors. No sooner had the band of pitiful marauders set foot aboard the vessel when a bright object slipped from the clothing of one of them and fell, landing heavily on the foot of a crewman and making him roar with pain. Too late to prevent other crewmen from locking eyes on the cause of the ruckus, the careless mercenary had snatched it up quickly and stowed it with his other gear. It was soon discovered that several of these survivors also had gold bars in their possession, and at hearing this Cardoza had consulted with the ship's captain to devise treachery that entailed killing them. The secrets the cove held belonged to him and no one else, and he was not going to let knowledge of its treasures fall into other hands. But these were dangerous men and catching them off guard would not be easy. They needed to be lulled into a state of complacency before the *San Pedro's* crew could dispatch them. So, while the mercenaries were feasting in the ship's galley, the crew had made its move. Unfortunately, he had lost two of his men in the short firefight that had preceded the execution, but at least he had possession of the bars, positive proof that gold actually existed within the cove.

The *San Pedro* had also brought back another prize. Immediately upon casting the raiding party's bloodied remains into the sea, an enormous shark had risen up from the depths to feast upon the carcasses. Cardoza had been told it was another great white even larger than Scylla. At hearing this, he had ordered the crew to drop a net and capture it. The shark was to be another addition to the moat's growing horde of ferocious denizens, making him wonder how receptive Scylla would be to the new occupant once the *San Pedro* arrived back.

Cardoza dropped these thoughts and focused on the scene before him, wanting to savor every aspect of it. Ever so slowly, Rico's feet neared the water, now thrashed into a frothing maelstrom of pandemonium as sharks fought for position directly under him. Rico screamed again, his pleadings exploding from his lips in an incoherent stream of gibberish as he stared down in wide-eyed terror.

Equally immersed in the event, Van Heflin watched with glazed eyes. The sound of something intruded its way into his awareness, and he turned his head to espy Ermstine laughing hysterically. The laughter was infectious, and he quickly joined in, unable to hold back the uncontrollable giddiness that had descended on him.

By now, Rico was bringing his knees to his chest in a vain effort to keep his feet beyond the reach of snapping jaws, every few seconds kicking down furiously to fend off a rising snout. But his actions for survival were futile, and inevitably his lower limbs could no longer be kept from the frenzy. Sharks pressed in bumping and jostling one another, the congestion of massed bodies so tight that it was impossible for any of them to get a clean open-mouthed strike on the dangling prey. Nevertheless, their teeth were slashing and raking those limbs, darkening the water a deep crimson that expanded outward.

Van Heflin continued to stare in rapt fixation, utterly captivated by the scene. He realized Cardoza had not exaggerated. The teeth of a tiger shark were like scalpels, able to flay and eviscerate with little effort. Suspended like a side of beef, Rico wailed in agony as flesh was stripped from his legs as though by a swarm of monstrously sized piranha.

And then something unexpected happened. The shark pack suddenly bolted, moving away quickly under the drawbridge upon which the senator stood. Lifting his gaze, Van Heflin saw the reason for the mass exodus. A fin considerably larger than all the rest cleaved the water, charging down the canal from the opposite direction. He perceived it was Scylla, the leviathan great white that had scrutinized him as a meal. She had sensed the commotion and was coming to claim her share. It was apparent she was the queen of this little kingdom, and sensing her approach her subjects had fled to get out of the way of that enormous maw.

By this time, Rico was waist deep in the moat, wallowing in his own blood and looking dazed, though he was still very much alive. Scylla surged past him before swinging around to make another pass, and Rico's orbs immediately widened yet again when he saw her huge dorsal slicing the surface. Looking up, he locked eyes with Cardoza one last time, managing to spit a thick wad of phlegm up at him that fell well short of its target. His momentary display of bravado dissolved as Scylla rose from the water and turned sideways to snare his torso in her massive jaws.

The pole supporting Rico, though having the diameter of a moderately sized tree trunk, bent under Scylla's three-ton mass as she pulled her meal down, and the rope tied to Rico's wrists vacillated erratically as it strained against the excessive load. Rico let out a final agonized scream as both his arms were torn free of their shoulder sockets, the pole jerking upward by the sudden release of tension, and his detached limbs were flung high as he was swept below the surface.

Van Heflin looked on, mesmerized by the bloodied arms falling back down and quivering to a stop, still tethered snugly at the wrists.

"Drop the rest of him!" Cardoza ordered, looking to his henchman manning the pole.

A rush of tiger sharks immediately swarmed back as Rico's arms were lowered into the murky water, and within seconds the limbs vanished, the rope holding them jerking violently.

The drug lord took a few steps toward the individual he had referred to as 'the prisoner' and smiled cruelly. "Would you like to join Rico, Mr. Osgood?" he asked bluntly. The prisoner said nothing, continuing to stare wide-eyed as the water turned crimson, clearly terrorized by what he had seen.

Cardoza moved closer to the man, keeping his voice low so as not to be overheard by his guests. "I'll give you three more days to reconsider my offer," he stated airily. "In the meantime you can continue to enjoy the delightful accommodations I have provided you. But if you refuse to give me what I want, you can look forward to the same fate as Rico."

Cardoza turned, his eyes sweeping the small throng of spectators to study their reactions to the lurid event, his gaze finally coming to rest on Van Heflin. "Perhaps I'll find better ways to entertain each of you in the future," he said, a broad grin clinging to his face.

Van Heflin maintained his composure, his Adam's apple bobbing only slightly at the implied threat. "I'll look forward to it," he said, managing to return the grin, his mind roving over the possibility of someday superseding Cardoza in the cabal's rigid pecking order. Certainly that would be possible once he occupied the Oval Office.

Chapter Twenty-three: Phillipe Missing

Sitting at a table in the *Angel's* salon, Jake studied the plans Belachek had meticulously sketched, not liking what he was seeing. "If the drawbridge is in the up position, the only way in is over the walls."

"I don't advise that," Belachek said.

"Why not?"

Belachek showed him the circles he had drawn in at evenly spaced intervals along the fortification's perimeter. "There are towers that extend up from the outer walls, six of them. I saw movement in two of those towers during my visit. It is probable Cardoza keeps men in them armed with heavy weaponry to ward off an assault."

"But you're not sure?"

Belachek leaned back in his chair. "It is a reasonable assumption. What defensive measures would you take if you were Cardoza?"

Jake let out a deep sigh and shook his head. "I guess that rules out using the chopper to get in."

"There is another way," Belachek offered, placing a finger on the moat abutting the east side of the fortress. He looked up to give Jake a crafty smile. "You have a problem with sharks?"

"I don't, but they might have a problem with me." Jake held up a forearm to show him the jagged puckered scar caused by a mako attack. "So Cardoza keeps sharks in the moat. That doesn't surprise me."

Belachek brought his mismatched eyes back to the paper. "Cardoza likes showing his pets to guests. I was with Zinova when he met with him. We were led to a room on a lower level where a meeting was held.

The room borders the moat, and we could see sharks swimming by, big nasty ones."

"A viewing window like an aquarium?"

Belachek nodded. "If you can get through the glass, that is your way in."

"What's this?" Jake asked, pointing to a structure well away from the stronghold.

"I believe it to be an aircraft hangar since it is at the end of the runway. It is large enough to house at least three commercial jetliners. I saw quite a bit of activity taking place there when we landed. Crates were being unloaded from trucks."

"Any idea what was in those crates?"

"None."

At that moment, Zimbola entered the salon, ducking his head down to avoid catching it on the doorframe. "A call has come in for you, Jay Jay." The Jamaican handed him the encrypted satellite phone they routinely used.

Jake shoved himself out of the chair. "Why don't you make our guest feel at home while I take it up in the pilothouse." He stopped at the door, turning to look back at the mercenary. "Do I have your word you won't give us any trouble, Victor?" He had studied the man closely during the last half hour, assessing his reaction to the three albino creations decorating the salon walls, all of them painted by Achilles, and he could not detect any signs of nausea or illness in the man. In fact, Victor appeared happy and at peace with himself as though a great burden had been lifted from him.

"You don't have to worry about me," Belachek avowed sedately. "I owe my life and that of my son to you."

"I'll accept that for now," Jake said dryly. With that, he strode out the door.

Zimby sat down heavily in the chair Jake had vacated, casting wary eyes on Belachek. He was not as trusting as Jake and needed further assurance. Indicating one of the paintings on the port side wall, he looked Belachek squarely in his mismatched orbs. "Look at the painting and tell me what you see?" he said, his voice deep and demanding.

Upon reaching the privacy of the *Angel's* pilothouse, Jake put the phone to his ear. He had expected the caller to be Jacob, but was surprised when he heard Mat's voice.

"I heard you came close to buying it, good buddy."

"Close is a meaningless word unless you're talking horseshoes and hand grenades," Jake replied glibly.

"Zimby tells me you're back at the cove."

"Seems I happened to be in the right place at the right time. Our old pal Cardoza is a persistent bastard. This time he hired mercenaries to take this little sanctuary. From what I've learned, they were part of the same team that was laying for me aboard the *Southern Star.*"

"A coordinated operation?"

"Yeah, does the name Zinova ring a bell?"

"Not really."

"How about the Reaper?"

A moment's hesitation ensued before Mat responded, his tone animated. "You just jogged my memory. Karloff Zinova used to be a Spetsnaz operative. During the Cold War, he was the Soviet's most decorated soldier. The Afghans were the ones that came up with that moniker for him. Following the Soviet collapse, he turned mercenary, offering his services to anyone willing to meet his exorbitant fee."

"Well I guess Cardoza was willing to pay it," Jake replied.

"That guy's becoming a nuisance," Mat grumbled. "So how'd you make out?"

"I got lucky and managed to capture one of his lieutenants, a guy by the name of Victor Belachek, also a former Spetsnaz operative. But he's been very cooperative, giving me the big picture."

"How'd you manage that?"

"It's a strange story, one I'll fill you in on later. But from what I've learned, the Hind we captured was piloted by none other than Zinova. What did you do with him and his crew?"

"Locked them up in the ship's brig."

Silence ensued on Mat's end, and Jake was forced to press him. "So what happened after I left you?"

"Things fell apart, I'm sorry to say."

Jake cut in quickly before Mat could go on. "Is Phillipe okay?"

"Relax, buddy. You should be proud to know he saved my ass. Bashir was badly wounded, but your mother-in-law was able to pick him up in one of our choppers. Last I saw, she was heading toward the Haitian coast rather than back to the colony. Any idea where she went?"

"She came here."

Another bout of silence befell the conversation. "I'm confused," Mat said. There was a sudden edge to his voice. "Isn't Phillipe with you?"

"No."

"I had Phillipe carry Bashir up to the *Star's* helipad," Mat uttered sharply, his tone consumed with panic. "I specifically ordered him to get on the chopper."

"He's not here." Now it was Jake's turn to evoke panic.

"Oh, shit!" Mat shot back. "That means he's still on the ship."

"You're not on the ship?"

"I had to abandon her. The blue helmet captain accompanying Allotey, I believe his name was Alvarez. He and his gang were sent to take back the ship, making a HALO on her. Phillipe and I were mostly successful in taking him on, but unfortunately Kalid also got wounded. With a second wave of UN reinforcements dropping down on us, I had no choice but to get Kalid out of there."

"I hope to god Phillipe's still not aboard her," Jake shot back dismally. "Any word from Ez? Surely she would have heard something from Perseus about his whereabouts."

"So far nothing! But the kid's smart. He's still got a cloaker and a Masker, so if he's still on the ship, Alvarez and company may not know he's there."

"This is not good," Jake groaned, "but at least the *Star's* not going anywhere. Maybe we-"

Mat spoke quickly before Jake could go on. "Another ship arrived to tow her away."

"Great, just great! Do you know which way they're headed?"

"Ez has been tracking them using satellite surveillance. They already made the turn below Haiti's lower peninsula. She thinks they may be headed for the Bay of Anse-Milieu. The water's deep enough there to accommodate large container ships like the *Star*."

Jake was puzzled. As far as he knew, there were no ship repair facilities at that location. "Why does she think that?"

"Because that's where Cardoza's yacht is right now. Ez got a bird's eye view of the vessel and has positively identified her as the *Usurpar*. She's currently sitting at anchor near the town of Tiburon."

"Did you say Tiburon?"

"Yes." Mat paused. "You sound as though you know something."

"That's where Cardoza stays holed up when he comes ashore. There's an old fortress located there that overlooks the bay. If that's the *Star's* destination, then I'm betting she's carrying something Cardoza wants unloaded right away."

"Any idea what it might be?"

"Not a clue."

"I hate to be the bearer of more bad news, Jake, but it's starting to heat up over here. The UN is mobilizing forces to invade us. Seems someone has gone to great lengths to vilify our operation, using the news media to label us as eco pirates. The media also claimed we hijacked the ship. Makes me believe your conspiracy theory is right on the money."

"I wish I were wrong about that. Ez give you any feedback on Big D?"

"She says there's a one-in-twenty probability at best in bringing it on line without blowing the system. Something to do with the crystal array not being large enough yet."

"If only we had more time to grow them bigger," Jake lamented.

"No sense crying over spilled milk," Mat rejoined.

"Listen, Mat, you're going to have to stay put and do whatever you can to defend the city."

The momentary silence that followed told Jake his longtime friend wasn't happy about this. "Aren't you coming back?"

"Not just yet. I'm going to Tiburon to take care of some business that should have been taken care of long ago, but first I'll need a few things from you."

Mat knew exactly what that meant, and he sighed in resignation. "What do you need?"

"Has Dr. Grahm gotten *Johnnie* up and running yet? Last I spoke with him, he was troubleshooting the auto-guidance system and hydrodrive power inducer."

"I believe he solved both problems. Why do you ask?"

For the next two minutes, Jake elaborated on the plan he had formulated. "You think you can get those things to me in the next few hours?" he finally asked.

"I'll take care of it right away."

"Don't let me down, buddy."

"When have I ever done that?"

"I suppose never would be an appropriate answer."

"You better keep that in mind." Another pause. "And Jake?"

"What?"

"Don't do anything stupid."

Jake sighed. "Doing something stupid is sometimes the only option we have," he riposted flippantly.

Chapter Twenty-four:
A Deceiver Felled

Standing at a railing along one of Aquaria's outer esplanades, Amelia cast a pensive stare at the translucent indigo sea, feeling very much alone and wondering if her own obstinacy had dashed her hopes of a prolific career. A barrage of conflicting thoughts hammered away at her. Could it be that she was far too naïve and idealistic for this business? Bolder's words came back to haunt her. *"My job is to record events on camera, and yours is to provide commentary, nothing more. What the editors do with it is their business."* The idea that Bolder might actually be right tormented her. Even so, all her previous ambitions to become a top-notch news commentator now seemed insignificant when compared to the aspirations of these colonists. Idly she glanced in the direction where she had last seen the *Southern Star*, though it had vanished hours earlier, towed over the horizon by another large container ship.

"I wonder what thoughts lay beneath those beautiful tresses."

Startled, Amelia spun around to find herself looking into a bronze, masculine face. A pair of mirthful limpid eyes regarded her, seemingly matching the very color and clarity of the surrounding sea. Separating them was the bridge of a perfectly straight nose perched above a mouth turned upward at the corners in an amused smile, and below that mouth was a square chin shadowed with dark stubble that hadn't seen a razor in several days. A thick crop of unkempt jet black hair fluttered lazily in the mild Caribbean breeze, nearly reaching the man's eyebrows.

Amelia continued to stare slack-jawed, lost in those self-assured, appraising eyes.

"I assume you are the Amelia Amhurst I've heard so much about." Mat held the smile and stuck out a hand.

Dazedly, Amelia accepted it, still unable to pull her eyes from his. "Yes, I'm Amelia."

"Name's Mat, Mat Daniels. How do you like our little kingdom?"

Amelia quickly gathered herself in and returned the smile, suddenly aware of how she must look. "Little is not the word I would use to describe this facility. Enormous would be more appropriate. My head is still spinning over what has been accomplished here." She paused, noticing the jump suit he wore was damp, clinging to a trim, athletic body. "Do you always go for a swim fully clothed?"

Mat widened his grin. "Only when circumstances dictate." He knew he badly needed a shower, shave and change of clothing, but habits he had acquired in the Seals were hard to suppress. Even though his battle aboard the *Southern Star* had ended hours earlier, he had spent over an hour in one of Aquaria's infirmaries to make sure Kalid was out of danger. Then he made the call to Jake, following through on his requests. The thought that he should go against Jake's wishes and leave for the cove at once nagged away at him, but he knew he had to stay put to do whatever was necessary to defend the colony. To alleviate his growing edginess, he had opted to go back in the water to secure a loose cable holding down one of the OTEC water intakes. He knew he could have delegated the task to one of the dolphins, but he needed to keep himself busy to avoid thinking too much about what was brewing.

"Do you work here?" Amelia asked.

"Not really. I don't consider it work at all. When you love doing something, it's hard to classify it as work. To my way of thinking, play would be a better choice of words."

"Then would it be impolite to ask what you play at?" Amelia felt her pulse quicken. Normally she was unaffected by attractive men, but there was something about this man that made her heart race.

Mat shrugged. "Some say I oversee security around here, but then there are others who might disagree."

"Then you must know what's happening."

Mat sighed in resignation, then laughed as though the matter were of no consequence. "Yes, but we knew this sort of thing was bound to happen sooner or later. When you push for something good in the world, there are some that are going to push back."

"I hope you don't think I had anything to do with those deceitful newscasts."

"Jacob briefed me. Said they were doctored by your editors."

"What are you going to do?"

"What any organism does when threatened. We defend ourselves."

Amelia's jaw dropped. Mat seemed way too complacent in the way he said this. What was about to befall the colony was serious, and he seemed to be taking it lightly.

"Aren't you worried?"

A nonchalant smile flashed briefly across Mat's face. "We still have a few tricks up our sleeve."

"They're going to throw a ton of military might against this place," Amelia reminded him. Mat's utter complacency shocked her. "How can you be so calm in the face of that?"

Mat leaned up against the rail, setting his gaze on the horizon. "When a gun is held to a person's head, he has two choices. He can either whine like a baby and beg for his life, or he can look his foe in the eye and grin. I prefer to grin."

Amelia was about to throw more concerns at him but pulled up short when her cameraman suddenly appeared.

"Just got a call from headquarters, sweetheart, and they want us to get footage of the island," Bolder said, speaking as though Mat were not present.

Amelia stared at him in disbelief. "I told you I'm through. I will not abet such despicable deceivers."

"You're gonna blow a huge bonus, Amhurst, for me as well as yourself. If you don't care about it, that's your business, but don't take money out of my pocket."

"I guess you'll have to deal with it."

Bolder scowled darkly, then reached for her wrist as if to drag her away with him, but Mat stuck out an arm to prevent it from happening. "You heard the lady. She said she's through."

Bolder stared up at him, the whites of his eyes streaked red with veins. He gave the impression of a bull fixated on a matador just before charging. Though he was shorter, he outweighed Mat by at least seventy pounds. He had once cleaned house in a wild melee that had broken out in a Beirut bar a few years back, pummeling seven men senseless and sending four of them to the hospital. Regretfully, he had been drunk at the time and didn't remember much about the brawl. But fully sober as he was now, he was keenly aware of his own brute strength and physical prowess. They didn't call him the Boulder for nothing. "I don't know who you are, pal, but if you want trouble, you found it."

Amelia watched as Mat produced that same lighthearted smile. "Now why would I look for trouble in a place like this?" he proclaimed innocently. "Peace and tranquility is more my speed."

"Then I recommend you mind your own business," Bolder growled, not understanding why his superior size failed to intimidate this pipsqueak.

"If you insist." Mat lowered his interceding hand.

Bolder nudged him out of the way with a powerful shoulder and reached for Amelia again, but before he could clamp onto her wrist, his eyes mushroomed wide and he sank to his knees.

"I'm terribly sorry," Mat apologized. "I have this problem with my right foot. I just can't seem to control it."

Bolder rolled onto his back, holding his crotch, his eyes squeezed tight in obvious pain. "You fuck!" he gasped, struggling to suck in air. "You're gonna be sorry for that."

"You're absolutely right," Mat conceded flippantly. "I'm sorry for not using my left foot instead. It packs more kick."

Mat turned to Amelia. "How would you like a tour of Aquaria's lower levels? Jacob tells me you haven't seen them yet."

Amelia looked at him in amazement. "I would love it."

Gallantly, Mat stuck out an elbow. "Then latch on and follow me."

By the time Bolder was able to stand again, both Mat and Amelia were gone.

Hunkered down in the tight quarters of the *Avenging Angel's* forward hold, Jake busied himself by putting together the gear he would need for the Tiburon mission.

A familiar voice, soft and mellifluous, interrupted his concentration. "I'm going with you!"

Jake stared back, seeing the same stubbornness he had come to know so well. "No way! Too many unknowns, way too dangerous."

"But you're going to need help," insisted Destiny. "You can't do this by yourself."

Jake continued loading shells into the Sledgehammer's detachable drum magazine. This time he would use frag-12 rounds. "I'll have Fernando and Jimenez with me. Victor has also volunteered to help. They'll be enough to get the job done. Too many players will only complicate the mission."

As soon as he said this, another insistent voice rang indignantly in his brain. *You're forgetting someone, JJ.*

Jake shot a look at Destiny, noticing that she had heard it too. "You're not coming either, Achilles!" he said aloud.

Something akin to a sulk impinged on Jake's awareness, but he ignored it. "Who's going to take care of the twins?" he felt it necessary to add.

"Mother can do that." Destiny was not to be dissuaded. "This is my fight as much as it is yours."

Jake stopped what he was doing, his reply gentle and consolatory. "I don't want you tarnishing your soul with what has to be done. It wouldn't suit you." He let his eyes linger on her a moment longer, then went back to loading cartridges. "And besides, I don't want to find myself in the heat of battle worrying about you. It could make me careless."

At that moment, Destiny's mother crowded into the hold to stand next to her daughter. "We are approaching another nexus, Jay Jay, and from what I'm able to foresee, both Destiny and Achilles must accompany you."

Jake looked up, caught completely by surprise by this unexpected intrusion. For one prolonged moment, he could only stare before a sudden surge of understanding took hold of him. A mother would never intentionally place her offspring in harm's way unless there was a damn good reason. But this was not the Harriet Grahm he had come to know since the demise of Ternier. There was now an added dimension to her, the same psychic aura he had encountered long ago. Though it wasn't visible, he could actually feel it, strangely attuned to its glow. Standing before him was Amphitrite, the same enigmatic personage who had played a crucial role in the past in bringing about the chain of events that had led to the building of Aquaria. At this moment she was invoking a jumble of conflicting thoughts within him. Abruptly, all his doubts, fears, and reservations about what he was attempting to undertake loomed in his mind's eye, and he realized a great deal of uncertainty hung in the balance. Complete failure was still possible with or without Destiny's participation. But there was one thing he was certain of, and that was to trust what was being revealed to him, for if he failed to heed Amphitrite's words, the mission would be doomed from the very start.

"I have to know something," Jake said.

Amphitrite stared back, looking solemn. "You want to know why Phillipe elected to remain aboard the *Southern Star* and if I had anything to do with it."

"Yes."

"No, Jay Jay, I played no part in his decision. I don't know why he decided to remain aboard. All I can tell you is that it felt right at the time."

"Is he still aboard the ship?"

"I don't know."

The sun was low on the horizon when something bobbed to the ocean surface forty miles west by southwest from the cove.

Jake shielded his eyes from the sun glare shimmering off the water, then checked his watch. "Right on schedule," he said.

Zimbola held the *Angel* steady as *Johnnie* came around their starboard side. Nearly the size of a bus, the underwater vehicle had been originally designed by the albinos as an interdiction craft capable of capturing large marine predators. But it served other purposes as well. The craft was incredibly maneuverable and streamlined to reach speeds far greater than even Achilles could achieve. At its heart was a specially grown crystal, a power inducer that drew energy directly from the surrounding salt water environment. Jake had trouble wrapping his mind around its operating principle, something to do with quantum entanglement. The scientific explanation was difficult for even Jacob to understand, a manifestation of the superior albino intellect that tended to hinge more on the metaphysical rather than the physical.

What Jake did know was that *Johnnie* had to first achieve a threshold speed of seven knots before the crystal was able to draw energy from the sea and provide the necessary power for the craft to move at higher speeds. It was basically an electric motor that gave *Johnnie* the kick start it required to go faster. Once the power inducer was engaged, the electric motor shut down.

"Be seeing you, big guy," Jake said, giving a farewell to his longtime friend.

Zimby scowled. "I should be going with you."

"We already discussed this. I need you to stay with the twins and their grandmother."

Jake left quickly, not wanting to debate the issue any longer, eager to get going. Leaving his children in Zimby's care would ease his mind considerably, for no one was better suited to protect them than the black giant. And he didn't have to worry about Bashir either, though he would have preferred to use him rather than Jimenez on the upcoming mission. Though Amphitrite, Destiny and the dolphins had managed to heal Bashir, he would need more time to fully recover, and it was shortly after Jake had been revived from his own critical injury that they had told him Bashir had already been transferred to the nearby village of Malique to be nursed back to health by Samuel's mother, Louwanda. Bashir would need at least another day to get back on his feet, at which time Kobe would take him back to Aquaria aboard the *Exoco*.

Jake let out a deep sigh. So many things to consider and worry about. All he wanted at this moment was to get aboard *Johnnie* and commence with the mission. With UN forces being mobilized to take control of the colony, time was no longer a luxury.

As he climbed down from the pilothouse, he thought about the name oddly bestowed on the submersible. It was Phillipe who had first begun calling it *'Johnnie'* shortly after its construction two years earlier.

"Why *Johnnie*?" Jake recalled asking the boy at the time. Phillipe had merely shrugged, saying, "I just like the name. It reminds me of a friend I once had back in Port-au-Prince." From then on the name had stuck, with all members of the colony, including the dolphins, using the moniker whenever it came up in conversation.

A sense of apprehension gripped Jake as he thought about Phillipe, wondering if his protégé was currently safe. Hopefully he would find out soon enough as he shouldered his way past the two men stationed along the stern railing, their eyes fixated on the strange looking watercraft as it bumped up lightly against the vessel's swim platform. Almost immediately, a hatch on top of the craft's hull opened with a slight hiss.

"Let me make sure everything's in readiness before you climb aboard," he said, glancing briefly at Jimenez and Victor. With catlike agility he jumped down onto the swim platform and then bounded onto *Johnnie's* hull. As he descended through the hatch, he was shocked to see Franklin Grahm sitting at the controls.

"There was no need for you to come, doctor," Jake said. "This baby should have been programmed to get here all by itself."

Normally carrying a cheerful, upbeat demeanor, enhanced all the more by a thick mane of shaggy white hair reaching to his shoulders, the aging scientist appeared apologetic. "Sorry, Jake, but I just don't trust the auto-guidance. Still seems a bit twitchy if you ask me. I wanted to make sure it got here."

Jake glanced at the control panel with its array of multifunctional displays, which glowed with a colorful mix of vibrant luminosity. "The hydrodrive give you any problems?"

"None whatsoever. Had her up to seventy-nine knots at one point."

Jake noticed the canvas bags tied down firmly in a storage rack to the rear of the cabin. "Mat give you everything I asked for?"

"It's all there. Mind telling me what you need all that explosive for? Mat says you could sink an entire armada with what's in those bags."

"I'm worried it won't be enough."

Franklin nodded stoically when Jake failed to offer more. He could pretty much guess what Jake had in mind. Not wanting to press the issue, he changed the subject. "Is Harriet with you?"

"She's here." Jake refrained from mentioning her transformation, wondering if she had completely lost sight of her actual identity as she once did before. As the Amphitrite of old, she had forgotten who Franklin was, failing to remember he was her husband until she met up with him again after an absence of twenty-two years. But as far as he could tell, her memory seemed to be intact this time around.

Franklin arose from the control panel seat, seemingly ready to vacate the sub but appearing deep in thought. "Mat told me Phillipe may still be aboard the freighter and that you're going after him," he said.

"That's right."

"He also said you were planning on settling a vendetta with Rafael Cardoza."

"It's not a vendetta."

"Listen, son, I had a lot of time to think about this on the way here." Franklin let the statement hang before going on. "I'd hate to see anything happen to the father of my grandchildren. You sure this is necessary?"

"I have to stop Cardoza once and for all, otherwise he's just going to keep coming after Destiny and the twins. If I do nothing, sooner or later he's going to succeed, ransoming them in exchange for Aquaria's wealth. If that ever happened, I'd never be able to forgive myself." Jake had thought long and hard on what he must do, and he voiced his decision adamantly. "The time has come to bring the fight to Cardoza on his own turf. I doubt he will be expecting that."

Franklin stared, saying nothing for several seconds. "Who's going with you?"

Jake was now cornered with no way out. "I've got a capable force."

"May I ask who?"

"If you must know, Destiny will be coming."

The alarm Jake had anticipated did not materialize on Franklin's face. "I see," the scientist said softly. "I rather expected this."

"You did?"

Franklin nodded. "She's too much like her mother and can be stubborn as a mule at times. Deep down, I knew she wouldn't let you go by yourself."

"As her father, I can understand your concern, but even though she's coming, I intend to keep her well away from the danger. I have two others who will accompany me, one with military training on a par with my own." Jake grew impatient. "Listen, doctor, it's critical I get underway without any further delay."

"I'm coming with you."

"Are you crazy?"

Franklin gestured to *Johnnie's* control panel. "Someone's got to be on hand to protect this asset and keep it intact."

Jake realized the suggestion wasn't such a bad idea. Franklin's presence might very well be the insurance he needed to keep Destiny from doing anything rash. Nevertheless, he felt it necessary to persuade him otherwise. "Tell that to your wife."

Achilles brushed against his awareness as he said this. *She already knows, JJ.*

Are you telling me she condones it?

She senses he must also come with us.

"Is something wrong, lad?" Franklin asked. "You look lost."

Jake broke from his reverie. "Climb aboard the *Angel* and say hello," he said.

"Give me your word you won't leave without me?"

Jake sighed as though he were hefting a colossal load. "You have it, doctor."

Franklin began climbing through the hatch, but stopped. "Don't you think it's about time you stopped calling me doctor. After all, we are family."

Jake smiled. He had a great deal of affection for the man. "You're right. I should be calling you dad."

Franklin beamed broadly, then ascended through the hatch.

Jake climbed up after him, poking his head above the outer hull. "Time to get aboard the *Tiburon Express*," he said. Victor and Jimenez stared back, still trying to make sense of the strange looking craft.

Chapter Twenty-five: Sterilis

With his cloaker deactivated, Phillipe crept along a dimly lit corridor within the bowels of the ship, every so often stopping and listening. Illumination was poor, provided by a battery-powered emergency lighting system that was apparently running low on juice. With the *Southern Star's* engine and main generator disabled, it was eerily quiet. The hum and rumble of machinery that normally accompanied a ship underway was completely absent. Only the occasional creak and groan of steel bulkheads and hull plates cut through the silence as the vessel was towed through the sea.

The thought that he had disobeyed Mat by remaining aboard the ship continued to peck away at him, and he had initially tried to rationalize it by telling himself that Mat would still have needed his help in getting Kalid off the ship. But that had only been a partial explanation for his actions. Upon getting Bashir aboard the chopper, Phillipe had at first meant to climb aboard, but then held up, setting his gaze on Harriet at the controls. Time seemed to stop at that moment, and in that timeless interval she had calmly looked back at him without any hint of urgency in her eyes. In that moment he knew he would not be leaving with her, but somehow it felt right. He could not explain the why of it, he only knew he had to remain with the ship. Stepping back from the whirling blades, he had watched as the main rotor gained momentum, and with Harriet's eyes locked on his, she had given him a slight nod of her head as she pulled up on the collective. And then she was gone.

An inborn need to protect Aquaria burned fervently within Phillipe. He wanted to prove himself, to measure up to the deeds of his father. Stories told by Jay Jay and Mat of their days in the Seals further sparked this need, and to strengthen it, he had taken to heart an inspiring quote by Theodore Roosevelt that compelled him to pursue it with a tenacious hunger. '*Far better is it to dare mighty things, to win glorious triumphs, even though checkered by failure than to rank with those poor spirits who neither enjoy nor suffer much, because they live in a gray twilight that knows not victory nor defeat.*' The words drove him on, adding to his resolve.

A short time earlier, he had made his way to the engine room fully cloaked to observe the ship's engineer and several assistants having a discussion in Spanish as they pondered the inner components of a partially disassembled control panel. Fluent in Spanish, Phillipe had listened.

"I don't get it," the engineer said. "All the circuitry is completely fried."

"I never saw anything like this," one of the assistants had uttered in amazement. "The whole system is shot, and unfortunately we do not have the parts to repair it."

Hearing enough, Phillipe had moved on, revisiting the ship's brig where he and Mat had locked up the Hind's crew, only to find the cell vacant. After that, he had wandered almost aimlessly through the hold of the ship until a series of crates caught his eye. Stamped on the wood of the nearest one was the word *Sterilis*. Curiously he pried the lid open, noticing eight keg-like barrels within the crate.

Does the word hold any significance to you, Perseus? he had asked his bond mate, who was still nearby and keeping pace with the ship.

The word is Latin and translates to barren or useless in English.

Phillipe had frowned at the inanity of it, wondering why cargo would be labeled with a word meaning useless. And even now he found himself continuing to ponder the word.

At hearing the approach of footsteps, Phillipe froze. Urgently, he darted into an adjacent corridor that was completely dark and flattened himself up against a wall, waiting for whoever it was to pass and keeping his weapon at the ready. Wanting to conserve the remaining power in his cloaker, he refrained from turning it on. The sound of voices reached him, and from the strained tones he perceived an argument was taking place.

"I have to get off this ship immediately." The voice was deep and gruff, tinged with a heavy accent that sounded Russian. "I have men out there who require evacuation."

"When we reach our destination," another voice replied petulantly, this one sharp with a thick Spanish overtone.

"Have one of your choppers pick me and my crew up," the first voice demanded hotly.

"That is not possible, I have my orders."

"How much longer before we get there?"

"Not long."

Phillipe held to his concealed position as the men passed, their heated bickering continuing and trailing away as they trooped down the passageway. At that moment he sensed the deck under his feet shift a tad, and abruptly he petitioned his bond mate, requesting an update on their heading.

We appear to be turning into the Bay of Anse-Milieu, Phillipe. I can see an exceptionally large stone structure overlooking the bay.

Phillipe digested this information, feeling the ship begin to lose momentum.

Zimbola was not happy. He was afraid for Jake and Destiny, fearful of what might happen. Dolefully he had watched *Johnnie* submerge a half-hour earlier, leaving the safety of Harriet and the children in his care. Nevertheless, he knew it was a necessary precaution under the present circumstances. But now he was plagued with anxiety.

Broodingly, he looked to the west, setting his gaze on the sun just as it slid below the horizon. Holding to a course that would take the *Avenging Angel* to the outskirts of the Bay of Anse-Milieu, he was in no hurry to get there, chugging the North Sea trawler at a steady five knots and saving fuel. With the onset of dusk, his growing edginess suddenly mushroomed to newfound heights, and he craned his head out the larboard door to the pilothouse to scan the sea behind him.

"What are you looking for?" Melody asked, standing next to him. She had grown bored and decided to keep him company.

"A sailor must always be vigilant in the open sea," the black giant said, forcing a broad, toothy grin.

Melody scrutinized his face. "Even when the sea is calm like it is now?"

"Especially when the sea is so gentle. A sailor must always be alert."

For emphasis, he leaned his massive frame out the opposite door to check out their six again. Worried as he was, he did his best to keep the child from picking up on his nervousness. Fifteen minutes earlier he had spotted the distant vessel off his port side as it passed him on a northerly heading. It had been moving fast, an ultra-large luxury yacht the size of a cruise ship with distinctive lines. But then it had made a wide turn, swinging around and hanging two miles back off the *Angel's* stern. He had recognized the vessel, for he had seen it just before pulling Jake and Fernando from the inflatable raft the dolphins had placed them in, and he remembered the unusual name emblazoned along its stern. *Numquam Satis*. But now the rapidly descending dusk was beginning to mask the yacht in a darkening gloom.

"*Omega* lets me know when to be vigilant," Melody said. She glanced lovingly at her bond mate keeping pace with the *Angel* off its port side. "She's very watchful and can sense the approach of danger."

Zimby stared down at his godchild, giving her a reproachful look. "It is not good practice to rely on others to ensure one's safety. Self-reliance is also important." As he completed the statement, he felt a set of tiny hands latch onto one of his tree-trunk legs, and he glanced down in surprise.

"Gotcha!" Troy Jacob said. "Snuck right up on you and you didn't see me coming."

Melody laughed, looking up at Zimby with an accusing grin. "What were you telling me about vigilance?"

"It is difficult to notice someone so tiny creeping up on me," Zimby said.

"Can I steer?" Troy Jacob asked eagerly, reaching for the lower portion of the helm.

"After you grow another foot," Zimby replied sternly. "You're way too small."

"But I can do it!" TJ insisted.

"You can't see over the windshield. How will you know what's ahead?"

"Alpha will tell me. He's out in front of us."

Zimby knew what the boy was saying to be true. Reluctantly he let go of the helm wheel. "Okay, but just for a minute. Hold her steady."

"I want to steer, too," Melody said, not wanting to be left out.

"You'll get your turn," Zimby said, taking the moment to look aft again. Though the sky had darkened further, he was startled to see the silhouette of the shadowing vessel much closer now, less than a mile back.

Zimby turned to TJ. "Do not deviate from our present course," he instructed, knowing Jake had familiarized both children with the *Angel's* helm, letting each of them steer the vessel every so often. "I'm going aft and will return in a moment."

Quickly, he climbed down from the pilothouse and strode briskly toward the stern, only to be met by Harriet.

"Remain calm," Harriet said. "Do not put up a fight with these people. To do so could be disastrous."

Zimby stared down at her for a prolonged moment. He had seen that same look on her face in the past, and it suddenly dawned on him what was happening now.

"You knew this was coming?" he said.

"Yes."

"So what do I call you, Harriet or Amphitrite?"

When Harriet did not answer, Zimby turned his gaze to the rapidly approaching shadow coming up on their stern, now feeling helpless.

How are you and Hercules doing, Achilles? Jake asked.

Being imprisoned like this is no great shakes, as you like to say, JJ, but we'll survive. How much longer?

We're entering the bay now. Jake looked over Franklin's shoulder, checking the GPS display on Johnnie's control panel. *Get ready to stretch your fins, Johnnie's going to spit you out?*

It's about time.

An air gap within the holding compartment fitted with carbon dioxide scrubbers and fed with a continuing supply of breathable air had sustained the dolphins during the trip.

Franklin eased back on the power, allowing the craft to slow down. With his eyes fixed on the digital velocity indicator, he watched as their speed quickly plummeted. As soon as it dropped below five knots, he flooded the holding compartment, then punched the release that opened *Johnnie's* retractable maw, and both dolphins bolted from their confinement, happy to be free.

Jake could well understand what it must have been like for them to be cooped up like that for the last two and a half hours, but now they had reached their destination.

Don't forget my status report, Achilles! Jake reminded him.

Nag, nag, nag!

Jake nearly burst out laughing at the reply, and he shot a quick glance at Destiny to catch the smile that came to her face. This was an ongoing source of amusement between them. Achilles had picked up on many of Jake's ways during the last several years, frequently echoing back the same phrases Jake tended to use.

As Jake waited for Achilles' report, Franklin worked the hydraulic controls that closed *Johnnie's* maw and purged water from the compartment. The scientist swiveled his head, looking to Jake for instructions. "What now?"

"We wait!"

As soon as Jake uttered the words, Achilles thoughts reverberated in his skull. *It's just as Ez predicted, JJ. The Southern Star is here with another ship moored next to her called the Northern Comet, most likely her sister ship and the one that towed her. Cardoza's yacht is anchored closer to shore. I also see another vessel. From her profile, she appears to be a tuna trawler. When I get closer, I'll give you her name.*

Any activity? Jake asked.

Yes, a tug is berthed alongside the Star and appears to be taking on cargo.

What about Perseus? Is he here?

When Achilles did not immediately answer, Jake grew uneasy.

I've just made contact with Perseus, JJ, and he tells me Phillipe is safe and has so far gone undetected aboard the Star.

Jake let out a deep sigh of relief before sending out another telepathic thought. *By any chance, does Perseus know the nature of cargo being offloaded?*

Another moment passed before Achilles answered. *Phillipe is currently monitoring the operation. He says crates are being offloaded that contain small drums labeled Sterilis.*

Sterilis?

Yes, it translates to barren or useless in Latin.

Jake picked up the satellite phone from the control panel and put in a call to the colony. "Ez, you were right on the mark about the *Southern Star's* destination, but I need you to find out what Sterilis is used for and who manufactures it. Crates of it are being offloaded from the *Southern Star* at this moment"

"I'll get right on it, JJ. Why do you need to know?"

"Something tells me it's important." Ending the call, he looked to Franklin. "Dad," he said, making sure to place extra emphasis on the moniker, "bring us to the east side of the fortress, as close to shore as possible."

Franklin smiled back appreciatively before setting his gaze on the control panel to engage the electric motor. The craft gathered momentum smoothly, then surged forward with more authority as the hydrodrive kicked in.

Turning, Jake looked back at Belachek and Jimenez. "Are you gentlemen ready to go ashore?"

Both men nodded. Jake locked eyes with the former Spetsnaz operative, searching for signs of last-minute misgivings about switching loyalties, but finding none. No bells went off in his head, and some deep-rooted instinct told him he could rely on this man, at least for the time being.

Two more minutes elapsed before *Johnnie* slowed once again and rose to the surface, upon which Franklin punched the button that opened the hatch.

"Good luck!" Jake said, watching as both men climbed out onto *Johnnie's* hull. Bending, he hefted two waterproof backpacks and shoved them through the hatch, letting each man grab one. Reaching down for other items, he lifted several other bundles and pushed them up into waiting hands, one at a time. Climbing a few more rungs, he rose halfway through the hatch as Belachek pulled a cord on the largest bundle. An audible hiss ensued as the small raft inflated, and both men climbed into it.

Jake glanced around, letting his eyes adjust to the semi-darkness. The shadow of Cardoza's fortress loomed above, overlooking the sea as though it were an evil sentinel. Hanging low and still rising in the night sky was the disk of a gibbous moon. Partially obscured by low slung clouds, it cast a feeble light on the water. A distant flash winked briefly off to the east where no stars were visible, and he felt a sudden rush of air against his face coming from that quarter. Another moment passed before a dull boom reached his ears, and he knew a thunderstorm was headed their way, hopefully a powerful, noisy one.

Bringing his eyes back to the water, Jake saw a fin break the surface in front of the raft. It floated there momentarily as Jimenez tossed out a length of rope attached to the raft's bow. As planned, Hercules would tow the raft the remainder of the distance to shore. In seconds, the two men receded into the darkness, and as he watched, a raindrop dashed against his forehead, heralding the storm's rapid approach. Quickly, he dropped back down into the craft, instructing Franklin to close the hatch and head back in the direction of the *Southern Star*.

Jake looked at Destiny. "A storm is headed this way," he said. "It may work to our advantage."

"Won't that be a problem for Jimenez and Victor?" she asked. "Cloakers don't work well when they get wet."

"That's true, but a nice hard blow with ear-splitting thunder will make a great distraction."

Jake was well familiar with the electrical storms that could suddenly crop up in these waters. They were loud and violent, but tended to pass swiftly. It would provide another element of cover to carry out this mission.

Abruptly, the familiar essence of his bond mate cut into his thoughts. *I'm able to read the name of the fishing vessel, JJ. It's called the San Pedro. There's activity on deck, and there appears to be a large container being readied for unloading.*

Thanks, buddy. Have Perseus pass the word to Phillipe to evacuate the Star. Let's all rendezvous near her stern.

Jake immediately turned to procure several more backpacks. "I wasn't counting on a fourth vessel," he said, "but hopefully we'll have just enough to go around."

Destiny appeared pensive, and Jake could tell she was having second thoughts about what they were going to do. "I know what you're thinking, but we've got to create as much pandemonium and chaos as possible. We've got to keep Cardoza and his thugs off balance in order to succeed."

"What if they're not all bad?" Destiny said. "What if some of them are like Fernando and Antonio?"

Jake had also given this issue much thought. Both men had once worked for Cardoza, but the employment had been against their will. "That's why we have the hologram projector."

"I hope you're right."

Jake sighed. "So do I."

Phillipe continued to monitor the unloading process as the wind picked up, standing off to one side on the *Southern Star's* deck with his cloaker activated. Though Perseus had passed along Jake's instructions, he was hesitant to leave the ship just yet. Remaining unseen, he had observed members of the UN troops that had taken back the ship assisting in bringing up crates from below. At the moment, most of them had gone back into the ship's hold to retrieve the last of the crates, leaving two blue helmeted men standing at the railing. Both men had taken the opportunity to light up cigarettes.

Phillipe crept closer, listening to their conversation as the men looked down at the tugboat with crates stacked up on the rear deck. With the wind gaining strength, the vessel was rocking more heavily in the growing swells.

A squat, powerfully built individual raised his voice loud enough to be heard above the rising wind, speaking in Spanish. "What's so important about these crates anyway?" he asked his taller companion.

The taller man appeared to cringe, turning around sharply to see if anyone was lurking nearby. The unexpected move caused Phillipe to jump back, but the man appeared to look right through him as though he were a ghost. "Quiet down!" he said irritably, turning back to the shorter man. "Do you want Alvarez to hear?"

"So what if he does?"

"Are you stupid, Poco? This operation is classified. We're under strict orders not to discuss or have any knowledge about this cargo. To do so will be a breach of security."

"Ha!" Poco ridiculed. "When did that ever stop you?"

The taller man did not immediately answer. He looked to his rear again, then turned to face his partner, speaking just loud enough for Phillipe to hear. "I overheard one of the ship's crew talking. He said the crates contain aerosol canisters that are used for crop dusting."

"Then why all the hush-hush?"

"This crewman thinks they're filled with highly toxic herbicides used for killing crops."

Poco stood quiet for a moment, turning his gaze toward the coast. "If they're being taken ashore, then they're probably going to be used here in Haiti. Why would they want to do that?"

The taller man shrugged. "How the hell would I know?"

"Herbicides can be dangerous," Poco said. "They can cause pollution and kill people. And if enough crops are destroyed, people will end up starving."

The other man snickered, swiveling his head to observe a series of lightning flashes illuminating the night sky just off to the east and rapidly advancing. "Since when did you become an environmentalist?"

"I'm not," Poco disavowed. "A bunch of Haitians being poisoned is probably a good idea seeing as how the country is so-"

Poco's discourse was abruptly drowned out by the cannonade boom of thunder, and the first spattering of raindrops came down, driven sideways by the wind. It was immediately followed by a drenching downpour.

Both men turned, looking to escape the ferocious blast of wind and rain, but stopped short. Dumbstruck, they gawked at Phillipe.

Phillipe met their confused, gaping stares, suddenly aware that his cloaker had been compromised. In that instant he made a decision, and that was not to use his weapon. He had already killed one man and had no desire to kill another. Instead, he leaped for the railing, intending to launch himself headfirst over it and dive for the water below. With the onslaught of rain, however, the deck had become wet, and his feet slipped out from under him. Off balance, he crashed headlong into the railing. Recovering quickly, he tried rising, but before he could get his legs under him, something slammed into the nape of his neck with brutal force. Dazedly, he felt strong hands haul him roughly to his feet and drag him along.

Regaining his senses, he found himself bound hand and foot and strapped to a chair. A deeply pockmarked face hovered before him. Captain Alvarez grinned sadistically. "Welcome to hell," he said, running a thumb lightly over the edge of his corvo. His grin expanded further when he saw Phillipe's eyes go wide at seeing the blade. "We will have much to discuss once I have finished with some important business," he went on, "especially some of the toys you carry." With his free hand, he picked up a Masker.

Startled, Phillipe shot a glance to his left wrist and realized the device had been removed.

"One of your compatriots also carried one," Alvarez said. He picked up a second Masker and dangled it before him, and Phillipe knew it had been taken from Bashir.

Strapping the second Masker onto his own wrist, Alvarez pressed one of the buttons on the device. Almost instantly his features and clothing appeared to change, bulging and deforming hideously before taking on a new shape. Fully transformed into the image of Malikai Allotey, Alvarez looked down at Phillipe with the same stern expression the UN envoy had exhibited at the colony. "A most ingenious little invention," he lauded smugly. "I must admit that even I was fooled when it was used against me by one of your accomplices."

The two men that had apprehended Phillipe stared at Alvarez's morphed image in amazement. This was their first viewing of one of the device's hidden functions.

Alvarez lifted the tiny cap strapped to his right thigh and slapped down on the plunger that lay beneath it, injecting the potent mix of dextroamphetamine and a non-hallucinogenic LSD derivative into his femoral artery. "I've had some time to play with this," Alvarez went on, "and discovered it can be used to first confuse an enemy before making him severely ill."

Turning his attention to his men, he pressed another tiny button on the gadget. Allotey's eyes immediately flamed, emitting a burst of interlaced light that swirled and danced in upon itself. Both men gawked for one brief moment before clutching their temples and screaming out in agony. Overcome by extreme nausea, they fell to the floor where they vomited copiously, their bodies juddering as though being jolted by a severe electric shock.

Alvarez ignored the convulsing men and focused beyond the convoluting lights. In spite of the drug's potency he felt a trace of disorientation creeping up on him. Fighting it back, he studied Phillipe closely as he let the hologram continue for several more seconds before deactivating the device on his wrist. Allotey's image abruptly faded, leaving the Chilean captain standing in his place. "You seem to be immune to what this device holds," Alvarez muttered reflectively. "Why is that?"

Phillipe gazed back starry-eyed, a contented smile on his face. "Only those who are truly evil become sick when they look at it."

Alvarez stared back in deep thought before his expression turned dubious. "More likely you take an antidote as I did." He shifted his gaze to the fallen soldiers. With the hologram no longer visible, their screams had given way to soft moans. "Idiots!" he scolded contemptuously. "You were briefed on what you saw, yet you did not use the drug to counter it."

Both men rose meekly to their feet, wiping off the vomit soiling their clothing. They were still wobbly, recovering slowly.

Alvarez turned to retrieve something on a chair behind him. Facing Phillipe again, he said, "I would like to know what function this serves?" He was hefting the cloaker, and Phillipe could see it was still wet from the rain.

When Phillipe did not answer, Alvarez set down the cloaker and pulled his corvo, his demeanor suddenly dark and ominous. He moved the blade close to Phillipe's face, but stopped short as a blue helmeted lieutenant entered the room. "Captain!" the junior officer barked crisply, addressing his superior in their native tongue. "Ambassador Allotey requests that you come ashore immediately."

"What does he want?" Alvarez growled irritably.

"He does not say, only that it is important."

Grumbling peevishly, Alvarez re-sheathed his corvo, then looked back at Phillipe. "I want you to think about the answer to my last question until I return," he advised stonily, reverting back to English. Turning, he looked at the taller of the two men that had apprehended Phillipe. "Do not take your eyes off him until I get back," he ordered gruffly.

"How much longer are we to stay aboard this ship?" the man asked anxiously, still a little unsteady on his feet.

"Only until the arms shipment goes ashore," Alvarez said. "Once we load it aboard the tug, our job will be finished here." The Chilean captain brought merciless his eyes to bear on Phillipe again. "Then we can get on with other business." Just as he was about to leave the room he pulled up short and reached for the cloaker, folding it up and taking it with him.

Dismally, Phillipe watched him go. The thought that he had chosen to remain aboard the ship plagued him, and he realized it had been a mistake not to obey Mat.

Riding their bond mates, Jake and Destiny approached the *Southern Star's* stern, keeping below the churning whitecaps stirred up by the storm. Jake noticed a sudden change in Achilles' switchback motion. The dolphin twitched convulsively under him as though agitated, and he immediately knew something was amiss.

What's wrong, Achilles?

There was a strong emotional edge to Achilles' reply, bordering on a wail within Jake's skull. *Perseus informs me Phillipe has been captured, JJ.*

A vision of a nasty corvo abruptly loomed in Jake's thoughts, and he saw the leering face of Alvarez behind it. This was not his imagination at work, this was real. Perseus had seen what was taking place through Phillipe's eyes and had relayed the image to Achilles.

Jake did his best to remain calm. I assume he's still aboard the *Star*?

Yes, they've got him in a room amidships, one deck down.

Jake's thoughts went into high gear, and he knew their planned assault had now been compromised. As he mulled this, a revised plan quickly came together in his mind's eye, and he shared the rudiments of it with his bond mate before asking the crucial question. *You think you can do it, Achilles?*

Achilles' despair suddenly shifted to one of vexation. *Of course I can,* the dolphin replied indignantly. I*f Hermes was able to do it, so can I.* He was referring to a feat carried out by Hermes several years earlier, one that had allowed Jake to dispatch Sebastian Ortega and Cardoza's evil nephew, Pedro.

Does Destiny and Hercules know what's required of them?

Yes, JJ.

Satisfied with the answer, Jake's resolve turned to granite as they pulled abreast of the massive ship.

Chapter Twenty-six: Invading the Fortress

The full brunt of the storm seemed to stall, hanging directly above the *Southern Star* as the tugboat cast off and headed for shore. The vessel rocked clumsily in the churning swells with its unwieldy payload of stacked crates and squad of blue helmeted commandos massed together on its rear deck. The men would be needed to unload the cargo once the tug reached the pier that stretched out into the bay. The men were soaked to the bone and miserable, pelted unmercifully by riven rain and heavy spray from waves crashing over the gunwales. They were soldiers, not day laborers, and this was reflected on their faces as they looked up in alarm each time a bolt of lightning cracked overhead with disconcerting closeness.

Two men watched the tug depart, also members of the UN strike force that had taken back the *Star*. Both had been ordered by Captain Alvarez to remain on deck in spite of the downpour, and as a result, both men were completely drenched.

"Do you notice how Alvarez stations himself with the Russians in the tug's pilothouse while everyone else is made to stand out in the elements?" one of the men remarked. He had to shout to be heard above the thunderous din.

His partner suddenly flinched, ducking down as a jagged bolt of lightning met the sea less than a hundred meters away. The bolt lit up his features, revealing a mottled patch of unsightly skin on one side of his face that resembled a pepperoni pizza, the remnants of a severe burn wound acquired earlier in his military career. "Alvarez has always been a poor leader," the man commented contemptuously. "He likes to see his men suffer while he remains comfortable. He always-"

The shadow of something leaping up from the water directly in front of them made him stop in mid-sentence. He followed the object's trajectory as it splashed back into the sea. "Did you see that?" he exclaimed.

The other man nodded. "I think it was a dolphin."

Pizza face looked down at the water again. "If it was, I didn't know dolphins got that big."

Both men recoiled as another lightning bolt sizzled the air, this one missing the tug by less than ten meters as it struck the water. It was immediately followed by a crackling cascade that ended in a colossal boom. Blinded by the intense lingering flash, they failed to see the shadow rise up from the sea a second time. But this shadow was different, appearing longer than the first. By the time both men regained their vision, it was too late.

On a smooth trajectory impelled by Achilles, Jake soared over the ship's railing, separating himself from his bond mate like the second stage of an Atlas rocket. He had once executed this same maneuver to reach Ortega's low-flying helicopter, with Hermes providing the impetus with his snout positioned precisely under Jake's feet to drive him upward from the water in a gravity-defying leap. At the time, Achilles had been an adolescent, lacking the necessary size and power such a feat required. But now Achilles was fully matured and up to the task.

Jake reached the apex of the aerial assault, coming down feet-first. With perfectly timed accuracy, he slammed the heel of his right foot into the nose of pizza face, knocking the man cold and sending him sprawling. The move cushioned Jake's fall, and he landed lightly on his feet. Caught off guard, the other commando failed to react in time to avoid a jaw-cracking right cross. Stunned, the man staggered backward but did not go down. Surprised at the man's resiliency, Jake followed up on the attack, snapping a vicious front kick to the man's crotch and feeling the scrunch of testicles. This time the man slumped, falling to his knees, and holding his groin as Jake drove a knee into his face to finish the job.

Jake looked down at the results of his work. Both men were out cold. Not wanting to take any chances, he gathered their firearms and tossed them over the side. Next, he removed their corvos, doing the same. Expertly, he used plastic ties to bind both men hand and foot.

Nice work, JJ! Achilles remarked when he was done. *Now I'll guide you to where they are holding Phillipe.*

Listening to Achilles' instructions, Jake raced between cargo containers to find a door that opened to a short flight of stairs. Though Phillipe had been dazed, he had been conscious enough for Perseus to see through Phillipe's eyes and memorize the route his captors had taken him on. This he had relayed to Achilles.

Just follow the hallway at the bottom of the stairs, JJ, Achilles explained. *At the end of the hall you'll find a room where Phillipe is being guarded by two men.*

Jake sidled up to the door, his USP-9 at the ready. Glancing back down the hallway, he made sure no one followed. A vision of the room's interior suddenly sprang into his mind's eye, and he saw Phillipe's perspective of the two men holding him prisoner. Both men sat in chairs, appearing bored, every so often eyeing the door that accessed the room. From the look of them, these men were professionals. They held their Uzis in readiness, seemingly prepared to fend off a potential assault by other foes sneaking about the ship as their captive had. Phillipe was currently relaying the image to Perseus, who was able to transmit it to Jake through Achilles.

Jake thought quickly. *I'm going to need a distraction, Achilles. Tell Phillipe to insult these men in the most vile terms he can come up with.*

What do you suggest, JJ?

Tell him to say they look and smell like sewer rats, that one Navy Seal is worth a thousand of them in battle. Tell him to spit in their direction.

Jake put his ear to the door. A few seconds passed before Jake heard Phillipe's voice, and he was surprised to hear the strength of venom issuing from the lad's mouth. Phillipe was hurling invectives at the men in their native tongue, a language in which Jake had little fluency.

Is he saying what I suggested, Achilles?

That and more, Achilles shot back. *He's telling them their mothers are whores that continue to work in backwater Chilean slums, though I don't have any inkling what the inference means.*

Another image of the men flashed in Jake's mind, and he could see the insults were having the desired effect. They rose from their chairs, moving to stand over Phillipe, their demeanors pugnacious and growing darker with rage. But now they were facing away from the door.

The perspective gave Jake an unobstructed view of the door, and he could see it had no bolting mechanism or latch with which to prevent entry. Emboldened, he gripped the doorknob, turning it slowly and hoping it would not squeak. Phillipe did his part, providing the necessary cover the situation demanded by continuing to taunt his captors, jabbering away in a loud provocative manner.

The image of both men as seen by Phillipe stayed fastened in Jake's thoughts, and he saw the shorter man suddenly unleash a nasty backhand that caught the lad flush on the mouth.

In that instant, a whirlwind of anger welled up from the pit of Jake's stomach and he flung the door open to level his weapon at the commando delivering the blow. "Drop your weapons!" Jake growled.

Both men spun, completely startled by this sudden intrusion, and in that fleeting moment of time, Jake could see not the slightest bit of surrender in their expressions. Without hesitation, he squeezed off a shot before they could retaliate. The shorter man's head snapped back as a bullet caught him squarely between the eyes, and before the taller man could raise his Uzi, Jake fired again. His second shot was not as precise, the round striking the man high on his forehead before exiting out the back of his skull. The man keeled over backwards, revealing a splattering of blood and brains on the wall behind him.

Phillipe looked up dazedly as Jake pulled out his K-bar to cut him loose. His lower lip was cut and bleeding.

"Why did you remain aboard this ship?" Jake grumbled peevishly, working quickly to slice through the rope binding Phillipe to the chair. "You could have gotten yourself killed."

Phillipe's eyes refocused. "They're going to use herbicides!" he blurted.

"What are you talking about?"

"They loaded herbicides onto a tug. They're going to poison the land so that crops cannot grow."

Jake cut through the final strand of imprisoning rope, now fully understanding what the word Sterilis implied, and he couldn't help but wonder about the odd set of circumstances that had led him here. Abruptly, he cast the coincidence aside, not attempting to analyze it any further.

"Then we have to stop it!" he said, his expression hardening further.

Franklin sat glumly at *Johnnie's* multi-functional display panel, keeping tabs on sonar images of the surrounding sea. Just after Destiny and Jake had left the sub, he had leveled *Johnnie* off at a depth of twenty feet, letting the craft float idly with its homing beacon turned on and sending out periodic pulses that would let the dolphins know his exact position. The thought that his daughter was out there now troubled him to no end, and he tried not to think about the first twenty-two years of her life he had missed. But now he needed to stay close, to do what he could in keeping her safe and out of harm's way. The fact that she was with Jake only increased his anxiety, for he was well acquainted with how the former Navy Seal dealt with matters such as this. There was no denying that Jake would prefer to look death in the face rather than back away from a dangerous situation, and this was certainly a potentially dangerous situation.

Worriedly, Franklin continued to ponder these things, not immediately recognizing the sudden faltering hum of the sub's generator. It was only when the lights on the MFD suddenly blinked erratically that he became aware of the problem, and as he broke from his reverie, the hum of the generator died altogether. Abruptly, the sub's interior was plunged into an inky darkness.

Franklin groped in a pocket, pulling out a pen light to scrutinize the controls. "Just what I didn't need!" he said aloud. Reaching over, he lifted a toggle guard and flicked the underlying switch that would turn on the emergency power provided by a bank of batteries. Nothing!

Frustrated, he flicked it back and forth several times. Still nothing! It was then he realized the growing magnitude of the system failure and the ensuing problems it would bring on. Without power, the homing beacon would not function. And without power, the air scrubbers would not work. The last thing he needed was a buildup of carbon dioxide in *Johnnie's* sealed cabin.

Johnnie was also outfitted with a Delphine Translator which could send and receive acoustical signals, converting hear-see water-based dolphin speech to English or English back to the Delphine speak-see language. But now lacking the necessary power to operate, the DT would not work. With the help of the albinos during the last few years, Franklin had finally succeeded in perfecting the highly complex computer algorithm he had been developing when he had first met Jake, and it allowed those Aquarians who didn't have a bond mate of their own to converse directly with the dolphins. Unfortunately, Franklin did not have a bond mate, so he could not communicate the problem to the dolphins.

That left him only one course of action. He would have to bring *Johnnie* to the surface and open the hatch. Packed within his utility belt, he carried a small handheld transducer he often carried with him to summon a pod member, and this one put out a sonar pulse that basically asked for their assistance, to please come now.

Moving to an emergency throw-valve, Franklin pulled down on the handle to direct pressurized air into *Johnnie's* ballast tanks. A barely audible hiss met his ears, and he sensed the craft begin to rise. It was only as it met the surface that he felt the severity of the storm. *Johnnie* was being tossed around hard in the wind-driven turbulence.

It suddenly dawned on him why the sub had lost power. The storm was the cause. He was only partly familiar with the quantum principles behind *Johnnie's* extraordinary design, but he knew that too much electrical energy being discharged into the surrounding water could conceivably disrupt the sub's operating system. This, of course, was only conjecture, a theory that was now being put to the test. But he also knew that if the theory was actually true, which seemed to be the case, there was another side to it that also might prove to be accurate. Once the storm passed, it was possible *Johnnie* would once again be fully functional.

Franklin steadied himself, gripping the crank wheel that would manually open the hatch cover. With waves crashing over the hull, water spilled into the cabin as the circular lid came up. Thoroughly doused and blinded by the spray, he extended his torso through the hatch opening and retrieved the transducer unit from one of the utility belt pouches. Gripping the handle, he squeezed the trigger. The small transducer immediately ejected from a stubby launch tube to arc out over the water. Tethered to a retrieval string, it disappeared in a cresting whitecap forty feet away.

Salt water and rain buffeted Franklin's face as he waited with his body halfway out of the hatch opening. It was important he give the transducer sufficient time to send out its message before he pulled in the line and closed the hatch. A lightning bolt suddenly flashed, lighting up the coast like an exploding nova, and he was able to perceive Cardoza's stronghold looming above a rocky shoreline where a pier extended out into the bay, the end of it now less than seventy meters away. It occurred to him that if the wind shifted, it was possible *Johnnie* could end up being driven into the pier or onto the rocks.

The electrical discharge hung for perhaps a second before flickering out, and a pervading tumultuous darkness reasserted itself once again. Franklin felt terrible. He had become a liability and was now compromising the mission. As he thought about this, something slammed into *Johnnie's* hull, jarring him to the bone and sending the back of his head into the hatch cover. Abruptly, he slumped forward, his head ringing with the sound of a thousand cathedral bells pealing in concert. Barely conscious, he perceived the chatter of voices through the roar of wind, and he felt himself being lifted as spray pelted him.

Hercules was the first to hear the sonar pulse echoing through the sea. *Your father beckons us,* Hercules said.

Is he alright? Destiny shot back.

I don't know. He calls with his portable transducer.

Then we must go to him at once, Destiny replied, a sudden bout of uncontrollable anxiety building within her. A vision of what she had seen on the chamber ceiling behind the falls suddenly came back to assail her with cruel, piercing lucidity, and she knew the vision had not been a figment of her imagination, for it had been a glimpse into the future.

I'll inform the others, Hercules said, turning his large body to follow the pulses to their source.

Jake and Phillipe rode side by side, their bond mates keeping well below the surface to avoid the worst of the storm driven turbulence. Only when their mounts sensed they needed to breathe did they streak upward, leaping high above the waves so their riders could suck in another lungful of life sustaining air. Jake sensed the storm had stalled, its forward thrust slowing to hover directly over the bay. Every so often an electrical discharge would flood the sea with a flickering light, this to be followed by a crackling thunderclap that echoed into the depths.

Not having encountered anymore blue helmets or ship's crew after leaving Phillipe's holding cell, they had made their way back to the same location where Jake had boarded the vessel. Once there, Achilles had bolted from the water, rising up to toss each of them a face mask. Even before he had left the sub, Jake had had enough foresight to bring an extra mask with him for Phillipe.

But now they were running late. Jake had checked his watch just before they had left the *Star*, and he realized they were behind schedule. In formulating the plan, he had not anticipated having to rescue Phillipe. And to make matters worse, they were now being summoned by Franklin. What else can go wrong? he wondered.

Achilles suddenly barged into his thoughts. *Uh, JJ, I hate to tell you this, but Destiny has just climbed aboard Johnnie to find Franklin missing. The hatch was still open, and the launcher to his portable transducer lay on the cabin floor with its tethering line still out. All of Johnnie's systems are dead.*

A wave of fear abruptly coursed through Jake's veins. *Search the surrounding water with your sonar, Achilles. If he's fallen overboard, he can't be far away.*

Destiny says she knows where he is.

Where?

He's being taken to Cardoza's lair.

How does she know that?

She just knows, JJ. Call it a vision.

The thought of Franklin in Cardoza's hands increased Jake's dread. *How much farther before we reach Johnnie, Achilles?*

Three minutes thirty-eight seconds.

There was an element of inconsolable despondency in Achilles' reply, and Jake knew at once there was an additional component of this unexpected news, perhaps something the dolphin had just learned. Achilles began to quiver uncontrollably as they sped along, and a quick glance at Perseus beside him showed a similar change in body language.

Jake's dread immediately escalated into the realm of panic, and he let loose a thought as though hurling a grenade. *Tell Destiny to stay where she is!*

Achilles' was now quaking horribly, and Jake knew what he was going to hear even before the dolphin responded. The reply that came back engulfed him like a floodtide of overwhelming anguish. *She has already left, JJ.*

Calmly and without fear, Destiny made her way up the slope toward the looming shadow of Cardoza's fortress. The storm still had not passed, now hanging tenaciously over the bay where it met the land and continuing to unleash crashing bursts of lightning and torrential rain with unabated fury. With Hercules fighting his way through a pounding, swirling surf, she had managed to come ashore, leaving her bond mate behind in a state of inconsolable sadness. Hercules had tried to dissuade her from going ashore alone, but she had refused to listen. For reasons she could not rationalize, some vague, adumbrate notion was compelling her onward.

When she had first stepped onto the beach, she had remained hidden behind an outcropping of bedrock. With thunderbolts intermittently exploding the night sky into daylight, she had witnessed ten men enter a van at the foot of the pier. Her heart had cried out when she discerned a white-haired individual put up a struggle before being shoved roughly into a rear seat. The van had then left, and she had watched dolefully as it made its way up through a series of winding curves on the road leading to Cardoza's stronghold. Another twenty or so men had been left behind, crowding the end of the pier where a cluster of floodlights showed them hastily offloading crates from the tug as it rocked precariously alongside the platform. Waves washing over the tug's deck had hampered the operation, and she had seen two of the men swept over the side before being pulled from the water by their comrades.

Destiny had stayed hidden, continuing to observe as the last of the crates were hoisted up and loaded onto the back of a large flatbed truck. With the task completed, the men had climbed wearily aboard the vehicle and departed. But as she watched the direction of its headlights, she had noticed it did not take the same road as the van. Instead, it veered off on another road that seemed to head off farther to the east. Only when it was well away did she venture from her concealed position and make her way directly up the rocky slope, only crossing the road at those places where it snaked back to intersect her path.

Lightning continued to erupt overhead as she ascended higher, seemingly growing fiercer each minute, and she found solace in the violent discharges. To her, it was not a strange notion. While she was still developing in her mother's womb, lightning had been one of the ingredients that had made her into the unique person she had become. Lightning was her ally. Lightning was one of the forces that had forged Amphitrite.

Undaunted, she continued on, her resolution escalating with the storm's growing intensity, and the more savage it became, the stronger she felt. Bolts were now striking the edifice above her, scorching and raking the stone that formed it.

Finally reaching the outer bank of the moat that girthed the fortress, she made her way to the area directly across from the portcullis. Seeing that the drawbridge was in the up position, she moved to the center of the road facing it, making herself clearly visible under the flaring electrical bursts.

Staring up, she saw movement in the observation tower directly above the entrance. Another explosive discharge revealed the head of a man looking down at her. He was speaking feverishly into a walkie-talkie raised to his lips. A rapid succession of several more aerial bursts gave animated snapshots of the man's face breaking out into a leer. And then the drawbridge began to swing down.

Destiny waited calmly as the end of the bridge finally came to rest on her side of the moat. Another moment passed before the portcullis gate lifted to reveal the silhouettes of five men rushing out to meet her, their bodies backlit from lights set back in the entrance.

A subtle smile crossed her face seconds before they reached her. Amid the din of wind riven rain and booming thunder, the sound of rotor blades could be discerned cleaving the air.

Achilles swam hard through the turbulent surf, allowing Jake to make landfall near the place where Belachek and Jimenez had come ashore. Upon searching the area well up from the wash of whitewater, he found their inflatable raft near a cluster of boulders. As planned, the items he would need had been left within it, one of them being a waterproof backpack which he quickly donned. The remaining item was a tubular object sealed in plastic wrap. Hefting it, he grabbed the strap attached to both ends and slung it over his right shoulder.

Squinting against the heavy downpour, he eyed the imposing mass of the fortress looming above him, his face a mask of determination. "Harm a single hair on her head, Cardoza, and you'll wish you were never born," he vowed aloud.

Doggedly, he began heading up the slope at a brisk trot. Bolts of lightning erupted haphazardly, many of them hitting the stone structure as he strode higher. "Even nature despises you," he found himself saying, his mind suddenly embracing a concept Jacob had expounded on years earlier during a fireside discussion in the cove. Perhaps the Gaia theory was true after all. Perhaps the earth was indeed a living organism, capable of purging itself of malignancies through preemptive initiatives before irreversible damage could be done. Didn't that provide a plausible explanation for the new breed of dolphins coming into existence? Wasn't that the reason for the building of Aquaria?

In spite of these musings, the thought that Destiny was already up there intensified his anguish, and Amphitrite's prophesy only added to his dark mood. "We are approaching another nexus, Jay Jay, and from what I'm able to foresee, both Destiny and Achilles must accompany you."

Almost reaching the plateau upon which the fortress stood, Jake stopped, turning to look back at the sea. Amid the cacophony of driving rain and thunder, he heard the muffled drone of an approaching whirlybird. Grimly, he checked the luminous dials on his wristwatch. Only a minute late, he thought. Not bad considering the magnitude of the storm.

Jake immediately set his gaze toward the middle of the bay, just catching sight of the aircraft as another bolt of lightning flashed. *Time to activate your transponder, Achilles*, he said.

It's already on, JJ. Let's hope it's still functioning.

Yes, let's hope so.

"Time to pay the piper!" Jake said, springing up the remaining distance to the plateau above.

With wraith-like stealth, Belachek and Jimenez made their way unseen to the hangar at the east end of Cardoza's private runway. The storm had come on swiftly, and both men were completely drenched from the violent downpour. As they neared the enormous structure, they saw it was ablaze with lights and buzzing with activity.

Just beyond the lights of the hangar, they came upon a huge aircraft sitting on the tarmac, intermittently revealed by intense flashes of lightning. Belachek recognized the type immediately. It was a Chinook CH-47F twin-engine, tandem rotor, heavy lift helicopter. Painted in bold letters on its side was an emblem designating it as the property of the United Nations. It was a military helicopter manufactured by Boeing and primarily used for transporting troops. So, even a faction of the UN is tied in with Cardoza, Belachek thought bitterly. This did not surprise him at all. In his dealings with Zinova over the years, he had been involved in several clandestine operations in which the Reaper had been commissioned by corrupt factions within the world body. Seeing that the Chinook was currently unguarded, he retrieved something from his backpack, and upon setting a timer, placed it under the belly of the aircraft near the fuel tanks. According to Javolyn, it was a highly potent explosive ten times more powerful than TNT per unit weight, and he knew the former Navy Seal had brought enough of it with him to sink every one of Cardoza's vessels currently in the bay.

Moving to the rear of the facility, Belachek and Jimenez found an unlocked door that opened to a dimly lit stairway. Hastily, they shed their jumpsuits, wringing as much water from the cloth as possible before stuffing them into plastic bags taken from their backpacks. Avoiding conversation, they pulled another item from their packs, donning them rapidly. Jake had instructed them thoroughly on the use of the cloakers while they were aboard *Johnnie*, and Belachek had been awed by the invisibility they invoked. With their cloakers activated, they ascended seven flights of stairs to find themselves on a steel catwalk that overlooked the hangar's cavernous interior. The view was panoramic, allowing them to observe what was taking place on the floor below.

More than fifty men were scurrying about, pulling canisters the size of scuba bottles from crates situated on pushcarts and installing them into compartments under strange looking aircraft. There was a whole fleet of them, row after row and all identical, each about six meters long by Belachek's estimate. Taking a quick count, he tallied forty-two in all. Seemingly directing the men loading the aircraft were another twelve men wearing white laboratory smocks, several of them sitting before a bank of computer consoles positioned at the center of the hangar.

Having heard Jake's conversation with someone called Ez while he was still aboard the sub, Belachek looked directly below him to scrutinize the nearest pushcart. Though his orbs were mismatched, he had exceptionally good eyesight. He had been born with brown eyes, but with the intent of enhancing their finest soldiers, the Soviets had used him as a guinea pig while training him to be a Spetsnaz warrior, and one of his eyes had been surgically altered to give him telescopic vision whenever he closed the normal eye. The crate on the pushcart had not yet been opened, and displayed on the lid in small letters was the word Sterilis, the same name Jake had mentioned.

Turning, Belachek reached out to touch his invisible partner, holding his voice to a whisper. "Whatever these men are doing, it cannot be good." With a practiced gaze, his telescopic orb fell on a medium-size tanker truck slowly working its way between rows of aircraft. As it came to a stop, a man extended a hose from the truck to refuel the next aircraft in line. Two similar tanker vehicles were doing the same in rows further away. "But I see we have the means to stop it."

Something else grabbed Belachek's attention, and he scrutinized the Hind set off to the far side of the sprawling facility. Zinova had purposely left the helicopter behind as backup for his troops, but at the moment it had no crew. As Belachek studied it, he noticed the airplane tug positioned directly in front of its nose bubble. Two men had just completed connecting the hitch, and one of them waved the tug driver forward. With a slight lurch, the Hind began to move as it was towed toward the hangar doors.

The doors parted as the tug neared them, and it was then that Belachek glimpsed an SUV enter the hangar to intercept the towing vehicle and block its path. The tug came to a halt as nine men filed from the SUV, and Belachek immediately recognized Rafael Cardoza as the first man out. Close on his heels were Zinova and Drakov. The rest of the men were members of Zinova's team.

Curiously, Belachek continued to watch as Cardoza moved quickly to the side of the tug, his face contorted with a dark scowl as he exchanged words with the tug driver. Relying on his telescopic eye, Belachek saw the tug driver nod vigorously as Zinova and his men climbed aboard the Hind. Seconds later the tug began to crawl forward again, working its way through the hangar doors and out into the stormy night with the two men who had connected the hitch following on foot.

Cardoza stood fast for a brief moment, eyeing the Hind's passage before getting back into the SUV and saying something to the driver. In seconds, the car zoomed to the center of the hangar, men leaping out of the way to avoid being run down. As the drug lord exited the vehicle again, Belachek noted a look of extreme displeasure on his face as he confronted one of the white smocked supervisors, apparently the man in charge of the operation. The supervisor appeared to wither as Cardoza threw his arms wide, gesturing wildly before pointing to his watch. Based on the display, Belachek could only conclude that the operation was running behind schedule. With the reprimand over, Cardoza got back in the SUV, glaring belligerently at the supervisor as the man began issuing heated orders to the other men in white overcoats.

Through the car window, Belachek saw the driver hand something resembling a phone to Cardoza, who raised it to an ear. The drug lord appeared to listen intently before his petulant expression changed over to a sneering grin. Abruptly, he lowered the phone and barked something to the driver, who abruptly gunned the vehicle and sped away. Once again, men were forced to leap clear of the SUV to avoid being hit, and seconds later the vehicle left the building.

Belachek reached out to grasp Jimenez's shoulder. "I'll take the nearest two fuel trucks," he whispered. "You take the truck at the far end of the hangar. Plant your charge on the underside of the tank."

Jimenez seemed to hesitate. "Some of these men may be worth saving," he replied. "We must use the hologram first."

Belachek paused, allowing himself a moment to mull the merit of this. Certainly he was tired of killing, but time was running short. "Okay," he conceded. "Perhaps they are not all bad." He was thinking of how he, himself, had abetted Zinova. Though he had been an accomplice of such a wicked man, he had grown weary of pernicious acts.

Jimenez pulled the PHP from under his cloaker and positioned it further out on the catwalk before activating it. This particular unit was much smaller than the one Jake had used aboard the Hind, an upgraded version of the bazooka-shaped Portable Holographic Projector. It was the size of a cell phone and originally developed to display the dolphin art in a fashion much more dynamic than that depicted in the two-dimensional paintings. For conscientious reasons, Jake had had the foresight to have Mat pack a few of them aboard *Johnnie* before Franklin sailed from the colony. And Jake had made sure Jimenez was equipped with one just before sending him on this mission, instructing him to employ it if he thought a situation warranted its use.

Pressing the activation button, Jimenez stepped back, making sure to avert his eyes from the projected image that immediately sprang into view just below the hangar roof. Jimenez was one of those people profoundly affected by these enigmatic artistic creations of the albino mind, and had he taken in the three-dimensional shimmering vision, he would have been rendered ineffective by its seductive narcotic influence. Instead, he focused his gaze on the people below.

A cry of intense pain suddenly erupted. The cry had come from one of the technicians sitting in front of a computer screen. The man had looked up, distracted by the glowing thing snaking and intertwining above him. He had stared for one brief moment before his eyes widened as though viewing some monstrous form hurling itself at him. Abruptly, he had clutched his temples before falling from the chair and screaming out in agony. Several of his peers followed his gaze just before he collapsed, only to suffer the same reaction. A chorus of shrill screams quickly ensued, and men were jerking violently as though being electrocuted. The display spread rapidly, gathering momentum as more and more men broke from their tasks to look up. A growing number of Cardoza's thugs lay sprawled in their own vomit, screaming and writhing and continuing to regurgitate copious portions of their last meal, while others had collapsed to their knees to clutch their skull.

Jimenez scanned the floor rapidly, looking for different symptoms. He spotted two people staring up at the far end of the facility, rapturously drinking in the scintillating vision. Both of them stood near one of the fuel trucks. Directly below him, he became aware of another man gazing up as though in worship, one of the white frocked technicians. From where he was positioned, he could clearly see that the infection had now spread to all quarters of the facility. With the exception of the unfallen three men, all the others appeared severely stricken with sickness.

Satisfied that there were no others to be saved, Jimenez moved back to his original place on the catwalk, reaching out to touch Belachek's invisible form. "I will guide the two men who stand near the far truck to safety once I plant the charges," he said. "Perhaps you can do the same with the man directly below us once you plant your charges."

"Yes, my friend, I will do as you suggest," Belachek readily agreed. Though he desperately wanted to, he also avoided looking at the hologram, managing to keep his eyes focused on the debilitating chaos taking place below. While formulating the plan, Jake had warned him about gazing directly at it. "Three-dimensional representations of the dolphin art are far more powerful than their two-dimensional depictions," Jake had stated while laying out the plan. "Staring at them will cause basically good people to become far too lethargic to be effective in a fight," he had gone on to emphasize.

Belachek had trouble grasping the concept, for he had never thought of himself as a good person. Nevertheless, he had no desire to test Jake's claim. Shaking off his reverie, he checked his watch. "We must hurry!" he said. "Set your timer for two minutes. That should be enough for us to get these men clear." Quickly, he moved back the way they had come.

Jake remained hidden behind the trunk of a fallen tree as errant electrical discharges spiked all around him, many of them striking Cardoza's fortress. Having just reached the moat three minutes earlier, he had arrived just in time to witness a lone SUV cross over the shark-infested water and enter the stronghold. Too late for him to sneak in behind it, he watched regrettably as the drawbridge came up to seal off the portcullis.

How you doing, Achilles? Jake queried, barely making out the sound of rotors above the storm's raging cacophony. The noise of blades chopping the air grew progressively louder, adding to the raucous mix of exploding thunder, blasting wind, and pounding rain.

Achilles' reply was swift. *Having to hitch a ride like this is no fun, JJ, I can tell you that. If not for the rain, my skin would be dried out and cracking by now.*

Well you're almost here, so hang tight, Jake said, finally able to discern the chopper bearing rapidly in on his position with a sizable object slung beneath it. Reaching out, he placed the portable holographic projector he had been holding on the tree trunk in front of him and pressed the button, hoping the rain would not impede it. He had set the range function on maximum so that the image would coalesce directly in front of the stone structure's nearest tower. He made sure to look away as the PHP sprang to life, projecting the vision it held to the required height.

Time seemed to hold still as Jake waited uncertainly for something to happen, but the scream suddenly emanating from the closest tower was like chamber music to his ears. The moment passed quickly as the chopper flared and came to a hover directly above the moat, its suspended cargo hanging ten feet above the water.

Jake checked his watch again, noting the time. A horrendous boom suddenly cut through the air, sounding different from the thundering discharges. It caused a dark smile to come to his face as he looked in the direction of the blast. A distant fireball rose up above the citadel's eclipsing bulk, throwing out a coruscation of orange and yellow flames into the roiling night sky. The blast was immediately followed by several more explosions, each one sending up a billowing, swirling ball of hot gas similar to the first.

Jake snatched up the PHP and stuffed it into a waterproof pocket on his utility belt. Pulling down his face mask, he bolted from his concealed position just as the chopper's sling parted to release its ponderous load. Taking three bounding leaps before hitting the water, he made sure to hold on tight to the gear he carried. A heavy blast of rotor wash accosted him as the chopper veered away, causing him to smile inwardly. Fernando had carried out his portion of the mission precisely as planned, flying from the cove at a prearranged time several hours after Jake's departure aboard the *Avenging Angel*. But now he was to stand by until needed again.

Achilles reached Jake in less than a second, and a moment later Jake sat anxiously astride his bond mate. With Achilles now under him, the dolphin immediately submerged.

Let's hope those sharks don't give us any trouble, Jake commented, handing Achilles the explosive they would need to breach the stronghold.

I think it's too late for that, JJ. I'm picking up an exceptionally large shape with my biosonar. The profile tells me it's a female great white better than twenty feet. I'm projecting the hear-see image so you'll have an idea just how big she is.

The reflected image that formed in Jake's mind startled him. The shark had to be somewhere close to three tons, an eating machine of sheer aggressiveness.

There's a plus side to this, JJ. The other sharks are keeping their distance from her.

Just plant the charge and use your speed to stay clear of her, Jake ordered. The back side of the charge was coated with a water-resistant adhesive that would readily stick to any submerged surface. Once pushed up against the Plexiglas window Belachek had described, a timer button would be activated that was set to trigger the detonator thirty seconds later. Jake was not worried about the deadly shock wave that would propagate through the water following the blast. Strapped to his bond mate's body was a Pressure Wave Inhibitor that would protect both of them.

I'm afraid that won't be immediately possible, JJ. She's coming directly at us. Hold on tight.

Jake felt Achilles turn sharply and accelerate with a burst of speed. Though the water was dark and murky, a sudden electrical discharge from above sent a flaring burst of light into the depths. A massive set of jaws armed with murderous triangular teeth flashed by, narrowly missing them in that fleeting instant of time, and Jake realized how close they had come to being a meal for the huge carnivore.

She's quick, JJ, almost as fast as me. I'm going to try luring her away from our objective before backtracking.

Do whatever you have to, but just make it quick. We have little time to waste. The thought that both Destiny and Franklin were now in Cardoza's hands tormented him like an auger being driven into his skull, for there was no telling what that sadistic bastard was doing to them at this moment.

Are you able to contact Destiny? Jake asked hopefully as his bond mate moved rapidly with darting evasive action.

Achilles did not immediately respond, and Jake felt the nervous shudder go coursing through the dolphin's body. *Well are you?* Jake demanded impatiently.

Yes, JJ, Achilles quailed, *and her situation is not good.*

Chapter Twenty-seven: Saving a Prisoner

Destiny took in the dispiriting sight with heartbreaking despair. Nevertheless, she knew she had to remain strong. Five of Cardoza's thugs had brought her to a musty chamber deep within the stronghold. They had shoved and prodded her along, all the while leering and laughing and groping her lewdly. She had not resisted, distancing herself from the fear that should have consumed her. Instead, she had locked onto the guidance Esmerelda had given her back in the cave. "You must cleanse your mind of the fear that shackles it," Esmerelda had maintained. "Have faith. Faith and fear will always be at war, so you must choose one or the other. You must have patience and steadfastness, continuing to believe with all your being until the belief is physically manifested. Once you possess it, all is possible."

Destiny clung to the words as she looked at her father, reminding herself that she had to remain strong. She would not let herself get compromised again. She would not let herself fall victim to negative thoughts. She would not deceive herself by forgetting who she was. Esmerelda's words continued to empower her. "Your unconditional love for those around you has made you even stronger. It is a source of great power."

Franklin turned his head, his eyes widening with shock and fear at seeing Destiny in this place. The fear was not for himself, but for his daughter. The men in the chamber were cruel and sadistic, capable of any heinous act. With his body stretched out on the medieval torture rack, he had no doubts she would be subjected to the same atrocity once they finished with him.

The sound of approaching footsteps echoed dully within the confines of the hallway leading to the chamber, causing heads to swivel in that direction. A brief moment passed before Rafael Cardoza emerged, his expression lighting up in a victorious grin at seeing Destiny. "So this is the dolphin girl," he declared expansively.

Destiny stood still, not saying anything as Cardoza made a show of sauntering around her to look her up and down.

"You have caused me many problems over the last several years," he suddenly spat, "you and all those associated with you." Coming back around to look her in the face, he stared implacably. "And yet I find it rather amazing that someone so beautiful would have the means to do that."

Destiny stared back calmly, remaining quiet.

Cardoza turned to gaze thoughtfully at Franklin strung out on the rack. "This man must be very special for you to come here alone like this."

"He is my father," Destiny said, her voice low and dulcet.

Cardoza's eyes lit up with apparent delight. "Your father, you say!" He let out a giddy laugh over his unexpected good fortune, and several of his cohorts joined in. He had expended considerable time and expense in planning the girl's capture, with the effort ending in a complete failure. But now here she was, walking right into his midst. "You are either terribly naïve or incredibly stupid if you thought you could save him by coming here."

"I ask that you release him at once," Destiny said without emotion.

Cardoza studied her as though she were insane. There was not a shred of fear showing on her face. "Do you know what this device is?" he asked, turning to indicate the rack Franklin was immobilized on.

When Destiny did not reply, Cardoza answered for her. "It is called a rack. It was developed in medieval times for interrogating and extracting confessions from prisoners. During that era, it was considered to be the ultimate instrument of torture."

Cardoza scrutinized her closely, looking for the fear to well up in her expression. "It can induce the most excruciating pain imaginable," he went on, carefully choosing his words to invoke the optimum psychological distress.

At seeing no reaction in the girl, he turned his gaze on Franklin again and continued the discourse. "As you can plainly see, your father's ankles are fastened to the lower roller, while his wrists are chained to the other." Reaching out he grabbed the long handle extending from the device, applying just enough pressure to move the ratchet attached to the top roller one additional notch. The ratchet moved with an audible click, and as it did, Franklin gasped out in pain.

The drug lord turned to address Destiny again. "Through a stepwise process, the tension on the chains can be gradually increased by means of the lever and pulleys connected to the rollers. They strain the ropes and chains until the victim's joints are eventually dislocated." Pausing, he studied her again, a depraved leer plastering his face.

Destiny barely managed to keep her features composed, though she wanted to scream out in tearful frustration.

At seeing no fear, Cardoza reached out and grabbed the lever handle again, this time yanking it hard. The ratchet advanced two clicks, causing Franklin to elicit a sharp intake of breath.

Destiny's expression did not waver. "With each cruel act you commit, you seal your own fate even more," she said. "I beseech you to release him at once if you wish to live."

Cardoza's jaw abruptly dropped, amazed by the potency of Destiny's audacity. This show of defiance was utterly alien to him. He was used to getting what he wanted by invoking fear in others. He fed off the fear, drawing strength from it.

All at once, Cardoza stopped gaping and let out a raucous laugh. "Salt water must have addled your brain, girl. It is you who have sealed your fate by coming here. But first I want you to see your father's arms pulled from their sockets. Only then will you comprehend who is in control here."

Gripping the rack lever, Cardoza kept his gaze fixated on Destiny's face. "Listen carefully. One aspect of being stretched too far on the rack is the loud popping noises cartilage, ligaments and bones will make when subjected to such severe stress. And when muscle fibers are stretched excessively, they lose their ability to contract."

Before Cardoza moved the lever, a tremor suddenly rumbled underfoot. Startled, he shot a look to one of his men. "What just happened?" he demanded.

The man mirrored his boss' startled expression, but before he could say anything the floor shook again, this time more forcefully.

A vision invaded Destiny's thoughts with flaring lucidity. Through Hercules' eyes, she glimpsed the rising fireballs, seeing parts of the hangar and what it contained fly high into the air under the scorching light of the blasts. It was understandable that the force of the explosions would be felt within the castle even though the hangar was more than a mile away. The shock waves would travel through the bedrock, which both structures were founded on.

"Pull that lever again, and this structure will be destroyed just as your hangar was," Destiny warned.

Cardoza stared back, not fully comprehending what she was saying, but before he found his tongue, a handheld radio carried by one of his thugs suddenly squawked. The thug winced as he lifted the radio to an ear, nearly deafened by the strength of the caller's panicky tone. "El hangar se ha ido!" a disembodied voice cried out in Spanish, loud enough for everyone to hear.

Cardoza grabbed the radio from the thug's hand and spoke angrily into the speaker. "Is this some kind of joke?" he asked in English. From the caller's voice, he knew it was Lamont stationed in the east tower, a man known for an occasional prank on some of the other men. If it was a joke, Lamont would pay dearly for it. "What do you mean the hangar is gone?"

Hearing Cardoza, the caller reverted to English. "No, this is no joke. The hangar has been completely destroyed. I saw it explode. All that remains of it is in flames."

"What about the drones?" Cardoza demanded, a shocked look befalling his features. "Did any get out?"

"I did not see any leave the hangar."

In a fit of rage, Cardoza hurled the radio against the closest stone wall, narrowly missing one of his men, who ducked just in time to avoid being hit in the head. The radio shattered, with pieces flying off in various directions. Spinning around, Cardoza turned venomous eyes on Destiny. "You did this!" he accused in a low, guttural hiss.

As Cardoza spat out the words, another vision suddenly coalesced within Destiny's thoughts. Achilles and JJ were being hounded by a huge shark within the moat, impeding them from reaching their objective. Probing with her mind, she extended mental tendrils into the shark's brain to supplant its hardwired primeval instinct with another urge. It was an old trick she had mastered from a young age, an ability to control the actions of sea creatures. She had utilized it once before to cause a massive school of barracuda to disable a boat in order to keep the men aboard it from attacking Jay Jay. Sensing a change in the shark's disposition, she reengaged her telepathic link with Jake's bond mate. *You're clear to go, Achilles.*

Cardoza continued to glower at her, his rage building like a volcano about to explode. "You did this and now you are going to pay," he repeated, this time screaming out the threat. "We will see how brave you are after I put you in the tiger's cage." Shooting a glance at two of his men, he screamed again. "Bind her!"

Feeling rough hands grab her, Destiny pressed the mental trigger, unleashing the energy her body had gathered in from the storm. Following the birth of the twins she had lost this ability, but now she sensed it was back. Like the *thurentra*, she was capable of storing a charge.

An abrupt flash accompanied by a loud crackling resounded as both men were flung backwards to land unconscious on the floor. The biting smell of ozone hung in the air as Cardoza gaped dumbly at their sprawled forms, trying to make sense of the scene he had just witnessed. With bulging eyes, he swiveled his head to look back at the girl. "I don't know what you are, but you haven't won yet," he uttered in a sibilant whisper. "At least I will have the satisfaction of seeing you watch your father's arms ripped from his body." Turning, he reached for the rack lever again, his face consumed with insane hatred.

"Then you have sealed your own fate," Destiny avowed.

Just as Cardoza's fingers made contact with the lever, a deafening boom rocked the chamber. Dumbfounded, Cardoza dropped his hand, his eyes drawn to the heavy cast iron door leading to the antechamber where his last meeting had taken place. An escalating rumble could be heard gathering strength on the opposite side of the door as a gush of water spewed out from beneath it.

Knowing what the sound heralded, Destiny bolted to the side of the rack, taking advantage of the situation. With Cardoza and his three remaining henchmen staring at the door in confused fixation, she quickly disengaged the ratchet, easing the strain on her father's limbs. In moments she had Franklin free, and helping to support him, she was able to guide him to the hallway leading from the chamber just in the nick of time.

With savage ferocity, the door burst open. Unable to withstand Scylla's three-ton mass driven forward by the force of the water, it was torn from its hinges. Like a battering ram, the door was swept forward by the onrushing torrent, slamming into two of the thugs and killing them outright. Knocked off his feet by the deluge flooding the chamber, Cardoza floundered frantically as Scylla's enormous jaws chomped down on the third henchman. Shaking her head savagely, she tore a huge chunk from his torso.

Moving hastily down the passageway, Destiny and her father barely managed to escape the initial onslaught as water from the moat gushed in. Turning her head, Destiny looked back. Carried along with the flood were other large predators, their jaws snapping as they were driven into the chamber by the powerful surge. Within their midst, she caught sight of Jake clinging tightly to Achilles, his head swiveling in her direction. In seconds he was at her side.

"Climb aboard!" Jake shouted, his voice carrying above the rush of water. Reaching out, he grabbed Franklin by the elbow to pull him in. Destiny followed, and with her father now sandwiched between her and Jake, Achilles began fighting his way back against the flow.

"We're going out the way we came in," Jake bellowed, and as he yelled out the words, Cardoza was suddenly before him, his head just above the water, a rabid snarl on his face. It was then Jake saw him raise an arm to level a snub nose revolver directly at him, but before Cardoza could pull the trigger, the drug lord rose up suddenly, lifted clear of the surge. Clearly stunned, Cardoza looked down to find half his body within Scylla's massive maw, and as he did so his eyes bulged out in terror.

For a seemingly endless moment, Cardoza continued to stare down in horrified silence before a hideous wail escaped his lips. Abruptly, he dropped the revolver and pushed down hard on the edge of the entrapping jaws, squirming frantically in an effort to free himself. His struggles proved futile as Scylla's mouth snapped shut, her serrated teeth cutting through flesh and bone with little effort. Cleaved in two at the waist, Cardoza let out a final piercing scream as the upper half of his body fell away to disappear in the torrent.

Glad to be rid of his longtime nemesis, Jake was perplexed by Achilles' next move. Instead of swimming against the current, his bond mate had turned to drift with the flow. Jake was about to question the dolphin's motive for doing this, but before he could object, Destiny spoke.

"There's a person trapped down here," she shouted. She had sensed him moments before Scylla's timely arrival.

"Where?" Jake yelled back, his voice almost lost in the deafening rush of whitewater crashing into the hallway's confined quarters.

"In one of the holding cells further back."

Jake looked in the direction she indicated. Only one electric light bulb situated at the far end of the passageway still burned, casting just enough illumination for him to see, and he was able to make out a set of stone steps where the hallway terminated. It was then he noticed the rusted doors strung out at intervals along both sides of the corridor. Achilles let the flow carry them past three of the cells on the right before pivoting around. Now swimming against the current, he kept them abreast of a fourth door on their left.

"He's in there," Destiny yelled.

Straining his eyes, Jake discerned the grim smudged face of an elderly white man plastered up against the door's small grill, his hands clutching the bars, his expression filled with fright.

Reaching for the latch handle on the door, Jake discovered it would not budge. Scrutinizing it further, he found the reason why. "We're going to need a key to open this door," he shouted, gauging how quickly the water level was rising. In another minute, the hallway would be completely flooded. "If we're going to get him out, we need to do it now."

"You know the drill!" Destiny yelled back, the deluge's thunderous roar nearly drowning out her words. "Concentrate!"

She was reminding him about an episode aboard Loomin's boat years earlier. It had been his first encounter with telekinesis. Locked away in a storage locker, he and Destiny, aided by two of the albinos swimming alongside the vessel, had merged their thoughts to move the locker's sliding bolt that imprisoned them. But he knew this was different. The lock was ancient and, in all probability, rusted on the inside. It was doubtful it could be moved without the use of a key.

Achilles' essence shrilled within his brain. *Think positive,* his bond mate reprimanded. *Negativity is not an option here.*

Sorry, Achilles, Jake apologized. *I should know better.* Focusing all his mental energy, he threw his entire will into disengaging the door's locking mechanism, and as he did so, he could feel Destiny's, Franklin's, and Achilles' thoughts intertwining with his own.

Something resounded within the lock, and the door suddenly sprang open, the imprisoned man swinging out with it as he continued to hold onto the bars. With his head just above the rising water, the man was clearly on the edge of panic. By this time, only one foot of overhead clearance remained in the flooded corridor.

"I hope you're good at holding your breath," Jake shouted at the man, who flinched in terror as Achilles reached out to grab him about the waist from below the waterline. From the look in his eyes, Jake could tell the man had spotted the fins racing down the passageway. Frozen with fear the way he was, Jake instinctively knew the man would drown if Achilles dragged him along in this manner.

Thinking quickly, Jake petitioned his bond mate. *This guy's too much of a liability in his present state, Achilles, and carrying four of us against this flow is going to be too much for you.*

But I can do it, Achilles protested indignantly.

I'm not going to risk your life, nor that of Destiny and Franklin, Jake shot back adamantly. *I'm taking this guy out by the same route Destiny took to get down here.*

But more of Cardoza's men will be up there, Achilles pointed out.

Maybe so, but it's the only option I'm willing to take. Now stop arguing and get going! Jake ordered, grabbing hold of the terrified man.

The exchange of thoughts was swift, taking place with an urgency the situation demanded. Reluctantly, Achilles began to move against the surge, leaving Jake behind. Destiny turned to look back at him, her head barely above the water. A concerned expression consumed her face, her lips moving in a silent plea. But Jake could tell she was in agreement with his decision and nodded a reply, as if to say "I'll try to be careful." By now, only an air gap of less than six inches remained, which was closing fast.

"Let go of the door!" Jake shouted in the man's ear.

The man continued to grip the bars with a strength born of terror, too traumatized to heed Jake's command. "Let go or I'm leaving you for the sharks," Jake threatened.

The words seemed to galvanize the man, and with a suddenness Jake had not anticipated, he let go of the bars. Swept back by the powerful surge, Jake kept a tight grip on his charge, having enough presence of mind to inhale sharply just before the air gap closed. With the passageway now completely filled with rapidly moving water, he was carried along its length with a violence that surprised him, twisting and turning out of control like a blind man caught in a sandstorm. Continuing to hold onto the man, he could feel him clawing frantically to get away. The sandpaper hide of one confused predator brushed rudely against him, and had the shoulder strap of his slung gear been less tight, he would have lost it.

Jake was again jostled, this time much harder than before. With unyielding tenaciousness, he managed to hold fast to the man, whose struggles had now abated. Something slammed painfully into his shoulder, jarring him to the bone, and he felt himself tumbled end over end. Throwing out his free hand to fend off the obstruction, he felt a series of ridges sweep by, and kicking hard, he sensed he was moving upward. Several moments elapsed before his head broke the surface. The water was rising, whisking him up the steps he had seen at the end of the hallway. But now he perceived an ebbing of the flow as the water pressure in the moat equalized with that in the fortress. Managing to stabilize himself on one of the steps, he climbed the remaining distance to the floor above, dragging his charge with him.

Jake lifted his face mask, pulling the limp and unmoving man onto a stone landing. Light from somewhere above cast just enough light for him to see. Quickly, he laid the man on his back and went to work, pumping the man's chest before applying mouth to mouth resuscitation. Several seconds passed before the man came around, and with an unexpected suddenness, he sat up and coughed out a small amount of water.

Jake placed a hand over the man's mouth to muffle the sound. "Easy there, fella! Try to be quiet," he admonished in a whisper, "otherwise you'll bring the bad guys down on us."

The man stared back vacantly before Jake's words fully registered in his expression. His short immersion in the tunnel had cleansed some of the grime off his face to reveal at least three days' growth of gray stubble clinging to his cheeks, chin, and lips. What remained of his slacks and dress shirt was tattered and filthy.

"I'm going to try and get you out of here. Can you walk?"

The man gave a weak nod and rose slowly with Jake helping him to his feet.

Jake unslung the tubular bundle strapped to his shoulder, removing the watertight plastic wrap covering it to reveal the Sledgehammer with its drum magazine. Lowering it to the granite floor, he pulled his USP-9 submachine pistol from the holster hugging his right thigh and removed the clip, replacing it with another from the waterproof utility belt girthing his waist. Slipping it back into its holster, he placed a hand on the hilt of his K-bar at his calf to make sure it was still there. Satisfied, he picked up the Sledgehammer and set the firing mode on semi, hefting the weapon to make sure it balanced comfortably in his hands.

The man he had rescued monitored his every move with curious though fearful eyes, making Jake wonder how he would hold up against the potential conflict that was about to ensue.

Thinking to check on his bond mate, Jake sent out a mental query. *How you doing, Achilles?*

We're back in the moat, Achilles answered back. *What's your status?*

Getting ready to blast my way outta here, Jake replied, setting a stony gaze on the next flight of steps, a narrow medieval stairwell that spiraled up into the dim light cast from above.

Achilles intruded into his thoughts again. *We'll wait for you.*

Don't wait! Get out of there now.

Sorry, JJ, but Destiny insists on waiting.

Jake sighed in frustration, knowing it was an argument he could not win. Even though Achilles was his bond mate, Destiny held dominion over the actions of every dolphin in the pod. She and not he would ultimately have the final say. No matter what the circumstances, her decision would trump his own when telling Achilles what to do.

As an afterthought, Jake queried Achilles again. *Are you in contact with Hercules and Perseus?*

Yes, JJ, they have planted the charges just as you instructed. They are all set to go off simultaneously in exactly three minutes twenty-two seconds.

Jake needed further verification. *Does that include all of Cardoza's water-based assets?*

All of them, JJ. Even his yacht and tugboat.

What about Johnnie? Jake was thinking about their mode of transportation once this business was finished. There was no way Fernando could fly all of them back to the colony in a single trip. The Bell Ranger was not big enough to do the job. It was not designed to carry sizable loads even after Fernando's exceptionally skilled tweaking of its power train. It had barely enough lift to carry Achilles' 1,200 pounds to the moat without over-stressing the engine.

The tugboat towed Johnnie out to the Southern Star and left it tethered to the freighter without anyone guarding it. While the Blue Helmets were offloading more cargo, Phillipe managed to untie the ropes and sneak aboard. By that time the storm had passed, and without any electrical discharges to scramble the systems, he was able to start the motor and move away.

Where is he now?

He waits for us near the end of Cardoza's pier.

And Fernando?

Hercules saw him set down on the beach two hundred meters west of the pier. Fernando was fortunate to land when he did.

Jake's gut involuntarily tightened, and he interrupted Achilles before his bond mate could add more. *Did he have mechanical problems?* He sensed Achilles wince under the force of the question. He was intensely aware that the Bell would be needed to retrieve Achilles from the moat.

You should refrain from stressing yourself like this, JJ. No, he did not have a mechanical failure. Right after he landed, Hercules observed another chopper fly out to meet the San Pedro. He believes it was another Hind.

Jake's gut tightened further. This was little consolation. The bad news he had anticipated had now taken on another form, one that was potentially worse. *What was it doing at the San Pedro?*

It lowered lifting cables to that large container I told you about earlier and is bringing it this way as we communicate. Got to submerge, JJ. It just turned on a spotlight and is directing it at the water.

Before Jake could ponder this new turn of events, Achilles burst in on his thoughts yet again. *Consider ourselves lucky, JJ.*

What do you mean lucky?

Had Fernando been summoned to lift us out of here, we would have been caught in the Hind's searchlight.

I can't argue that Achilles. Keep out of sight, but keep me informed. I've got work to do.

Turning back to the man he had rescued, Jake spoke softly. "I think it's only fair that I know your name if I'm going to get you out of here."

"Mort…you can call me Mort," the man stuttered hoarsely.

"Well, Mort, I need you to stay right behind me, so please don't lag if you're set on living. It's gonna get ugly up there."

Mort nodded, his eyes still wide with trepidation.

With a sudden lust for battle building in his veins, Jake ascended the stairs with the Sledgehammer's muzzle pointed upward.

To find out what happens next in this on-going saga, read Part 5 of the Dolphin Riders Series -
Dolphin Riders, 3rd Edition
Survival.

Acknowledgments

No one deserves more credit for their support in the writing of this tale than my wife and soul mate, Harriet, my biggest fan. Her indomitable spirit and encouragement was indispensable in keeping me focused on completing a work that could have otherwise gone unfinished, a story that could have conceivably transpired in an alternate universe closely paralleling our own. As the novel progressed, it was always a delight to gauge her reaction, which was never disappointing as I read proceeding entries to her over breakfast each and every Saturday morning.

But the thing that finally compelled me to actually write it was the way Harriet was able to cope with her illness. Harriet is tough as nails and since the year 2000 she's been battling CML - chronic myeloid leukemia - and so far she's put up one hell of a valiant fight, absolutely refusing to yield to what most doctors would describe as a devastating, life-threatening malady. Thus, she made up her mind long ago to live out a normal existence, avoiding hospitals completely and refraining from seeing doctors as much as possible. Consequently, it was her grit and determination that inspired me to take pen to paper and flesh out an adventure imbued with these admirable qualities of the spirit. In its basic subliminal form, I wanted to honor her with something unique, essentially a literary work that came from the deepest part of me, something only I could give her, but something which would reflect her iron will and indomitable strength. This is initially mirrored in the book's opening scene where we find a woman adrift and marooned in a thunderous, tumultuous sea. She is alone and clinging to a piece of flotsam, and the reader finds the woman to be pregnant. By all rights, she should accept her fate and succumb to the elements, but she continues to fight on in the face of overwhelming odds, clinging to life, and refusing to quit until she has nothing left within her to resist the battering forces of a sea gone mad. Later in the book we learn the woman survives with the help of a dolphin and that her name is Harriet Grahm. And although she has no recollection of her former life, she ends up taking on a new identity, becoming Amphitrite, one of the cornerstone characters of the story. During her ordeal at sea, something incredible has happened to Amphitrite, and her failure to remember her past has somehow given her the power to glimpse the future. Henceforth, she becomes an arrant believer in this power and what the future holds, convinced her visions are real, and it is this ability that spills over and infects the reader to make the story palpable and real.

Writing the novel was a labor of love that took four years to complete. In creating it, I had to constantly challenge myself to come up with new ideas, not always knowing where the story was headed since some of the characters within the developing plot started taking on a life of their own. I only knew I wanted to take the reader on a journey to high adventure, an escape from the often mundane routines of everyday life most of us encounter, and in adhering to this I kept imagining what I'd like to see on the big screen if the novel was ever made into a blockbuster movie. My heartfelt appreciation also goes out to my daughter, Melissa, for her added encouragement to keep me moving forward with this project. And I certainly would be remiss if I left out her three little progenies, Troy Jacob, Solomon, and the latest addition to the family, Jayna Jocelynne, each of whom provided me with the personality traits and inspiration to create the mischievous impish characters which have now come alive to play an integral part within the sequel to this tale.

And lastly, I want to thank my sister, Barbara, for showing an enthusiastic interest in my creativity. Whenever she picked up the uncompleted manuscript, she always seemed to have trouble putting it down, totally absorbed and fascinated by the plot's intrigue and explosiveness.

About the Author

Michael J. Ganas is a licensed professional engineer. Following a stint in the U.S. Army, he earned a degree in civil engineering from Cornell University. Shortly thereafter, his love of the sea prompted him to pursue a career as a deep-sea commercial diver, heading a wide array of marine construction projects. This eventually led him into his current occupation, which takes on the challenges of civil engineering in underwater environments. Having published over twenty technical articles involving marine engineering, he decided on writing his first novel, an epic action adventure titled ***The Girl Who Rode Dolphins***, which eventually merited seven literary awards and has since been subdivided into the first three books of the on-going ***Dolphin Riders*** book series. ***Creation*** is the fourth book in the series.

www.ingramcontent.com/pod-product-compliance
Lightning Source LLC
LaVergne TN
LVHW020654110826
845149LV00012B/1995

* 9 7 8 1 9 6 6 1 9 1 1 0 0 *